WE ARE THE
MARTIANS
THE LEGACY OF NIGEL KNEALE

WE ARE THE MARTIANS

THE LEGACY OF NIGEL KNEALE

Edited by NEIL SNOWDON

WE ARE THE MARTIANS
THE LEGACY OF NIGEL KNEALE

Copyright © Neil Snowdon 2017

COVER ART AND DESIGN
Copyright © David Chatton Barker 2017

Published in July 2017 by Electric Dreamhouse, an imprint
of PS Publishing Ltd. by arrangement with the authors.

All rights reserved by the authors.
The rights of each contributor to be identified as Author of
their Work have been asserted by them in accordance with
the Copyright, Designs and Patents Act 1988.

FIRST EDITION

ISBN
978-1-786361-03-5
978-1-786361-04-2 [signed edition]

Design & Layout by Michael Smith
Printed and bound in England by T.J. International

PS PUBLISHING
Grosvenor House
1 New Road
Hornsea, HU18 1PG
England

editor@pspublishing.co.uk
www.pspublishing.co.uk
www.electricdreamhouse.co.uk

For Lili and Mina, candles in the dark.

To Alan, Linda, Ella and Bill:
I got there eventually.

Thomas Nigel Kneale 1922 - 2006

OBITUARY

Science Fiction Mourns Nigel Kneale

LAST NIGHT, OR EARLY THIS MORNING, JUST AFTER MIDNIGHT, Monsters HD started running its annual HALLOWEEN Marathon and I watched a bit of **HALLOWEEN III: SEASON OF THE WITCH** (1982), a film originally scripted by Nigel Kneale. After the disappointment of **HALLOWEEN 2**, series producers John Carpenter and Debra Hill tried to kill off Michael Myers and convert their popular franchise into an anthology that would celebrate the holiday in different ways each year. Carpenter—an avowed admirer of Kneale's "Quatermass" films for Hammer—had approached him to conceive the first chapter in **HALLOWEEN**'s new direction. Kneale turned in what was, by all accounts, his customary thoughtful, thought-provoking job, but Carpenter infamously rejected the script ("It was old-fashioned," he later told me), though some of Kneale's ideas remain in the lopsided but occasionally interesting work that resulted.

How strange, then, that I should come online today to discover, in an e-mail from Kim Newman, that Nigel Kneale died last Sunday, October 29th, at the age of 84. To resort to an overused but fitting phrase, it feels like the end of an era—one of those events that bookmark one's life.

We Are The Martians

As a boy who spent his weekends at the movies and his weekdays in front of a television showing movies, I came to understand the importance of the director by the placement of his name at the end of the main titles. The director's name was the one left to resonate in your thoughts during the dissolve that would brighten into the telling of the story. On the other hand, I never gave much thought to the screenwriter's job, other than to wonder where all of these horror movie stories (as in "Story by so-and-so" as a distinct credit) had been published; I later realized that they were mostly written expressly for the screen, sometimes on the back of an envelope or bar napkin. As an habitué of horror, science fiction and fantasy films, I didn't begin to appreciate the craft of the screenwriter until I caught up with Nigel Kneale. He was one of the earliest writers whose name I sought out in newspaper movie ads, and thus more than just a writer to me. He was one of my childhood heroes, along with the first generation of NASA astronauts and Dr. Christiaan Barnard.

Mr. Carpenter's opinion to the contrary, Kneale's work remains rare in my experience of, shall we say, speculative screenwriting in that it has never become old-fashioned. Even when his stories date from another era, such as the time when we stood on the threshold of space travel, they hum with urgency—an urgency of discovery—and take us through experience that leaves us brighter, more aware and speculating of all the mysteries about us that remain to be clarified by the avatars of art and science.

Such a legacy! He wrote the famous BBC teleplay of George Orwell's NINETEEN EIGHTY FOUR (1954) starring Peter Cushing, and his affiliation with Hammer Films was to predate even that of Cushing. His byline appeared on such feature films as **THE QUATERMASS XPERIMENT** aka **THE CREEPING UNKNOWN** (1955, based on his teleplay "THE QUATERMASS EXPERIMENT"), **QUATERMASS 2** aka **ENEMY FROM SPACE** (1957), **THE ABOMINABLE SNOWMAN OF THE HIMALAYAS** (1957), **THE ENTERTAINER** (1960, one of Laurence Olivier's finest screen portrayals), **THE FIRST MEN "IN" THE MOON** (1964, one of the few Ray Harryhausen films to engage us as something more than an excuse for stop-motion magic), **THE WITCHES** (1966, not a favorite Hammer of my childhood but one that interests me today), the magnificent **QUATERMASS AND THE PIT** aka **FIVE MILLION**

MILES TO EARTH (1968, based on his 1959 teleplay), and of course those brilliant and often prophetic other teleplays written for British television, many of which are now available on import DVD: THE YEAR OF THE SEX OLYMPICS (1968), THE STONE TAPE (1972), BEASTS (1976), THE QUATERMASS CONCLUSION aka QUATERMASS (1979), and the marvelous goosebumper THE WOMAN IN BLACK (1989). THE QUATERMASS EXPERIMENT was remade last year as a live BBC broadcast starring Jason Flemyng. The presence of his name on a project was always indicative of quality, indeed of a quality and character that could supercede even indifferent direction on the sheer power of its language and ideas. Thus, Kneale is one of the very few screenwriters who fully warrant identification as one of the genre's auteurs.

Kneale's TOMATO CAIN AND OTHER STORIES (1949) predated his work in television and points to a promising literary career sidetracked by television — but, as I'm sure he would say, "I never had a career, only work." Thirty years later, he complemented his miniseries teleplays of the 1979 finale to his "Quatermass" saga with a novel version, titled simply QUATERMASS — one of the most effectively written, elegiac and moving science fiction novels I've read. Largely on the strength of this novel, and of course the "Quatermass" series of stories as a whole, I've always regarded him as one of Britain's greatest literary visionaries, on par with J.G. Ballard.

Science fiction mourns Nigel Kneale because he was one of the genre's most illuminating humanists — not a sentimentalist like Bradbury, or a myth-maker like Frank Herbert, but a confrontational writer in the tradition of Orwell and Huxley, who used the genre as a metaphor for the problematic times in which we find ourselves. He often painted cynical landscapes of our future, and found fault with us as a species, and he developed into a masterful satirist whose tweaks at Mankind's expense proved just as prophetic as his works undertaken in a more somber mood. He predicted our dire fascination with "reality television" in 1968's THE YEAR OF THE SEX OLYMPICS; the cosmic "ball of twine" narrative of QUATERMASS AND THE PIT, which puts forth a frightening theory about the origin of our species, was a startling forebear of stories like THE DA VINCI CODE; and even his **HALLOWEEN III** script, as I noticed last

WE ARE THE MARTIANS

night or this morning, is every bit as critical and satirical of the television medium as David Cronenberg's contemporaneous **VIDEODROME**.

There is no replacing a talent of this magnitude; we can only thank Nigel Kneale for the many inexhaustible gifts he left behind — on film, on videotape, and on paper.

—Tim Lucas. *Video WatchBlog.*
Tuesday, October 31, 2006

CONTENTS

1. *Foreword* — Mark Gatiss
5. *Introduction* — Neil Snowdon
11. **THE KING OF HAUNTOLOGY** — Mark Chadbourn
25. **THE LITERARY KNEALE** — Tim Lucas
95. **THE QUATERMASS CONCEPTION** — Stephen Bissette
153. *A Conversation With Judith Kerr* — Neil Snowdon
169. **ON NIGEL KNEALE** — Ramsey Campbell
177. **THE QUATERMASS LEGACY:** *A Personal Reflection on Kneale and his Influence* — David Pirie
187. **CREEPING UNKNOWN PT1:** *Wuthering Heights, The Crunch, Nineteen Eighty-Four* — Kim Newman
197. **PHENOMENA BADLY OBSERVED, AND WRONGLY EXPLAINED:** *Quatermass, The Pit, and Me* — John Llewellyn Probert
209. **UNDER THE INFLUENCE:** *Kneale's Dramatic Legacy* — Maura McHugh
223. *A Conversation With Joe Dante* — Neil Snowdon
243. **BRIEF ENCOUNTER** — Stephen Laws
253. **ADAPTATION AND ANGER, OR:** *The Nigel Kneale / John Osborne Synthesis* — Richard Harland Smith

WE ARE THE MARTIANS

261. **THE PROMISED END:** *Nigel Kneale's Lost Masterpiece THE ROAD* — Jonathan Rigby

271. *A Conversation With Mark Gatiss* — Neil Snowdon

293. **COOL THE AUDIENCE, COOL THE WORLD** *Media, Mind Control & The Modern Family* — Kier-La Janisse

309. **PUSHING THE DOOR HE UNLOCKED: *GHOSTWATCH** and THE STONE TAPE* — Stephen Volk

319. **BEASTS:** *An Overview* — Mark Morris

343. **"IT WOULD HAVE BEEN SUCKLED, YOU KNOW":** *BEASTS and 'Baby' An Appreciation* — Jeremy Dyson

355. **QUATERMASS:** *Rebirth & Resurrection* — Jez Winship

397. **THE QUATERMASS CONCLUSION:** *An Interview With Nigel Kneale* — David Sutton.

409. **CREEPING UNKNOWN PT 2: KINVIG** — Kim Newman

413. **IN PURSUIT OF UNHAPPY ENDINGS:** *Chris Burt & Herbert Wise on THE WOMAN IN BLACK* — Tony Earnshaw

435. **WHERE'S KNEALE WHEN YOU NEED HIM?** — Thana Niveau

451. **CREEPING UNKNOWN PT3:** *"Sharpe's Gold" & "Ancient Histories"* — Kim Newman

455. **ON WISHING FOR A NIGEL KNEALE CHILDHOOD** — Lynda E. Rucker

466. *Contributors*

FOREWORD

Mark Gatiss

"*B*ring something back..."

One fine day I met Nigel Kneale.

I recall it vividly. The charm and courtesy of the great man and his lovely wife Judith Kerr, a pristine white carpet, the striking modernist painting of him which hung over the fireplace, like a 50s portrait of an atom scientist. Where to begin? I had so many questions!

Though I was too young to have grown up with the original Quatermass, Kneale's influence on me was immense. He was, as characters would often say of his most legendary creation, 'the rocket man'. A writer with a soaring and unique imagination, an almost eerie gift of prophesy and an extraordinary ear for delicate, creepy dialogue. And though Quatermass loomed over his work like a colossus, there was so much more to him. The string of intriguing and dystopian TV plays, his prize-winning collection of eerie short stories, his screenplays for **THE ENTERTAINER** and **LOOK BACK IN ANGER**. I venerated him as one of the giants of television writing. And on that fine day in Barnes, I was on my way to discuss the possibility of remaking a lost play of his called THE ROAD.

But where did it all start for me? It must have been the screening of the Hammer Quatermass films on TV which became the talk of my school playground. This in turn had aroused much nostalgia from my parents about the whole Quatermass phenomenon. Of how, back in the impossibly distant, murky 1950s, pubs had emptied as people raced home to catch this ground-breaking and brilliant sci-fi landmark. How the whole nation had jumped as one as the dead Martian carcass fell to the floor of the buried space-capsule ("It's alright. They're dead. They've been dead a long time...") Then, for me, had come BEASTS, six ITV plays from 'the Quatermass man', a series so weird and troubling that they left an indelible mark. The sheer horror of the witch-suckled 'Baby', the nerve-jangling suspense of 'During Barty's Party', the suffocating modernity of 'Special Offer'. Here was a very special imagination at work. Then there was KINVIG, perhaps the strangest sitcom ever broadcast and the repeat of Kneale's shattering adaptation of '1984'. Each time, I was attuned somehow to the name of the great man and his place in the pantheon of fantastical writing. Finally, in 1979 came a new Quatermass story, produced by the great Verity Lambert, shot on film and starring Sir John Mills. I ate up this staggeringly bleak production with alacrity and fell with glee upon the republished scripts for the original first three serials. Here, in the deft and charming introductions, I first began to discover a little about Nigel Kneale himself.

Born in Lancashire but raised on the Isle of Man he had, intriguingly, once been an actor. His short story CLOG DANCE FOR A DEAD FARCE paints a picture of a shambolic, uninspired company hauling themselves through a leaden and laugh free production. It was clear Kneale's true talents lay elsewhere, as a storyteller. His Somerset Maugham prize-winning collection of short stories TOMATO CAIN brought him to the attention of the BBC and it was there he met his great collaborator Rudolph Cartier. THE QUATERMASS EXPERIMENT was the fruit of this, though originally, it had a very different title. In reference to the parting words of astronaut Victor Caroon's wife it was called 'Bring Something Back', a wonderfully grisly joke. Caroon did indeed bring something back from his trip into outer space. Something terrible...

Foreword

I remember seeing Kneale's pugnacious face with its quizzical eyebrows staring out at me from black and white production photos in those script books. And now it was looking at me again, older and white-haired as we discussed THE ROAD—his brilliantly original 18th Century ghost story with a startling twist, which tragically no longer existed in the archives. But our conversation ranged far and wide. His abiding contempt for Hammer films, his antipathy towards the BBC, his delight in THE ROYLE FAMILY, his memories of his father's death which had coincided with production of THE ROAD, how he had written the marvellous script for THE WOMAN IN BLACK in only ten days. He answered all my questions with a twinkling smile, with the sagacity born not just of age but of a deep humanity.

Undoubtedly a prophet, like his hero H.G. Wells, Kneale possessed an uncanny gift for looking just around the corner, of predicting what fresh horrors humans might conjure and of brilliantly exploring them, most often through science fiction. It was a term he disliked yet could not escape. He preferred to think that he used the genre to explore his personal concerns. It's ironic that, although he can lay claim to having invented popular TV, the fact that he wasn't known as a "straight" writer has forever kept him in the "cult" bracket, legendary to some but never considered alongside Dennis Potter, Alan Bennett, David Mercer, Alan Plater and all the others. And though there were many non-genre pieces (a late flowering and happy relationship with Central TV led to episodes of SHARPE and KAVANAGH QC, the latter of which, a terrific case involving the Holocaust, was appropriately entitled 'Ancient History') it is for YEAR OF THE SEX OLYMPICS, the brilliant modern ghost story THE STONE TAPE and numerous other dystopian visions that Kneale is best remembered.

In almost all his work, there's an appealing quality of strangeness. It's our world but with something not quite right. Perhaps Kneale's unique position was always to remain slightly outside, taking a Manxman's view of the world: a sceptical, measured vision, frequently bleak but never entirely nihilistic. As troubled and troubling as Professor Quatermass himself.

WE ARE THE MARTIANS

Though the proposed remake of THE ROAD never got off the ground (see inside this splendid book for more details), that afternoon Nigel Kneale gave me something very precious. A memory of a brief time in the company of a truly brilliant and original mind. So I really did get to bring something back.

Mark Gatiss
London
November 2015

INTRODUCTION

Neil Snowdon

IN MANY WAYS, WHAT YOU HOLD IN YOUR HANDS IS A DREAM, coalesced out of passion and goodwill.

Passion for a writer not given his due is perhaps the fiercest passion in fandom, and the greatest motivator for critics. Certainly it was mine when I conceived this book and pitched it to the contributors. Passion for the work, and a sense of injustice, of incredulity, that a man who created so much, who changed lives and opened minds, should have so little written about him; should seem so little known.

Quite apart from his achievements as a storyteller and a dramatist, he is ground zero for the development of the televisual drama as a powerful medium in its own right. Not an approximation of theatre or the poor cousin of cinema, but a medium that could take the best of it's narrative forebears—the intimacy of theatre, the visual drive of cinematic story-telling, the length, breadth and depth of the novel—to create something new. Not the 'lean in and listen' safety of Radio (which no matter its content will always approximate the tale around the fireside of old) but something that projected its light into your living room. That broke into your home and embraced or assaulted you, something that was—in a way—the fire itself. Lean in close and look into the flames... but not too close, or you might get burned. That was what Nigel Kneale offered.

WE ARE THE MARTIANS

There is nothing passive about his writing. Nothing 'cosy'. He wants to make you think and feel.

And he does just that. In spades...

It says an awful lot, I think, about how much Kneale's work means to the contributors herein (how deeply he made them think and feel) that they stepped up to write for this collection so willingly. That each of these immensely talented writers would throw their lot in with a newbie editor without a second word. Indeed, in some cases, they came knocking at my virtual door, asking to come in.

I was overwhelmed by the response of the writers you will find between these pages. Humbled and thrilled in equal measure. And the work that they've put in is staggering.

If you're new to Nigel Kneale, I hope this sends you straight to his work (*run*, don't walk, to your viewing device of choice). I hope it helps contextualise the work too. Not that it needs it: the ideas, the characters and the situations are as potent and as urgent as ever they were. But methods of production change. In some cases they have dated, and I know that can be an obstacle. For those who find such elements an issue, I hope the passion of the writers will help you past it. That the context the writers provide — anecdotally, historically, critically — will help unlock the modes of making, scrape away the tarnish of accreted years to expose the thrumming primal core within: Kneale's writing. His ideas.

For those of you who *know* Kneale's work, and come to this as fans, I hope you feel we've done him justice. Gone some way to correct the imbalance. However you come to this book, know this: it's just the beginning. We are not done with Nigel Kneale. We have not covered all his work. In an effort to properly embrace the passion and fervour of my contributors, I did not force them into a scheme to cover every title or every topic. I let their passion guide them. That was always foremost in my mind. With luck, there'll be a Volume 2 to follow, because there's more to tell. And besides, the amount of people who — having gotten wind of the project — came forward and asked if the could be involved, has been thrilling to me. And not a little touching. Nigel's work means so much, to so many people, to practitioners within his field and beyond. He has inspired writers, film-makers, musicians, doctors, scien-

Introduction

tists...there's a great deal more to come. I hope that you'll come with us too.

This book is about the Work. The Legacy of an incredible talent and a unique mind. But I'd like to say a word or two about Kneale 'The Man'.

There's a common misconception that he was 'Difficult'. 'Curmudgeonly', 'Cantankerous', 'Misanthropic' even.

I don't buy it.

This is a man who was at the peak of his field. In television, he *created* his field. And he knew it.

I don't think he was arrogant, and he wasn't a show off (he was too British for that). But he knew how good he was, and his standards were high. And he didn't mince words about anything he saw as failing to meet those standards. He set the bar high, for himself and for others.

Interference from people (film and television executives) who were less experienced and less talented, must have frustrated him. Indeed, at times, I'm sure infuriated him. Certainly, I think that was the case with **HALLOWEEN III**, with which he was forever associated despite removing his name (at cost to himself) from the film. Because the changes that were made fell below the standards he held to his work and his name.

Unfortunately, for contemporary readers, because John Carpenter remains (rightly) a popular figure among film fans today, I think that particular bad experience overshadows everything else. Kneale's name and work is so little known in pop culture circles, that this is the example that comes up again and again...'he wasn't happy with what they did to his script', 'he wasn't nice about the final film', 'he didn't get along with Carpenter'. All of which is true. He did not like what was done to his original script. And as a result he removed himself from the production and his name from the credits (losing any residual payments he might have received for his involvement with the film in the process). It's also true that he disliked the final film...and let's face it he was not alone. But having removed himself from what he saw as inferior work, his name stuck. I can't think of a review or an article that doesn't mention him. And I think the more that went on, the more annoyed he got and the less kind he became about the film. Because this fly in his ear just wouldn't go away.

This image of Nigel Kneale pervades internet culture, and that's a shame. Because as a man and as a writer, Kneale was SO much more...

I've read people talk about Kneale as a misanthropic writer, but I don't read the work that way at all. He is a deeply humane writer. Concerned with human drama as well as big ideas. Indeed, all his big ideas are profoundly linked to what it means to be human.

If, as they say, drama is conflict, then Kneale's dramas deal with the conflict of what most afflicts us not only as people, but as a society, and as a species. They may seem pessimistic, and there is often an ambiguity to them, a queasy uncertainty... but there is *always* hope. The potential to overcome our worst aspects is always present. Literally, as in the Quatermass stories, or implicitly, as if by showing our worst, by confronting us with our fears and foibles and failures, Kneale is offering a warning. A plea... *must we be like this!?*

Kneale is a profoundly emotive writer, his ideas are never divorced from emotion. He makes us *feel* the idea (its implication, its meaning for us as people), not just think about it.

It seems to me that, in his combination of the emotive and the intellectual, Kneale not only demonstrates what great drama can do at its best, but what we as thinking, feeling beings can be...

Humane, emotive and intellectual in equal measure. These are the things that typify Nigel Kneale and his writing. These are the things that cracked my head wide open when I first saw **QUATERMASS AND THE PIT** at roughly 9 years old.

I'm not usually an advocate for violence, but I hope he does it to you too.

Neil Snowdon
York
November 2015

leg·a·cy
[leg-uh-see] **noun, plural leg·a·cies.**
1.
Law. a gift of property, especially personal property, as money, by will; a bequest.
2.
anything handed down from the past, as from an ancestor or predecessor: the legacy of ancient Rome.
3.
an applicant to or student at a school that was attended by his or her parent.

THE KING OF HAUNTOLOGY

Mark Chadbourn

'Hauntology is not just a symptom of the times, though: it is itself haunted by a nostalgia for all our lost futures.'

—Andrew Gallix

'To tell a story is always to invoke ghosts, to open a space through which something other returns.'

—Julian Wolfrey

THE FUTURE IS BEING FORGED ON THE WEST COAST OF ENGLAND. Arcs of promethean fire cut through the dark of a long, long night. Hammers pound iron, tolling the end of one age, heralding the arrival of a new one. In the Vickers yards of Barrow-in-Furness, they are building sleek machines to probe the inhospitable reaches. Their conical noses and fins, their missions into silent darkness, these things will soon find an echo in the works of the British Experimental Rocket Group.

But for now it is 1922, and the vessels are submarines. Their promised future of technological marvels is just beginning to take hold. King George V is on the throne, David Lloyd George is in Downing Street, and

We Are The Martians

Nigel Kneale is being born within the sound of those shipyard hammers, born into a liminal zone, between the sea and the land, between a past that is still clinging on, and a shining future, between superstition and science. It is a place he will inhabit for the rest of his days.

In the midst of life, it's impossible to see the connections, the patterns. But rise above and look down and all becomes clear. Nigel Kneale is a baby. Nigel Kneale is an old man, acid and angry in public, kind in private to friends and family. He writes, books and TV and movies. He acts and marries and has children, thinks and complains and inspires. Somehow he finds a way to listen to the voices haunting his unconscious, and through their guidance manages to articulate a particular time and place, as all the best writers do. He doesn't see that, of course. Hanging in the amniotic fluid as he focuses on this moment, and then the next one, and then the next, he hears only the distant boom and the thrum without realizing the invisible forces that pull and shape. But at the end, rising above it, looking down, we can see, we can understand.

In that Lancashire town, in 1922, those submarines *are* the future to all who lay eyes upon them. Yet still they are christened for luck, in the same way that the Babylonians did five thousand years before, and the Egyptians, the Greeks, the Romans, the Vikings. Five thousand years of blood and wine to buy the fortunes of the gods. They will never begin their journey on a Friday, the day of the crucifixion. No women can sail with them, for fear they will bring bad luck. Every man who steps on board is drilled in the forbidden words, the words of power that were never to be uttered. *Goodbye* and *drowned. Good luck* brings only bad luck. The only way to break the spell is a punch that draws blood. Another sacrifice for the gods.

The submarines sail off into the future, one that comes hard on October 2nd 1925. John Logie Baird is successfully transmitting the first television picture. In the laboratory, the greyscale image is chilling, the head of a ventriloquist's dummy named Stooky Bill. Silent, staring, jaw agape at what the world is coming to. Baird drags office worker William Edward Taynton into the experiment because he wants to see what a human face would look like. Taynton enters history. Baird enters the offices of the Daily Express, seeking fame. The terrified news editor thinks this is a madman. "Get rid of the lunatic," he tells one of his reporters. "He says he's got a machine for seeing by wireless. Watch him — he may have a razor on him!" Baird flies out of history, but only for a while. The future is coming, faster by the day. The future is here.

But still there is no escape from what was. High over Barrow-in-Furness looms the Giant's Grave, two standing stones raised five thousand years ago in the shadow of the brooding Black Combe Hill. Now, this is a place of legend, of giants in the earth, and ghosts seen on moonlit nights. But the men who set those stones were the first men of science, mapping the stars and creating a network of old straight paths, leys, marked by these stones, by age-old religious sites, and wells, and cairns.

Ley comes from an old English word meaning fire. Paths of flickering blue flame, traversing the land, crossing time, reaching into the imagination, linking us to the home of the gods, to dreams, creating patterns and structures that envelop everything. We learn this as we walk them, as we rise above them and look down upon the weft and weave of life. Look: there is Nigel Kneale aged six, leaving Barrow with his family, in the past, in the eternal now, inadvertently following one of those leys, across the sea, west to where the dead go, west to the Isle of Man, the old Kneale home. It is 1928, and Frederick Griffith has just discovered the proof that DNA is genetic code material.

The Isle of Man, in the Irish Sea midway between Britain and Ireland, still holds tight to the passing age. It is a place of stories. At the other end of that ley lies the Meayll Circle of standing stones, where the sound of a tolling bell rings out on lonely nights and travellers mysteriously lose their way. On the Castletown Road out of Douglas, where the Kneale family is moving, young Nigel crosses the Fairy Bridge. It is the home of the Mooinjer Veggey, the Manx term for the little people. Never call them fairies. Never speak their name. The Mooinjer Veggey are mischievous, spiteful. Around two feet tall, they look like mortals. They wear red caps and green jackets and often ride horses followed by packs of little hounds. Like the wild hunt of the mainland, the wish-hounds hunt souls. The Mooinjer Veggey are Manx, but they have counterparts everywhere in the mainland. You cannot escape them. Nigel greets them as all who cross the Fairy Bridge must greet the Mooinjer Veggey, with *Laa Mie*– Good day —

or risk bad luck. Before the annual TT races, which have claimed many a life, the motorcyclists visit the bridge to make a plea for good luck, like ancient pilgrims.

Nigel Kneale writes stories, by day, while his father is editing The Herald newspaper in Douglas, and by night, by candlelight. He hears stories too, everywhere. The doors open, bringing things in. The demonic black dog that stalks Peel Castle. Gef, the talking mongoose, which haunts a mountain farmhouse. On the eve of May Day, Walpurgis Night, Nigel's neighbours fix a wooden cross bound with sheep wool on the inside of their doors. It will ward off the Mooinjer Veggey. And on Peel Hill that same night, horns blow to banish evil spirits. The old world stays and stays.

In his home, Nigel understands the darkness. Since childhood, he has suffered from photophobia, an intolerance to light. Imagine: to sit on sunlit days, when the light dapples the grass beneath the trees in the garden, and yet you seek out only shadows for comfort. Sunglasses in the day, the world darkens around you. Turn inwards, where the light does not hurt. Turn to the stories that burn brighter than anything. Nigel writes.

At school, he is apart, as all boys who read are apart, but more so. The photophobia draws him away, draws him in. After St Ninian's High School in Douglas, he seeks solace in books and a small world, an office. The law seems a solid profession, ordering a world that cannot be ordered, through a precise arrangement of words and ideas. Kneale is an advocate at the Manx bar. But the order he prefers to impose comes from his own mind, his own ideas, his own words. This is not a profession for a man who opens doors to ghosts.

Peer down, now, on 1938. Ignore the distant tramp of boots, the harsh voices in the night, and watch the new world begin to take shape as it emerges from the dark. Otto Hahn and Fritz Strassman have discovered nuclear fission of heavy elements. The hiss of science begins to match the chant of prayer and spell. In his small office, Nigel is bored. When war breaks out, he tries to enlist in the army. But a man who shies away from the light is no use to them.

The fighting makes the world too big a place. Through the headlines, barely-recognised locales become as familiar as the fields outside Douglas. A small island tossed by storms in the Irish Sea is claustrophobic, even

The King of Hauntology

with leys radiating out across the globe, into the deep past, into the imagination. When Kneale broadcasts a reading of his short story 'Tomato Cain' on the BBC's North of England Home Service, it opens a door for him too, and he darts through it, to a new home, and a bigger world.

London is "an enormous anthology of possibilities", Iain Sinclair says. Stories are the city's bones. They thrum through its arteries. They join then and now, day-city and night-city, science and superstition. Though the stories abide, Kneale finds a city trapped in the post-war stasis, like the rest of the UK. Beige light, ration book hunger and near-horizons. Rubble and bomb craters and the fading strains of Glenn Miller, who himself has been cut adrift from time and space. There are no dreamers here, only sharp elbows, only gutter eyes. The nation needs strong arms to rebuild, strong hearts. But that is the least of it, though it does not yet know it. Britain needs a clearly-imagined future, one filled with hope, possibilities, but it also needs to remember who it was and from where it came.

Here, Kneale can tap into the deep past, where the stories are formed, and use those bones to help shape his view into days yet to come. Beneath the streets, lies Londinium where Boudicca led the Iceni to crush their oppressors. Londinium, burned to the ground, only to rise again. Here, the world turns. Here, Brutus of Troy defeated the giants Gog and Magog a thousand years before the Christian era and founded New Troy, Caer Troia. Here, King Lud ruled, and here, too, the Trinovantes tribe renamed the town Caer Ludein. These are all stories. Historians know nothing of these things. And so they are more potent than facts. London is founded on stories. The ghosts were let through a long time ago.

London is the most haunted capital city in the world, filled with old ghosts, and new. As Kneale begins to study acting at the Royal Academy of the Dramatic Arts, an underground worker finishes some paperwork at Bethnal Green Station. All his colleagues have gone, the last train has left. In the lonely silence, he hears children sobbing. Then women's voices, and screams, and panicked cries. The station is empty, and he runs into the night. During the blitz, sixty-two children and eighty-four women suffocated there while they were sheltering from German bombs. The screams are heard again and again, and are still heard.

All around, the future is coalescing, part-myth, part-mundane, as all

WE ARE THE MARTIANS

times are. It is 1947 and Kenneth Arnold sees nine flying saucer aircraft over the Cascade Mountains in Washington State. Two weeks later, Roswell shudders. It is 1948. Richard Feynman forms an idea of a new reality and quantum electrodynamics emerges into the light. Later, Feynman takes LSD, marijuana and ketamine and floats in sensory deprivation tanks to understand consciousness. He wonders if he can somehow reach the deep unconscious, beyond the mind that he knows.

Kneale graduates from RADA and takes an appointment as a professional actor in Stratford upon Avon. Heading north out of London to his new place of work, he passes the Rollright Stones, a three thousand five hundred year old stone circle where many leys converge. Once these pitted stones were alive, a king and his army marching across the Cotswolds, so the stories tell. The monarch met a witch, who said, "Seven long strides, thou shalt take, and if Long Compton thou canst see, king of England thou shalt be." Though the king marched forward, on his seventh stride, the ground rose up in a long mound, hiding any sight of the village ahead. The witch turned them all to stone, with the king overlooking Long Compton, his men standing in a circle not far away, and five knights whispering treachery further off. They stand there to this day.

'Ley line' came into common usage in 1921, one year before Nigel Kneale starts his journey. The historian Alfred Watkins reads a paper to the Woolhope Club in Herefordshire, expounding his theory about 'the old straight track'—prehistoric trading routes based on straight lines between sighting points, standing stones, religious sites, barrows, wells.

Dragon Lines, they are sometimes called, mythological beasts, real and unreal and symbolic. For centuries, it was believed that there was a power in the land beneath these routes and that strange things happened on them. Others call them death roads and spirit paths, to mark the route taken by funerary parties to bury the dead. And the path the soul takes when it journeys back. Ghosts walk these roads.

The Incas had these lines too. So did the Egyptians, and the nomadic tribes of North Africa. In Australia, the aboriginal people walk the lines they call turingas to keep the world alive. Formed by the creative gods, the paths connect the waking world with the dream-time, the source of everything. For those who understand the secrets, messages can be communicated along them over great distance, and at certain times of the year, energies flow through them to bring the countryside alive. All stories come from the dream-time, even this one.

There is no escape from ghosts. In Nigel Kneale's new home, the Stratford Ripper haunts the White Lion inn, and a dead pilot from the war wanders into the Dirty Duck pub for yet another last drink. Stories are published, a collection of them, and Kneale begins to understand who he is and what he must do. He sees the world around him, still drained of blood by the teeth of the war. He senses a need throbbing in the chests of the men and women at the Lyons tea shop. His publishers tell him, write a novel, people like novels. But Kneale likes the cinema and its flickering spectral lights. Human faces reveal stories better than words, he says. He wants to write television. In book-lined offices, faces crumple in horror. He does not tell his publishers that he has never seen any television.

But first: radio drama, a story that formed on the Isle of Man, a story that was real, that was in his head, a mining disaster. And then he knows he can do this thing, and he should be doing it, and he signs a contract to be one of the first staff writers for BBC Television. He learns the basics, one foot in front of the other. Adaptations of books and stage plays, scripts for light entertainment, children's shows. Sharpening the words, understanding how to open doors.

Years later, Princeton University physicist Dean Radin examines a mountain of data published in scientific journals and says, "Reality built out of imagination, which in turn is a manifestation of a primordial 'substance' that is both mind and matter? It sounds like science fiction. But there is evidence that this may be so, and if true, it might explain a number of persistent puzzles, from legends of the siddhis, to psi in life and the laboratory, and even, as unlikely as it may seem, to 'unidentified flying objects'."

It is 1951. High in the Himalayas, the air carves into the lungs and Eric Shipton takes a photo of a footprint in the snow. It is massively bigger than any human footprint. The photo travels around the world. People think, we live in a strange place. Is it real, this Abominable Snowman? Is it just a story?

It is 1952. In the New Forest, in Hampshire, John and Christine Swain

WE ARE THE MARTIANS

are driving through the back lanes with their two sons. They chance upon a lake swathed with mist, not far from Beaulieu Abbey. In the middle of the lake, there is a rock with a sword embedded in it. Awed, the family whisper about the legend of King Arthur. A memorial to him, they say, it must be. Once every three weeks, for the next seventeen years, the Swains drive from their home in Somerset to the New Forest to find the lake, and the stone, and the sword again. They never do. It is not there.

Now, here in 1952, it is time. Kneale has work to do. Writer's work. This world he sees is threadbare and dreary, still clinging on to the deprivations and spiritual destruction of the war. There is not enough humanity. But beneath the surface, other worlds exist, truer worlds, he knows this to be true. We all do. Kneale creates a character with one foot in the past but a gaze turned high, and to the future.

In this story, Professor Bernard Quatermass of the British Experimental Rocket Group supervises the first manned flight into space. BERG is informed by the peculiarly-British sensibilities of the civil service and government ministries, and of how public service by committed individuals of the kind that worked so well in the war years could lead to a new common good. The design of its rockets harks back to those sleek machines of the future that slipped from their moorings beneath the black waves off Barrow-in-Furness.

Professor Quatermass, though, is something different, something new. He is a dreamer and a man who sees hope for humanity by shackling science to that common good. He looks up and out, always. Through Quatermass, Kneale believes, the public will find an antidote to the benighted years of the recent past in this new vista that science is rapidly opening up. Quatermass can conquer the fear within us that is the legacy of that dark, superstitious past.

It is one year later, as the six-part BBC series airs in a sweltering summer, and a huge proportion of the TV viewing audience tunes in at some point across the run. THE QUATERMASS EXPERIMENT is a success. But its prescient underlying message that new threats to Britain's security will come with this new openness is already finding an echo in the wider world. The public is struggling to comprehend the ramifications of President Truman's announcement that the hydrogen bomb has been developed. As Quatermass speaks, Russia announces that it, too, has the bomb.

The world is in upheaval now. New myths are emerging. Crick and Watson have already published Molecular Structure of Nucleic Acids: A Structure for Deoxyribose Nucleice Acid. Aldous Huxley is hard at work opening THE DOORS OF PERCEPTION after trying hallucinogens. The spirit of exploration that Kneale tapped into continues, out into the universe, into the very fabric of existence, into the architecture of the mind.

Kneale is not blind to the threats that lie in the future. He writes an adaptation of Orwell's NINETEEN EIGHTY-FOUR which cements his reputation. And when he turns his attention once again to the British Experimental Rocket Group in QUATERMASS II, one of the themes is a conspiracy corrupting the political establishment.

New myths, and old. Kneale has seen Eric Shipton's photo taken high in the Himalayas, and writes his teleplay, THE CREATURE, about the Abominable Snowman. It is a seemingly simple story about a monster, yet one which is infused with both a belief that the universe offers hope, and a fear that humanity will never claw its way out of its self-destructive state. Afterwards, Kneale wants freedom for himself. He does not seek renewal of his BBC contract, stating, "Five years in that hut was as much as any sane person could stand."

Set free, Kneale begins writing what many, including the BBC itself, consider his greatest work, and one of the best works of TV drama. QUATERMASS AND THE PIT is also the point where Kneale forges perhaps his most powerful idea. He remembers that fairy bridge on the Isle of Man, those stone circles with their millennia-old legends. He understands how myth has shaped every aspect of human development, but he also understands people. They see strange things, lights in the sky, footprints in the snow, shadows with no source. But they are not liars. They are not fools.

The world seems caught between a misty shape in the shadowed ruins of an old church and the ghostly blips on a radar screen, each summoning their own form of existential dread. Perhaps there are demons, perhaps there are Martians, perhaps we are both of them. Everything is connected,

We Are The Martians

lines running through the world, through space, through history, through the human mind.

It is 1957. Analytical psychologist Carl Jung publishes FLYING SAUCERS: A MODERN MYTH OF THINGS SEEN IN THE SKY. He explores the theme of myth manifesting as real and suggests that experiences of angels, aliens, fairies, sprites, elves and demons, all may be psychophysical, a blurring of conventional boundaries between objective and subjective realities. The imaginal and the real are not as separate as they seem. It is 1957, and Kneale starts to write this new story, QUATERMASS AND THE PIT, developing his life's philosophy—that science underpins the strange. We do not throw away all those centuries of accumulated experiences of the bizarre, we do not dismiss the people who claim these things. We understand them in the fierce light of this new world.

And in QUATERMASS AND THE PIT, everything is connected. Not only scientific exploration and age-old legends, but also the world that is unfolding all around, the racial tensions that had been building across the decade, the cloying bureaucracy that still lingered after the war, the politics as the military tries to lay claim to the British Experimental Rocket Group in this developing Cold War.

It is 1960. Near Otterburn in Northumberland, at the site of a fourteenth century battlefield, the engine of a taxi dies. As silence falls on the lanes, the driver and passengers see a phantom army marching towards them. As the soldiers close on the car, they fade away.

It is 1961. There are aliens, we know that now. Betty and Barney Hill told us. In Portsmouth, New Hampshire, a reporter interviews them about how they were abducted by beings from another world as they drove home from a vacation in Niagara Falls. They are taken aboard a flying saucer, they say. Ten days later, Betty starts to experience vivid dreams of small men with dark eyes and grey skin who took them away. They look like the fairies of the Isle of Man, and act like them too.

Kneale has already imagined the future, and found the lines that join it to the past. For the sixties, he takes a long holiday, adapting plays and novels for the cinema. He earns a BAFTA nomination. He has a comfortable family life, a wife Judith Kerr, children Matthew and Tacy.

The King of Hauntology

It is 1964. Arno Penzias and Robert Woodrow Wilson provide experimental evidence of the Big Bang. Now we start to understand how the biggest story of all was created. It is 1967 and Jocelyn Bell Burnell and Antony Hewish discover the first pulsar. In the Cairo suburb of Zaitoun, at the same time, crowds witness the first of many visions of the Virgin Mary appearing over the Coptic Church.

Yet the Britain of the 1970s seems to be going backwards. After the collapsing boundaries of the sixties, the white heat of technology, the rushing torrent of optimism and change, all that is left is the mud-flats of political strife, ugly fashions, collapsing economies and corruption. 'Without You' by Nilsson is on the radio, the soundtrack of loss. So is 'Take Me Back'Ome' by Slade, and Alice Cooper's rebellious 'School's Out'. History seems to be ending. The future has been stolen, and Britain is haunted by the ghosts of those promises made only a few years ago.

It is 1972. After a grey autumn, Britain lumbers into a cold December. The air reeks of coal fires, everywhere. Saturdays are long treks home from the football, through dark terraced streets throbbing with the threat of violence. Bovril, flat caps on old men, piss beer and nicotine-stained fingers.

Somewhere a government ad-man is conjuring up a campaign to terrify children with a public information film, 'The Spirit of Dark and Lonely Water'. The hooded figure of Death stalks kids at play near a lake. It is thought that this ad is a good idea.

Christmas Day, and children awake and rush to the tree to tear cheap paper off Action Man and Sindy, Space Hoppers and roller skates. Their parents think it is a good idea to let them stay up to watch some festive BBC programming, THE STONE TAPE by Nigel Kneale. There are a lot of nightmares in the seventies.

THE STONE TAPE is a nerve-jangling ghost story that is the purest evocation of Kneale's evolving philosophy. The tradition was old—a ghost story for Christmas, another example of the writer drawing on the past and finding its relevance to the modern. In the story, an electronics company research team descends on a haunted mansion. Science collides with the supernatural as the team starts to realize that stone is a recording medium for moments of heightened emotion. Ghosts are no more than a replaying of what has been, preserved forever in the environment. Old stories flickering into life again and again and again.

The production is a masterpiece. Kneale's tale reaches out across the years, influencing new generations of writers. It reaches out across the world, too. In America, the horror director John Carpenter sees it and dreams up his film, **PRINCE OF DARKNESS**.

Kneale has had his fill of the BBC. The corporation has rejected several of his scripts and plans for a new Quatermass serial. But he still has much to say about the confluence of myth and science, and how those dark supernatural beliefs still shape the modern mind. He moves to ITV and writes BEASTS, where horrors that would have been at home in medieval times find a new place in the kitchen sink seventies.

ITV also produces Kneale's final Quatermass story, one centred on the megalithic sites that surrounded his childhood homes. It is loaded with the writer's distaste for the hippie movement and the occult beliefs they had made common currency, perhaps even a dislike for young people in general. Nigel Kneale has no truck with ley lines. Woolly-headed New Age thinking sets his blood pumping. His Neolithic standing stones are not nodes of earth energy, but markers for beacons left by an alien force. The four-part serial is not critically well-received.

Kneale does not see himself as a science fiction writer, he tells people. He does not really seem to enjoy the genre. He has nurtured a loathing for DOCTOR WHO. "It sounded a terrible idea and I still think it was," he says. "The fact that it's lasted a long time and has a steady audience doesn't mean much. So has CROSSROADS, and that's a stinker." It is the tail end of the twentieth century and Kneale is asked to write an episode of THE X-FILES. He turns it down. No one is surprised. He has a lot of anger in him, Nigel Kneale. He does not seem to like the light very much. He simmers and carps and pokes sticks. So what? No one wants a writer to be their friend. They want them to see things that no one else can see.

Jeffrey Kripal, professor at Rice University, says the mystical, the paranormal, the supernatural may be thought of as symbols that illustrate "the irruption of meaning in the physical world via the radical collapse of the subject-object structure itself. They are not simply physical events. They are also meaning events." Writers know everything.

The King of Hauntology

Writers know nothing. J.R.R. Tolkien thought THE LORD OF THE RINGS was not a reflection of the Great War. J.R.R. Tolkien thought he was writing from a Christian perspective while creating a sprawling, powerful evocation of the pagan greenwood. Writers know their conscious mind, which is next to nothing. Stories are made in the unconscious mind, where the ghosts live. They come through doors, unbidden. No one knows the unconscious mind, what works are done there. Not even writers.

It is 1993 and Jacques Derrida is finishing his work, SPECTRES OF MARX, in which he discusses an idea within the philosophy of history. Hauntology is "the paradoxical state of the spectre, which is neither being nor non-being." Derrida is intrigued by this idea, which suggests that the present exists only with respect to the past, and that society will eventually begin to form itself around the "ghost of the past", or, seen in another light, the ghost of imagined futures that never materialized. In his book of essays, GHOSTS OF MY LIFE: WRITINGS ON DEPRESSION, HAUNTOLOGY AND LOST FUTURES, Mark Fisher says hauntology is a "refusal to give up on the desire for the future".

Nigel Kneale never did give up on that desire, and his visions still haunt the world of today. We dream of the British Experimental Rocket Group that we never got, and the aesthetic design sensibility of his sleek 1950s-finned vessels. We yearn for the wide-eyed sense of hope that we need to be looking 'out there'. Nigel Kneale captured an idealized view of what could have been, should have been but never was. But he also delineated a darkness that itself haunted the human condition, one that was perhaps always self-inflicted and which would prevent us reaching those great heights he imagined. Hauntology, the first new critical theory of the twenty-first century, exists in this tension between two poles.

The past and the future. Science and the supernatural. Myth and the mundane.

Kneale may not have known his own deep mind, but he mapped Britain's unconscious at a time in our history when all sorts of lines were blurring. He understood, instinctively perhaps, how everything was connected, and by doing so, he started to sketch out new myths that owed everything to what had gone before, but were relevant to the way we live our lives now.

We Are The Martians

It is 2015 and Massachusetts Institute of Technology professor Bradford Skow publishes his book, Objective Becoming. Skow talks about the Block Universe theory, and that all time exists simultaneously. Rise above it, look down, he says, and you will see what was, what is, what will be, all happening in an ever-present instant. It is 2006 and Nigel Kneale is gone. And it is now, always now, and there is Nigel Kneale, striding across the land, across time, from the real world in to dreams, into the world of ghosts, shaking his fists, flickering with blue fire.

> 'If the evolution of knowledge in this century exceeds that of the last, which seems likely, then we can look forward to a future that's likely to redefine our concepts of reality far beyond any of the stranger concepts we've encountered so far.'
>
> —physicist, Dr Dean Radin

THE LITERARY KNEALE

Tim Lucas

THOMAS NIGEL KNEALE WAS A YOUNG MAN OF EIGHTEEN WHEN Nazi Germany raided the skies of London on the evening of September 7, 1940—the beginning of a 57-day "blitz" that toppled and gutted over one million homes and left more than 40,000 men, women and children dead.

Eighteen marks the advent of adult life in bloom, a time when the future unfolds before us in the forms of vocation, romance, and opportunity. But for those Britons who reached maturity in the ashen rubble of the London blitz, such promises were violently revoked by a hellstorm of apocalyptic proportions. A resident of the Isle of Man, Kneale responded to this rape from the sky as many others of his generation did, by attempting to enlist in the Royal Air Force; unfortunately, since the age of two, he had suffered from an allergic reaction to direct sunlight, which made him unsuitable for active duty. And so he sat out the war years, bearing witness as his fellow countrymen were shipped out to meet head-on Mars, God of War—doubtless keenly aware that he lacked the inner armour that made soldiers of other men, that warrior gene.

It was during this period that Kneale began to write short stories, while still living on the Isle of Man and working in a lawyer's office. He found opportunities to read one or two of his stories on radio programmes, and

this attracted the interest of the British publishing house of Collins, who contracted him for a book of stories. His pleasure thus became an obligation. He continued to write stories in fits and dribbles; they would accept one or two and return the rest.

After the war, in 1946, Kneale relocated to London—now a shambles. It was there, with the third acts of so many of his future scenarios strewn prophetically around him, that he began to study acting at the Royal Academy of the Dramatic Art, while dashing off the odd short story on the side. In 1949, TOMATO CAIN AND OTHER STORIES was finally published to considerable critical acclaim; the following year, it won two of literature's most prestigious prizes in a two-month period—the Atlantic Award in February, and the Somerset Maugham Award in March. A second volume of Kneale fiction would not appear for almost another thirty years, another lifetime really—not until his novel QUATERMASS appeared in 1979.

With TOMATO CAIN, Kneale had a taste of print and the traditional intimacy of communicating with readers—but it wasn't enough to satisfy him. With his background in stage drama, he was becoming more interested in writing for live audience. He wanted to write stories for broadcast. By 1953, he was doing just that for the BBC.

There is a great deal to be said for the immediacy of live television, for having the whole country discussing your work around the office water cooler the next morning. However, regardless of such ready gratifications, it must be remembered that Kneale's work for British television *stayed* in Britain. In some cases, it was even erased. His Quatermass teleplays for the BBC were subsequently made into feature films by Hammer, and these received exposure all over the world, but Kneale was always highly critical of them—even so, given the limited reach of television, these (in his estimation) inferior productions are what represented him and his best ideas abroad for decades. That is, until fairly recently, when unauthorized uploads of Kneale's television work became accessible to the world at large through YouTube. Prior to that, the only people outside the United Kingdom who could see Kneale's original teleplays were those home video obsessives who owned multi-standard equipment, who sought out bootlegged videocassettes, DVD-Rs, or imported DVDs of his programmes.

In short, for the better part of half a century, the most reliable source for the voice of Nigel Kneale was in the two books he would write. Sadly, they have become the most neglected part of his considerable legacy.

In point of fact, TOMATO CAIN is two books. It differs significantly in its respective British and American editions, the latter published by Alfred A. Knopf in 1950. The US (or 'To-may-to') edition omits two stories ('The Terrible Thing I Have Done' and 'Charlie Peace and the King') from the UK ('To-mah-to') edition while adding three ('Essence of Strawberry', 'Mrs. Mancini', and 'The Patter of Tiny Feet.') Should you care to read them, you'll have to pay dearly. It is possible to find the Knopf edition for under $200, but if you want to read the omitted stories, the state of the market may require you to double that figure. Regardless of what you pay, neither edition of the book can be considered integral.[1] TOMATO CAIN has not been in print since a Fontana Books trade paperback appeared in Britain in 1961, following the success of the BBC Quatermass serials. Even this reprint (if you can find it) will likely set you back $100 — your cheapest option, short of a lending library.

The long-term unavailability of TOMATO CAIN has led to its being too often mentioned in passing rather than discussed in-depth, even by Kneale's most devoted followers. (THE ENCYCLOPEDIA OF SCIENCE FICTION miscounts its number of stories as 26, rather than the UK edition's 28 or the American edition's 29.) It has also prevented Kneale from being rightly recognized as the originator of some of the most successful ideas to be expressed in horror and fantasy films over the past sixty years.

The purpose of this monograph is to bring some long overdue attention to Nigel Kneale's overlooked achievements as a published author, whose recurring themes and command of style are not as well-known among his admirers as his facility with ideas.

TOMATO CAIN AND OTHER STORIES (1949/50)

Nigel Kneale began writing in his early teens but his short stories did not

---

[1] It should be mentioned that another, more modern, edition exists: *Tomato Cain and Some Other Stories*, a bilingual Manx/English edition published in January 2015 by The Isle of Man Arts Council, with translations by Dr. Brian Stowell. However, this volume further reduces the number of stories from the total 31 to only those seven stories that deal specifically with life on the Isle of Man.

achieve publication until he reached his early twenties. He explained the origin of his first book in a 1998 interview: 'I'd written a couple of stories during the war, and they put me under contract to write enough to fill a book. I'd send in three or four stories and they'd say, "Oh yes, one of them's very good, we'll keep that." This went on, year by year, and I got interested in other things. I really didn't believe they'd ever publish it!"[2]

The earliest of his published stories appears to have been 'Lotus For Jamie', which appeared in the February 1944 issue of the British magazine *Convoy*. 'The Calculation of N'Bambwe' appeared in the March 1945 number of *The Strand Magazine*, when its author was 22. Another story, 'The R.A.F. and the Sleeping Beauty', marked Kneale's *Argosy* magazine debut; the story, which appeared in their February 1946 issue, would be retitled 'Enderby and the Sleeping Beauty' for its appearance in TOMATO CAIN.) The collection's title story dates back to at least as far as early 1946; it was on March 25 of that year that Kneale made his BBC Radio debut, reading 'Tomato Cain' to the listeners of the North of England Home Service programme *Stories by Northern Authors*. At that time, it had no previous print publication; nor did 'Zachary Crebbin's Angel', which also became the subject of an author's reading, this time on the *BBC Light Programme* — Kneale's first national radio exposure, broadcast on May 19, 1948.

Because it is long out-of-print and generally unavailable, any discussion of TOMATO CAIN AND OTHER STORIES must incorporate synopses if the interested reader is to follow and appreciate the fine points of commentary and criticism. My goal has been to represent the stories, to quote them to evoke something of their flavour without usurping their magic.

'TOMATO CAIN'

The period piece that gives the collection its name concerns Eli Cain, a 'sidesman' (or usher) at the Ballaroddan Methodist Church and takes place on September 28, 1883 — the day of the church's annual Harvest

---

[2] Newman, Kim and Petley, Julian. 'Quatermass and the Pen: Nigel Kneale Interviewed', *Video Watchdog* (#47, 1998), p. 42.

Festival. It details the consequences of the superstitious disharmony that Eli—'a good man'—feels when a fellow parishioner, the well-to-do John James Quilleash, adds to the home-grown vegetal contributions of local farmers and gardeners a basket of tomatoes cultivated in his home conservatory. Eli, internally stewing over these 'love apples' as a freak not of nature, something 'not fruit nor vegetable', impulsively and covertly bundles them up and carries them away with the intent of burying the lot. However, in the attempt, they burst and he is left to pile the soil by hand over the seedy glop of his abortive intentions. Cain returns to the assembly and, as others begin to question Mr. Quilleash about the disappearance of his bounty, all eyes slowly turn to Eli, who stands before the congregation with his 'dark grey Sunday suit with the long tails' stained with the red juice of his crime.

The reader may wonder, on first reading, why this particular story, so deceptively slight in its construction, was chosen to represent the volume as a whole. But 'Tomato Cain' shows the germs of Kneale's most famous works already in place. One of Kneale's Manx stories, it is keenly attuned from the very beginning to Cain's paranoia. The opening sentence invites us to peer through his windows at him, as his neighbors do, and he walks to church alone, tipping his hat when he passes neighboring houses 'in case' others happen to be looking, and finally taking a road he can walk alone, 'where his face . . . was seen only by the creeping things that lived by the roadside.'[3] A pious man, Cain sees himself as very much of the land, of the earth; however these prideful feelings mask a deep-seated sexual revulsion, a fear of contact and contamination that is unintentionally expressed when he refers to the tomatoes as 'love apples' and when the sight of them piled under his church roof prompts the comment 'Next they'll be havin' one of those stage-dancin' women in the pulpit.'[4]

Though Cain is anything but gregarious and favours the unknown watchful denizens of the woods to his own kind, his own sense of islanded purity is all he has to call his own. He feels he must maintain it, to the extent of feeling repulsed by anything that has not been grown naturally— a distrust of science later echoed in the ethos of the Planet People in

[3] Kneale, Nigel. *Tomato Cain and Other Stories*, UK edition, p. 15.
[4] Ibid., p. 18.

Kneale's 1979 novel QUATERMASS, which also features a kind of harvest festival. Cain is himself as far removed from his own humanity as he can be, and it is not too far a stretch to see kinship between his raid on Quilleash's tomatoes and the ethnic cleansings on the planet Mars in QUATERMASS AND THE PIT, as they are carried out for the same reasons. (Note that, in both cases, Kneale gravitates to 'Qu' surnames to represent scientific progress or those who stand apart from common folk.) What terrifies Cain most is contamination by outsiders, by innovation, by the future—and his contact with them is finally unavoidable, leaving him stained with a mark symbolic to that of his Biblical namesake. He has committed thievery, not murder, but the two sins are equal on the tables of the law and in the eyes of his God), thus branding the story with one of Kneale's signature touches: the underpinning of the everyday with the mythic.

'ENDERBY AND THE SLEEPING BEAUTY'

The foreshadowing of QUATERMASS AND THE PIT is stronger still in this wartime story, in which Frederick Enderby, an LAC (leading aircraftman) in the Royal Air Force, is broadsided by a sandstorm while driving through the Sahara and survives a crash that kills his fellow passenger. Stumbling through dunes whose very shapes are forever shifting under the weight of the winds, Enderby finds a long-buried structure unearthed by the storm that he is able to enter. Inside are labyrinthine tunnels that lead to a central chamber wherein the sculpture of an irresistibly beautiful woman appears to lie in repose. Enderby is unable to resist kissing it upon the lips, which has the effect of activating it to life along with the containing structure itself, which seeks to fatally entrap him with a system of deadly sharp poles that begin to emerge from the walls of the corridors, gradually filling all of its interior space, which explains the presence of so many skeletons scattered around its chambers. He barely manages to make his escape before the structure, now hovering, vanishes into the sky.

The brilliance of this story lies as much in its structure as in its substance. It is triple-layered, as it were, punctuating its main story with flash-forwards to contrapuntal remarks from Enderby himself, as recorded during his later debriefing. The airman's voice is characterized in colloquial Eastender English, which allows Kneale to inject his asides whenever the main text runs the risk of rhapsodising as Enderby swoons over the memory of the mysterious structure's goddess-like inhabitant. Adding yet another layer to the story is the assertion of the opening paragraphs that the following story contains 'the factual core of a legend that every child can tell when it has reached half a dozen years.' It speaks, of course, to the legend of Sleeping Beauty and supposes that the resonance of certain myths and legends may be traceable to certain truths buried not only deeply underground but also in our own DNA.

This story has much in common with Colin Wilson's 1976 novel THE SPACE VAMPIRES, and also Tobe Hooper's **LIFEFORCE**, the 1985 film made from it. Many reviewers of the Hooper film have compared it in vague terms to the *Quatermass* films, but because Kneale's collected stories have been so long out of print, the film and novel's more specific debt to this story has not previously been clear.

It should also be mentioned that in 1963 the British novelist Anthony Burgess published (under the pseudonym 'Joseph Kell') one of his best-received novels, INSIDE MR. ENDERBY, which resulted over time in three sequels. Burgess' Enderby was a dyspeptic, flatulent poet whose Muse often came to him in the lavatory. TOMATO CAIN was published a decade before Burgess became a book reviewer for various newspapers and magazines; he left no record of familiarity with Kneale's writing in general, nor this story in particular. However, INSIDE MR. ENDERBY and the other books in its series are very much related to a style of writing that Kneale may have originated in TOMATO CAIN, particularly in its dramatic monologue stories ('Oh, Mirror, Mirror', 'Jeremy in the Wind', 'Chains', etc). Indeed, Burgess's novel opens with a chapter in which the body of the sleeping Enderby is prodded and poked by a ghostly group of dead children supervised by a spectral schoolmarm—which can be read as an inverted analogy of Kneale's Enderby adventure (in which the airman interferes with a slumbering presence), just as Kneale's story can be read, like Burgess's novel, as a metaphor for the artist's relationship with an elusive Muse.

'MINUKE'

This widely anthologised story is one of Kneale's most cleverly structured, its fifteen pages encompassing what feels like an entire film's worth of thrilling events rather than the sketches of life afforded by some other stories in the collection.[5] The inventive structure presents the main story as backstory, which is bookended at beginning and end by present-tense addenda, in which a listening character briefly sets up and then offers closing comment on a history related in first person at much greater length by a real estate agent.

The story's title, seemingly primitive and evocative of some ancient or possibly Third World language, is deceptive. It is the name bestowed by the Pritchard family on their new home, described as 'one of those coast road bungalows...put up by one of those gone-tomorrow firms' (p. 34), 'one of those light, hollow frame-and-plywood jobs' (p. 41). Minuke is actually nothing more exotic than a punny homonym of 'My Nook.' As the agent drives a new client to visit this property, he offers a full disclosure of the problems that prompted its former abandonment. These began two weeks after the Pritchards first moved into the house, when their kitchen water tap began to selectively withhold its flow only to release it all at once with tremendous force. The agent was summoned, witnessed the problem at first hand, and was later informed—ten minutes after he left— that the plaster ceiling in the master bedroom came loose and crashed onto the bed below. The family's initial anger at the shoddiness of the house's construction turned to terror as they awakened to find all the furniture in their bedrooms rearranged overnight, fresh foods turned rotten, and particularly when Mrs. Pritchard nearly lost her hands to a dropping metal shutter while speaking to her family through a window connecting the living room and kitchen.

The agent remembers tracking down the residential development's contractor, who recalled that the ground underlying the real estate was

---

[5] Groff & Lucy Conklin's *The Supernatural Reader* (Longmans, 1953), Bryan A. Netherwood's *Medley Macabre* (Hammond, Hammond & Co., 1966), Herbert van Thal's *The Eleventh Pan Book of Horror Stories* (Pan Books, 1970), and Peter Haining's *Poltergeist: Tales of Deadly Ghosts* (Severn House, 1987) are just a few of the many horror fiction anthologies that have preserved 'Minuke.'

We Are The Martians

found to be composed of large, heavy stone slabs that seemed to mark 'a giant's grave' and which resisted any attempt to be fused with freshly poured cement. On another occasion, the agent arrived to find a policeman handling the family in the wake of a sudden landslide that forced its way through their back door, followed by the sudden explosion of their front door in his presence. The agent was next summoned to the house by a panicking phone call from Mr. Pritchard, taking time off from his job to protect his family, who was startled by his arrival as he made no such call. The house then began to breathe, slowly and stertorously, causing everyone to evacuate. Realizing that the family dog had been left behind, the agent had doubled back to collect it, only to discover the pet in the kitchen, strangled to death by an animated length of pipe. As they gathered at a safe and distant vantage, the agent and the Pritchards watched in awe as the entire quaking property was suddenly smashed as flat as a swatted fly. In closing, the listener and the agent arrive at the cleared remains of the property, where the prospective buyer is nearly struck by a white hot steel nut, which flies past him to bore through the entire width of the agent's parked car. They find it sizzling on the open road like a final warning, and flee.

Clearly, this story has much in common with that told by another Tobe Hooper film, **POLTERGEIST** (1982), scripted by Steven Spielberg with Michael Grais and Mark Victor, from a story by Spielberg. In this film (more recently remade by director Gil Kenan, working with no less than five screen-writers, in 2015), a house in an Indiana residential development falls victim to spectral mayhem including the abduction of the family's young daughter into another dimension through a television set—activities eventually explained with the revelation that the entire neighborhood was built atop a desecrated Indian burial ground. **POLTERGEIST** was frequently cited as owing a debt to Richard Matheson's TWILIGHT ZONE teleplay 'Little Girl Lost', but to my knowledge, its more conspicuous debt to 'Minuke' has heretofore gone unnoted. Though Hooper's film overlooks Mrs. Pritchard's harrowing near-accident with the shuttered window, the scene is effectively staged in Mario Bava's final feature film **SHOCK** (1977), itself a polter-geist story. Kneale himself would again explore the idea of ancient subterranean templates inviting contemporary disaster in QUATERMASS.

The Literary Kneale

'CLOG DANCE FOR A DEAD FARCE'

This is a particularly ambitious story, comic in nature, that details a disastrous 'tour version' staging of a West End play entitled 'O, Frabjous Night—A Comedy in Three Acts.' Framed as a reminiscence of the 'opening night of our last week,' it finds Kneale drawing on his personal experience as an actor in small roles in the Stratford Memorial Theatre in Stratford-on-Avon, following his 1946 graduation from the Royal Academy of Dramatic Art. Like a good many of his written works, it depicts a varied community and how they manage to navigate a path through disaster.

Everything goes wrong in this performance, a fact that Kneale foretells by having one of the acting troupe, 'old Arnie,' lose his good luck mascot Kangaroo, *'it was made of coloured pipe cleaners and wool, and it had always looked to me like some kind of dry fly.'* (p. 49) As the evening proceeds, the stage manager's nerves begin to fray because a man is waiting outside the theatre to serve him with a writ for unpaid alimony. The lead ingénue has sprained her ankle and must be replaced by her understudy, Little Dolly, who takes the stage in stark muttering terror. The audience is composed of old ladies who watch 'in rigid silence.' In the third act, just as the cast begin to find their feet, constables invade the stage in search of the manager and the set dressings of 'the old Chateau' begin to wobble and collapse—with old Arnie doing his back an injury by trying to hold up the backdrop single-handed. At last, as the actor falls to the stage in crippling pain, the audience shows its first signs of life—with harsh, derisive laughter.

As with 'Minuke,' this story incorporates three levels—bookending reminiscence, the remembered main story, and the *faux* text of the play itself. The latter is particularly inventive and looks forward to other *faux* texts (and variations thereof) in Kneale's work, such as the radio show in the BEASTS teleplay 'During Barty's Party.' The story is a progenitor of sorts to THE YEAR OF THE SEX OLYMPICS and the disastrous outcome of its *faux* text, 'The Live Life Show,' which likewise incites unintended audience laughter.

'LOTUS FOR JAMIE'

Kneale's earliest published story to be included, 'Lotus For Jamie' concerns a mentally impaired man of 40, who lives with his sister and caregiver, Emily. The exact nature of Jamie's condition is never specified; it could be brain cancer because he suffers from debilitating headaches ('Your brain was upset, dear' —p. 60), but it could also be mental retardation because his development seems arrested in most ways. Emily is called away to attend to their ailing Uncle Jacob, requiring Jamie to be left alone in their house for most of a day. Knowing that Jamie has been complaining of headaches, Emily instructs him to keep quiet, to eat the meals she will provide in advance, and to go to bed if she has not returned before 8:00.

In her absence, Jamie tires of reading his comics and, finding some money, decides to take a bus into town. Drawn to a bakery, he buys a cream cake and eats it so messily that he leaves cream in his beard that a passing child notices aloud. He then goes to a chemist's and, not understanding either the money he carries or how many aspirin are contained in a bottle, buys far more than he actually needs. At a newspaper shop, he buys three comic books, which he discovers during his bus ride home to be three copies of 'a kind of comic that had no stories and many pictures' (p. 63). Infuriated, Jamie tears them up. While passing by a neighbouring farm, he befriends and pockets 'Mister Mole.' When Emily finally returns home, she discovers her brother in bed, having swallowed some two hundred aspirin, a wild animal scurrying around his room.

One often meets characters in Kneale's stories that foreshadow Victor Caroon, the returning astronaut of THE QUATERMASS EXPERIMENT who has been changed by contact with alien space spores outside our atmosphere. In the character of Jamie, a sense of relationship is particularly strong in the way he is depicted as alienated from his own world, perhaps by some disease that is gradually robbing him of his humanity. Emily likewise relates to Caroon's wife Judith, and Jamie likewise experiences encounters with a child and another species.

The Literary Kneale

'OH, MIRROR, MIRROR'

Prefaced by a quotation from the Grimm Brothers' 'Snow White and the Seven Dwarfs' that underscores the Old Queen's pleasure at being called 'the fairest in the land' by her magic mirror, this story is not so dense as to require such explication. Artful in its indirection, it is presented as a first-person monologue spoken by the doting aunt of Judith,[6] who, at age 15, has been locked in her room in a brooding, high-walled mansion following an earlier attempt to run away. Her aunt proceeds to gingerly break the news that Judith has been deliberately denied the society of her peers because she was born different, so ugly as to be intolerable to their sight. Auntie (whose words seem never less than loving) holds up a mirror to her poor niece, presenting her 'Ugly Duckling' with a litany of her physical offences—her thin blonde hair, her '*soft, curvy*' body and '*swollen little breasts*'—while impressing upon her the norm of the coarse black hair, brown leathery skin and general shapelessness that she herself physically represents.

If 'Oh, Mirror, Mirror' now reads as predictable, it is because it anticipates by a full decade Rod Serling's 1960 TWILIGHT ZONE teleplay 'Eye of the Beholder', not only in its carefully choreographed inversion of the standard definitions of beauty and ugliness but in its narrative emphasis on a lone female voice. As such, it is one of the stories in the collection that most exquisitely delineate Kneale's gifts as a writer of dramatic monologues.

Like other stories in this collection about children who are being raised protectively, sequestered away from others of their age group, 'Oh, Mirror, Mirror' has some autobiographic bearing worth discussing. Kneale himself had been a sickly child, since a family beach outing at the age of two made his parents aware that he suffered from an allergic reaction to sunlight. He would not only suffer terrible burns, but high temperatures

---

[6] In case the reader is wondering, the story's protagonist was not named for Judith Kerr, Kneale's future wife; they did not meet until some years after the publication of *Tomato Cain*. They married in 1954. However, Judith's later success as the author of many popular children's books makes it very serendipitous indeed that her name should appear in a story predicated by a quotation from the Brothers Grimm.

WE ARE THE MARTIANS

and nausea. As a boy, he had to wear gloves and a hat when moving about, but he could only watch other children playing in the sun from afar. This explains the recurring sympathy found in his writings for the secluded, the different, the eccentric, and the alien.

This story's particular value as a key to Kneale's work is its gentle emphasis on the unreliability of the subjective view, and the exposed disconnection between the truth of a matter and what one is led to believe. There is in the surprise revelation of Judith's beauty a tacit relationship to the many things in Kneale's writings that are introduced as commonplace and unworthy of notice, which are gradually revealed as having cosmic significance — the rubble scattered around Winnerton Flats in QUATERMASS II, the supposed 'Satan' bomb of QUATERMASS AND THE PIT, the basement wall of THE STONE TAPE, the disused Finnycity aquarium of BEASTS' 'Buddyboy' episode. Here, as in the 'Huffity, Puffity' children's rhyme of QUATERMASS, the truth governing Judith's sad world has always hidden in plain view, in the pages of one of her children's books.

'Oh, Mirror, Mirror' was produced as a radio play by John Whiting for KPFA in Berkeley, California sometime in the 1960s, with the role of Auntie played by Eric Bauersfeld. The recording has been preserved and was aired as recently as November 2012 as part of the macabre spoken word programme *The Black Mirror* at www.radioriel.org.

'GOD AND DAPHNE'

This is a four-page short, also about manipulative aunts and innocent nieces being judged as wicked. It's the fourth birthday of little Daphne, who is being raised by her elderly spinster aunts Janet and Susan. Daphne doesn't care for the dried apple rings served to her as a special treat, and drops them out the window of her upstairs room, watching as a striped cat passing by pauses to sniff and ignore them. Her aunts decide that it's high time Daphne was introduced to the Bible, which they tell her was written by God, who speaks to people through signs, and who sees to it that all good people go to Heaven while bad people do not. Worried because she has been raised to think it's bad to not clean her plate, Daphne later goes outside and buries the apple rings, praying to God that He might accept her sincerest apology and to give her a sign that she will someday be let into Heaven to be with her aunts. Something wet falls from the sky—not a raindrop, because *'except for one of God's birds flying ever so high above, the sky was quite empty and clear.'* (p. 77)

The placement of 'God and Daphne' directly after 'Oh, Mirror, Mirror' encourages the attentive reader to draw connections between the two narratives. The ugly aunts in both stories clearly were drawn from the same model, and the two unmarried aunts of this story seem to point ahead to the Barlow spinsters of the later 'The Excursion.' 'God and Daphne' is, like its precedent, evidence of the vast gulfs that often exist between truth (which Kneale always depicts as unknowable in its unimaginable enormity) and belief. Her aunts decide for her that, at age four, 'Daphne is old enough to know about the Bible' (p. 75). She is presented with the book (*'it had no pictures, and the pages were covered with tiny words'*) but not truly introduced to it, as its importance must be explained to her through the distortions of her caregivers' beliefs. By the end of the story, Daphne has been duly intimidated, even damned to eternal Hell in her own senses, but—most importantly—kept so in line by fear, that the child confuses a bird dropping with the word of God.

This ironic, scatological expression of impatience with religious dogma should not be taken to equate spiritual signs with bird shit, only their characterization as 'the word of God.' Kneale's work revels in spiritual mysteries, connecting them to eurekas that resonate on the deepest levels of our human and spiritual makeup. However, Kneale does stand in rational opposition to belief systems grounded in fear and superstition, which presume to know things that cannot be known, whose ultimate truth is typically self-interested and motivated by public or personal politics. It is not surprising, given his apparently strong feelings on the subject of religion, that his work assumed over time a more scientific grounding and that the very essence of his collected work lay in finding connections between points of mystery and logical arguments for occurrences mistakenly interpreted in faith. In this story, Kneale demonstrates how, with very little effort (remember, only four pages), even the most rudimentary belief system is sufficient to separate Daphne from the reality of the world around her—an alienation from her own world that will only become

WE ARE THE MARTIANS

more inculcated in her with the passing years. She is expected to understand the abstractions of holy scripture before she is old enough to comprehend the most basic workings of her own world and *that*, the story seems to wink, is how they get you.

'JEREMY IN THE WIND'

Mistaken belief is also at the core of this first-person narrative, which attends the amok friendship of an addle-pated young man and his best friend, who, though never explicitly described as such, is a pumpkin-headed scarecrow. Mice leap from its mouth and its arms wave animatedly in the midst of a field on a windy day. The unnamed protagonist steals Jeremy from the field and carries him into town, taking violent exception to anyone making fun of him, or to their friendship with one another. He assaults a laughing, mocking carriage driver to the point of bloodshed, threatens a woman grocer, and leaves a policeman bent on arresting him unconscious. The story concludes in the manner of a direct threat, with the storyteller and Jeremy having forced their way into a private home — yours — where they intend to stay forever.

Reading 'Jeremy in the Wind', one is reminded of the character Sladden in QUATERMASS AND THE PIT, played by Richard Shaw in the 1958 teleplay and by Duncan Lamont in Hammer's 1968 feature: a rugged farmer driven mad by Martian information invading him on a cellular level, who prances and leaps through open fields as though driven by an unearthly wind.

'THE EXCURSION'

One of the longest stories in TOMATO CAIN, and unusual of the collection in its avoidance of superstition and other forms of dark psychological undertow, 'The Excursion' is one of Kneale's most exemplary pieces of prose writing. The events of the story are quite simple: Mr. Clucas, a widower of sixty-two years, harnesses his old horse Robert to a seldom-used carriage (the leather seats need cleaning for mildew) one Sunday morning for the uncommon adventure of a ride into

The Literary Kneale

the town of Peel. He's not going alone; he's more or less acting as driver to a young married couple, Jeremy and Nellie Callister, who are expecting their first child and for whom he feels a *'fatherly'* affection. As they climb aboard, with Mr. Clucas fretting about whether the jostling of the carriage might upset Nellie's pregnancy, the group are joined unexpectedly by the *'big-bosomed'* widow Mrs. Kaighin and her two children, Grace and Edward John, who, after a prolonged negotiation of the available space, join in. With the children consigned to various laps, Mr. Clucas is further able to accommodate *'th' ould women'*, Misses Anne and Ethel Barlow, visiting spinsters from England who have ill-advisedly been invited along by Mrs. Kaighin, so long as everyone agrees to climb out and walk when they come to an uphill path, so as to spare old Robert's heart the strain.

> *"What age is he now?" asked Callister.*
>
> *"Ah—he's gettin' on." Mr. Clucas felt that his age should be Robert's secret. To give it, amid head shakes, would be like shortening the animal's life.* (TC, p. 86)

Mr. Clucas's internal logic is one of the story's few concessions to superstition, which also briefly surfaces in the three threats used at different times by Mrs. Kaighin to pull her misbehaving children back into line (*'Hush! The bugganne'll get ye!'*—p. 86[7], *'Be still, or the black man'll get ye!'*—p. 87[8], *'Don't go in deep now, d'ye hear! Or the tarroo-ushtey'll get ye and pull y'under!'*—p. 89[9]).

---

[7] According to *The Manx Note Book* (Volume 1, April 1885), "The BOGGANE is a general term for any frightful apparition."

[8] The 'black man' is most likely a reference to the Phynnodderee of Manx superstition, which is said to be half-man and –beast, with flaming red eyes peering out through its shaggy, black hair.

[9] According to the *Myth Beasts* website at www.mythicalcreatureslist.com, the Tarroo Ushtey is 'a water bull from the folklore of the Manx people of the Isle of Man. It was similar to the Tarbh Uisge but less vicious and it lived in the lowland pools and swamps rather than the ocean. It was a black bull with fiery nostrils. It would emerge from the pools and swamps to mate with the cattle on farms. Its calf when it reached adulthood would cause trouble and be a nuisance to farmers.' It is also the subject of its own story in *Tomato Cain*.

WE ARE THE MARTIANS

The visit to the *'little sandstone town'* of Peel, with its *'broad, empty bay and the crumbling red castle on its islet'* is mostly uneventful: Mr. Clucas sits on the shore with Mrs. Kaighin (*'She lay on her back and her big bosom shook.'*—p. 88) until he feels her conversation about the difficulties of raising two children alone and her physicality unwelcomely tugging at his emotions, and walks away. The two English spinsters have a petty argument likely born of more deep-seated frustrations, the older Ethel complaining that Anne has contradicted everything she has said today and finally blaming her for their abandoning England for *'this horrible place.'* The Callisters spend their time in Peel exploring the remains of the castle, where the expectant Nellie finds herself disturbed by the implications of its dungeons and cannon (*'It would be a terrible killin' thing once.'*—p. 95) and concerned that her reaction to these dark things might *'be puttin' a mark on the child...'*

Just as everyone regroups for the return trip home, Nellie suffers a collapse. Mrs. Kaighin takes charge, separating her from her husband and the others in case she should miscarry, but her ailment turns out to be nothing more than a kickback from some kippers she ate. On the way back,

Gaiety grew all the way.

The younger Miss Barlow started it, with the softest singing of a hymn, as a form of lullaby. Her sister took it up, still almost as clear as in a Wiltshire choir-stall. And soon the singing of all of them, scandalous and happy, was bringing people to their cottage doors to wave good-night. (*p. 99*)

'The Excursion' is utterly charming in its carefully observed portraiture and painterly landscaping, worthy of comparison not only to Maupassant (as Elizabeth Bowen notes in her Foreword to the book) but to other bards of English country living, including Thomas Hardy, H.E. Bates, or D.H. Lawrence. It captures perfectly the pleasures, dreams and concerns of a group of ordinary people brought together by random proximity, and shows how a neighborhood of this place and period could be counted upon to look after their own.

'FLO'

The story of a man and his dog, possibly the most heart-rending tale in the book, 'Flo' finds Kneale testing the limits of how far he can go without his reader turning completely against a protagonist. Percy Hurd is a man out of work on the tenth anniversary of his wife's death, who is living in the open with his aging, rat-catching dog, Flo.[10]

As the story opens, Percy is pawning his overcoat for *'three cold half-crowns'*, which he spends on a bottle of cleaning fluid, explaining that his overcoat needs cleaning, but which he then takes to a hidden spot in a bleak field and judges to taste like fire. As the effect of the blue liquid sets in, Percy becomes nostalgic, his thoughts turning to his late wife (*"'My old woman didn' like dogs. No, she didn', no. Funny about that: why shouldn' she like—? But she died and it didn't matter.'"*). In an effort to divert his thoughts from anguish, he tries to engage Flo in fetching stones, but the hungry, bleary-eyed dog soon tires. Percy goads the animal until it snaps at him out of exhaustion and fear. Angered, the drunken Percy drags Flo to a nearby veterinarian, complains of the attack, and uses his remaining coins to have the bitch put down.

He awakens in the field the next morning, calls for the dog out of habit, and is quickly recalls the awful thing he has done. He races to the vet, but it's too late. Insane with grief and remorse, he takes the dog's carcass with him, carrying it through the town on his shoulder till nightfall. He is found the next morning, sodden with chemical spirits, sitting beside his lifeless companion. Told by a policeman that he cannot stay there, Percy rises to his feet and leans on the officer, muttering through his tears about the death of his wife that very afternoon, caused by a bite from the dog, whose body he kicks savagely.

If 'Flo' narrowly escapes notoriety as the cruelest story in this collection, it is partly because its finale reveals the burden of guilt and resentment invested in Percy's relationship with his pet, and that the dog's death at the hands of a caring doctor is a kindness in contrast to the prolonged life she

---

[10] Notice Kneale's tendency to name certain of his stories after the animals in them, rather than their human characters.

would have had with her master. This is finally less a story about a man and his dog than about buried feelings ritually revisited through libation, and how those nostalgic indulgences can overtake the attention paid to one's present life. Percy, in effect, drinks to 'become' his late wife, to feel as one with her again, though she hated the only other thing he loved.

This is also the first 'beast' story of six in the collection, addressing an already present fascination with animals that would later flourish in the form of Kneale's 1976 ITV mini-series BEASTS.

'THE PUTTING AWAY OF UNCLE QUAGGIN'

This is another picaresque Manx story about a congregation of eccentric characters, who this time gather in the wake of Ezra John Quaggin's death on the day of Queen Victoria's diamond jubilee in June 1897, for the old man's funeral and the reading of his will. Tom-Billy Teare, the husband of Ezra's niece Sallie, was assured by him before his death that he had provided for them in his will. Indeed, a document leaving them the farm is found in an unlocked deed box on the premises. During a wake held at the farm, *some sort of cousin* known as Lawyer Quaggin appears and, as the time comes for the will to be read, the document is found missing—meaning that the bequest will have to be evenly divided amongst a large family crazy as coots. Knowing Lawyer Quaggin to be the most likely thief, Tom-Billy undertakes a clever plan to force him out into the open—starting a fire in the kitchen, chasing everyone out-of-doors, and entrusting the unlocked deed box in the hands of Lawyer, saying so all can hear, 'Here, take this! An' keep it safe! Uncle Ezra's will is inside it!' When all settles down for the reading, the long, sky-blue document is back in the box where it had previously been.

A companion piece of sorts to 'The Excursion', 'The Putting Away of Uncle Quaggin' shares with it many quaint and colourful characteristics, particularly its double-edged details of funeral food like tasteless cold beef and the refreshments served in pickle glasses, but also its way of teasing the reader with the possibility of dark prospects. Elizabeth Bowen notes in her Foreword to TOMATO CAIN that Kneale's children and animal stories 'focus on suffering' and 'dangerously approach the unbearable' ('Flo' meets it full-on), but this is also true of these two stories involving young married couples who are expectant — of a child in the former story, and of domestic security here.

The family name of Quaggin, and the story's passing mention of '*Quine the draper*' — not to mention the collection's recurring character John James Quilleash — indicate that the queerness of 'Qu' names had attracted Kneale long before Quatermass, a name that he recalled fishing out of a telephone directory.

'THE PHOTOGRAPH'

This story recalls 'Oh, Mirror, Mirror', in that its focal point is a sickly child living in a more privileged, but far less free, environment than the working class characters who inhabit Kneale's stories in greater number.

Raymond has limbs '*sore in the places where they bent*' and has evidently been bedridden for some time. He glimpses '*a terrible, thin face . . . that belonged to a thing, not a person*' in the mirror, unfamiliar with his own long-neglected reflection, as he is fussily dressed by his mother and sister Gladys for a sitting with a professional photographer. The unspoken imperative behind the appointment, which is life-endangering, is his mother's desire to have a picture of the boy before he dies. During the photo session, Raymond finds the cameraman repulsive, yellow-eyed with fingers stained and nails cracked by dark room chemicals, and he feels that these traits have the power to contaminate his work when the resulting photograph displays, once again, '*that terrible face.*'

Left alone in his room with the portrait illuminated on his mantel by a flickering candle, Raymond begins to intuit his own pending metamorphosis: '*He felt cold and small. Then, in the same instant, he was enormous. His head stretched from the pillow until it touched the walls.*' — (p. 129) The terrible face in the photograph smiles at him '*with little bony teeth.*' '*Just-keep-quite-quite-quite-still,*' it tells him. '*You won't be anything at all.*' The sound of cries coming from his room interrupts a downstairs argument between Raymond's mother and the family physician, the latter angered that the woman would endanger her child's precarious health by moving him from bed to have him photographed. They race upstairs and find the boy half-dressed in his nightshirt, half-dressed in the clothes worn in the photo. He tells them he won't go on the mantelpiece.

This is plainly the tale of a child who senses his own imminent demise and the fact that his place in his mother's life has already been occupied by the photograph of a likeness he cannot recognize as his own. There is, in this story of alienated love and alienation from self, a foreshadowing of Victor Caroon's affected relationship with his wife upon his return to Earth in THE QUATERMASS EXPERIMENT. Indeed, it is something shared in common with each of the Quatermass serials and films: the infected characters of QUATERMASS II, the Martian possessed characters of QUATERMASS AND THE PIT, and also Clare Kapp in QUATER-MASS/THE QUATERMASS CONCLUSION, whose comparative youth makes her psychically attuned to Isabel, a survivor of the cosmic harvesting of a gathering of Planet People, a gift that ultimately separates her from her husband. The character of Isabel herself relates to Raymond in that her contamination from the alien ray—a metaphor for the sunlight that afflicted Kneale throughout his life—causes her limbs not only to crystallize but to distend, to expand, much as Raymond perceives his own metamorphosis.

'CHAINS'

Another of the book's first-person narratives, 'Chains' consists of the ramblings of Samuel, an unwholesome dealer in used chains, who leads a prospective customer—cleverly, played by the reader—to a wharf-side shack where his goods are precariously arranged. (*'Crush a man's head like a barnacle if they come down sudden.'*—p. 135) Attended by his rat-hunting dog Crabber, Samuel details his routine of obtaining, cleaning and storing chains of all sizes and makes, and the dangers of unsettling them with sudden noises. It gradually emerges from the monologue that the buyer being addressed is the captain of the Lampedusa, a shipmaster working in the illegal slave trade, seeking manacles as well as heavy chains, and none too particular about their condition so long as they can restrain prisoners. The six-pager concludes with the expected unsettling of some heavy chains and the death of a character.

The Literary Kneale

Perhaps the most bedeviling writing experience of Kneale's career was his thwarted attempts to develop a project called CROW, the story of the real-life Manx slaver Hugh Crow, which he wrote as a mini-series, feature film and stage play in the mid-1970s. The unnamed customer in this story might well be Crow. Kneale might well have been inspired to write this story by a viewing of the 1943 Val Lewton production THE GHOST SHIP, directed by Mark Robson, in which a character is memorably dispatched by being trapped in a ship's hold, unable to call for help as it loudly fills with heavily piling chains.

Deeply informed by Kneale's theatrical experience, this is above all a masterful and unsettling study in voice, worthy of Poe; one that communicates not only a vivid sense of character—encompassing Samuel's family history, his appreciation of solid craftsmanship, his brutish relationship to his dog (including this story among TOMATO CAIN's 'beasts' tales), his peculiar morality, and racism—but also eerie, salt-laden, coastal atmosphere.

It is surprising that, so far as can be determined, it has never been adapted to a dramatic or radio performance. Editor Christine Bernard included 'Chains' in her anthology THE FOURTH FONTANA BOOK OF GREAT HORROR STORIES, published in 1981 by Harper Collins.

"THE TAROO-USHTEY'

Of all the stories collected in TOMATO CAIN, 'The Taroo-Ushtey' is perhaps the most fundamentally Knealean, insofar as that adjective is commonly deployed. The focus of this character study is another 'Qu'—Charlsie Quilliam, the fattest inhabitant of an unnamed but obvious island, the sort of misfit whose peculiarities might make him a target of cruel sport in more civilized environs, who has become a formidable and unassailable source of superstitious truth for its other people. Kneale sets up his tale magnificently:

'In the far-off days before the preachers and the schoolmasters came, the island held a great many creatures besides people and beasts. The place swarmed with monsters... As the generations went by and people took to

> *speaking English on polite occasions, the old creatures grew scarcer. By the time that travellers from the packet boats had spread the story about a girl named Victoria being the new queen of the English, their influence was slipping; at night people put out milk for the fairies more from habit than fear, half-guessing it would be drunk by the cat; if they heard a midnight clamour from the henhouse, they reached for a musket, not a bunch of hawthorn. But back hair could still rise on a dark mountain road.' (p. 138)*

Offering civilised counterpoint to Charlsie is one Duncan McRae, a Scottish, peg-legged peddler dealing in buttons and elastic who is reliant on good stories to get his foot in the door of the closeted Manx people. When he hears that a new-fangled device called a 'fog horn' is to be tested on the English side of the channel, 'less than thirty miles away', he hastens with his bag of buttons to the nearest village, and hears the eerie bellowing of the horn through the lowering fog. Unfortunately, he finds the village curiously empty of people and cannot make a sale.

Kneale then backtracks through the story to present Charlsie's side of it, as he was brought to the door of his cottage earlier by a hubbub of visitors led by the elder Juan Corjeag. Charlsie's neighbors have heard a fearsome sound offshore requiring his knowledgeable identification. As he shepherds the group downhill to a place with a clearer view of the sea, the sound becomes clear enough for Charlsie to balefully identify the bellowing as the cry of a *tarroo-ushtey*, a mythic creature with a bull's head and webbed feet, known to drag unsuspecting land dwellers to their doom. Charlsie ceremoniously lays a charm of herbs on the water to quiet the thing.

As he returns uphill to their homes, Charlsie finds his neighbors still gathered outside and gabbing about the 'nonsense tale' being told by the Scotch peddler. The story culminates in a showdown-of-sorts between Charlsie and McRae, simple truth versus elaborate superstition, that ends when the bellowing of the horn ceases for the night, for which Charlsie and his charms take full credit.

In a final twist, Charlsie is revealed to be something more, and less, than artful in white magic when he laughs McRae out of town and proposes, before the others, to write a letter to the government, advising them that it might be a good idea to devise a machine to make the sound of the *tarroo-ushtey* to guide ships through the fog. When the fog horn makes no further sound for the next week, this plays into Charlsie's plan to save his own smug hide. The story ends with Charlsie's fame as an inventor spreading through local gossip, as he takes credit for all manner of devices in common use outside the village.

In telling this deceptively simple but beautifully woven story, Kneale charts at grassroots level the ancient relationship between superstition and politics, terror and power; he shows how easily people have been manipulated by others through the centuries with rumours inspiring fear and dread, others motivated by great ambition or, in this case, a more rudimentary need to be respected. At the same time, Kneale never presents the more mythic past to which he alludes, or its native creatures, as mere illusion devised to delude the simple and malleable; he permits their reality as a boon of consensus, a consensus that evolved over time to exclude old information as new information was included as communication between peoples extended.

Kneale's conflation of the fog horn with the call of the *tarroo-ushtey* significantly predates Ray Bradbury's more famous story 'The Fog Horn', which first appeared in the June 21, 1951 issue of *The Saturday Evening Post* and was subsequently included in his 1953 collection THE GOLDEN APPLES OF THE SUN. In the story, a sea monster arises from the deep to demolish a lighthouse with its attentions, evidently drawn to it by the sound of its fog horn, which it has confused with the love cry of its own kind. The story was acquired by Warner Bros., which filmed it (none too faithfully) as **THE BEAST FROM 20,000 FATHOMS** (1953), the picture that launched the solo screen career of legendary stop-motion animator Ray Harryhausen. It became arguably the most seminal work of 1950s science fiction cinema.

'CURPHEY'S FOLLOWER'

Like 'Flo', this is an animal story but it's of a more uncanny, magical realist caliber, a foreshadowing of the quirkier stories Kneale would later tell in

WE ARE THE MARTIANS

his BEASTS miniseries. 'Curphey's Follower' is also uniquely related to other stories in the collection, with "Tomato Cain"'s John James Quilleash mentioned as the employer of its protagonist, Lot Curphey. Quilleash will also have a cameo role in the subsequent story 'Zachary Crebbin's Angel.' For Kneale to have begun interlacing and cross-referencing his stories in this manner may indicate that having some of his stories cover a broader fictional canvas—much as John Cheever would later do when he wove various *New Yorker* stories into his first novel, THE WAPSHOT CHRONICLE (1957). The idea might have worked out well for Kneale, as it won Cheever the National Book Award for Fiction.

Lot Curphey is described as *'a small man, chiefly from shortness of the legs, with a tufty hairiness about the face,'* who limps on a left leg injured in a ploughshare accident years before, and wears a yellow overcoat given him by his employer, Quilleash. While limping home to his cottage one night, he makes the unlikely acquaintance of a kindred duck: *'It stood on the rough slate step boldly, but with its right leg oddly twisted, like a bored corner boy. One eye looked in his face; the other was closed and hollow. Its feathers lay many ways; in patches there were none. Those that remained were black.'* (p. 151) Curphey claps his hands to scare the bird away, but still finds it awaiting him in the same spot the morning after. It waddles after Curphey's yellow coat on its *'twisty leg'* as he limps his way to work.

By the fourth day, Curphey's head is ringing with his neighbours' giddy chants of 'Mary Had a Little Lamb.' He takes the devoted fowl with him to the village pub, where he uses it as a novelty to entice free drinks from the locals. It occurs to him, hours into the merriment, to treat the duck to some corn meal doused in gin, which inebriates it. As drink continues to flow, Curphey grows more and more resentful of the animal but the barkeep sends him home before the scene can turn ugly—but it does, just before he leaves, when one of the patrons, Moughtin, dares to point out the obvious: that *'The thing is; he's—he's the bloody spittin' image of the duck!'* The unspeakable eureka, now spoken, gnaws at Curphey on his besotted walk home. He tries to take out his anger on the mocking fowl, but gets the worst of it himself.

'Curphey's Follower' reads uncomfortably, teasing the reader inces-

50

santly with the portent of animal cruelty, as it moves inexorably toward some final accounting as all doppelganger stories must. That said, the entire piece is possessed of a quirky, twisty-legged humour that seems to emanate from the duck, who, for all its misshapenness, is possessed of an innate nobility somehow beyond the ken of the man whom it dogs to his doom.

'THE TERRIBLE THING I HAVE DONE'

A rare disappointment among the TOMATO CAIN stories, 'The Terrible Thing I Have Done' is a darkly comic monologue delivered by the unnamed royal taster of a Pharoah of ancient Egypt, who unburdens himself to one Iranamet about the circuitous circumstances that led to his poisoning their leader (known as 'the Good God') and then himself. The comic element is derived from his story being told in colloquial English, with an occasional intoxicated belch worthy of the Burgess Enderby.

The story fails in the uncolourful language chosen to tell it, in its unusual aggression to please, and in going nowhere that isn't readily obvious from the moment the speaker is identified. Also, by the time we reach this point in the book, we've already had a few stories that culminate in medicinal or alcoholic poisonings. Though it could reasonably be argued that the story's conflation of ancient times with contemporary speech conveys something of Kneale's recurring interest in the present's unconscious co-existence with the remote past, this minor work was wisely omitted from the US edition, where 'Essence of Strawberry', a rather more pleasing poisoning story, replaced it.

'QUIET MR. EVANS'

Reasonable jealousy and romantic nostalgia are the themes of this story, whose namesake is a Fish & Chip shop owner and cook, prompted by the gossip-mongering of his customers to interrupt a private conversation between his wife Megan and a young admirer, John Phillips. Ordering the clucking geese out of his shop, Owen Evans—crook-legged like Lot Curphey and his duck—sends his wife to her room like an errant child and has what he intends to be a subtly cautionary talk with Phillips. Unfortunately, his temper takes a turn for the worse and the talk ends with him dumping some freshly fried, salted and vinegary chips over the younger man's head. After throwing him out to the amusement of the locals, Evans heavily mounts the stairs to his bedroom, where he discovers that Megan has left him—'*Her coat had gone from behind the door. Drawers stood open.*' (p. 177) He takes to the streets in search of his wife, hastening through '*the wild spaces of heather and bracken … where he used to walk with her before they married*' (p. 178) until the sound of the night's last train whistle inspires him to try the station. The train has departed and there is no one there but Old Thomas, the station master, and a couple of chips on the platform.

> '*Old Thomas spoke gravely. "Those fell out of his clothes when he went to pay for the tickets. Like confetti. She never let go his arm."*
> '*He gave a dry cough. "You're better rid of her," he said, "if she would go like that."*' (p. 179)

It is common for the stories in this collection to tease us mercilessly with the possibility that the worst might happen, only for Kneale to step in at the last moment to shed some deserved grace on his characters, sparing them the losses that have hovered like storm clouds over the preceding pages. Nellie Callister doesn't lose her baby in 'The Excursion', the thief of the will doesn't get the best of Tom-Billy Teare in 'The Putting Away of Uncle Quaggin', and the duck comes out on top in 'Curphey's Follower.' Yet in this story, Owen Evans doesn't fare so well, perhaps because he doesn't handle its central situation as well as we expect, the expected airing-out of Megan's flirtation with Phillips giving vent to unsuspected depths of sadism in his character—which, truth be told, are also evident in the forceful way he orders his wife to her room. Introduced to us as a 'quiet' man, Mr. Evans is nothing more than a possessive, controlling bully—his last words in the story are '*Megan's my girl*'. He shows a different face to the world, and so receives his just desserts.

The Literary Kneale

'TOOTIE AND THE CAT LICENCES'

In some ways, this story is the most successful of the many character monologues in the book, but Kneale cleverly embeds it within another first-person account, in which a narrator—possibly Kneale himself—arrives in a Manx village overrun with cats and seeks respite from *'one of the hottest afternoons of the year'* in a pub. Before going inside, he passes by *'a low, fat man, erecting with red-faced energy a narrow signboard'* at the side of what appears to be a duck pond—a possible nod to 'Curphey's Follower.' In the pub, the narrator sees the sign-maker enter, where he is approached at the bar by a *'tall, lean person with an expressionless face and hair like string'*—who finagles a pint out of him.

'How's the cat licences, Tootie?' the other man asks, irritably, before leaving.

At this, the narrator strikes up a conversation with one of the pub's regulars, a colourful speaker, who is persuaded to share the 'private story' about Dicky-Dan Watterson, the sign maker, and Tootie Taggart (*'He pointed to his forehead. "A touch clicky is poor Tootie."'*) The narrator assures us that the privacy of those involved in the story has been protected with the use of false names, the only reference to him being a writer.

The man whose voice temporarily takes possession of the tale explains that, one night when the patrons were talking as patrons will do, Dicky-Dan announced that the village was becoming a disgrace and that something needed doing about Gob Kelly, a violent drunk, and the cats that where turning up everywhere. Everyone was in agreement *'but nobody was terrible eager to actually do anything'* about Kelly, so they turned instead to the cat problem. It was promptly passed on to Tootie for handling; he was named 'Licence Inspector Taggart,' to whom anyone with a dog or cat would be answerable—with no one in town having a cat licence, needless to say; a job with no salary but good for the occasional pint courtesy of Dicky-Dan. It all turns out to be a preamble, cooked up by Dicky-Dan in his cups, to await Kelly with a group of other men in the fields where the Irishman was known to sleep it off, ambush him, and tie

WE ARE THE MARTIANS

a sackful of feral cats captured by Tootie to his head. "*He showed up in one o' the towns with a face like a junction of the railways. The cats had cleaned most of the red hair off him too. He wasn't a quarter of the lady-killer that he had been.*" The bar patron asks, "*Would it surprise ye to know he never come back? Would it now? Well, 'tread on the divil's tail and he'll eat ye; laugh at his horns an' he'll cry...*" (p. 187)

In a haunting coda, the story's original narrator exits the pub and sees Dicky-Dan putting the finishing touches on the sign beside the duck pond, painting the word 'DANGER' upon it in red. '*A duck stood in the middle of the drying slime, watching him; the water came half-way up the bird's legs. But perhaps in winter it was deep.*' (p. 188)

There is in this closing sentence an allowance for the sake of entertainment. It admits that not all stories, nor all narrators, are reliable, but what's the harm in believing a story for the sake of passing time?

'PEG'

A third-person story so intimately entwined with its protagonist's inner thoughts as to feel like a first-person account, 'Peg' is the shortest story in the book, yet one of Kneale's most endearing delineations of character. Indeed, though only one character figures in the story proper, it feels teeming with them as the hotsy-totsy Peg, swinging her handbag, strolls along a busy market street, heading toward the arcade where people her age gather, taking in the sights. She's an outgoing sort, saying hello to everyone, showing off her knees, looking for fun, even taking a good-looking gentleman by the arm, but she feels ignored, invisible—like Claude Rains in a movie she saw back before the war. The story implies, virtually on its first page, that Peg is a ghost, and it transpires that she is, the ghost of a young teenager killed in the blitz. She was evidently bombed into some shade of purgatory, where she has been left to watch life continue on without her, as hemlines descend, as jukeboxes blast, as other ladies are gifted with the mink shawls of postwar prosperity, her legs never tiring, her soul never maturing, her yearning heart never satisfied. '*She would always be fourteen.*'

In the hands of another writer, Peg's status as a ghost would be withheld

The Literary Kneale

till the final page, paragraph or sentence, but Kneale alludes to her disembodied condition on the first of his story's four pages. To build to such a revelation could only lead to a quickly surpassed surprise; to get the revelation out of the way early allows him to explore the psychology of someone who has paid the ultimate price of war without attaining the maturity to understand even the basics of how life, relationships or commerce work. Peg is forever stuck in a young teenage girl's moonstruck view of the world, and the idea that the stars can never leave her eyes is this story's ultimate horror.

In the story's collusion of ghosts from the past and the fallen bombs of the blitz, there is also a whiff of QUATERMASS AND THE PIT about this story, in which one extinct is the only extant character. Furthermore, in QUATERMASS, the aging title character reflects that all the greying and whitening men and women of his generation, the generation of the blitz—invisible to the young—are ghosts. The real ghost, of course, was Kneale himself, rejected by the RAF, who surely invented this story as metaphor for his own sense of displacement from the war effort.

'ZACHARY CREBBIN'S ANGEL'

This is a touching story about a nondescript, elderly man who obtains a moment of celebrity when word gets about that he was recently visited by an angel. Agreeing to tell the story, old Zachary crowds his humble living quarters with a half-dozen visitors—all male, because to invite women into such cramped quarters with men would be asking for trouble (one of them is named Quirk, another of Kneale's queer 'Qu' names)—and entertains questions from them about the encounter. When he describes the skin tone of the angel as 'yellow', one of the visitors—John James Quilleash, no less!—is outraged and exits the place in an offended outburst, but the others remain enchanted and inquisitive. Putting the questions aside, they plead with the old man to simply tell them what happened, and then they ask if the angel left anything behind to prove he'd been there. Zachary then produces a pressed flower from under his family Bible, unlike anything the others have seen. In the moment that he held it, we are told, his guests collectively witnessed a momentary

55

miracle: the old man appeared to them as young. Zachary died three days later, and the neighbours who looked after his belongings later found pressed in his Bible, in addition to various examples of known flora, one or two that were not familiar and yet not of the kind Zachary had shown to his guests. Nothing was ever said to diminish his presentation, the cottage was eventually picked clean by lawyers and locals, and its ruins remained a point of superstition for children who came to know it as 'the Wizard's house.'

'Zachary Crebbin's Angel', then, is a sweet account of how superstitions take shape (through storytelling), and how what we credit as supernatural can sometimes be traced to something perfectly natural but uncommon, something that has perhaps naturally died out and inspires a fanciful explanation. It discounts the miracles of religion though not as scatologically as 'God and Daphne' does; it takes a more sympathetic view of how our basic need to communicate with others, indeed to hold their attention, may lead to the invention and sharing of tall tales—the very foundation, after all, of literature. As one reads the story, the leap that the heart makes upon the disclosure of the first flower shows how much we want to believe in such things, and Kneale stops just short of disqualifying Crebbin's account, for which he pays with his life anyway.

'BINI AND BETTINE'

Reminiscent of Tod Browning's **THE UNHOLY THREE** (1925), this story rather surprisingly sketches the criminal underbelly of sideshow entertainment. It's written in reflective first-person from the perspective of Sam, a song-and-dance entertainer in a seaside pavilion show, who reminisces about two of his fellow performers, a midget (Bini) and full-grown woman (Bettine) whose act consisted of them portraying a mother wheeling her infant son around in a perambulator, the two of them simultaneously producing and concealing a vast number of items—rattles, feeding bottles, teething rings, and so forth—in the pram or on the person of the baby. Sam had no particular rapport with Bini, who was in fact 25 years of age and kept to himself, but he and Bettine quickly fell in love and married. Alas, their marriage burned out just as fast, as Bettine demonstrated her

The Literary Kneale

predilection for finding and pressuring the weak links in other people, belittling Sam's act and talent until he felt himself cowering under her cold scrutiny.

Several years later, 'during the war', while touring with an ENSA show, Sam happens to meet Bettine (whom he never divorced) again, catching her in an argument with another woman in a public place, both women wheeling prams. Bettine's baby is being hotly accused of having stolen the silk cover off the other pram, which Bettine haughtily denies. Sam intervenes, says hello, and — without the slightest show of surprise — is immediately introduced into the argument as Bettine's husband and character witness, as she breaks down on his shoulder, thus winning the sympathy of the assembled onlookers. The reunited couple are allowed to go. As they push the heavy pram away, Sam asks how long this new racket has been going on, and Bettine admits that she's been doing well with it, lifting handbags and whatnot. Figuring that it's time Bini had some fresh air, Sam lifts back the pram cover to discover *a normal child of four or five* inside, staring him out *like a little cornered animal.* He knows immediately who the little fellow must be.

This is one of two stories (along with 'Peg') that Elizabeth Bowen singles out in her Foreword as 'masterpieces in a genre particularly this writer's own.' That said, its atmospheric associations of salt air, beachside entertainment and small time criminality suggest the likely influence of Graham Greene's best-selling novel BRIGHTON ROCK, which was published in 1938, but also staged in 1944 and successfully filmed by John Boulting in 1947, around the time this story was likely written. These associations would surface again, many years later, when this story's initial *seaside pavilion show* setting recurred in Kneale's unexpectedly seedy BEASTS episode 'Buddyboy', which is set in and around an abandoned seaside pavilion theatre called Finnyland, as well as the countercultures of strip clubs and pornography.

Like several of the TOMATO CAIN stories, 'Bini and Bettine' documents a romantic relationship in collapse, which can be read as a domestic reduction of the cataclysmic subjects that obsessed Kneale throughout his career, not to mention historical touchstones like the London blitz.

57

WE ARE THE MARTIANS

While the story is ostensibly about its two namesakes, it is most importantly about Sam and arranged in two halves, before and after the blitz, which occupies the dead zone of 'several years' separating his two encounters with Bettine. She is described on the story's first page as *'drowsy-eyed and very beautiful in that heavy, sexy way that doesn't last'* (p. 203) — and indeed it doesn't. Met again after the war, Bettine inspires in Sam only a few hard stabs of sharpened focus: *'All the beauty of the pier pavilion days had gone'*, *'I saw now she was shabby too'* (both p. 207), and *'Her eyes were all over my face; they were harder eyes than I had known.'* (p. 208) Sam doesn't describe the ways in which the war years have changed him, but he doesn't have to, because the story amounts to a map of entrapment for him. As soon as he recognizes Bettine's child and partner-in-crime as his own, he is — to use the word Henry Green used for the title of his own novel about the London blitz, *caught*.

'THE STOCKING'

The darkest of the TOMATO CAIN stories is set on Christmas Eve. As a mother and father are preparing to celebrate the holiday at the local public house, their young invalid son — described as having no feeling in his legs and bedridden in a cot affixed to a wall — pleads with them to hang a stocking, so that 'Daddy Christmas' might leave him something like the big bag of sweets he got the previous year. Pa quickly hammers one of Ma's long stockings to to *'a wooden beam that ran across the room above the cot, a little below the ceiling.'* The hammering stimulates sounds of activity in the ceiling, caused by what the parents call 'the Minkeys', the 'Mickey Mouses' that live in the rafters and hate the sound of noise. When the adults leave, the house falls into silence, and the Minkeys slowly emerge, climbing down the stocking into the cot, where they bite, bleed and begin to devour the abandoned child.

This story has genuine merit but is uncharacteristically merciless in terms of the horror it unleashes on an unsuspecting, invalid child. One particularly Knealean aspect of the storytelling is how the source of horror and danger is given a friendly, funny nickname that draws the unsuspecting closer. 'The Minkeys' are very much a forerunner of the likes of

The Literary Kneale

Baby, Buddyboy and even the 'Stumpy Men,' the megalith formation near Ringstone Round. Kneale would later ratchet his horror of rats up to nearly an hour with the BEASTS episode 'During Barty's Party.'

'WHO—ME, SIGNOR?'

Another of the lesser stories in the collection, this is a first-person monologue delivered by a Italian male being interrogated in the wake of the Liberation of Italy. The speaker is a none-too-bright but crafty fellow who is forever passing the buck to absolve himself of the crimes he committed in the wake of Mussolini's downfall — *'but only to the extent of raising funds for the necessities of life.'* The buck is most often passed to the man's friend — no, more of an acquaintance! — named Giuseppe Cavallini. The crux of the story is his account of how Giuseppe coerced him into advertising and setting up a program in a disused hat shop, where *'special concessions'* would be made to blind men, under the supervision of Colonel Smit of the Allied Military Government — in fact, Giuseppe disguised in a makeshift uniform that *'bore the badge of a part of the liberation forces called Salvation Army,'* and tricking the sightless out of their clothing, which they intended to resell, under the pretense that they would be reclothed. The scam was undone when two of the supposedly blind men looked at each other in disbelief — the scam falling victim to another backfired scam.

The story itself is a clever farce about survival, but in this instance Kneale doesn't quite succeed in creating a believable or remotely sympathetic character, resulting in a caricature that somewhat overstays its welcome at six pages.

'THE POND'

Another beastie tale, 'The Pond' is the story of an old man who lives in the woods and poaches from its ponds as many frogs as he can catch, which he then meticulously skins, boils, preserves and arranges into dioramic still-lives. *'All had been posed in human attitudes; dressed in tiny coats and breeches to the fashion of an earlier time. There were ladies and gentlemen*

WE ARE THE MARTIANS

and bowing flunkeys. One, with lace at his yellow, waxen throat, held a wooden wine cup. To the dried forepaw of its neighbor was stitched a tiny glassless monocle, raised to a black button eye. A third had a midget pipe pressed into its jaws, with a wisp of wool for smoke. The same coarse wool, cleaned and shaped, served the ladies for their miniature wigs; they wore long skirts and carried fans.' (p. 225)

The greater part of the story details this eccentric's conversations with himself as he works on these projects that no eyes but his own are likely ever to see. He has just caught what he believes to have been the last frog in his favourite pond, but as he works, he hears something. *'He knew it was coming from the pond. A far-off, harsh croaking, as of a great many frogs.'* (p. 227) He takes a lantern, walks out to the pond in the dark, listens closely, and then *'the whole pond seemed to boil.'* Like the poor child in 'The Stocking,' the old man is slowly consumed by nature. When his waterlogged remains are later discovered by a constable, they are found held together by *'tiny green stitches.'*

The beauty of this story—which foreshadows an area of horror cinema that could be termed the 'ecological revenge' story that only came into fashion with 1970s films like **FROGS, SQUIRM** and **NIGHT OF THE LEPUS**—is that, from a human perspective, the old man is elevating nature to the level of art; that he is ennobling these creatures and identifying with them in the expression of his art, by giving them human characteristics and the traits of his own remote past; and in its dominant assertion that nature is its own perfect expression.

Though not really one of the best stories in the collection, 'The Pond' had the distinction of being chosen as one of the 100 stories included in *THE CENTURY'S BEST HORROR FICTION*, a two-volume collection edited by John Pelan and published by Cemetery Dance in 2001.

'THEY'RE SCARED, MR. BRADLAUGH'

Kneale took a deceptive approach to telling this story, opening with third person dialogues that gradually reveal a first person reminiscence. It's primarily a deathbed argument between Ralph—a supposed rational 'Freethinker' influenced by the pamphlets of prominent atheist Charles

Bradlaugh—and the aunt who raised him, who seeks comfort in what he sees as the humbuggery of prayer and belief as she awaits the inevitable. As Ralph wastes their last moments together railing against her weakness and superstitious savagery, she suddenly raises up and embraces him in despairing pity, just before the light in her eyes goes out. In the wake of her death, neighbours come and tidy up, caring for the mourning—'*Silly conventions!*' thinks Ralph. But, as time passes, Ralph finds himself turning more and more toward the beliefs of his late aunt, as a means of keeping her memory close by. The story ends with Ralph cursing his aunt, affectionately.

This story says something discerning about one of the peculiar powers wielded by organised religion—the comfort of its familiarity to those raised in it, the feeling it offers of remaining connected with family members who have died, and so forth—but it is not so easily discerned if the author is being kindly or critical toward the later inclinations of his protagonist. Bradlaugh himself is mentioned only briefly and in passing, and never by his full name, so Kneale leaves to his readers the choice of whether or not to learn more about the causal source of this discord in Ralph's familial harmony.

By choosing to learn more about Bradlaugh, we discover that the story is not a contemporary one, which it may seem to be, but set in the latter part of the 19th century, as Bradlaugh lived from 1833 to 1891. The founder of the National Secular Society, Bradlaugh was an elected member of Parliament who refused to take the sacred Oath of Allegiance necessary to taking office, which made him famous as an atheist and encouraged his depiction as an anti-nationalist because taking the Oath was meant as confirmation of one's allegiance to the Crown. This was only the beginning of a six-year struggle that encompassed a period of imprisonment and his eventual acceptance into Parliament.

One of the feelings one takes away from the story is that people who dare to be free-thinkers are not making life easy for themselves, and not least of all because they must spend their lives under their own uncharitable watch.

'THE CALCULATION OF N'BAMBWE'

Written at least five years before the publication of TOMATO CAIN, this is one of the collection's earliest stories yet it has the distinction of pulling off a literary trick that, much like the closing paragraph of Vladimir Nabokov's 'The Vane Sisters,' cannot be played to the same effect twice. In Nabokov's case, he concluded a story about the attempts of two dead sisters to communicate from beyond the grave with a paragraph that, read acrostically, sends a message to the reader from those absent protagonists. In this story, Kneale uses his entire story—a colorful, character-driven sketch of a women's book club session—to set up its conclusion, which unfolds in a distinctly literary way.

It's a small but distinct gathering, consisting of Miss Tandy, the tea-serving hostess; Mrs. Berrilee, who dotes on ghost stories; Miss Morgan, timid in life yet somewhat more adventurous in her tastes; and Mrs. Churchman, the most conservative of the bunch. The story builds, over well-observed conversation, to the point where Mrs. Berrilee shares a story about her brother-in-law Gerald, an engineer presently residing in Africa. In a recent letter to her husband, Gerald mentioned his meeting with a 'witch doctor' named N'Bambwe who arrived at his own calculations by means of arcane gadgets and methods—one of which was, according to the present position of the planets, that seven days following the next equinox, time itself was going to stop. Indeed, the story never ends but reaches a point, almost coinstantaneous with the women's calculations, when words we have read begin to cycle, to repeat themselves, when words we have read begin to cycle, to repeat themselves, when words we have . . .

Unfortunately, when the TOMATO CAIN collection came to be published in America by Alfred A. Knopf, the editors outsmarted themselves by 'correcting' what they wrongly interpreted as a misprint. In the American edition, the story ends with the blunt, serial repetition of the word 'chewing,' which hasn't the same meaning or impact as the original. Why this matter wasn't corrected in galleys is anyone's guess, but a second edition never happened to set the record straight.

Though it would be unseemly trespass for another writer to attempt this

The Literary Kneale

trick in another story, Kneale's clever finale can be seen repeated some-what—possibly independently of the story's influence—in the closing minutes of Ib J. Melchior's 1964 film **THE TIME TRAVELERS**.

'NATURE STUDY'

Miss Bunnary, an overly strict schoolteacher with crooked teeth, leads her young class of twenty-five students on an expedition to the nearby woods to conduct a nature study. She supplies these young and often unruly students with paper bags, telling them to collect only clean and intact examples of however many different kinds of leaf they can find lying on the ground. After a variety of leaves are brought forth for her approval (and seldom get it), three students—including Albert Johnson—disappear without a trace. After much excited calling, the children soon return, explaining that they were examining a hedgehog they had found, which works their teacher into such a state that she has a cardiac episode.

This is a playfully critical denouncement of educators placed in charge of teaching subjects without much direct experience of, or regard for, life. Miss Bunnary's view of nature is the nature preserved in textbooks, where leaves are intact and perfectly preserved, where animals are separate from their own dirt, and all that she succeeds in teaching her impish charges, who seem to embody the wild of the wilderness, is respect for their own curiosity and disregard for authority.

'CHARLIE PEACE AND THE KING'

There is nothing else to do in the rainy town of Oglethorpe, dominated by its pickle factory, but to spend one's evenings at Charlie Peace's *'Cinema House,' a former 'cart and carriage shed for the richest man in town'* that entertains the locals each night with a featurette, cartoon and main feature. The whole town crowds in, children and adults alike, so infor-mally as to make shadow figures on the screen should it happen to turn white during reel changes.

Starting promptly at seven, the evening programme on this particular night begins with 'God Save the King,' as played on a Panatrope phono-

WE ARE THE MARTIANS

graph set up behind the screen. When the story's first-person narrator inquires of a nearby couple if this misplacement of the national anthem (which traditionally ends ceremonies rather than commences them) is usual, they reminisce. They recall a time when the King was once due to visit Oglethorpe, when Charlie, imagining there wasn't much else to see there but the pickle factory, edited together a visual accompaniment to the national anthem—a wonderful montage that might please His Royal Highness should be so kind as to peek in:

> 'He made it in his back room yonder, where he has snippets of owd films. King and t' family, he had o' course, and guns and palaces. Soldiers, aeroplanes, boxing matches, jungles, dancing niggers[11], dog shows, ghosts, soccer, weddings, dam-buildings, Roman gladiators, volcanoes, collisions, hunger strikes, murders an' all,' they say. 'O' course, the King got no further than Manchester when he came up this way.' (p. 254)

The programme proceeds through a Donald Duck cartoon—the book's last quacking triumph of Curphy's follower, and in that quack one last recapitulation of the 'Qu' prefix that Kneale assigns to uncanny beings—and an unnamed main feature, after which 'God Save the King' is played at even greater length, ostensibly to make the audience stand and take their time leaving the cinema. Then the figure F9 is flashed onscreen from a black slide. The neighboring couple explain that the ticket holder holding that ticket number gets in free the next time—'As Mother here said awhile back, people like a bit of try-your luck... and ba' gum, it keeps 'em quiet for t' King.'

Once again, this closing story is rich in the voices of small town, working-class England, and its placement seems to point prophetically toward Kneale's pending transition away from prose to visual entertainment. It also makes the ironic point of equating the national anthem with

---

[11] The word 'nigger' appears a few times in Kneale's stories, always in dialogue spoken by coarse characters, which may be disturbing to some contemporary readers. In Britain, the word didn't always have the inflammatory character it acquired through its perjorative usage in America. The word's etymology is usually traced to the Spanish/Portuguese negro, but Kneale's local colour use the word more than once to liken black people to the black fly, an insect known for its ubiquity and nuisance.

The Literary Kneale

an opportunity of cheap winnings, and puts his readers in mind of that anthem as they rise to put the book down.

Taken as a whole, TOMATO CAIN AND OTHER STORIES is a wondrous and wonderful confection, sufficiently rich in the macabre to warrant consideration as a genre debut, but so accomplished in its delineations of character and country as to herald the arrival of an important new naturalist. The writers brought to mind by its collective qualities are all staunch individualists—Saki, John Collier, Flannery O'Connor, James Purdy—which makes it all the more tragic that Kneale left behind so little material in this mode. A reader familiar with his later work could be forgiven for expecting to find in these stories some influence of M.R. James (for whose collected ghost fiction Kneale later wrote a Foreword)[12], but if it's there, it's artfully concealed. Published when Kneale was closer to 30 than 25, TOMATO CAIN has the integrity of a writer fully grown, who writes in his own voice and uses it only to speak for himself and those specimens of humankind who attracted his compassion.

On the strength of Kneale's work, his publisher Collins was able to secure a commending Foreword by the revered Anglo-Irish author Elizabeth Bowen (1899-1973). Bowen had once said of her own work that she was most interested in 'life with the lid on and what happens when the lid comes off,' marking her as a kindred spirit to Kneale. She makes the insightful comment that Kneale's writing in the short form had appeared in the short story's 'present rather fascinating position half-way between tradition and experiment'. Bowen was likely speaking of the experimentation that was creeping into traditional fiction in the wake of writers like James Joyce and Virginia Woolf, and there is a persistent sense throughout Kneale's stories of tradition and something older and more mysterious than mere tradition, yet ever-present in the present lives of common people; something that resides within nature as well as human nature. This is where his debt to M.R. James perhaps lingers. This quality could be described as superstition or the fabulous, or that may only be

[12] James, M.R. Ghost Stories of M.R. James, edited by Nigel Kneale (London: Folio Society, 1973).

the texture of it; something long concealed by the blinders required by organised religion, of which only science was likely to make concrete sense. Kneale's subject matter here can be boiled down to queer people (in the classical sense), people made strange by lack of travel and communication, by remaining close to the land of their birthright. Their folkish natures and language make his stories superficially traditional, but they also move beyond the forms of traditional literature to show as much as he dare about what gets habitually swept under the carpet of the traditional.

Bowen also seems to predict the future course of Kneale's work when she writes, '"Tomato Cain' itself, "The Excursion" and "The Putting Away of Uncle Quaggin" have (for instance) a naturalism not unworthy of Maupassant: the supernatural never raises its head, but eminent human queerness is at its height.'

'This is a first book,' Bowen summarised. 'Nigel Kneale is at the opening of his career; he is still making a trial of his powers. To an older writer, the just-not-overcrowded effect of inventive richness, the suggestion of potentialities still to be explored, and of alternatives pending, cannot but be attractive. That the general reader will react to Nigel Kneale's stories, and that the perceptive reader will relish what is new in his contribution to fiction, I feel sure.'

Kneale would later assert that he went into writing for television because there was 'no money' to be made in writing short stories, yet he achieved more financial reward and recognition in his first two years of print publication than many writers manage in a lifetime. TOMATO CAIN AND OTHER STORIES was a significant success, both for a writer's first book and for a collection of short stories. As mentioned before, it won the Atlantic Award for Literature, which brought with it a cash prize of £250, which was then trumped in May 1950 when Kneale was honored as the fourth recipient of the Somerset Maugham Award. This prize, presented annually to a worthy British author under the age of 35, included a cash prize of £12,000, which was to be used exclusively toward

---

[13] Kneale is one of only two winners of the Somerset Maugham Award whose son has also received it (Matthew Kneale got it for his novel *Whore Banquets* in 1988); the others were Kingsley and Martin Amis, who won respectively in 1955 and 1974.

the broadening of one's mind with foreign travel.[13] According to the notes included on the Knopf edition dust jacket, Kneale used the money to visit France, Italy, and other parts of Europe for the first time. However worldly he became as a result personally, his future work remained unaffected, remaining contentedly within those boundaries he had already mapped in his first—and, for many years, only book.

After its publication in Britain, some of TOMATO CAIN's contents were placed in American magazines to create interest in the coming US Knopf edition. 'Minuke' and 'Jeremy In the Wind' both appeared in *Argosy* (February and April 1950, respectively), while *Harper's Magazine* published a pair of its stories as "Two Manx Tales" twice later in the year: 'The Putting Away of Uncle Quaggin' and 'Oh, Mirror, Mirror' (June 1950), followed by 'Minuke' and 'Curphey's Follower' (September 1950). The *Harper's* stories continue to be available online to that magazine's subscribers as downloadable pdfs.

When the Knopf edition finally appeared, it was not quite the same book that had performed so well in Britain. Though it is not known whether the idea came from his Knopf editor or from Kneale himself, two weak stories (one of them particularly Anglocentric) were replaced by stronger material that Kneale had likely produced since placing the initial collection with Collins—three new stories amounting to 40 additional pages. Exclusive to the US edition are 'Essence of Strawberry' (positioned fifth, between 'Clog Dance...' and 'Lotus For Jamie'), 'Mrs. Mancini' (positioned sixteenth, between 'The Taroo-Ushtey' and 'Curphey's Follower') and 'The Patter of Tiny Feet,' which replaces 'Charlie Peace and the King' as the book's finale.

'ESSENCE OF STRAWBERRY'

This tragic vignette is also about issues of faith and belief, in its own way. It details a working class love triangle set in the deceptively wholesome environment of a milk bar. Middle-aged, graying Fred runs the shop, which is owned by his invalid, bedridden wife May. Fred dotes on May, turning sentimental whenever he prepares for her sweet tooth a favorite drink each afternoon consisting mostly of raw strawberry essence, the kind

WE ARE THE MARTIANS

used in phosphates. However, having physical needs his wife can no longer satisfy, Fred has been having an affair with Valerie, the hired help. Bored and eager to have Fred all to herself, Valerie proposes that Fred poison May, as her death is inevitable anyway, and that they run away together while they are still young enough to savour their freedom. Fred is briefly tempted, but as he takes May's strawberry drink upstairs, his wife speaks to him lovingly and warns him that she is dying, which she then does before Fred can leave the room. The heartbroken husband informs Valerie, who misinterprets the news and believes Fred responsible. This outrages him in front of customers, and after Valerie is violently chased away, local gossip has spread and Fred is arrested on suspicion of murder. In time, he is cleared, and Valerie returns to awkwardly tend her apologies, hinting that they might still have a future. Fred tentatively agrees and prepares two glasses of strawberry essence to seal their agreement, a gesture that soon proves that Valerie still doesn't quite believe him incapable of murder. Fred drinks both and goes to bed.

'MRS. MANCINI'

This remarkable character study focuses on an afternoon in the life of Mrs. Rose Mancini, a middle-aged widow who has had to sell her former home and now lives in a flat with a pet parrot. The story begins with Rose being wakened early by an errant ray of sunlight, then continues with her fussy morning rituals, during which she is driven out of her home by thoughts of having her furniture repossessed and the parrot's belligerent chants of 'You got my shoes?' — something her late husband, a waiter, asked her only once that she can remember. As Rose wanders further away from her apartment building — did she even bother to dress before going out? — her behaviour and thoughts become increasingly erratic, causing the reader to slowly realize that she is schizophrenic, known as such by her neighbours, local shopkeepers and the patient constables, mistaken for a beggar or trouble maker by others, and coming around to the idea of putting her head in a gas oven.

Kneale succeeds perfectly in placing the reader inside this poor soul's consciousness as her mind darts from one fleeting concern to another, be

The Literary Kneale

they questions concerning the future or reproaches about mistakes she made in the past. The possibility is also delicately raised that Mrs. Mancini, in her younger days, may have conceived a child out of wedlock which she gave up for adoption.

'THE PATTER OF TINY FEET'

The US edition of TOMATO CAIN concludes a good deal more memorably than its British counterpart, with a fresh, amusing and somewhat unsettling variation on the poltergeist tale. Thus, it provides a welcome reminder and complement to one of the volume's key achievements, 'Minuke.'

A newspaper reporter named Staines and his photographer Joe Banner drive out to the English suburbs to investigate and confirm a story being offered by a man named Hutchinson, who works in a restaurant as an assistant headwaiter. We are not thrust into the nature of the story right away, but patiently await its unfolding through acquaintance with the characters, with Hutchinson and his backstory particularly, as it is filled in by his answers to Staines' practical questions. It is revealed that Hutchinson is a widower, that he was once married to an *unworldly* young woman of nineteen — at least twenty-five years younger than himself — *a distant cousin, actually* — who came from a strongly religious background (unlike himself) and suddenly passed away seven months ago. When asked if their marriage was happy, Hutchinson admits that it was not, because his wife very much wanted to have children and they could never conceive. Insisting that her failure to conceive was not his fault (when he offers to submit to tests, Staines replies that there are limits even to the curiosity of the press), he points out that the time is approaching when things typically starts happening...and he leads the two visitors upstairs, with Staines handling Banner's Leica camera as he carries the lights. They are then witness to a series of auditory phenomena suggesting that the house is haunted by children — the children that Mr and Mrs Hutchinson never had.

This story, a first-person account by Staines that often takes the form of a third-person story, shows that Kneale's facility for yarn-spinning was

WE ARE THE MARTIANS

continuing to advance impressively, but it also shows that it was very much advancing in the direction of drama. 'The Patter of Tiny Feet' is a story that reads as though each of its characters' movements, each of their gestures and positions within the described floorplan as they speak their perfectly measured lines, was meticulously and spatially worked out beforehand, like a play. Even the pauses in their speech are carefully noted, and measured in ways to inch the reader ever closer to the edge of their seat. Hutchinson himself is meticulously described as though Kneale had the very actor in mind: '*A pale pudding face and a long nose that didn't match it, trimmed with a narrow line of moustache. He had the style of a shopwalker, I thought.*' (TC Knopf edition, p. 286)

Particularly clever is Kneale's handling of ratcheting up the breathless tension experienced by the two visitors—one memorably calm and descriptive paragraph unexpectedly ends with Staines' confessional aside '*Every vein in my head was banging*'—and also his kindly but firm insistence about not drawing a definitive conclusion. The point of the reporters' visit to the house (which is described as personally as its inhabitant: '. . . *Number 47. It was what the address had suggested: a narrow suburban villa in a forgotten road, an old maid of a house with a skirt of garden drawn around it, keeping to itself among all its sad neighbours*') was to determine whether or not the house is genuinely haunted, but Banner is the first to reject what he experiences, and he's followed out of the house by Staines. Their departure cuts to a coda of the two men talking later, when Staines presents his colleague with a winking explanation that could just as easily be the doing of Hutchinson as his late wife.

In summary, TOMATO CAIN AND OTHER STORIES is a grand read in either version but—despite the unfortunate editorial error in 'The Calculation of N'Bambwe'—is strongest in its American edition, whose three bonus stories provide compelling evidence of the continuing growth and deepening of Kneale's narrative powers.

There is an entire school of writing known as 'British postwar fiction,' and though Nigel Kneale is rarely discussed as part of that movement, TOMATO CAIN proves him very much part of it. British postwar fiction

The Literary Kneale

is generally distinguished by its working-class realism, as typified by the novels of Kingsley Amis (LUCKY JIM), Alan Sillitoe (THE LONELINESS OF THE LONG DISTANCE RUNNER) and John Braine (ROOM AT THE TOP). Its stories are usually about rough-hewn individuals striving to make something of themselves and their unpromising circumstances, either getting ahead or merely surviving. Of course, there were other voices in postwar British fiction, as well—George Orwell, William Golding, Anthony Burgess, Doris Lessing, Roald Dahl—voices that were generally more escapist yet also confrontational. In reading Kneale's stories, we can see that he played both sides of this movement; he wrote about everyday reality, but what interested him most were the quirks in life, the doomed eccentrics—and the lies with which they lived, which made life possible for them.

> 'I like to think of them as strange or mystifying stories,' he once said, 'but they can be anything from social satire like [THE YEAR OF] THE SEX OLYMPICS and WINE OF INDIA to what I like to think of as funny or just plainly human.'[14]

The war, the destruction of London—these are not often mentioned in Kneale's stories, yet the trauma of war is deeply imprinted on most of them, primarily in the cracks and fissures of its characters. The contemporary stories describe what could be called the uncertain, day-to-day survival of a victorious but shell-shocked people. Without being told what has knocked them off-center, without *having* to be told, we see Kneale's characters trying to recover and perpetuate a lifestyle and sense of humour that are no longer quite possible, because no one still standing has remained quite so innocent. They depict people scrabbling about in the rubble, toward the looming light of futures they dare not wish for. In a few of his stories, particularly those with Manx settings ('The Excursion', 'The Putting Away of Uncle Quaggin'), he describes people inhabiting a time further back, in the years before global conflict changed

---

[14] Sutton, David A. 'The Quatermass Conclusion: An Interview with Nigel Kneale', originally published in Fantasy Media (Vol 1 No 5), December 1980.

We Are The Martians

everything, when people had enough of a war going on with their own shadows.

Indeed, Kneale's greatest literary distinction may be his love for common people, for their quirks and conversation—for 'the Weird Old England', to coin a phrase. In his way, he is a perverse poet of isolation, charting the strangeness that takes hold of personalities deprived of societal order. His attention dotes beyond them and the worlds they've fashioned for themselves, to the real turf underlying it, the world they (and we) inhabit without ever fully knowing. He knows that place where the wilderness of the woods and the wilderness of the human spirit seem to flickeringly become one, and is not afraid to end a story there. His stories also delight in the inexplicable, as if the inability to explain something makes it far purer than we, in our worlds of self-invention, can ever hope to be. However strange they may be, however enticingly real he may make the possibility of a supernatural explanation, his stories are remarkable in their ability to make the natural seem far eerier and unknowable than the self-delusions we term the supernatural. It may well have been this practical quality—and his rejection of simple ambiguity in favor of resonant questions—that allowed such a peculiar collection of arcane stories to be so warmly embraced by the literary establishment and award committees of its day, usually closed to books of more conspicuous genre.

The unexpected rewards of reading TOMATO CAIN today encompass not only the discovery of how much of Kneale's own later work is projected by its initial range of interests, but also the extent to which its fertile ideas have pollenated so much other genre entertainment over the past fifty years. In this single volume, Kneale gave us stories of poltergeists, cursed houses built on ancient burial grounds, ghostly children, twisted subjectives, animal revenge, and also the I-am-dead, I-see-dead-people, and even the nature-strikes-back scenario. Of course, some of these pre-existed TOMATO CAIN in the broadest terms, but Kneale finessed them to the point where they become readily identifiable. In this way, he is comparable to the French novelist Gaston Leroux, who is principally remembered for writing only one thing, THE PHANTOM OF THE OPERA, but whose broader body of work contributed a remarkably vast

The Literary Kneale

array of ideas to popular entertainment—locked room mysteries, human-ized apes, killer robots, biomechanics, reincarnated killers, wax museum horrors, lost civilisations of fish men, and much else besides. For all this, Kneale was adamant that he not be considered a horror, science fiction or fantasy writer.

In addition to receiving the endorsement of a major novelist, publishing contracts in London and New York, widespread publicity, the printing of his stories in major magazines and newspapers on both sides of the Atlantic, and two major literary awards, several of Kneale's stories continued on to a busy afterlife in the pages of various short story anthologies and magazines. They sometimes appeared under different titles, as in the case of 'Minuke', which became 'The Trespassers' for its appearance in the September 1958 issue of the British fiction digest *Suspense*.

'It got a prize, but it didn't bring any cash in,' Kneale complained about TOMATO CAIN. 'I thought "How many years can I crawl around living in cardboard boxes?" I went back to RADA and said almost despairingly, "Can you help me keep alive?" They said there was this very nice ex-student [Michael Barry] who had taken over the drama department at the BBC, and why didn't I go and talk to him?'[15]

And, to fall back on a much overused phrase, the rest was history. For the most part, so was Kneale's career as a writer of prose—though there would be exceptions.

QUATERMASS II (1955) AND THE PUBLISHED SCRIPTS

Sometime shortly after the BBC's telecast of the second *Quatermass* serial in late November 1955, a circulation war between two London newspapers, *The Daily Express* and *The Daily Mail*, precipitated the writing of what might be termed a 'lost' novella.

[15] Newman & Petley, p. 34.

WE ARE THE MARTIANS

Kneale jovially reminisced about the project's origin: 'It was immediately after we'd put this thing on screen, and they said "Can you do us a serial?" Each rang up, and so my agent bid them up against each other — to an amazingly small sum. The Express won, and so they said "Can you think of one?" I couldn't, so, in the end, they said "Oh well, write the thing you've just put out on the telly." It was very lavishly illustrated, but after about ten days of it, it gradually drifted further and further towards the end of the paper! One day, they rang up and said "How much more is there?" I was only halfway through and they said, "Can you just wrap it up?"'

Kneale's novelisation of QUATERMASS II ran in the *Daily Express* newspaper from December 5-20, 1955. It has never appeared in book form, nor been reprinted in any way.

Possibly due to his status as an award-winning author, Kneale's BBC teleplays for his original stories THE QUATERMASS EXPERIMENT, QUATERMASS II and QUATERMASS AND THE PIT all appeared in Penguin paperback editions between 1959 and 1960, each with eight-page photo inserts, the first two coinciding with the original telecast of the third serial.

In 1976, a collection entitled 3 TV PLAYS was published by Ferret Fantasy Ltd consisting of Kneale's original texts for THE ROAD, THE YEAR OF THE SEX OLYMPICS and THE STONE TAPE, one hundred copies of which were bound in buckram and signed and numbered by the author.

In 1979, Hutchinson Publishing Group marked the twenty-fifth anniversary of THE QUATERMASS EXPERIMENT's initial broadcast by issuing the three Quatermass teleplays in new paperback editions from their subsidiary imprint Arrow Books Ltd, featuring new Forewords written by Kneale. Their publication also coincided with Kneale's first new Quatermass serial in almost 20 years, and his dissatisfaction with the result prompted him to undertake the writing of his first and only novel.

[16] Newman & Petley, p. 42-43.

The Literary Kneale

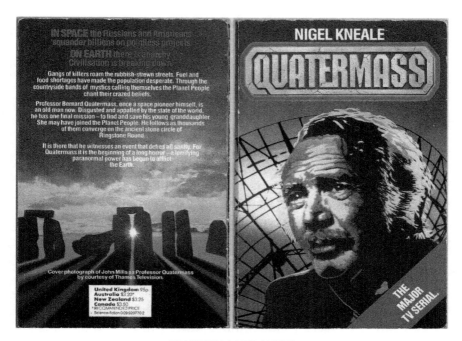

QUATERMASS (1979)

After a fruitful collaboration lasting more than twenty years, Nigel Kneale and the British Broadcasting Corporation parted ways in 1978. His last script for their airwaves was the *LATE NIGHT STORY* episode 'The Photograph,' which aired the night before Christmas Eve, 1978. The straw that broke the camels back in this regard appears to have been Kneale's most ambitious project in years, a four-hour miniseries that would resurrect Professor Bernard Quatermass—the protagonist of his famous BBC teleplay trilogy of the 1950s—for one last challenge from the cosmos.

Ronnie Marsh, BBC's Head of Drama Serials, first commissioned the miniseries, which came to be called simply QUATERMASS, on November 21, 1972.[17] Kneale delivered his completed scripts by the

---

[17] Or perhaps not so simply. The title *Quatermass* may seem generic at first glance, but Kneale may have chosen it for its etymologic resonance. Quater means one-fourth of something, and it was the fourth and last of Kneale's teleplays about the eponymous character. The third syllable, *Mass*, has bearing on themes of human sacrifice, transubstantiation and requiem, all of which are relevant to the story at hand.

WE ARE THE MARTIANS

contracted deadline of February 1973 and production in fact commenced the following June, under producer Joe Waters. After some days of preliminary special effects filming, BBC pulled the plug on the project having become daunted by location problems and the overall cost of production, then estimated at £200,000. Their option was good through 1975 and prevented Kneale from taking it elsewhere.[18]

Kneale believed that the tone of the piece—a bitterly dystopian drama set in the near future—was more responsible for its cancellation than funding. 'They [the BBC] gradually went sour on it,' he told director John Das in his documentary short THE KNEALE TAPES, 'and said they found it too gloomy.' To this, he later added in another interview: 'Well yes, it was supposed to be gloomy. Stripping the Earth of its population is a gloomy thought. But maybe it was just not destined to be jolly.'[19]

In QUATERMASS, the eponymous rocket scientist is an elderly man who has left the safety of his loch-side cottage in Scotland to search for his runaway orphaned niece Hettie in the trashed, gang-lorded urban landscapes of near-future London. He is shocked to find private homes barricaded, bloated corpses strewn about the streets, conditions far worse than the media ever reveals. Invited to appear on BTV as a commentator about the 'Hands Across Space' programme, on the occasion of the docking of US and USSR spacecraft ('the symbolic wedding of a corrupt democracy to a monstrous tyranny—two super-powers, full of diseases'), Quatermass and fellow commentator Joe Kapp, a younger radio astronomer, are stunned when a live video feed of the docking turns catastrophic. Before their eyes, the joint Spacelab crumples and space-walking cosmonauts are sent adrift into the void. It is later discovered that the disaster coincided perfectly with another catastrophic event on the earth's surface: a spontaneous gathering of 12-13,000 young people at a megalithic arena formation in Brazil, everyone there reduced to a crys-

---

[18] Pixley, Andrew. 'All the Rage of the World. Flashback: The Quatermass Conclusion.' *TV Zone* (#161, April 2003): p. 48–54.

[19] Kibble-White, John. 'The Magic Word Here is "Paradox"' (November 2003). The interview text is posted on the website offthetelly.co.uk.

talline dust by an absorbing ray fired from the extreme depths of space. The space program just happened to get in the way of it.

By the time this coincidence comes to light, Quatermass and Kapp— having abandoned London for the safety of Kapp's radio observatory base and family cottage in the countryside, where he lives with his wife Clare and two little daughters—have been witness to the phenomenon at closer hand. Megaliths abound in Kapp's area—a small formation known as 'The Stumpy Men' within view of his observatory and, further on, a formation more on the scale of Stonehenge called Ringstone Round, made famous as the subject of a children's rhyme in a picture book. While driving Quatermass out to Ringstone Round for a view of it, the Kapps find themselves caught up in the spontaneous arrival of a hippie cult known as the Planet People, pagan idealists hateful of learning who believe that they can collectively wish themselves away from dying Earth, sick with science, to the new hope of another planet.[20] In the midst of a skirmish with 'pay cops,' Quatermass and the Kapps make their escape—only to hear and see a powerful beam drop from the sky and, within 20.2 seconds, erase all sign of the thousands of lives just assembled there. They drive back and find the stones of the formation chipped and riven, their circle clotted with the seething dust of pulverized human remains from which *something* has been subtracted. Not all of the Planet People were killed; their leader, an alpha male known as Kickabout, had been arrested with some followers and now break free of their paddy wagons to feel their insane belief confirmed by the disaster scene at Ringstone Round. Quatermass discovers the still-living body of a pubescent girl at the very outer edge of the location, blinded by what she calls 'the lovely lightning,' the limbs on one side of her body distending and turning semi-crystalline. To the displeasure of Kickalong and the other surviving Planet People,

---

[20] There is actually precedent for this 'religion,' if you want to call it that, in the popular youth culture of the 1970s. In 1970, Paul Kantner – rhythm guitarist, singer and mentor of the San Francisco-based rock band Jefferson Airplane – released his first solo album *Blows Against the Empire* (RCA), credited to Paul Kantner/Jefferson Starship. The songs composing the second half of the record formed a suite, telling the story of a group of hippie radicals who hijack a starship awaiting take-off and escape into the ultimate irresponsibility of space ('All the weight gone from your heavy mass / all the years gone from your age…'). The album made pioneering use of sound samples from numerous science fiction films and was actually nominated for a Hugo Award for Best Dramatic Presentation.

WE ARE THE MARTIANS

Quatermass and the Kapps abduct her to evaluate her condition scientifically.

While tending to the girl's needs, Clare begins to develop an almost telepathic bond with her, chanting the mindless chants of the Planet People to comfort her, and soon intuiting that her name is Isabel. Clare begins to act irrationally, her husband sending her back home when he finds her leaving their children unattended to venture out to the Stumpy Men, ostensibly to dig for pottery. Quatermass realizes that the girl must be taken away, partly to better identify her physical state, but also to get her away from the Kapps, and prevails upon Annie Morgan, the district commissioner, to drive them to a London hospital when she pays a visit.

Shortly after reaching London, Annie and Quatermass unwittingly drive into the midst of a war between two street gangs, the Badders and the Blue Brigade. One of the Blues succeeds in pulling Quatermass out of the truck and he makes a long, dangerous trek through the battlegrounds, badly injuring his ankle before being found and accepted by a group of elderly men and women living in a camouflaged underground fortress. Hoping to locate another man of science, he is introduced to Chisholm, who once worked for a perfume company, his nose able to differentiate and identify well over a thousand smells. Meanwhile, Annie has succeeded in getting Isabel to hospital, where the girl is seen to spontaneously levitate toward the ceiling, as if in rapture, before exploding into a mass of crystalline confetti.

Quatermass is successfully tracked by the military and reunited with Annie, by which time he has determined from the continuing reports of megalith incidents around the world, each involving beams 20.2 seconds in duration, that the source must be a machine. Among the new reports is a recent catastrophe at a megalithic formation known as 'the Stumpy Men'... It was while adding water to his car radiator that Joe Kapp happened to hear and see the beam, which covered not only the small stone formation but his home as well, killing his entire family and leaving his house in powdered ruins. Assuming all of his friends lost, Quatermass remains in London with Annie, setting up a kind of laboratory to combat whatever is killing the earth's young — with the help of exclusively elderly

The Literary Kneale

scientists, including Chisholm, who, after vividly recalling the scent of the first girl he ever lay with as a teenager, succeeds in synthesizing the essence of what the alien beacon is seeking. He determines that the beacon is not attracted by the megaliths, but that those ancient stones were raised to mark certain meeting grounds as 'terrible' in the remote past, and that the beacon may not be restricted to megalith formations but any area on the planet, large or small, where people are known to gather—likely drawn by vast magnetic templates buried far below ground.

Quatermass's worst fears are confirmed when a new gathering is found to be underway, with more than 70,000 young people congregating at Wembley Stadium—in this future state, a kind of government-countenanced killing ground like the arenas of ancient Rome, an attempt to channel carnage away from the streets. Hatherly, a young government official—young enough to believe in the Planet People angle—tries to have Annie's van gunned down to prevent her and Quatermass from interfering. Annie manages to flee the attack into an underground car park, where her neck is broken shortly before light and noise flood the area—the decimation of tens of thousands in the stadium above. When Quatermass resumes consciousness the next morning, the sun rises in a sky the colour of vomit—the atmosphere strewn with the biologic refuse of the beacon's last gigantic taking.

In the wake of this most appalling disaster, Quatermass conceives a plan to synthesize enough young human scent and noise to attract the beam and subject it to a nuclear detonation, which he stages at Joe Kapp's radio observatory. There, Kapp himself is found, still alive but deeply traumatised by the loss of his family. The bomb can only be triggered manually, which Kapp offers to do, but Quatermass feels he's had his time and assumes responsibility. Just as the nuclear bait underlying the synthesized pheromones is about to be taken, a new group of Planet People arrive in response to the recorded sound of a million gathering kids, and Quatermass sees his granddaughter Hettie among them. He is doubled over by a sudden pain in his chest but rushes to the button with Hettie beside him. One last kiss from her gives him the vigor to complete the task—and the 35 kiloton message is taken. What used to be Joe Kapp's farm is left a deep smoking crater, but in time, children would be born and

WE ARE THE MARTIANS

grow to have children of their own, the rhyme of 'Ringstone Round' continuing to pass down through the generations.

QUATERMASS was eventually produced by Euston Films for Thames Television, at a final reported cost of £300,000 per episode, and broadcast in four episodes from October 24 to November 14, 1979. Sir John Mills was cast as Quatermass, with Simon MacCorkindale (Joe Kapp), Margaret Tyzack (Annie) and Barbara Kellerman (Clare) in support, all working under the direction of Piers Haggard, who had achieved notable success as a director of features (in particular 1970's **THE BLOOD ON SATAN'S CLAW**, a 17th century story in which a young farmer has the Knealean experience of unleashing a satanic power of vast consequences when his plough unearths something ancient from the ground) and Dennis Potter's PENNIES FROM HEAVEN (1978).

QUATERMASS was able to be so lavishly produced because it was undertaken to yield not one, but two end products—a four-part miniseries for ITV and also an independently distributed feature film version, which came to be known as THE QUATERMASS CONCLUSION. The latter had a running time of 102 minutes. One might assume that the distillation of the feature from the miniseries was the usual hatchet job, a necessary evil left to the hands of the director and editor, but Kneale actually claimed to have done the majority of the work on paper, writing scripts for both miniseries and feature simultaneously. THE QUATERMASS CONCLUSION supports his claim, being quite a skillful piece of dramatic surgery, one whose tightness actually serves to clarify the original's sometimes muddled geography and to punch up the various plot points. The only faults of this version are owed to the simple facts of subtraction, the most notable being that *Conclusion* is a feature film that shows only half its budget onscreen. Between this and the bargain basement special effects provided by Clearwater Films and Effects Associates, it was poor competition for the other science fiction releases of its year— **ALIEN, STAR TREK—THE MOTION PICTURE, THE BLACK HOLE**, and **MAD MAX**—though it was by far the most intellectually stimulating of the lot.

Kneale spoke of the project with professional enthusiasm in promotional interviews anticipating the initial broadcast, but later interviews find him speaking far more critically. He accepted some of the blame for the result himself, admitting that 'The script went through a lot of changes, one way or another. Frankly, I was never really happy with the whole idea in the first place... although the setting of the country fallen into social disaster was hugely interesting to write, the outer space bit was just too ordinary. Once we knew what was causing all the trouble, the story couldn't carry any further surprises... The theme I was trying to get at was the old coming to redress the balance of the young, which I thought was a paradoxical, ironic idea after the youth-oriented Sixties. The problem with the Planet People is that they were too harmless and really rather nice people, too much like flower people, when they should have been more like punks. I wanted them to be aggressive, mad, dangerous and out of control—a cross between punks and whirling dervishes. These were people the gods had driven mad in order to destroy.'[21]

Kneale also became quite outspoken in his criticism of Sir John Mills and Simon MacCorkindale, both of whom deliver noble and driving performances, but he never seemed to mention those areas where the film is genuinely weakest—for example, the interminably grating and cheapening synth score of Nic Rowley and Mark Wilkinson, or the terrible depictions of the street gangs in their obvious longhaired wigs. The project was shot by Ian Wilson, a commendable director of photography whose past work included Robert Fuest's **AND SOON THE DARKNESS** and Hammer's **CAPTAIN KRONOS — VAMPIRE HUNTER** and whose future work would include **THE CRYING GAME**), but for some reason, it looked terrible on television, like videotape converted to 16mm, an ugliness that persisted when it was released to home video.[22]

A promotional machine was in place to strike when the programme reached air, with Hutchinson Publishing bringing the teleplays of

[21] Newman and Petley, ibid.,p. 42.

[22] In July 2015, Network Video released Quatermass and The Quatermass Conclusion on Blu-ray, remastered for the first time from the original 35mm camera negatives, with the miniseries presented in 5.1 sound from its original three-track audio masters, and the feature making its home video premiere in its original screen ratio of 1.78:1. The results were absolutely illuminating.

Kneale's original trilogy of Quatermass stories back into print with new introductions by the author. They were also keen to have a new book to complete the grouping.

'When the idea came up of doing a book, neither I nor the publishers wanted the usual sort of crude novelisation of the script,' Kneale recalled. 'So I tried to imagine I hadn't written the script and that I was starting on it from the outset as a book. It wasn't easy because I was simultaneously doing routine amendments to the screenplay, while shooting was in progress, and also working out the shortened *Conclusion* script, which was far more than just a matter of cutting. So there were three versions in play at once. It was very confusing for a while. But I think the book's come out as a separate entity, as intended. It's got a number of characters and a lot of action that don't even appear in the TV or film version. I like it the best of the three now.'

The novel QUATERMASS is the hidden-in-plain-sight triumph of Kneale's overlooked literary output. Tragically, it never quite found its audience because — packaged, as it was, with the likeness of Sir John Mills and "The Major TV Serial" emblazoned across the cover of the paperback edition — it was generally mistaken for a novelization, possibly even something ghost-authored. 'I was hoping some creature would review it,' Kneale later admitted, 'but not a one did.'[24]

It was a terrible oversight. While Piers Haggard's **THE QUATERMASS CONCLUSION** isn't quite able to compete with other theatrical science fiction of its day, Nigel Kneale's QUATERMASS fares extremely well on the playing fields of 20th Century dystopian science fiction. In literary terms, it is wholly comparable to George Orwell's NINETEEN EIGHTY FOUR or Aldous Huxley's BRAVE NEW WORLD (both of which Kneale adapted), Ray Bradbury's FAHRENHEIT 451, Michael Moorcock's Jerry Cornelius or 'Dancers at the End of Time' novels, or any of Anthony Burgess's work in this area, from A CLOCKWORK ORANGE to THE WANTING SEED, 1985 and THE END OF THE WORLD NEWS. In this writer's opinion, QUATERMASS has a broader scope than any of these, and at least equal depth; it's an angry, elegiac novel encompassing the best

---

[24] Newman and Petley, ibid., p. 42.

The Literary Kneale

and worst of the human species, presenting a remarkable chain of bold, original ideas, which it then proceeds to deconstruct in speculative dialogue as the story continues to move forward with remarkable briskness and confidence. Much as Kneale's speculation in QUATERMASS AND THE PIT about possible Martian involvement in the evolution of life on this planet has gained scientific favour over the past fifty years, his speculations here—about the possibility of templates buried far below our known megalithic structures—have also begun to receive some unsettling support, with archaeologists in late 2014 discovering below Stonehenge some 17 theretofore unsuspected stone monuments, dwarfing the centrally positioned Stonehenge itself, including a burial mound more than 90 feet long and 6,000 years old. Some scientists have speculated that the structure was used to strip bodies of their flesh and organs, a process called 'excarnation,' prior to burial. With just these two stories, Kneale warrants our recognition as one of the most unnervingly prescient science fiction authors of all time.

The novel hits the ground running and never lets up, with Quatermass exclaiming 'That was a body!' as his taxi drives him through a dangerous area of London to keep his appointment with host Toby Gough at the studios of British Television. As the filmed version cannot do, Kneale's tightly wound prose phases in and out, from descriptive action into the protagonist's internal life—his thoughts, self-recriminations, even a passage from his published memoirs on Page 2. The novel also makes the most of its boundless capacity for art direction and landscaping, littering the smoking battlements of London streets with decomposing dead, car wrecks, barricaded housing, and so forth. The Badders-Mindoff gang (their name 'borrowed plumage' from the Baader-Meinhoff gangs of Germany) wear dreadlocks, rather than the abominable long-haired wigs of the film version, and are more believably lethal. Over the course of the book, more is written about the particulars differentiating the Badders from their better-armed opponents, the Blue Brigade, whose flag is an all-blue variation of the Union Jack, and their conflicts eventually erupt in a gang war that peters out when a magnetic procession of peaceful Planet People, sharing their youth, marches through the midst of their battlegrounds to reach Wembley Stadium. We also learn from

WE ARE THE MARTIANS

the novel that the chanting of the Planet People ('Lehlehleh!') has no meaning; these people are, as Joe Kapp says, 'violent to human thought' and the purpose of their chant is that of a transcendental mantra, to drive out any and all conscious, sequential, and consequential thought.[25]

Individual members of the Planet People are described in better detail, inside and out, while the mini-series can't take the time even to name them all. Caraway is introduced as their leader and he remains so until he is trumped by Kickalong, the one with a rock star's charisma, who makes himself known when he pushes himself to the fore at Ringstone Round, seizing the bullhorn from Quatermass to address the throng. One of the group who is paid particular attention and empathy in the novel is Fat Sal, a physically and mentally thick girl who is also mother to a sickly infant that slowly deteriorates into a grey suckling, its eventual corpse toted around like a tragic ragdoll till it's finally lost or discarded. Quatermass's granddaughter Hettie remains a cypher in both versions of the film, but the novel takes us further into her life with an examination of the only possessions she keeps on her nomadic person:

'Beneath her springy poncho she kept a small leather pouch. It hung between her breasts and in it were personal things. There was a lucky stone she had found as a child, a pebble that seemed to have something growing in it. She had kept it not for the luck but to remind her of the holiday when she had found it. There was a tiny photograph of her parents who were dead, killed in a car crash in the days when cars still ran on motorways... and a wadded letter she had kept less from affection than from canny sense that it might be needed some time. She had re-read it once or twice when she looked at the other things. "My dearest Hettie..."'[26]

The novel also makes matters of character more important in the early

---

[25] It is interesting, and perhaps ironic, that 'leh' should be the chanted syllable that attracts the alien beacon, as the olfactory scientist Chisholm later attracts it synthetically by producing an analogue scent of 'the first girl I ever lay with...' (p. 246)

[26] Kneale, Nigel. *Quatermass* (London: Hutchinson & Co., 1979), p. 83.

chapters in which Quatermass makes the acquaintance of Joe Kapp's colleagues at the observatory. Kneale drops early hints in his descriptive passages concerning Allison Sharpe (Allison Thorpe in the filmed versions) that foreshadow her later decision to join the Planet People; Frank Chen is identified as the son of the reknowned physicist Chen Teh; and Kneale places Kapp's second-in-command Tommy Roach under interesting scrutiny when he deduces that the 'Hands Across Space' disaster was not of earthly origin. *'He shouldn't look so pleased with himself, thought Quatermass. It's all very well to be right, but—'* (p. 87) In this minor passing detail, Kneale touches upon a subtle distinction between youth and age, enthusiasm and experience, that demonstrates a certain refinement of thought and consideration that comes with age.

And then there is the considerable added bonus of glimpses into the inner life of Quatermass himself, such as this reverie from Chapter 3:

> *'There had been other times when all the rules snapped. Men in a spacecraft crew who had been invaded and made over, to return as a single, obscene carrier of alien disease. That had been the worst because it was totally unexpected. No one had been ready for it. Perhaps no one could ever really be. One guarded against a future eventuality, only to be struck in the back by the past. That other time...an organic machine dormant in the ground since the Pliocene, warmed back to its purpose and activity of nightmarish irrelevance...Those things had happened. When one tried to recall the events clearly to write about them one suffered too much. One took to one's bed for a day or two and, going back to it, one abandoned that whole section, knowing that one would never complete it because one could not bear to.*"[27]

In terms of sheer added material, the novel's 12th chapter is its most remarkable. It opens with a description of the scene at 10 Downing Street, whose door is blocked by a heavy tank. *'After the curfew siren there was little movement on the streets below, only an occasional army pig [armoured vehicle] on patrol or a car carrying some of the Prime Minister's catamites*

---

[27] Ibid. p. 46-47.

home to Number 10.'[28] As Quatermass stands at the window of his quarters, looking down on this scene, Annie returns with food and the remarkable news of a more recent incident at Disneyland.(*'Thousands of young people again, the very fact that they had gathered there should have been warning enough.'*) As he ponders the whys surrounding the event, the scientist suffers a kind of *petit mal* seizure and begins clinging to Annie like a child. She puts him to bed, lies down beside him, and they fall asleep side-by-side, Quatermass waking in the middle of the night and failing to make love to her. Dreams bring Quatermass back into the living presence of his late wife, along with remorseful memories of how he neglected her during her pregnancy, his mind deep in work. He wakes to find Annie beside him, his waking mind already incredibly busy and fertile, and he feels certain that what is behind the incidents is a machine. As they talk about what differentiates life from mechanics, they begin to make love again — Quatermass looking at Annie as though she is the last living representative of all other life on the planet, which she seems to intuit, calming his urgencies with the words 'I'm only me.'

While the scene of Quatermass and Annie making love might very well have seemed gratuitous in the film versions, it makes sense in the novel where Quatermass more frequently berates himself for the failures of his process due to aging ('I'm too old! My brain must be drying!'). Just as the alien intelligence must derive something of value from whatever it syphons from these mass sacrifices, the novel shows Quatermass deriving what he needs to rally his own best resources from intimate contact with the life force of the younger, but greying woman:

> *'He was wide awake now. His brain was curiously busy. Nervously active in an undirected way, excited as a dog hunting rats in a field, jumping all over the place. Ideas kept popping up and vanishing, getting away from him before he could catch them. Then small, logical sequences came. And, in a sudden rush, lucidity.'* (p. 183)

---

[28] It should be noted that Kneale beat to the punch by one year Anthony Burgess's epic novel Earthly Powers, whose opening sentence – 'It was the afternoon of my eighty-first birthday, and I was in bed with my catamite when Ali announced that the archbishop had come to see me' – was praised by The Daily Telegraph as 'outrageously provocative.'

The Literary Kneale

We can see this also in the film versions, when Quatermass collapses and seems to die before detonating the bomb, only to be blearily resuscitated by a kiss from Hettie, which gives him the last ounce of strength he needs to push the button — with her loving help.

The lovemaking scene also offers healing counterpoint to the burlesque made of human sexuality earlier in the story, during Quatermass's return visit to the BTV studios, where he interrupts a taping of 'The Tittupy Bumpity Show':

'He peered past the monitor screens, through the thick glass to see exactly what was going on down there on the studio floor. Huge papier-mache breasts were being swung vigorously about by their invisible, black-clad operators. Tassels whirled from light-up nipples. Sorbo bellies bulged and rocked. Fibreglass buttocks swayed, and pubic hair made in great shocks of gaudy synthetic swirled extravagantly.

'But that was only the background. In front, live dancers dressed as comic animals were prancing through elaborate choreography. To maintain internal logic they too were fitted with outsized genitals, a cat with vast breasts, and elephant with a phallus like a drainpipe.

'It was a family show.' (p. 159)

This episode — in which Quatermass disrupts the bawdy broadcast to commandeer the air waves and make publicly known that in excess of thirty cosmic beam attacks around the globe have eaten hundreds of thousands of young lives around the world — is meaningful in the way it contrasts the television medium's abilities to narcotize and nourish its audience. Kneale had covered similar ground in THE YEAR OF THE SEX OLYMPICS and the BEASTS teleplay 'Buddyboy' but, in this context, there is a pointedly satirical indictment of the business of television, its catering to the lowest possible denominator to attract the highest possible ratings, and the residual effects on society in general and human relationships more particularly.

After the lovemaking scene, Chapter 12 continues as Quatermass makes a fateful exploration of the corridors adjoining the Parliamentary Annexe at Downing Street where he and Annie have been given quarters:

WE ARE THE MARTIANS

'There was a doorway, he found, that led from the quadrangle of Dean's Yard into the cloisters of Westminster Abbey... He made his way to the south transept, his footsteps clicking and echoing. Poet's Corner. This was the exact point. This is where he stood then. He looked up from the tombs of Chaucer, Spenser and Kipling to the high arches of the triforium. Dark gothic hollows, elegant stone tracery. Once there had been something else up there. He had stood on this very spot and had seen it... a being that was not a being, men gone wrong... an incarnation that had wrapped not hands but fronds round the columns of Purbeck marble. What had been three men had become a single, spreading fungoid mass, and it had dragged itself here to hide... It had been made to go. Not destroyed, made to go. The destruction of such a presence was impossible but it had been made to go.'[29]

This unexpected return trip to Poet's Corner performs the service of reminding us that, when Quatermass previously stood on this spot (in 1953's THE QUATERMASS EXPERIMENT), he had stepped forward to appeal to whatever might still be lingeringly human in the transfigured alien body of Victor Caroon, just as Caroon himself might have sought out this burial place of England's great poets in a desperate bid to hold onto what was still noblest and most essentially human in himself. At the beginning of this adventure, Quatermass describes himself as living in a cottage by a loch in Scotland, away from all this, where he seems to have neglected his orphaned granddaughter terribly in his academic distraction. This scene tells us, obliquely, that Hettie's escape from her grandfather's living death was necessary to his recruitment back into his own species. In THE QUATERMASS EXPERIMENT, Quatermass addresses what his still human in Victor Caroon; in QUATERMASS, with beautiful irony, he returns here to address what is still human in himself.

And extending this irony, he does so in concert with Pavel Grigorovitch Gurov, a Russian academician of his own generation with whom his original rocket experiments would have been conducted in direct opposition. The film versions of QUATERMASS are in fact narrated by Gurov, as if to

[29] Ibid. P. 190-191.

point out that we can never be certain of who may end up reading our eulogy.

Kneale dedicated QUATERMASS 'to Judy'—that is, to his wife Judith Kerr, whom he credited with informing the Jewish dimension of the story in all of its forms, as expressed through the devotions of Joe and Clare Kapp. Allowing that he was not a religious man himself, Kneale said 'I do know about Jews having been married to one for 50 years, and I love them. I thought these would be the probable survivors because that is their history. They would find a way of surviving and would keep their knowledge and apply it.'[30]

As Joe Kapp tells Quatermass early in the novel about the Jewish people and the importance of learning to their survival, in a way that summons back into memory all of the ignorant folk of Kneale's TOMATO CAIN stories and the weird fantasies born of their isolation, *'They knew it was the only way... to beat the dark.'* (p. 41)

But, this being a bleak novel of human sacrifice, the Jews don't win. Kapp loses everything, dies pointlessly, and doesn't finally beat the dark. However, the novel's closing recitation reminds us that knowledge will survive so long as we have literature, and so long as children find refuge in its light—which, lest we forget, can be blown out like a match:

> *Huffity, puffity, Ringstone Round*
> *If you lose your hat it will never be found*
> *So pull up your britches right up to your chin*
> *And fasten your cloak with a bright new pin*
> *And when you are ready, then we can begin,*
> *Huffity, puffity, puff!*

LADIES' NIGHT (IN UNNATURAL CAUSES, 1986)

The last of Kneale's original prose works to appear in print was LADIES' NIGHT, a novelette based on the teleplay he had written for the Central

---

[30] Kibble-White, Jack, *ibid.*

WE ARE THE MARTIANS

Independent Television series UNNATURAL CAUSES. The series offered different hour-long plays on the shared theme of murder and accidental death and ran for only seven episodes, of which Kneale's was the fifth, airing on December 6, 1986. The accompanying paperback book was a fascinating promotional item, in that four of the programme's contributing authors—Kneale, novelist Beryl Bainbridge, future PRIME SUSPECT creator Lynda La Plante, and Nicholas Palmer—adapted their scripts as novelettes, with the remaining teleplays (written by Ron Hutchinson, Paula Milne and Peter J. Hammond) were adapted by other writers. Kneale's contribution is, once again, outstanding.

It documents a Monday night at the venerable Hunters Club, which has for generations been accessible only by men who have distinguished themselves as hunters, who have furnished the premises with the mounted heads of conquered prey as proof of their good standing. It is tradition, upon entering, to pat the balding head of a stuffed aardvark named Eustace—*'mistakenly shot during a big game hunt by Major Wilfred Dawes in 1911'* in Southern Rhodesia, in apology. In recent years, the Hunters Club has had to ease up on some of its conditions for membership and has begun, for example, to allow businessmen of a certain stature to join even if they have no hunting experience—and now there is a Monday night experiment in play, allowing wives and girlfriends to dine at special guest tables in the club, to drink in a special anteroom to the bar area, and to make use of a special ablutions station down a separate corridor from that set aside for the use of the gentlemen. Wives are permitted to sleep over.

The club's oldest surviving member is Colonel Gordon Roberts Waley, now in his eighties, who is accustomed to riding roughshod over the other men, who kow-tow to him because the club affiliation can be helpful to them in business. But after offending one female guest quickly, and bullying another into drinking too much and then ordering her to leave for being drunk, he meets his match in Mrs. Evelyn Tripp. While dining with her husband at a guest table in the so-called Coffee Room, Evelyn is appalled as she overhears Colonel Waley holding court:

Waley leaned back in his chair. 'It was back in 1936. I was quite a young fellow then, on attachment in Berlin. I was invited to go shooting in East Prussia. My host was a chappie called Hermann Goering.'

He paused, knowing this usually sharpened interest. It did Evelyn's.

'He had his problems,' Waley continued. 'He was married to a Swedish woman, a neurotic invalid. But he'd just been appointed Reichsmarschall and he was celebrating. We shot 17 boar that day. Towards the end . . . I was standing near old Hermann when a huge tusker broke cover. Straight at us. He raised his gun — and it jammed!'

'My God,' said Monks.

Waley smiled. 'Mine didn't. Hermann turned to me and he said "Danke, mein Jaeger." Those very words. Thank you, my hunter.'

Those at the long table were deeply moved. The quantity of malt whisky they had drunk in the Bar helped.

Evelyn could hardly speak. She turned to Tripp and demanded, 'Did you hear that?'

'Yes.' He had been moved too.

'He saved Goering's life!'

It came out as a hoarse cry. She was on her feet, yelling on over the spluttered protests of Monks and Greenbow. 'D'you think that was a good deed, all of you?'

"You don't understand,' protested Summerland.

And passionately from Monks, 'They never understand!'

Even Foss's pale face had grown heated as he cried, 'It was a matter of honour!'

Evelyn spat it out, 'And what did you do for Hitler?'[31]

As Waley responds coldly, *'Hitler, Madam, was a vulgarian!'* the clubmen subject their guest to the worst vulgarities, demanding that she be ejected from the room. Tripp escorts her quietly to their room, where she berates him for not defending her, not realizing that each word is ratcheting his resentment of her ever higher. Evelyn is quick to see that the

---

[31] *Unnatural Causes* (Dorset: Javelin, 1986), p. 112. Of the various authors contributing to the book, only Beryl Bainbridge is noted on the front cover, for writing the book's introduction. Readers thinking of consulting abebooks.com for a second-hand copy are advised to search for it under her name.

WE ARE THE MARTIANS

men are enamored of the club because it takes them back to their school days, subservient to a hectoring headmaster, and that it offers them a fantasy shelter and temporary respite from the responsibility of being grown men. A letter from Colonel Haley, sent to the Tripps' quarters, written with *'proper pen, club paper'*, officially dismisses Tripp as a member of the Club—which so shakes him to his core that, at the first sarcastic word from Evelyn, he cracks her skull with a heavy silver candlestick holder.

Word of the murder is discreetly conveyed to Colonel Haley, who feels justified by Tripp's manly handling of the situation—which he has in fact cold-bloodedly provoked as a test of mettle. Visiting the scene of the crime, Haley proceeds to destroy and wipe clean any objects that might incriminate his member. As discussions are held in another room to decide how best to dispose of the 'thing' (Haley's word) upstairs, the 'thing' disappears—evidently only wounded, not killed—forcing the members of the Hunters Club to hunt her down on the premises.

'She came here to make fun of our manhood!' Waley cries before shooting the lock off the gentlemen's Ablutions, where Evelyn seeks shelter. The irony of the situation is that Evelyn is only present at the club because she gives her husband all too much credit for being a man. He sleeps overnight in the city once a week and she wants to confirm, by visiting the club, that he is sleeping alone. Whenever she objects to her husband's behavior, it is because he isn't jumping to her defence; he falls short of expectations, as she can plainly see, because Waley's towering ego doesn't leave room at the club for any other men. By the same token, Evelyn is portrayed as a bit of a Waley herself, which raises the valid question of whether the monsters who walk among us are self-made or enabled—making the reference of Nazism most apt.

Kneale's novelette, which runs 48 pages in print, enriches this story substantially by venturing under the skins and into the minds of its characters. Seven pages precede the first spoken line of dialogue in the teleplay, in which Colonel Waley wakes from a nightmare in a cold sweat; it is part memory, involving a beating dealt out to him by his childhood nanny—part imperialist race conquest fantasy, part admission of his abiding fear of women. Upon rising, he notes the yellow quality of the waning light on his wall, a yellowness he notes in his own aging reflection ('*Age brought a sort of gilding, the touch of a gentle and considerate Midas*'), and he then grooms himself and dresses for the evening with military circumspection. We receive the equivalent of a TOMATO CAIN short story in the first six pages, before the characters begin to meet and interact. Kneale also dotes on the details of the club itself, imbuing it with the weight and dust of its history and its many decorative, fanged and glowering appointments. The budget of the programme did not extend to cover much of what he so richly describes.

There have been many proper adaptations and loose cinematic nods to Richard Connell's story 'The Most Dangerous Game' over the years, in which a hunter sets himself the ultimate challenge of tracking his own species, but LADIES' NIGHT—particularly in its prose form—packs more gunpowder than most. Unlike most of these adaptations, the suspense of Kneale's piece has nothing to do with siding with its tremulous prey. Once Mrs. Tripp is clubbed (appropriate term!) to apparent death, we never see her again; instead, we are forced to share company with her boorish hunters and to imagine her frantic animal distress as they track her from one quickly abandoned hiding place to another, finally coming to an open window in the Ablutions area, a place she was pointedly forbidden to enter—her survival ironically dependent upon her breaking the rules laid down by men. And once again, this absurd human tragedy is underlined as such by the glass-eyed witness borne by various bears, boars, rhinoceros, and gnus—Kneale's beasties.

Like QUATERMASS, UNNATURAL CAUSES was judged by the critical establishment to be a promotional tie-in rather than a serious book and it sank without a trace.

It didn't matter.

Such was the impact of Nigel Kneale's overall achievement that, 50 years after winning the Atlantic and Somerset Maugham Awards for his first book, his visionary labours were honoured once again, in the last year of the 20th century, with a Lifetime Achievement Award from the Horror Writers Association.

The middle 1/7th of a £2.99 paperback, one that didn't carry his name on the cover except in the finest of fine print on the back? This was hardly the venue where anyone might have expected such an important fiction career to reach its final port. But, as Kneale's most famous character once grumbled, he never had a career—only work.

THE QUATERMASS CONCEPTION

Stephen R. Bissette

THERE ARE DAYS WHERE I FIND MYSELF GOBSMACKED BY HOW completely Nigel Kneale's powerful, at times prescient body of creative work continues to resonate in our day-to-day lives. When I am watching television with my wife or screening feature films in my home viewing room, the associative links sometimes prompt me to grab a scrap of paper and make a note.

The echoes are everywhere, in mainstream media and in the most obscure self-distributed productions.

My wife and I are watching the first episode of the Welsh detective TV series Y GWYLL aka HINTERLAND (October 2013/January 4, 2014), entitled "Devil's Bridge," the episode named after the titular village landmark beneath which a woman's body has been found after a suspicious disappearance.

And I think, "Hobb's End, QUATERMASS AND THE PIT."

Though there are no supernatural or science-fiction elements in Y GWYLL, the ominous association between the devil and a dark secret the village harbors smacks of Nigel Kneale to me.

A later episode of the same program has me thinking more than once of Kneale's ATV one-shot "Murrain" for the anthology series AGAINST THE

CROWD (broadcast July 27, 1975), which I'd finally seen on DVD (the UK DVD BEASTS anthology collection) a couple years back.

Is it just me?

On the advice of friends, I dive into the debut episode of the British sf anthology programme BLACK MIRROR, entitled "The National Anthem" (originally broadcast December 4, 2011). Series creator Charlie Brooker's provocative, pitch-black satiric script finds the British Prime Minister (Rory Kinnear, squirming more than his father even did for director Richard Lester) plunged into a brewing international scandal when a video of the just-kidnapped, much beloved member of the royal family (Lydia Wilson) is broadcast on YouTube with the demand that the Prime Minister fuck a pig live on national television, or the beloved royal family member will be executed.

I am galvanized—this is outrageous, terrific, incredible television, and absolutely brilliant science-fiction, the kind we never see in American television.

But I can't help but think that this brand of speculative faux–"reality TV" science-fiction began with Nigel Kneale and Randolph Cartier positing that in the same Westminster Abbey from which the Queen's coronation had just been broadcast live, a mutated British astronaut no longer recognizable as once having been human was about to reach reproductive gestation and the live broadcast of the explosive expulsion of its spores might be only minutes away—essentially, fucking us all, forever, live, on the BBC.

Am I delusional? *Is it just me?*

Months later, 57 minutes into the documentary MIRAGE MEN (2014, Perception Management)—written by Mark Pilkington, directed by John Lundberg, Roland Denning, and Kypros Kyprianou—journalist Linda Moulton Howe (filmmaker/author of A STRANGE HARVEST, 1980, STRANGE HARVESTS, 1993, and much else) is onscreen, describing a covert meeting with infamous (in UFO and paranormal circles) US government operative Richard Doty, who Howe claims privileged her with a look at "secret documents" in an OSI Consulting office in Kirkland, WA

("My superiors have asked me to show you something...you can read these; you cannot take notes..."). Howe reads portions of a document entitled "BRIEFING PAPER FOR THE PRESIDENT OF THE UNITED STATES OF AMERICA ON UNIDENTIFIED AERIAL VEHICLES," and finds therein a passage that reads, "...These extraterrestrials manipulated DNA in already-evolving primates to create *homo sapiens*." Howe cryptically says, "And I remember reading that sentence over several times trying to absorb the implications of its meaning...because if *homo sapiens* is a genetically constructed species by extraterrestrials, we are then by definition a planet of 6½ billion androids—if we are androids, what purpose are we serving?" MIRAGE MEN also references a document entitled "Project Garnet," and a sentence in that document that reads, "All questions and mysteries about the evolution of *homo sapiens* on this planet have been answered and this project is closed."

And I think, "QUATERMASS AND THE PIT."

No, it isn't "just me."

It *is* everywhere.

Was Nigel Kneale simply teasing out a speculative origin of the species (as Arthur C. Clarke had at about the same time, in his novel CHILDHOOD'S END, 1953) simply to entertain his BBC viewership, or did he suspect or *know* something? Or (*far* more likely), did a professional government-employed disinformation expert simply fabricate "government documents" using ideas cribbed from a late-night TV broadcast of Hammer Films' 1967 feature film version of Kneale's QUATERMASS AND THE PIT under its American title, FIVE MILLION YEARS TO EARTH?

I could play this parlor game all day. I could construct this essay entirely from such connective tissues and tendons and cartilage (perhaps some of my compatriots in this collection have done just that; read on).

Kneale's footsteps and fingerprints are everywhere, all about us, on the screens we're addicted to, the newspapers a few million of us still read, the books and comic books and TV shows and media we lap up like milk, day after day, all our lives.

It all began before anyone was so media-saturated, as television was just entering the homes of a lucky minority, before every hour of broadcast time was filled with countless programming options. It all began with Nigel Kneale's original Quatermass deadly duo—the teleplays broadcast on the BBC in 1953 and 1955, adapted to the big screen by Hammer Films and Val Guest in 1955 and 1957, respectively.

Our focus will be on the first of these, THE QUATERMASS EXPERIMENT.

Almost every creator, writer or critic who has written about Nigel Kneale's Quatermass TV serials has noted how each is rooted in Britain's then-recent WWII experience, and the peculiarities of post-war England's radicalized, ever-changing political and social environment. The echoes of the Blitz—the rocket plunging into a British home in THE QUATERMASS EXPERIMENT, the secretive military installation and covert operatives of QUATERMASS II, the subterranean "missile" erroneously identified (much to Quatermass' contempt) as an unexploded Nazi bomb or V2 rocket in QUATERMASS AND THE PIT—have always been self-evident.

The Quatermass Conception

It seems to me, though, that little attention has been given to two of the key sources of dread, suspense, and the central transformative horror of Kneale's seminal THE QUATERMASS EXPERIMENT. Britain was ruled by a Conservative government from 1951-1964, reflecting and determining much of the social and political climate THE QUATERMASS EXPERIMENT was conceived and received within.

Kneale's imaginative, innovative teleplay was first and foremost a speculative drama about contagion from "outside"—a central concern in the UK in the early 1950s, manifest even in the lowliest of cultural artifacts, the comic books that children and adults habitually purchased and read—[32] and how such contagions might fundamentally change England in the wake of the Second World War.[33] Kneale's brilliant conceit was to manifest such dire "change" as coming not from America (as media critics, the press, and Parliament feared) or England's European neighbors, but from *outer space*—specifically, a British exploration of space—and to characterize that contagion as one that functioned by *replacing* that which it fed upon.

It isn't much of a leap to identify Kneale cleverly exploring another expression of that *same* fear as the springboard for QUATERMASS II, in which the Conservative government in power *had already been supplanted* by an extraterrestrial invasion force, and was quietly having its way under a militarized cloak of secrecy hiding covert technologies intent upon altering the very atmosphere we breath and terrain of our planet. A short time later, Kneale reinterpreted the same premise yet again to propose that as a species we'd not only "lost" the war against contagion millions of years ago, but in fact owed our very existence and evolution into *Homo sapiens* to that contagion and transformation: the contagion

---

[32] For more on the language of that early 1950s British campaign, contemporary to the broadcast of THE QUATERMASS EXPERIMENT, how it unfolded, and the Act of Parliament it culminated in, see Martin Barker, *A Haunt of Fears: The Strange History of the British Horror Comics Campaign* (Pluto Press, 1984; US edition: University Press of Mississippi, 1992).

[33] Val Guest and Richard Landau's Hammer Films adaptation of Kneale's teleplay preserved and subtly amplified this Cold War dread of a contagion from "outside" changing England from within, and the fear that the change had already begun and was irrevocable. Note the slight change from Kneale's dialogue in Chapter Five of QUATERMASS EXPERIMENT, which Guest modified to "I have a very sick feeling it was something to speed up the change going on inside him" in QUATERMASS XPERIMENT. A close analysis of the latter half of this article will reveal much to the attentive reader.

had *already arrived* eons ago and *already* irrevocably changed Britain (and all of mankind) in the prehistoric past in QUATERMASS AND THE PIT.

By that point, Kneale had matured as a writer and specifically as a writer for television, making QUATERMASS AND THE PIT the densest, most ingeniously woven of all his contagion scenarios, looking backwards, forwards, and ahead at the same time. Kneale was diagnosing the social ills of the present (racism, xenophobia, tribal infighting, etc.) as symptoms of that contagion-past, the Martian transformation of the species, and the lingering after-effects of the hive-mentality that was hard-wired into our racial memories and behavioral patterns.

Before arriving there, however, Kneale had to start with a simpler contagion. These pathogens must be introduced carefully at first. Part and parcel of the still-resonant "body horror" of THE QUATERMASS EXPERIMENT and its film adaptation **THE QUATERMASS XPERIMENT** lies in Kneale's choosing as his first-ever sf infectious agent a primal life form that is omnipresent and all-consuming. The contagion that overtakes the doomed downed survivor of THE QUATERMASS EXPERIMENT is patterned after one of the most common life forms on Earth—yet so unlike any other life form that it is neither animal nor vegetable.

Prior to Nigel Kneale adopting that life form as a model for his new breed of televised dread, another British writer had already explored its potential for raising hackles and gorges. This writer was spreading his notion of contagions-from-outside many decades before Kneale put pen to paper...

It's fashionable in literary horror circles these days to fête the accomplishments of long-overlooked British author William Hope Hodgson, who back in the 1960s had been championed by scholars and anthologists like Sam Moskowitz for his novels THE NIGHT LAND and THE HOUSE ON THE BORDERLANDS (highly recommended, both). Less renowned, but now generally acknowledged, is Hodgson's pioneer role in what I can only call "contagion horror." Imaginatively drawing from his life experiences as a sailor (beginning as a cabin boy apprentice in 1891, as a teenager) and soldier (he was eventually killed by artillery during World War 1, April

The Quatermass Conception

1918), Hodgson scribed many a sea-survival tale, most of them horror stories. Though Nigel Kneale, to my knowledge, never specifically acknowledged any familiarity with (much less affinity for) Hodgson's fiction—the fact is, when interviewed Kneale rarely acknowledged any literary or media influences upon his work—there's no doubt that elements central to Kneale's seminal THE QUATERMASS EXPERIMENT have antecedents in Hodgson's published work.

Hodgson's most adapted story (long after his death) memorably involved fungal infection and death: *"The Voice in the Night"* (1907, debuting in *Blue Book Magazine*). Some of those elements echoed in passages of his novel THE BOATS OF THE "GLEN CARRIG" (also 1907). Hodgson tapped the fungal horrors in other stories, too, and (as 'blob' movies are also part of Kneale's QUATERMASS EXPERIMENT legacy) it's worth noting Hodgson later crafted a nasty seaborne ravenous "blob" story with *"The Derelict"* (1912).

Hodgson's earlier sea-faring photographs of maggot-infested food linger as precursors of these still-chilling tales of organic infestations and "supplantation"—unlike any other living thing on Earth, fungus feeds by replacing, or *supplanting*, its food-source, absorbing nutrients from plant or animal matter (living or dead) by "predigesting" the food material via enzymes produced in the thread-like *hyphae* veined into their host. This manner of feeding-by-replacement is central to THE QUATERMASS EXPERIMENT, as is the fact that fungus reproduces by producing spores that spread by breeze and wind currents to new host sites.

Hodgson's *"The Voice in the Night"* involves two survivors of a sinking ship who end up stranded in a lagoon festooned with a fast-spreading, all-consuming fungus, which eventually spreads onto their skins and triggers a craving to devour the fungus itself ("...day by day the fight is more dreadful, to withstand the hungerlust for the terrible lichen..."). This morbid tale is told by a lone "man" in a rowboat seeking supplies from a schooner, who refuses to come too close or to be seen; as the storyteller's boat departs with fresh supplies after telling his story, the dawn's early light reveals a misshapen, barely human figure rowing away ("...Indistinctly I saw something nodding between the oars. I thought of a sponge—a great, grey nodding sponge...").

It's hardly a stretch to trace how Hodgson's story impacted the cinematic (and televised) horror genre. *"The Voice in the Night"* was in fact filmed over half-a-century later: it was officially adapted by Stirling Silliphant for Alfred Hitchcock's Shamley Productions as one of their most unusual contributions to the 1958 TV anthology programme SUSPICION.[34] Hodgson's short story was included in the paperback anthology ALFRED HITCHCOCK PRESENTS STORIES THEY WOULDN'T LET ME DO ON TV (US: Simon & Schuster, Dell Publishing paperback editions in two volumes 1958 and 1959;[35] UK: Reinhardt, 1957, Pan Giant paperback edition, 1960), ghost-edited by Robert Arthur (Hitchcock name was on, but he hadn't written, the preface, per usual)—well, it *hadn't* been adapted to TV by Hitchcock's production team in 1957, when this book first saw print.[36] That was soon to change.

According to Silliphant, *"The Voice in the Night"* was originally to have been directed by Hitchcock:

"Except for one meeting with Hitch to discuss my scripting a one-hour SUSPICION, 'Voice in the Night,' I never, over the seasons I wrote for the show [ALFRED HITCHCOCK PRESENTS], met the man. My meetings were always with Joan Harrison, his series producer... Now, my single meeting with Hitch: Joan told me the master was actually going to direct one of his TV shows—this one his very favorite story—'The Voice in the Night,' to be the flagship episode for his one-hour SUSPICION series. Joan drove me to his home up Bellagio Road, one of those canyon streets off Sunset Boulevard where you drive in through a gate. Hitch was

---

[34] This was one of ten Hitchcock/Shamley-produced SUSPICION episodes. The late Patrick Macnee starred as the ship's captain who listens to the infected sailor's story, and a young James Coburn was his first mate. Another extraterrestrial-invasion fungal gem of sf/horror short fiction has an Alfred Hitchcock TV association, too: Ray Bradbury's *"Special Delivery"* was adapted for ALFRED HITCHCOCK PRESENTS (November 29, 1959). Almost three years later, the Bradbury short story finally was published as *"Come Into My Cellar"* (later retitled *"Boys! Grow Giant Mushrooms in Your Cellar!"* when collected) in *Galaxy* (October 1962).

[35] Hodgson's story was published in the first Dell volume; the original hardcover contents were split in half, with the remaining stories published in 1959 as ALFRED HITCHCOCK PRESENTS 13 MORE STORIES THEY WOULDN'T LET ME DO ON TV.

[36] Other stories in this collection that *did* make it to Hitchcock's TV show: Robert Arthur's own story "The Jokester" (adapted/broadcast October 19, 1958), Arthur Williams' "Being a Murderer Myself" (retitled "Arthur," broadcast September 27, 1959), and Robert Bloch's "Water's Edge" (broadcast October 19, 1964).

The Quatermass Conception

charming. Congratulated me on the scripts I'd done for the half-hour ALFRED HITCHCOCK PRESENTS shows, personally made me a scotch and soda and sat me down with my yellow pad.

"I wouldn't trade the hour that followed for anything I can think of at the moment—except possibly—no, not even that. The man was *brilliant*. He fucking dictated the script to me—shot by shot, including camera movements and opticals. He actually had already *seen* the finished film. He'd say, for example, 'The camera's in the boat with the boy and the girl. The move in is very, very slow—while we see the mossy side of the wrecked schooner. Bump. Now the boy climbs the ladder. I tilt up. I see him look at his hand. Something strange seems to have attached itself. He disappears on deck. Now the girl starts up, and I cut to the boy exploring the deck. I'm shooting through this foreground of—of *stuff*—and I'm panning him to the cabin door. Something there makes him freeze. He waits. Now the camera's over here, and I see the girl come to him. Give me about this much dialogue, Stirling.' He holds up his hand, thumb and forefinger about two inches apart. I jot down—'Dialogue, two inches.' As I say, the whole goddamned film—shot by shot, no dialogue—just the measurements of how much dialogue and where he wanted it. He left its content to me, since there is no dialogue in the entire short story. It's all introspection and the memory of horror, and the writer didn't want to spoil it with dialogue. Lotsa luck, screenwriter. 'Give me two inches of dialogue right there.' I went away and wrote what I still consider a rather neat piece of work; but lo and behold, Hitch decided to shoot a theatrical movie, and his presence was denied to us. Arthur Hiller directed..."[37]

Starring in that American TV production (broadcast on March 24, 1958) was none other than British character actor James Donald. He starred as the unfortunate unseen infected seaman in the boat, begging for supplies, whose wheezing voice[38] (and dramatized flashbacks) told the tragic tale of his and his beloved wife's (Barbara Rush) plight. At the time, American audiences might have recognized James Donald as the actor

---

[37] "Stirling Silliphant: The Finger of God," interviewed by Nat Segaloff, *Backstory 3: Interviews with Screenwriters of the '60s*, edited by Patrick McGilligan (1997, University of California Press), pp. 338-339.

[38] Ironically, James Donald eventually retired from acting due to his lifelong battle with asthma.

who'd recently played Theo van Gogh in **LUST FOR LIFE** (1956), though most would have associated him with his prominent role as the prisoner-of-war doctor who questioned the sanity of Colonel Nicholson (Alec Guiness) in David Lean's popular WWII epic **THE BRIDGE ON THE RIVER KWAI** (1957)—the man who spoke that multi-award-winning film's unforgettable last line, "Madness! Madness!" That cemented Donald's presence in a procession of iconic male action-adventure and military films: **THE VIKINGS** (1958), **THIRD MAN ON THE MOUNTAIN** (1959), **THE GREAT ESCAPE** (1963), **KING RAT** (1965), **CAST A GIANT SHADOW** (1966), etc. Throughout this period, Donald continued performing for the small screen in the UK and the US, including memorable performances for two episodes of ALFRED HITCH-COCK PRESENTS which Hitchcock himself directed, including the role of the man laying in bed paralyzed with fear because he believes a venomous snake is coiled on his stomach in a taut adaptation of Roald Dahl's *conte cruel* short story "Poison" (October 5, 1958). Most genre devotees remember James Donald as the heroic self-sacrificing Dr. Roney in Nigel Kneale and Hammer Films' adaptation of Kneale's teleplay **QUATERMASS AND THE PIT** (US title: **FIVE MILLION YEARS TO EARTH**, 1967). It always comes back to Kneale and Quatermass, somehow or other, doesn't it?

Five years after James Donald starred in the TV adaptation for SUSPI-CION, *"The Voice in the Night"* was unofficially adapted by Takeshi Kimura (with an additional credit onscreen to Masami Fukushima and Shinichi Hoshi) for Toho producer Tomoyuki Tanaka and director Ishirō Honda as マタンゴ/**MATANGO/ATTACK OF THE MUSHROOM PEOPLE** (1963).

Hodgson's fungus horrors spilled into other media in the meanwhile. EC Comics lifted the story, uncredited (as most Pre-Code horror comics publishers tended to do), to harvest *"Forbidden Fruit"* (THE HAUNT OF FEAR #9, September-October 1951; scripted by Al Feldstein, art by Joe Orlando), and other comic book rips followed.[39] Hell, *I* lifted Hodgson's concept for a pitch to DC Comics editor Karen Berger for SWAMP THING when I was still writing for and drawing covers for that comic book series. This pitch evolved (or devolved) into my script for *"Threads"* in SWAMP THING ANNUAL #4 (1988), illustrated by Pat Broderick, Ron

The Quatermass Conception

Randall, and Eduardo Barreto; writer Doug Wheeler (at my suggestion) then folded the concept into his scripting run on the comic book SWAMP THING, naming the fungal being Matango as a nod to the previously-cited Honda/Toho film. Some attentive SWAMP THING readers chalked my *"Threads"* script up to being a riff on Stephen King's *"Gray Matter"* (*Cavalier*, October 1973) or his *"Weeds"* (*Cavalier*, May 1976), which King adapted (and starred in) for his 1982 **CREEPSHOW** *"The Lonesome Death of Jordy Verrill"* episode,[40] or John Brosnan's novel THE FUNGUS aka DEATH SPORE (1985), published under Brosnan's *nom de plume* Harry Adam Knight. One SWAMP THING fan even wrote to accuse me of stealing from Brian Lumley's *"Fruiting Bodies,"* which wasn't remotely possible, as Brian's story first saw print the same year my SWAMP THING was published, my script having been written months earlier. This was a case of two writers an ocean apart concocting superficially similar tales — but for me, it was Hodgson that I was happily referencing.[41]

---

[39] How well known could Hodgson's stories have been? To my mind, we can divine the popularity of a given genre trope by seeking out not only those works derivative of a given story, but those works that *suggest* derivation (and an expected outcome) only to *deviate* from the expected derivation—surely, *that* is the measure of a well-heeled, overly-familiar narrative device or concept. Hodgson's pulp-era "fungus at sea" conceit was so well-known by the early 1950s that at least one Pre-Code comic book story set up its readers to *think* they were reading just another spin on *"The Voice in the Night"* only to offer a twist ending completely altering the premise. In *Mister Mystery* #14 (November, 1953, *Aragon Magazines*, Inc/Stanley Morse; art by Ellis Eringer, writer uncredited/unknown), "Terror of the Deep" posited a slime-covered wreck, harboring partially-dissolved-in-ooze dead sailors, and a doomed still-living narrator telling what led to such horrific conditions. It wasn't Hodgson's fungus: it was the result of a ship and its crew being swallowed whole by an enormous sea monster, and its corrosive digestive juices taking their toll even after ship-and-crew had been vomited up! The story can be read online at http://thehorrorsofitall.blogspot.com/2012/07/terror-of-deep.html

[40] . . . and which King lifted, almost verbatim, from an obscure Pre-Code 1950s horror comic book story entitled "Green Grows the Grass" in *Eerie* #10 (January 1953, Avon Comics, art by Alvin (A.C.) Hollingsworth; the story can be read at http://seductionoftheindifferent.blogspot.com/2010/02/black-history-month-pre-code-horror.html). More on this in a forthcoming article I am preparing on Lovecraft's *"The Colour Out of Space"* and its kith and kin.

[41] *"Fruiting Bodies"* was first published in *Weird Tales* #291 (Summer 1988), though I first read it in THE YEAR'S BEST HORROR STORIES #17 (DAW, 1989); both saw print months after I'd delivered my SWAMP THING script. When later asked where the inspiration for *"Fruiting Bodies"* came from, Lumley explained, "When I was living in London, a neighbor's house got dry rot. I watched the workmen gut the place! It literally fell apart before your eyes. From the ground floor you could see up through three flights and the roof! Monstrous! A living cancer that turns wood to dust! I made my cancer a little less selective, that's all." Lumley interviewed by Bob Morrish, "TSF Biblio File featuring Brian Lumley," *The Scream Factory* #11, Spring 1993, pg. 102.

WE ARE THE MARTIANS

Long before all this activity, there were already Hodgson imitations and successors. Phillip Fisher's *"Fungus Isle"* (*Argosy All-Story Weekly*, October 27, 1923) pitted shipwrecked sailors against a horde of "Weed-Men." More to the point of Nigel Kneale's THE QUATERMASS EXPERIMENT, H.P. Lovecraft echoed Hodgson's fungal infection to concoct the extraterrestrial meteorite-borne "colour" that crashed into a "blasted heath" and infected the surrounding farm, livestock, farmer and family in his classic *"The Colour Out of Space"* (completed March 1927; published in *Amazing Stories*, September 1927). With his dying breath, Lovecraft's infected farmer described the contagion as something that was "...suckin' the life out of everything...in that stone...it must a' come in that stone pizened the whole place...dun't know what it wants..." Perhaps Lovecraft was extrapolating from Hodgson's reference in this very first line of *"The Voice in the Night"* to "a dark, starless night," or perhaps it was simply the fact that the vastness of space had by the end of the Roaring Twenties replaced the expanses of the sea as a more believable abode for such abhorrent fungal infections to appear from. One no longer had to be a shipwreck survivor in uncharted seas to be contaminated: the damned stuff could fall onto you and yours at any moment, right out of the sky.

The confusion over what precisely fungus *was* as a life form—neither plant nor animal, and eventually deemed to be its own scientifically-defined kingdom—and the manner in which it seemed to spontaneously manifest from nearly-invisible spores, the manner in which it fed, and the insidious ways different fungi could infect and direct the behavior of living hosts lent fungi a disturbing "unnaturalness." All this made it entirely believable that fungi may have indeed originated and plunged from outer space in the prehistoric past, and proliferated from then into its myriad forms. Lovecraft's *"Fungi from Yuggoth"* sonnets (scribed 1929-1930, first published 1930-1947 in *Weird Tales* and various amateur press zines and publications) may have been risible to many as poetry, but the title alone resonated as an evocation of fungi being, inherently, *something* from space.

In any case, by the 1950s, space-borne fungus invaders had quietly established a moldy outpost in pulp sf/fantasy/horror, and began to mushroom in media beyond the pulps, comic books, and paperbacks. With the blossoming of the 1950s science-fiction and horror movie cycle, the "fungus was amongus" in movie theaters and drive-ins, by the 1960s spreading to late-night TV broadcast pastures.

The "science" in these science-fiction/horror feature films was as vague and dubious as any in the pulp tradition Hodgson initiated. All that mattered was the unsettling notion of an all-consuming saprotrophic 'absorption' of living or dead matter, and the primal dread of—and dire consequences of—the slightest exposure to such a rapidly-spreading, ravenous mass. If those narrative elements were in place, the story pot could boil. "You are what you eat" transmuting into "you are what eats you" was all even the least knowledgeable, most impressionable audience members needed to grasp for these horrorshows to work.

Kneale, more than any other teleplay author or screenwriter, dramatized the fungus-like 'feeding' method of his infected astronaut with remarkable precision and fidelity in his surprisingly sophisticated THE QUATERMASS EXPERIMENT teleplay. Fortunately, those elements were retained in Val Guest and Richard Landau's adaptation of Kneale's teleplay into Hammer Films' theatrical movie sensation **THE QUATER-MASS XPERIMENT** (US title: **THE CREEPING UNKNOWN**, 1955). Kneale's pathetic space-travel survivor Victor Carroon's condition manifested in his saprotrophic 'absorption' of living tissues—*absorbing* and incorporating completely his fellow astronauts, a potted cactus plant, zoo animals, and any living being he crossed paths with—like a true fungi. Kneale took imaginative liberties, however. Fungi, of course, do not then change their form to imitate or reflect their hosts (i.e., a mushroom growing on a rotting log does not become log-like; a fungus growing on a caterpillar does not become a surrogate caterpillar), as Victor Carroon did. Still, Kneale's gradual revelation of what Carroon had become after his jaunt in space was teased out and dramatized with conviction, and harbored its own internal logic with associative links to how fungi draw nourishment from their host materials, living or dead. Guest and Landau carefully maintained that same step-by-step revelation of dawning horror

WE ARE THE MARTIANS

for their feature film adaptation. There had never been anything like it before on the big screen (and certainly nothing like it ever before on the television, broadcast into homes).[42]

Such science was completely bungled or abandoned in the many imitations that followed Nigel Kneale's and Quatermass' lead. Most supplanted Carroon's plight with that of various cosmic-crap-encrusted, dissolving, or otherwise malignant downed astronauts or astronaut extremities (i.e., **FIRST MAN INTO SPACE**, 1959; **THE CRAWLING HAND**, 1963; **THE INCREDIBLE MELTING MAN**, 1977; etc.). Like spores, the concept had already spread and mutated long before those later media permutations/bastardizations of THE QUATERMASS EXPERIMENT tainted any screens.

Right around the time Val Guest/Hammer Films' **THE QUATERMASS XPERIMENT** opened in British theaters, Jack Finney's THE BODY SNATCHERS (initially serialized in *Colliers Magazine* in 1954, published in novel form in 1955, and adapted into the classic **INVASION OF THE BODY SNATCHERS** in 1956) established the most definitive 1950s sf spore-fueled invasion. As sf author Damon Knight later pointed out, Finney's "science" was rather lacking: how exactly *did* those spores-from-space grow into three-foot pods, which then sprouted surrogate humans, and then replaced their victims? It was all rather vague and suspect, but it had its own perfectly realized suggestive nightmare logic, and Finney's skillful writing made sense of it to the casual reader; however blurry the science, the conceit translated vividly to the screen, via Daniel Mainwaring and Richard Collins' screenplay and the steely conviction of Don Siegel's *film noir* direction. The "seed pod people" in Finney's imag-

---

[42] There had been transformations in cinema, dating back to the first silent era adaptations of Robert Louis Stevenson's THE STRANGE CASE OF DR. JEKYLL AND MR. HYDE, and lycanthropy had become a genre staple as early as he 1935 **THE WEREWOLF OF LONDON**, but disfiguring disease was quite another matter. Leprosy was a staple of Biblical motion pictures (as were leper colonies in adventure stories), but it was never shown in its progressive stages for shock effect, much less to slowly disturb and distress audiences with insidious, cumulative emotional impact; it was, in almost all religious narratives, something introduced only to be miraculously cured. Sam Newfield/Lawrence Williams/Pierre Gendron/Martin Mooney's **THE MONSTER MAKER** (1944) for poverty-row's PRC (Producers Releasing Corporation) was a precursor, exploiting the deformative stages of an artificially induced infection of a rapidly-spreading strain of acromegaly. A scientific miracle cure made for a comforting concert coda.

inary botanical contagion (supplanting human minds and bodies with plant surrogates, leaving behind withered husks in a resonant variant on saprotrophic 'feeding') seemed to be, ultimately, neither fungi nor plants, *per se*. They were and remain "something else" in all incarnations of Finney's scientifically incoherent concoction that has spawned remakes, sequels, and countless nightmares.

In the wake of Kneale's and Finney's inspired invaders, space contagion more often culminated in walking-dead outbreaks, from the 'aliens possessing corpses' of Ed Wood's **PLAN NINE FROM OUTER SPACE** (1958), Edward L. Cahn/Samuel Newman's **INVISIBLE INVADERS** (1959), Phil Tucker's **THE CAPE CANAVERAL MONSTERS** (1960), and so on through to the space-spawned zombie plagues that marched in the wake of **NIGHT OF THE LIVING DEAD**. The former were most often intangible energy creatures inhabiting corporal host bodies; the latter most often disease-like contagions sans fungi affiliations. By this point, Hodgson's distinctive brand of fungal phobia was manifest in films evidencing none of Kneale's influence, such as Charles Marquis Warren and Kenneth Higgins' lackluster **THE UNKNOWN TERROR** (1957), in which subterranean foamy-fungal parasitic infections turned men into soap-bubble-tinged monsters.

As in H. P. Lovecraft's *"The Colour Out of Space"* and Kneale's THE QUATERMASS EXPERIMENT, the *real* contagions yet to come arrived from above, not below. Edward Bernds/George Worthing Yates/Daniel Mainwaring's **SPACE MASTER X-7** (1958) and Hugo Grimaldi and Arthur C. Pierce's **MUTINY IN OUTER SPACE** (1965) imitated Kneale's QUATERMASS EXPERIMENT in that both were actually *contagion* movies, with their respective infectious menaces arriving from space.

Contagion movies were one of the curious subgenres that shaped Kneale's conception for and of THE QUATERMASS EXPERIMENT, as surely as shared recent WWII memories of the Blitz had. But these all had a common source beyond the fiction of Hodgson: it must be noted that Kneale scripted his innovative BBC serial in the wake of a series of real-life events and media based upon those events.

WE ARE THE MARTIANS

After World War II, rumors and reports began to spread of the now-infamous Japanese Kwantung Army's Unit 731 experiments in Manchuria with anthrax as a biological weapon and the use of prisoners-of-war as guinea pigs; under the code name "Agent N," the Allies, too, had investigated the use of anthrax as a potential biological weapon. Botulinum was also researched as viable bioweaponary, as were chemical and toxic organophosphorous nerve agents (after the war, the Allies were quick to capitalize on Nazi advances with nerve agents like sarin, suman, and tabun after the war).

Most visible of all to a Manxman like Kneale was the notorious 1942 British bioweapon experiments with a so-called "N-bomb" that rendered Scotland's Gruinard Island uninhabitable due to Vollum-14578 anthrax spores (the island wasn't decontaminated fully until 1990). "Operation Vegetarian" involved anthrax-impregnated animal feed intended to attack German livestock; planned for a 1944 deployment, neither the five million edible anthrax "cattle cakes" nor the N-bomb were even used, and the spore-infected cattle cakes were destroyed via incineration by the end of 1945. These deadly cattle cakes were stored all that time in Porton Down, a military science park in Wiltshire, England, the Ministry of Defense lab Nigel Kneale later used as inspiration for QUATERMASS II —shortly after the VX nerve agent was perfected at Porton Down in 1952.

There were deadly epidemics unassociated with government or military programs, too. Annual influenza outbreaks were unfortunately common, claiming a quarter-million to half-a-million lives per year, but the most devastating influenza pandemic of the 1950s didn't occur until after Kneale had scriped THE QUATERMASS EXPERIMENT (i.e., the Asian influenza pandemic of 1958). Other disease pandemics, real or threatened, dominated international headlines. "Smallpox: The Killer That Stalks New York" by Milton Lehman was published in *Hearst's International-Cosmopolitan Magazine* (1946), reporting on a potential smallpox outbreak in the city that prompted authorities to authorize millions of free vaccinations. Annual summer outbreaks of polio escalated to devastating proportions after WWII, exploding into the terrible 1952 U.S. epidemic (58,000 reported infections, leaving over 21,000 with

The Quatermass Conception

various forms of paralysis and killing over 3,000). Dr. Jonas Salk introduced his polio vaccine in 1955, prompting authorities to launch a vaccine trial involving almost two million school-age children which proved successful.

These post-WWII disease outbreaks, epidemics, and near-epidemics fueled Elia Kazan/Richard Murphy/Daniel Fuchs' **PANIC IN THE STREETS** (1950), in which Jack Palance starred as a bubonic-plague infected criminal on the run in New Orleans, fleeing authorities intent on finding him within 48 hours to avert an epidemic. A flurry of similar contagion features were produced and played theatrically in the UK and US.[43] In many ways, 1950 was the Plague Year for motion pictures, and surely Nigel Kneale, Rudolph Cartier, and their BBC compatriots would have noticed. For all of Kneale's interviews refuting any measurable influences from other media, it must be noted that his teleplay for THE QUATERMASS EXPERIMENT featured a vivid and sharply observed caricature of what was popular in 1953 UK cinemas—in Chapter Four's sequence with the little boy taking Victor Carroon to hide out in a theater matinee of the imaginary 3-D sf movie PLANET OF THE DRAGONS, Kneale satirized the populist space operas of the early 1950s, using the fabricated dialogue to such an opus to comment upon Carroon's sorry condition and fate. Clearly, Kneale and Cartier knew what was going on in mainstream cinema and media, making the associative links between the 1950 "contagion" thrillers and THE QUATERMASS EXPERIMENT impossible to ignore.[44]

---

[43] Note that **PANIC IN THE STREETS** remains the most well-known of these 1950 contagion films, but it did not initially perform well commercially. Despite the awards it won (Academy Awards for best writing, Venice Film Festival "International Award" to director Kazan) and its eventual fame and impact, **PANIC IN THE STREETS** had not been a hit for Fox—it in fact lost money at the box-office.

[44] Twenty years later, Kneale was at it again, digging into far more primal historical contagion roots. I mentioned in my opening paragraphs Kneale's ATV one-shot *"Murrain"* for the anthology series AGAINST THE CROWD (July 27, 1975); the word "murrain" was a non-specific blanket term referring to various contagions afflicting sheep and cattle, including anthrax, foot-and-mouth disease, streptococcus, etc. It also appears in some Bible translations of Exodus 9:3 in reference to the fifth of the plagues God visited on Egypt ("…there shall be a grievous murrain"), and in medieval Scotland it referred to a curse on one's land or livestock, hence a stigmatic reference to witchcraft. "Murrain" literally means "death." Kneale's absolutely brilliant, deceptively straightforward teleplay taps all meanings of the term, on all levels.

Movie concepts spread like fungal spores, feeding off one another before the initial growth has even reached market maturation. Per usual for Hollywood and independent filmmaking, once the subject matter was in the air—for whatever reason, considered timely and potentially lucrative—the imitations were in production before anyone had time to count boxoffice results. **PANIC IN THE STREETS** opened in June 1950, and even after a studio-imposed delay, Earl McEvoy's **THE KILLER THAT STALKED NEW YORK** was in theaters by December 1950 (reportedly withheld from release by Columbia until winter so as to avoid too-close proximity to **PANIC IN THE STREETS**). Based on the 1946 smallpox incident Milton Lehman had reported on in *Cosmopolitan*, the latter film involved Treasury agents and desperate Health Department officials trace a diamond smuggling operation in which a jilted courier (Evelyn Keyes), having contracted smallpox in Cuba, is haplessly spreading the disease as she stalks the double-crossing lover (Charles Kovin) who has stolen the contraband diamonds and scrammed with her sister (Lola Albright).

This was hardly a uniquely American phenomenon, either: contemporary to these US productions were the British sleepers Terence Fisher and Anthony Darnborough's **SO LONG AT THE FAIR** (1950) and the much more prominent production of Roy Ward Baker and Eric Ambler's **HIGHLY DANGEROUS** (1950). Though most critical attention afforded **SO LONG AT THE FAIR** is solely due to co-director Terence Fisher's later Hammer Films body of work, **HIGHLY DANGEROUS** is the more relevant of the two regarding the eventual production of **THE QUATER-MASS XPERIMENT**, if only as early fruit harvested by American producer Robert Lippert's development of American-British coproductions. Lippert co-produced the Hammer Films' adaptation **THE QUATERMASS XPERIMENT;**[45] the earlier **HIGHLY DANGEROUS** was produced by Lippert with Two Cities Film, a production firm launched as a joint venture between London and Rome by partners Mario

---

[45] Lippert signed his four-year production and distribution contract with Hammer Films in 1951, the year after **HIGHLY DANGEROUS** was released. It was Lippert who imposed Brian Donlevy on **THE QUATERMASS XPERIMENT** as a condition of production, a contractual condition of all the Lippert/Hammer co-productions beginning with **THE LAST PAGE** (US title: **MAN BAIT**, 1952), directed by none other than Terence Fisher.

The Quatermass Conception

Zampa and Filippo Del Giudice. Two Cities was launched in 1937 specifically to produce "very British" product—which included **IN WHICH WE SERVE** (1942), **HENRY V**, and **BLITHE SPIRIT** (both 1945)—before merging with the Rank Organization. **HIGHLY DANGEROUS** was a rather daft Cold War thriller starred Margaret Lockwood (playing against type) as a British entomologist reluctantly working undercover as an agent to investigate the development of insect-spread bioweapons behind the Iron Curtain, in the Balkans; with the help of an American reporter (Dane Clark), she of course succeeds. Unfortunately, many of the 1930s novels by screenwriter Eric Ambler had already been filmed, familiarizing audiences with his narrative tropes; and what wasn't filmed was quickly absorbed into the mainstream, popularizing Ambler's narrative devices via the work of numerous British filmmakers (including Alfred Hitchcock). By this time, Ambler was essentially stuck with imitating his own work—this film owed a debt to the author's first novel THE DARK FRONTIER (1936)—and only later would mainstream filmmakers tap the different flavors of Ambler's distinctive post-WWII work (i.e., his 1962 novel THE LIGHT OF DAY filmed as the popular **TOPKAPI**, 1964). Despite its title, **HIGHLY DANGEROUS** barely breaks a sweat—the biowarfare element takes a back seat to the risible, delusional side effects of a "truth serum" that convinces Lockwood that she *is* a competent super-spy—where the modest period Paris-in-1889-set **SO LONG AT THE FAIR** mounted (and still maintains) a fair measure of suspense.

Based on Anthony Thorne's 1947 novel, **SO LONG AT THE FAIR** pitted visting British innocent Jean Simmons against foreign hotel staff and Parisian authorities intent upon convincing her that her brother who has vanished (David Tomlinson) was never with her. An insouciant British painter (Dirk Bogarde) is the only person to believe her, eventually uncovering the truth—her brother, overtaken their first night in the hotel by the symptoms of the Black Plague, has been secreted away to ensure neither the contagion nor a panic might blight the Exposition Universelle's success.[46] Most writers who acknowledge **SO LONG AT THE FAIR** at all tend to cite it as a variation on Alfred Hitchcock, Sidney Gilliat, Frank Launder, and Alma Reville's **THE LADY VANISHES** (1938, based on the 1936 novel THE WHEEL SPINS by Ethel Lina White)—which just

WE ARE THE MARTIANS

happened to star future **HIGHLY DANGEROUS** heroine Margaret Lockwood—and hence, a particularly British narrative model. Film scholar/historian Michael H. Price (co-author and overseer of the venerable FORGOTTEN HORRORS book series) begs to differ. Price writes, "Its ancestor, of course, is **THE MIDNIGHT WARNING** (1932), which stems from an urban legend of the 19th century. A semi-remake in the interim is **MARSHAL OF AMARILLO** (1948). Seems like a fairly uncluttered line of descent, for once."[47] As cinema, perhaps. As literature and oral narrative, it's a stickier lineage than that: this is referred to as "The Disappearing Room" or "The Vanishing Lady" urban legend, and it has yielded multiple variants and interpretations. Folktale and urban legend scholars Paul Smith and Sandy Hobbs noted that Thorne's source novel **SO LONG AT THE FAIR** (1947) seemed to lift its setting from the German film **VERWEHTE SPUREN (LIKE SAND IN THE WIND**, 1938, was set during the 1868 Paris Exposition).[48] Hammer Films later adopted the narrative conceit for Don Sharp's **KISS OF THE VAMPIRE** (1962), the last variant to boast a 'contagion' element (albeit it vampirism).[49] This archetype interested Kneale not in the least—he was telling a very different story with THE QUATERMASS EXPERIMENT.

[46] The same tale, with the same 1889 Parisian setting, was adapted into the first-season episode of ALFRED HITCHCOCK PRESENTS, "Into Thin Air" (October 30, 1955); note that it's heroine Diana Winthrop (Patricia Hitchcock)'s mother, not brother, who was infected and "vanished" in this adaptation, scripted by Marian B. Cockrell (online sources cite "an uncredited story by Alexander Woollcott," which would be WHILE ROME BURNS (1934), not Thorne's novel SO LONG AT THE FAIR; see http://the.hitchcock.zone/wiki/Alfred_Hitchcock_Presents_-_Into_Thin_Air), directed by Don Medford. These peculiar Nigel Kneale/Alfred Hitchcock TV connections continue to pile up, don't they?

[47] Michael H. Price, from a June 5-6th, 2015 Facebook conversation with the author; quoted with permission. Subsequent quotes herein from Michael are from that same conversation.

[48] Smith and Hobbs, "Contemporary Legend on Film: The Vanishing Lady," FOAFTALE News #26 (June, 1992), pg. 4; they also note that a character in Evelyn Piper's novel BUNNY LAKE IS MISSING (1957) makes explicit reference to "The Disappearing Room" urban legend. Hobbs also wrote about "The Vanishing Lady" narrative, as one "dealing with feelings of uneasiness in strange places such as a foreign hotel," in "The Folk Tales as News," Oral History Vol. 6, No. 11 (1978), pp. 74-86.

[49] As David Pirie later noted, "**SO LONG AT THE FAIR** could easily have been re-shot, sequence for sequence, as a vampire movie without making any difference to its basic mechanics, for the same dualistic structure pervades every frame. Presumably the film would then end with the staking of the brother to purify and purge an Alien 'infection' to which he has succumbed." (Pirie, A HERITAGE OF HORROR: THE ENGLISH GOTHIC CINEMA 1946-1972, UK: Gordon Fraser, London; US: Avon/Equinox, both 1973, pg. 55).

The Quatermass Conception

Despite their borderline science-fiction and terror flourishes, none of these films were truly sf/horror films. These 1950 British and American contagion films were concerned with what film Michael H. Price characterizes as quelling "a threatened or forestalled mass contamination." This is *precisely* the thrust, structure, and narrative arc of THE QUATERMASS EXPERIMENT, with Quatermass himself both the catalyst for the contagion and the official who successfully contains the "threatened or forestalled mass contamination." Kneale was also embracing—and dramatically consolidating into his London-based urban contagion scenario—the far more global concerns of British apocalyptic sf contagion literature of the day. THE QUATERMASS EXPERIMENT was bookended by John Wyndham's THE DAY OF THE TRIFFIDS (1951, with its twin contagion of collective blindness and venemous, ambulatory plants) and John Christopher's THE DEATH OF GRASS (US: NO BLADE OF GRASS, 1956, in which the epidemic is a viral infection of staple food grains fomenting mass famine and collapse of civilization as we know it), among others.

Concerning the unusual eruption of 1950 urban contagion feature film narratives, Michael H. Price further notes that there are "...innumerable references to plague and disease (comparatively fewer to typhoid) in the AFI's [American Film Institute] subject-matter catalogue, but no full-bore citified epidemic business until these titles of 1950. James Cruze's **PRISON NURSE** (1938) comes close, what with its threat of an outbreak from a confined space...[though there may] be something lurking in a nook or a cranny. As usual. But these are a watershed. Notable carryovers into **NO PLACE TO HIDE** (1956) and **SPACE MASTER X-7** (1958), and into such [American TV series] epics as HIGHWAY PATROL and RESCUE-8 during same general period..."[50] In Josef Shaftel and Norman Corwin's **NO PLACE TO HIDE** (1956, the first US-Philippines feature film co-production), yet another city was placed in jeopardy when a boy— the young son (Hugh Corcoran) of a scientist (David Brian) developing germ warfare technologies for the US military—takes two lethal experimental pellets from his father's lab. Fearing punishment (including the loss of a beloved pet), the lad and his playmate (Ike Jarlego Jr.) elude adults and authorities, only to lose one of the pellets during their fugitive flight.[51]

The bioweapon/contagion genre went mainstream when Alistair MacLean's novel THE SATAN BUG (1962) became a best-seller, adapted to the screen three years later by James Clavell, Edward Anhalt, and director John Sturges. THE SATAN BUG spawned successors and imitators, including Gerd Oswald and Blair Robertson's AGENT FOR H.A.R.M. (1966, filmed as a TV pilot for Universal Pictures, which decided on theatrical release instead), which also revolved around bioweapons (a fungal spore that dissolves human flesh). In this case, the "spore" was ballyhooed in the ad campaign as "A *Blast of Blood-Curdling Terror From Outer Space!*" Michael Crichton's bestselling techno-thriller THE ANDROMEDA STRAIN (1969) involved a team of scientists investigating, isolating, and seeking to contain further lethal outbreaks stemming from an extraterrestrial biological contagion carried to Earth by a downed satellite. Robert Wise and Universal Pictures produced the handsome feature film adaptation (1971), further codifying the fusion of "extraterrestrial contagion" tropes and fear of military bioweapon programs into a genre staple. Many of these were essentially either *noir* police procedural riffs (in the 1950s) or globe-trotting techno-thriller spins (1960s) on Kneale's QUATERMASS teleplays and movies.[52]

To summarize: Nigel Kneale's original QUATERMASS deadly duo—

[50] Later American TV urban contagious disease scenarios include the HAWAII FIVE-0 two-parter "Three Dead Cows at Makapuu" (February 25-March 4, 1970). It's irrelevant to Nigel Kneale and QUATERMASS, but that two-parter was definitely a personal favorite (from seeing it when first broadcast) for its biological infection "The Q Strain," then quite a surprise on prime-time network television. Clearly, *something was* in the air: that very month of that same year, only three weeks earlier, British TV offered the far more creative and potentially cataclysmic DOOMWATCH debut episode "The Plastic Eaters" (February 9, 1970), which writer/creators Kit Pedler and Gerry Davis revamped almost immediately into their novel MUTANT 59: THE PLASTIC EATER (1971). This was contemporary to, and very similar in many ways to, Michael Crichton's THE ANDROMEDA STRAIN (novel 1969, film 1971), in which the extraterrestrial microorganism at one point mutated into a strain that destabilized and "ate" rubber and plastic rather than human blood.

[51] There were strikingly similar films and TV shows in which containers of highly-toxic radioactive materials rather than biological contagions were the dire threat, as in Ivan Tors' **MAGNETIC MONSTER** (1953), Robert Aldrich's brutal Mickey Spillaine adaptation **KISS ME DEADLY** (1955), Irving Lerner, Robert Dillon, and Steven Ritch's **CITY OF FEAR** (1959), etc. This became a very familiar narrative device still used (and parodied) by the likes of Alex Cox's **REPO MAN** (1984) and Quentin Tarantino and Roger Avary's **PULP FICTION** (1994).

The Quatermass Conception

QUATERMASS EXPERIMENT and QUATERMASS II, and their respective Val Guest/Hammer Films adaptations—were brilliant fusions of contagion films *and* sf/horror narratives. As such, they were precursors of everything from Michael Crichton's best-seller THE ANDROMEDA STRAIN (1969) and Robert Wise's surgically-precise film adaptation (1971) to George Romero's **THE CRAZIES** aka **CODE NAME: TRIXIE** (1973)[53] and David Cronenberg's **RABID** (1977) to **OUTBREAK** (1995) to **THE CRAZIES** remake (2010) to—well, **CONTAGION** (2011). We were, in effect, still in Quatermass territory. Given the fact that **THE QUATERMASS XPERIMENT/THE CREEPING UNKNOWN** had become a late-night TV movie favorite, it could be argued that as a culture we'd *never left* Quatermass territory behind.

So: we have covered the key antecedents to Kneale's and Cartier's bold television "experiment," what came before, and a bit of what followed.

It's time to probe what, precisely, Nigel Kneale's THE QUATERMASS EXPERIMENT originally was—and what it *became*, via the Hammer Films adaptation.

"An experiment . . . is an operation designed to discover some unknown truth. It is also a risk . . ."

So began the first original classic of made-for-television science fiction-horror, Nigel Kneale's THE QUATERMASS EXPERIMENT—an opening

---

[52] The fungi-like contagion infecting the 'contagion movie' **SPACE MASTER X-7** was referred to in the film itself as 'blood rust.' 'Blood rust' was the moniker for the extraterrestrial fungal menace in Ray Bradbury's 1948 short story "The Visitor" (in which "blood rust" was a virulent, terminal lung disease native to Mars), a story first collected and widely read in THE ILLUSTRATED MAN (1951). A decade later, Michael Crichton would adopt the 'blood rust' for his own use in THE ANDROMEDA STRAIN (memorably shown running like red sand from a corpse's severed wrist in the Robert Wise 1971 movie adaptation). Contrary to Nigel Kneale's QUATERMASS EXPERIMENT model, Crichton arguably brought the "alien contagion" template back to its less urban, more rural roots, fusing the remote outposts of "Who Goes There?" and its film adaptation **THE THING** (1951)—instead of an arctic outpost, THE ANDROMEDA STRAIN'S military complex is underground, deep beneath the American desert— with the small-town invasion targets of **INVADERS FROM MARS**, **IT CAME FROM OUTER SPACE** (both 1953), **INVASION OF THE BODY SNATCHER** (1956), etc.

[53] Given the movie's "Venus probe" news report, George Romero and John Russo's **NIGHT OF THE LIVING DEAD** (1968) is part of this chronology, too, but I didn't want to confuse this article by bringing that walking dead landmark into it.

line that accurately summarized the nature of the mini-series itself. Broadcast by the British Broadcasting Corporation in six 30-minute episodes between July 18 and August 22, 1953, the Rudolph Cartier production was a popular success that also broke significant new ground in the genre.

Alas, THE QUATERMASS EXPERIMENT is a "lost" classic. The first two episodes of THE QUATERMASS EXPERIMENT are all that survives today on kinescope (digitally restored on DVD, along with the complete second and third Quatermass serials, thanks to the April 2005 boxed set released by BBC Worldwide); the rest exists only in the illustrated paperback of Kneale's compelling teleplay (published by Penguin Books in 1959, with cover art by Nigel's brother Bryan Kneale; reprinted in 1979 by Arrow Books). Fortunately, the published script cements not only the serial's historical importance, but also Kneale's objections to Hammer Films' feature version **THE QUATERMASS XPERIMENT** (1955), a title which shrewdly exploited the X certificate awarded it by the British Board of Film Censors.

Despite Kneale's contempt for it, director Val Guest's film (scripted by Guest and Richard Landau) stands as creditable compression of the lengthy teleplay. It's impossible to overstate the influence of Guest's Hammer Films adaptation, which enjoyed international success, spreading Kneale's audacious "contagion" and "body-horror" concepts like Carroon-spores.

Consider, first and foremost, the production context from which the film itself emerged—a "conventionality" that was "a function of the industrial context within which" independent British film studios labored after WWII, wherein "budgets were low...schedules were tight and technical resources were extremely limited...there was simply not enough time, money and resources for them to be anything else," to quote British film scholar Peter Hutchings.[54] Within this context—as well as that of sf films released in the UK and US prior to 1955—it's still rousing to consider the alarming urgency of James Bernard's title music, the potent electricity it

---

[54] Hutchings was specifically writing about director Terence Fisher's early films for Highbury Studio in the late 1940s, but the same was true of Hammer Films in the 1950s at the time **THE QUATERMASS XPERIMENT** was produced. Quoted from Hutchings, TERENCE FISHER (Manchester University Press, 2001), pg. 43.

The Quatermass Conception

brought (and brings) to the first sequence Guest and Landau tease from Kneale's teleplay, as two young lovers have their late-night passion in a field interrupted by a screaming intruder from space. In this, Guest and Landau were adopting and adapting the jarring opening minutes of Jack Arnold, Harry Essex, and Ray Bradbury's 3D smash-hit **IT CAME FROM OUTER SPACE** (1953), an explosive opener that must have penetrated the doldrums of formula British black-and-white fare with indelible impact. There was, it turned out, no turning back.

Tempting as it is to once again dig into and sing the praises of **THE QUATERMASS XPERIMENT**, my purpose here is to analyze Nigel Kneale's THE QUATERMASS EXPERIMENT—so, we leave those lovers in that scorched field, for the meantime, and move on.

Given its truly "lost" status, it is easy to understand Kneale's frustration over the attention garnered by the film version—an historic touchstone whose success motivated Hammer to launch its classic line of Gothic horror films—an adaptation which, as we shall see, greatly distorted the depth and scope of Kneale's conception.

As the only complete dramatization, **THE QUATERMASS XPERIMENT** (hereafter QX) is crucial to our understanding and appreciation of the serial broadcast. By comparing the film with Kneale's published script, we can approximate what Kneale and Cartier achieved in our mind's eye, vicariously reconstructing what time has consigned to the memories of those lucky enough to have participated in the original broadcast.

THE QUATERMASS EXPERIMENT (hereafter QEX) opened with Professor Bernard Quatermass (Reginald Tate) auditing an experimental manned rocket which has strayed far beyond its prescribed orbit only to plunge back into South London. The downed rocket is found to contain only one surviving astronaut, though three had been launched. In subsequent episodes, the lone survivor—mute and tormented Victor Carroon (Duncan Lamont)—soon manifests disturbing side effects from his voyage into the uncharted regions of space, speaking with the voices of his missing comrades, suffering from unidentifiable skin eruptions, and absorbing a potted cactus plant that he happens to touch. The only physical remains of his missing colleagues seems to be a gray coagulated jelly, spread along the infrastructure of the rocket. After studying Victor's degenerative (soon

WE ARE THE MARTIANS

proven to be a transformative) condition and the surviving audio wire-recording of the flight, Quatermass theorizes that Victor is the host of an alien organism, able "to change, to remake other living things..." He is quickly proven correct, as Victor escapes into London, absorbing every life form he happens to touch. In the climax, Victor was spectacularly unveiled as a hideous bio-botanical monstrosity, preparing to generate countless self reproducing spores in the rafters of Westminster Abbey—where Queen Elizabeth's coronation had been held two weeks before broadcast!

Knowing that explosives would only scatter the infectious spores, Quatermass successfully appeals to whatever vestiges of the three astronauts remain buried in the creature, and it conscientiously destroys itself.

It is important to recognize how outrageous and fresh this material was in 1953, however unoriginal it may sound after forty years. One can now afford to laugh at the crudity of its special effects (the broadcast was live, necessitating simplistic on-camera effects and minimally enhanced by teleciné-incorporated film footage), or wince at the climactic conceit that has since been gendered ersatz by countless STAR TREK imitations, but Kneale was daring something never before seen—especially on television, most particularly British television.

The script melded a realistic appreciation of budgetary and live-broadcast limitations with devious intelligence, easing its rapt viewers from familiar signs of the times—rocket experimentation, memories of the London blitz, government secrecy—into completely unfamiliar and believably horrifying terrain.

The weekly live performances were transmitted "via TV cameras which dated back to 1936 [with] one fixed lens each...preventing quick cutting from camera to camera"[55] with minimal special effects inserted, all for a total budget of £3,500. Given the horrific content, BBC warned that QEX was an adult broadcast "thought to be unsuitable for children and persons of a nervous disposition." Despite the risk, its success was assured. At that time, "there was no competition," Kneale recalled. "You turned on the set, you saw the BBC, the only channel...if you put on a play like [QEX], you knew that was the only thing they would be watching...they had no

[55] John Brosnan, FUTURE TENSE: THE CINEMA OF SCIENCE FICTION (,St. Martins Press, 1978), p. 292.

The Quatermass Conception

choice."[56] ITV's broadcast of competing American and original science-fiction programming would not begin until 1956.

Having no such monopoly on the public attention, Hammer Films couldn't count on duplicating the success of the teleplay, and began remolding Kneale's source material as soon as they had purchased the property. Hammer had already suffered the failure of a previous radio adaptation, **THE LYONS ABROAD** (1954), and had no reason to expect Kneale's creation would fare any better. Robert Lippert, cagey as ever, was hardly open to squandering resources on a title that had no presale value or recognition outside of the BBC's broadcast reach: it was business-as-usual for Lippert, and best that Hammer get on with it per usual. Hammer's earlier science-fiction endeavors—Terence Fisher's rather turgid romance-dramas **SPACEWAYS** and **THE FOUR-SIDED TRIANGLE** (both 1952)—hadn't held their own against America's exploitable, energetic black-and-white fare or more lavish Technicolor space operas. As a result, the usual meager resources were allotted to **QX**. Director/co-scripter Val Guest most definitely made the most of what he had to work with.

The British version of **QX** (now available on DVD and Blu-Ray in both the US and the UK) runs 81m 21s; **QEX** was composed of six episodes of 30-40m each, meaning that the complete serial was between three and four hours long, "about 200m" by Kneale's own estimation.

Given this, for the following analysis I have chosen to break down **QX** in terms of Kneale's original scripts, comparing Landau and Guest's compressed narrative to each of the teleplay's six chapters, and noting the primary differences.

CHAPTER ONE: "CONTACT HAS BEEN ESTABLISHED"

QEX opens rather spectacularly, for its time and chosen medium, using "stock film library footage...of a V2 rocket blasting off, coupled with sub-orbital shots of the Earth's surface as seen from the stratosphere. These establishing sequences were on 16mm film... [inserted via] teleciné

---

[56] Bill Warren, "Nigel Kneale: THE QUATERMASS EXPERIMENT Part One," Starlog #139, pg. 34.

transfer—literally the cine projection of the film onto a small screen being [filmed] by a television camera."[57]

Reginald Tate as Professor Quatermass

The scene is a research station where Prof. Quatermass (Tate, John Paterson (Hugh Kelly), and Judith Carroon (Isabel Dean) track the wandering, descent, and crash-landing of their manned rocket. The significant changes begin immediately: Paterson's character, whose rivalry with Quatermass and regrets about not joining the rocket crew lend substantial weight to the teleplay, was cut from the Hammer script altogether. Nor does QX explain that Judith (played in the film by Margia Dean) is Victor's wife until much later, reducing this primary character's relationship to Quatermass and Victor into a mere cipher. In the film, Dr. Gordon Briscoe (David King Wood) arrives at the landing site with Quatermass' entourage; in the teleplay, Briscoe (John Glen) isn't introduced until midway through Chapter Two.

Also eliminated from QX was reporter James Fullalove (Paul Whitsun-

---

[57] Jeremy Bentham, DR. WHO: THE EARLY YEARS (W.H. Allen, 1986), pg. 31.

Jones)[58], whose office scenes and interplay with Quatermass allowed for integral exposition and comedy in QEX. In QX, the role of the

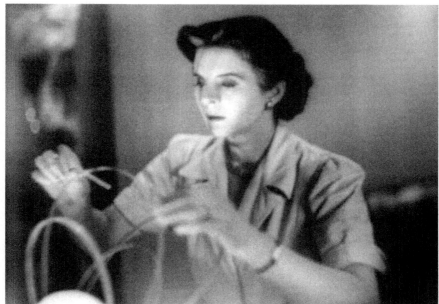

Isabel Dean as Judith Caroon

media is instead evoked with the archetypal shorthand of newspaper headlines.

While QEX began with exposition, characterization, and technical innovations, QX opened with a sexualized reinvention of Kneale's opening that "decisively... seem(ed) to record the intrusion of Hammer into the cozy middle class domesticity of the British Cinema."[59] Two lovers are shown enjoying one another's company in a haystack under the stars when the ear-splitting squeal of the returning rocket drives them indoors. After an earth-shaking crash, they step back outside to find the rocket stabbing the exact place they just fled.

[58] James Fullalove returned in Kneale and Cartier's QUATERMASS AND THE PIT (December 2, 1958-January 26, 1959), played by Brian Worth; for the Hammer film adaptation, Kneale himself had to excise the character from the screenplay. Another journalst, Hugh Conrad (Roger Delgado), played a pivotal role in the Fullalove style in QUATERMASS II, but succumbed to the alien parasites, which might explain why Kneale chose not to cast Fullalove in the sequel.
[59] Pirie, Ibid., pg. 29.

The rocket is never fully shown in QEX, which shifted focus to a rich tapestry of characters caught up in the event—elderly Miss Wilde (Katie Johnson) and her cat, who survive the rocket's plunge through their home; the neighboring Matthews couple (Van Boolen and Iris Ballard) who try rescuing her before the authorities arrive; the ensuing flow of reporters and onlookers, including a banner-wearing doomsayer and drunken reveler (Denis Wyndham). QX has Victor (Richard Wordsworth) quickly shuttled away in Quatermass' van en route to the research center at the close of Chapter One, which ends in both teleplay and feature with Victor's barely audible plea for help. In Kneale's original, Victor is taken by ambulance directly to the hospital; in Chapter Three, he returns to the ruins of Miss Wilde's home, where he absorbs a potted cactus belonging to her: our first indication of his transformative appetite.

Hammer's unsubtle approach to Kneale's work was personified by a radical reinterpretation of Quatermass himself. As played by the fading American star Brian Donlevy, Quatermass was a crass, cold-blooded brute—most unlike Reginald Tate's sympathetic interpretation—and signified the key tonal difference between film and teleplay. It was a difference so pronounced that Kneale would withhold his 1959 serial QUATERMASS AND THE PIT from Hammer for many years, until they allowed him to write the screenplay himself and have a decisive casting vote.

Throughout Chapter One, QEX carefully sketches Quatermass as a man consumed and emotionally detached by scientific curiosity, though he is capable of expressing affection and concern for his associates (particularly Judith, whom he paternally comforts and worries over in Chapter One); hence, their loyalty to him and his audacious experiments is rewarded and understandable. A reptilian charisma and ferocity of will is all that seems to galvanize Quatermass' associates in the Hammer film; efficiency, expediency, and abrasive forward drive is all the persuasion its time constraints will allow. Anything else is an obstacle to be confronted, pushed aside, or trampled over. Here, then, is the blueprint for Hammer's Baron Frankenstein to follow, the antihero of the studio's most characteristic works.

Marcia Landy accurately characterizes this Quatermass as being "like most of the creators of horror, unmoved by his creation's [Victor's] sufferings; he is more interested in prolonging its life for the benefit of science.

The Quatermass Conception

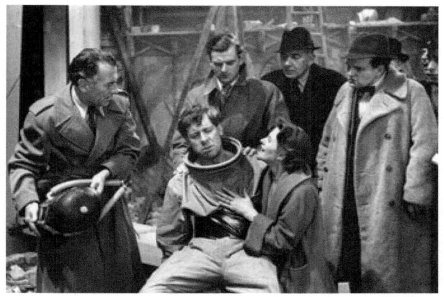

Duncan Lamont (centre) as Victor Caroon

A modern Prometheus, with full confidence in his power to know and control, Quatermass is free of any moral qualms. Victor's wife accuses him of having destroyed her husband [in Chapter Three], and he responds that there is no room for personal feelings in science and that she should be proud of her husband."[60] Guest remained ambivalent about his brash, belligerent Quatermass, chronicling his activities—here, and once again in **QUATERMASS II** (US title: **ENEMY FROM SPACE**, 1957)— with an amoral fascination that foreshadowed Hammer's Frankenstein series (wherein the scientist, rather than his monster, would also be the titular character binding the series together).

This narrative bracket, which runs 31m 15s in the surviving broadcast episode, occupies the first 15m 22s of the feature—a reduction by more than half. (Hereafter, I will note at the *beginning* of each section the condensation/running times comparing the respective Chapters of QEX—each originally broadcast at about 30 minutes per installment, give or take—with the respective running time of the same passage in **QX**.)

[60] Marcia Landy, BRITISH GENRES: CINEMA AND SOCIETY, 1930-1960 (Princeton University Press, 1991), pp. 410-411.

WE ARE THE MARTIANS

CHAPTER TWO: "PERSONS REPORTED MISSING"

Condensed in QX to 10m 36s.

As already noted, Chapter Two of QEX opens with Victor being ambu-lanced to the hospital; in the feature, Quatermass' van takes him to Briscoe's private research facilities. At this point, while at the crash site, QEX introduces Scotland Yard's Chief Inspector Lomax (Ian Colin; played in QX by Jack Warner) and Detective-Sergeant Best (Frank Hawkins), where—after a moment's hesitation—Quatermass grants Lomax's request for co-operation. It is Lomax who notes the empty pres-sure suits belonging to the two missing astronauts—Charles Green and Dr. Ludwig Reichenheim—and asks if he may take them for study; in QX, Quatermass' first inspection inside the rocket (without Lomax or Best) has him quickly make the same assessment. In QEX, Lomax probes the mystery of the empty suits well into Chapter Three, alerting the distracted Quatermass to the fact that the bodies have disappeared although the suits remain unopened.

Louisa Green (Enid Lindsay)—the distraught wife of one of the missing astronauts—is introduced in QEX during Victor's first interrogation; both her character and Victor's questioning are missing from the film entirely. Gone, too, are the essential interplay between Fullalove and his fellow reporters, as they jockey for the story that will motivate important action at the crash site in Chapter Three. In QEX, Victor is taken to a Christian hospital with Judith, where Lomax questions him until a nurse insists that he stop. Before Lomax departs, he furtively fingerprints Victor's spastically flexing hand; when Quatermass later hears of this, he is infuriated and leaves to confront Lomax in anger. None of this appears in the film.

Teleplay and film are rejoined as Quatermass confronts Lomax and Best at their office, where he asserts his control of the situation, delivering offi-cial staff records and the fingerprints of Victor (and his two missing comrades) to prevent any further interruptions; in the teleplay, Quatermass additionally discloses that Victor has been transferred from the hospital to his private research center. In the teleplay, this exchange ends with Lomax challenging Quatermass with the mystery of the missing

The Quatermass Conception

astronauts' linked suits and helmets, leaving Quatermass to ponder this overlooked detail. As Best comments, "That shook him." But nothing shakes Donlevy's Quatermass. He grudgingly allows Lomax the respect (and hence the power) necessary for them to interact, ground he gives no one else in the narrative. While this allows Lomax to function onscreen to some degree as he did in the teleplay, it hardly justifies Marcia Landy's claim that "the familiar battle in science fiction between science and conventional moral and theological wisdom is exemplified in the conflict between Quatermass and Lomax."[61] The only dramatic conflict in QX is that between the forces of chaos that consume Victor and threaten society, and the forces of control that Quatermass so potently personifies.

Guest sets the film's first engaging sequence with Victor in Briscoe's office at the research center, where only the rudiments of Victor's condition can be identified and treated; in the teleplay, Briscoe has yet to be introduced. A telling dialogue between Quatermass, Briscoe, and Judith (finally identified as Victor's wife) defines the sequence, as Judith expresses

Brian Donlevey as Quatermass, and Richard Wordsworth as Caroon in Hammer/ Val Guest's feature film version of **THE QUATERMASS XPERIMENT**

[61] Landy, Ibid., pg. 410.

WE ARE THE MARTIANS

her concern that Quatermass transfer Victor to hospital care. Judith's worries are dismissed by Quatermass, as Victor sits unnaturally erect in an examination chair, unnervingly gaunt and repeatedly flexing his hand. Quatermass' only concern is with the obstacle presented by Victor's silence, his sole curiosity intent upon Victor's physical, rather than his emotional or psychological, condition. Once he has convinced Briscoe and Judith to keep Victor out of the hospital, he leaves. This is a far cry from Tate's Quatermass, in whom Judith confides that she had intended to tell Victor upon his return to Earth that she was leaving him for Briscoe, a confidence Quatermass rewards with sympathy for both Judith's situation and Victor's condition:

"...there's not much I can say. Not much I ought to say. [looks to Victor] Poor creature. He's going to need you now if ever he did. Your care, anyway."

Victor now claims the spotlight, in both teleplay and film. Guest abandons Kneale's first genuinely chilling setpiece, which introduces both Briscoe and Mrs. Greene. Victor responds to interrogation with the voices of the two missing astronauts, first responding to Mrs. Greene in her husband's voice (using his pet name for her), then edging into German with Reichenheim's voice. This is the first suggestion of his powers of absorption in the teleplay, evoking both medieval (i.e., demonic possession) and contemporary fears (i.e., multiple personalities sublimating the individual). This uncanny ability to effectively blend ancient and contemporary phobias became one of Kneale's greatest strengths as a writer, and this crucial sequence is a primal moment in Kneale's ouevre, making its deletion from Landau and Guest's adaptation all the more unfortunate.[62]

---

[62] This sequence also uncannily anticipates chilling passages in two subsequent American films from producer Roger Corman's busy low-budget production line, Corman's own **ATTACK OF THE CRAB MONSTERS** (1957) and Bernard Kowalski's **NIGHT OF THE BLOOD BEAST** (1958). In the former, the outsized crustaceans lure new victims into reach of their pincers by speaking with the voices of those they have already devoured; in the latter, an alien invader that claims to be benevolent— though it has decapitated and absorbed the intelligence of its victims, and impregnated a living host astronaut's body with its embryonic offspring—speaks with the voices of its victims, too. The parallels to QX in the latter film particularly mark it as one of the earliest of the exploitation films to transparently adopt many of Kneale's innovative narrative concepts and "body horror" devices, anticipating the parasitic horrors of future works like David Cronenberg's **SHIVERS** aka **THEY CAME FROM WITHIN** (1976) and Ridley Scott/Dan O'Bannon/Ronald Shusett's **ALIEN** (1979).

The Quatermass Conception

In these scenes, Guest's diluted script is saved by Richard Wordsworth's powerful *presence* as the luminously alienated Victor, which gives the film its emotional core. Indeed, when trying to reconstruct a mental picture of the teleplay, it is impossible to shake Wordsworth's stark skeletal visage to imagine Duncan Lamont's beefier features in their place. Though Victor is clearly the film's "monster," Guest renders him mute whereas Kneale had given him terrible voice(s); it is a testimony to Wordsworth's characterization that Victor loses none of his heart-wrenching humanity.[63] The dynamics between Victor and his Promethean "creator"—that he is mute, in contrast with Quatermass whose power lays as much in his ability with words as in his actions—also foreshadows Hammer's definition of the schism between the speechless monster and its articulate creator in **THE CURSE OF FRANKENSTEIN** (1957); Christopher Lee's scarred and speechless fiend (another makeup creation by Phil Leakey) even resembles Wordsworth's tormented loner.

[63] Wordsworth left his mark on the other Hammer features he memorably appeared—but never again starred—in, including Val Guest's **THE CAMP ON BLOOD ISIAND** (1958), Terence Fisher's **THE REVENGE OF FRANKENSTEIN** (1958), **THE CURSE OF THE WEREWOLF** (1961), and others.

WE ARE THE MARTIANS

At this point in QEX, the mystery of the empty suits and Victor's altered fingerprints remain unresolved. In QX, Quatermass walks into his own office to find Lomax, who confronts him with Victor's altered fingerprints ("These prints aren't even...human," a momentarily incredulous Quatermass observes) before they are summoned back to the crash site. In the teleplay, Quatermass tells Lomax "you'd better come," confirming their alliance at this point in the narrative. In the film, Quatermass bolts past Lomax, snatching only his own hat from the rack before hustling out the door, leaving Lomax in the dust to make light of his rudeness. Chapter Two's movement ends, in both versions, with the discovery of a gray jellied matter spread within the rocket's frame. Briscoe takes samples, as does Lomax in QEX.

CHAPTER THREE: "SPECIAL KNOWLEDGE"

Condensed In QX to approximately 17m.

In QEX, Kneale follows Judith and Briscoe's observation of Victor's worsening condition in "sick bay" while, elsewhere, Paterson plays for Quatermass and Lomax the surviving audio wire-recording of the fatal flight. (During this scene, the friction between Quatermass and the embittered Paterson is asserted to the breaking point. When he next appears, Paterson is drunk and unloading himself to an eager press, much to the consternation of Quatermass and Lomax.) Instead of the wire-recording— a visually impoverished means of exposition—Guest provides a *filmed* record of the rocket's interior during flight. As Quatermass' assistant Marsh (Maurice Kauffmann; QEX: Moray Watson) develops the film, Briscoe reveals to Quatermass that his gray jelly analysis suggests it is the liquified remains of Reichenheim and Greene. In the background, Victor rises from his bed, reaching for a pot of flowers before collapsing and awakening Judith.

With both Paterson and the burgeoning press excised from its screenplay, QX nurtures a parallel conflict between Quatermass and Judith, who has grown furious at how Victor has been victimized by Quatermass' irresponsible idealism. Judith's angry frustration establishes her later attempt

130

The Quatermass Conception

to kidnap Victor, replacing QEX' s newspaper-related espionage. Briscoe convinces Quatermass to send Victor to the Central Clinic Hospital, though Quatermass insists on isolation, maintaining control.

QX proceeds to an eerie sequence in which Quatermass, Lomax, Briscoe, Blake, and Marsh watch the silent, stuttering footage of the rocket flight. However clumsy Guest's low-budget emulation of space travel has been till now, this pseudo-verité sequence has retained its power to disturb.

As the three astronauts move about the cramped quarters of the rocket cabin, a wave of bright light consumes them; inserted footage of the cabin's statistical gauges indicates an increase in temperature. One astronaut falls, then another as a second bath of light washes over them; with the third wave, only Victor remains standing as the footage abruptly terminates.[64]

Kneale's teleplay arrives at the same narrative point somewhat clumsily, though it is impossible to guess how effective its presentation may have been to an audience caught up in the spell of the event. Quatermass' decision to return with Victor to the crash site, to shock him out of his self-absorption, is conveyed in a brief telephone scene, where an exasperated Lomax says, "he seems to be a law unto himself, with a tame Ministry between him and the world. What doesn't help me is that he's probably

---

[64] Val Guest's inventive visualization of Kneale's concept here is also cinema history in the making, the wellspring of the entire so-called "found footage/reality horror" movement we're amidst today. The QX sequence was echoed in Riccardo Freda and Mario Bava's **CALTIKI – IL MOSTRO IMMORTALE / CALTIKI – THE IMMORTAL MONTER** (1959), when an missing archeologist's camera is found, the film developed on site, and screened: the compact 1 minute, 39 seconds of "found footage" echoes the in-ship "found footage" screened in **QX**, and serves the same purpose: a teasing reveal of "what happened" in a hidden chamber from which only one in-shock survivor emerged, in which the footage hides more than it reveals. Both 1950s sequences are the wellspring for the entire "found footage" horror subgenre: **CANNIBAL HOLOCAUST** (1980), **THE LAST BROADCAST** (1998), **THE BLAIR WITCH PROJECT** (1999), **PARANORMAL ACTIVITY**, [REC], (both 2007), CHRONICLE (2012), etc., here we come. This sequence in **QX** is also the inspiration for so many subsequent scenarios in which characters fired into space (or other dimensions) are transformed by their experience, only to return (either whole, fused, or fragmented) as "something else." The most obvious genre successors include those already cited — **FIRST MAN INTO SPACE, THE CRAWLING HAND, THE INCREDIBLE MELTING MAN**, etc. — but we're currently amid another pop culture wave that owes a vast debt to Kneale and this aspect of THE QUATERMASS EXPERIMENT. Kneale's concept was adopted by Stan Lee and Jack Kirby for their 1962 comic book series *The Fantastic Four* and all that followed — including animated TV series, four movies (to date), and an entire publishing/merchandizing/media empire, all their origin story (unacknowledged) to Kneale's QEX and Guest's **QX**.

WE ARE THE MARTIANS

quite right" This suggests Quatermass' decisive power without Tate having to resort to Donlevy's bullying tactics. After a brief sequence in which Fullalove and other reporters descend on the shambles of Mrs. Wilde's living room, Victor is hauled into the rocket cabin where Quatermass, Lomax, Judith, Briscoe, and Paterson play him the wire-recording of the flight. Here, the teleplay segues into Victor's flashback of the event, Greene (Peter Bathurst) and Reichenheim (Christopher Rhodes)meeting their fates as an unseen presence invades the craft.

"The sound!" Victor cries. "It's inside! It's in here with us—but there's nothing to see!" Victor's frightful screams end the flashback.

"Something...did get in," Judith whispers, concluding that it, whatever it was, got inside Victor's body.

Briscoe and an unnamed American journalist carry Victor into Mrs. Wilde's home, where the violent climax to Chapter Three erupts. Noticing that her potted cactus is agitating Victor, Mrs. Wilde moves it into the kitchen, followed by Judith and a trembling, incoherent Victor. An opportunistic photographer (Lewis Wilson) slips into the kitchen, offering Judith £500 to let photos to be taken. Victor barehandedly grabs the cactus, spasmodically clutching its flesh and spines. Judith screams as Victor raises his (unseen) mutated fist. In a flurry of offscreen chaos, Victor kills the photographer, whose companions outside shoot the lock off the door and kidnap Victor.

In *QX*, it is *Judith's* kidnapping of Victor from the hospital isolation ward that precipitates this first eruption of violence. Judith arranges for Christy (Harold Lang), a private detective, to pose as a night duty nurse— a sequence which Guest milks for maximum suspense. Christy momentarily leaves Victor alone in his room to summon an elevator to take them down to Judith's waiting car. Meanwhile, Victor glowers at a potted cactus in his room. As Victor plunges his fist into the (offscreen) plant, the camera closes in on his agonized features as he shudders orgasmically.

Christy returns and hustles Victor onto the elevator, noticing that Victor is hiding something under his coat, which he uncovers to his horror. After Judith hustles the solitary Victor into her car and drives off, a nurse discovers Christy's body, in the first moment of graphic Hammer horror

The Quatermass Conception

ever to bless the screen. The nurse's reaction is punctuated with a fleeting closeup of Christy's partially consumed face, his skull exposed where Victor struck his fatal blow, followed by an oddly upsetting glimpse of his smashed and rubbery hand.[65]

[65] Leslie Norman and Jimmy Sangster's **X THE UNKNOWN**(1956), Hammer's first Quatermass spin-off (prepared as a Quatermass project until Kneale denied permission for his character to be used, prompting a retraction and slight rewrite), featured an almost shot-by-shot recreation of this shock sequence. The proximity of the radioactive blob 'X' overcomes a hospital attendant—punctuated with a queasy closeup of his face dissolving to the bone and his hand swelling horribly. It's telling how in such quick order Hammer management and writer Sangster (this was not only his first screenplay for Hammer, but his first feature film script, period) were able to create a template based not on Kneale's teleplay, but on Val Guest's condensation of Kneale's teleplay; the "Hammer Horror" mold was, in part, codified. Sangster went on to refine his Kneale-centric genre chops to script the feature film adaptation of a TV serial Kneale 'knock-off,' **THE TROLLENBERG TERROR** (1958; US title: **THE CRAWLING EYE**) for producers Robert Baker and Monty Berman (itself a Quatermass imitator, produced for ITV as a "Saturday Serial" in 1956; both the teleplay and the feature film version were directed by Quentin Lawrence).

CHAPTER FOUR: "BELIEVED TO BE SUFFERING"

Condensed in QX to 7m 5s.

As Lomax and Quatermass realize what has happened, QEX fades to the kidnappers' car, where Ramsay (Jack Rodney) and an unidentified driver discuss Victor, who is babbling. A brief cutaway to the Wilde flat shows Lomax mobilizing a police search as the antagonism between Paterson and Quatermass is renewed. Back in the car, Ramsay forces Victor at gunpoint to uncover his hidden arm. Glimpsing his mutated limb, Ramsay brakes the car, knocking Victor forward onto the driver who, once touched, loses all signs of life. The car crashes offscreen.

In **QX**, remember, it is *Judith* who kidnaps Victor, and their drive through the rain is ominously restrained. Victor stares at her with indecipherable intensity as she promises him treatment and a happier life away from Quatermass. Judith nervously reaches for a cigarette in her bag, nearly brushing Victor's concealed hand, which she notices only after offering him a cigarette. Judith becomes concerned ("Your hand—are you in pain?") and stops the car to examine him. Victor flinches violently, threateningly lifting his mutated hand into the shadows as Judith shrieks. As Victor flees into the night, the film unceremoniously abandons Judith, who we never see again.

QX condenses the rest of Chapter Four into two setpieces joined by a typical police search montage. Cutting from Judith's screams to Lomax's examination of Christy's body in the clinic elevator, an investigator arrives to tell Quatermass, Lomax and Briscoe that Judith has been found "alone and in a severe state of shock." When Quatermass presses for details, he adds her description of Victor's hand being thorny as a cactus. Lomax immediately struts into Victor's empty room and finds the shattered remnants of the potted cactus, then phones for a citywide search for Carroon. The montage follows, ending with Victor emerging from some shadows as a patrol car has just passed. **QX** then returns to the pathology lab, where Briscoe is examining Christy's corpse.

Prior to this sequence's parallel in QEX, Kneale and Cartier staged a brief scene of Fullalove in his editor's office, followed by a shot of Victor

The Quatermass Conception

stumbling across a desolate V-bombed London landscape, finding shelter in an open cellar hole. QEX returns to Victor's hiding place twice during the subsequent expositions, accentuating his misery and loneliness. Between these tableaux, Best learns that Victor is alive from a barely coherent Ramsay (who survived the car crash), Lomax and Quatermass discuss the post-mortems of Victor's victims, and Paterson fails to convince Fullalove to print an attack on Quatermass in his newspaper.

The teleplay's conversation between Quatermass and Lomax (and Judith, who remains an active participant in QEX) is riveting because, unlike the film, the audience have not yet seen the bodies and are still unacquainted with the nature of Victor's attacks and his progressive transformation.

QX paraphrases QEX's densely informative post-mortem scene in characteristically glib fashion. Inferring that Victor's condition may be akin to an infectious disease, Briscoe describes Victor as "a carrier—the shell of a man being transformed... if one of these cactus plant [fragments] was subjected to the same mutation, there could be an affinity, a union between plant and animal—"With the ability to destroy." Quatermass interrupts, "And—*possess?*" a line lacking any but the most literal meaning divorced form the context of the teleplay, in which Victor has spoken with the voices of his absorbed comrades. Briscoe's announcement that Victor must have food to survive cuts to a garbage can being slammed shut. We are outside the chemist's shop that closes Chapter Four.

Immediately preceding the chemist's shop scene in the teleplay was one of its most suspenseful (and delightfully self-referential) setpieces, in which a young boy (Anthony Green) discovers Victor in the cellar hole. Kneale quickly establishes the boy as a likable little fellow who, after failing to engage Victor in conversation, plays with a space helmet and toy ray gun, forbidden by his mother, which he has secreted in the rubble. After awhile, the child coaxes Victor into following him to a better hiding place. That shelter is the Grand Cinema, a fleapit theater which the two enter through a side exit. Playing at the Grand is PLANET OF THE DRAGONS, a science fiction film "in Super-Real 3-D!" The rest of this remarkable sequence occurs inside the darkened cinema, where a matinee audience in cardboard spectacles watches the fictional space opera. When a talkative stout woman misplaces her 3-D glasses, the boy takes them for his own, the woman's ruckus attracting an usherette (Bernadette Milnes), who takes a long look at the boy and Victor before leaving. Throughout the sequence, the film's vapid dialogue is heard in the background, cruelly mocking Victor's "real life" situation.

The movie's Space Lieutenant's pompous soliloquy, about his duty to explore the unknown, is suddenly interrupted by a slide of Victor's face, captioned "Have you seen this man?" The boy glances over to Victor's seat, now empty, as the camera cuts to the side exit door closing. As Space Hero and Heroine embrace and profess their love onscreen, the usherette realizes the boy is without a ticket and drags him to the Manager's office.

QX replaces this inspired and timely sequence, further into the narrative, with Victor's memorable encounter with a little girl (Jane Asher, who would later star in Kneale's serial THE STONE TAPE, December 25, 1972). This corresponding scene begins much like that with the boy in the teleplay, as the child is introduced having an imaginary tea party with her doll alongside an abandoned boat hull in the shipyards, inadvertently

The Quatermass Conception

waking Victor. He stumbles out to confront her, but she is unafraid and tries to engage him in her imaginary playtime. Flinching from her offerings of tea and cake, Victor swats her doll aside, breaking its head off. As the girl handles her broken doll, Victor staggers away.

In both versions, the sequences of Victor's meetings with children are our *last* glimpses of his human form: after these pivotal shifts, the mutation's accelerated progress renders him truly monstrous. Where Kneale potently reasserts the humanity buried in the Thing at the climax of his teleplay, QX accords its final notes of sympathy here. After this scene, Victor essentially ceases to be human.

The teleplay continues inside the theater manager's office, where the Manager (Lee Fox) phones the police when he realizes that the boy's missing companion is wanted by the authorities. After a brief responsive sequence between Lomax and Quatermass in the Scotland Yard offices, the chapter dissolves to its conclusion in the chemist's shop.

The concluding sequence in the chemists shop is virtually identical in both QEX and QX. As in the teleplay, the chemist's scream terminates the scene.

CHAPTER FIVE: "AN UNIDENTIFIED SPECIES"

Compressed in QX to 24m 24s.

This passage of the film offers the most faithful transposition of the original broadcast episodes. Nevertheless, there are a few key differences.

QEX opens in the chemist's shop as Victor, hampered by his outsized arm, mixes a series of chemicals and drinks the dark concoction. It then cuts to the Manager's office at the Grand Cinema, where Quatermass and Lomax question the boy and the usherette. After the interrogation, Quatermass expresses his feelings of guilt and despair (these regrets are coldly related by Donlevy in Guest's chilling coda) and leaves the cinema with Lomax and Best as a muffled roar is heard from the movie playing in the auditorium—"the angry cries of dragons." At the Rocket Group laboratory, Judith and Briscoe labor over the cactus specimens, their analysis (from which Hammer's Briscoe distilled his dialogue in Chapter Four's conversation with Quatermass) gives way to their own expressions of guilt and grief over Victor's fate. Paterson intrudes, packing up his personal effects in resignation, raging at Quatermass and his "newfound tolerance for the impossible" (Paterson refuses to accept or believe what all available evidence indicates has happened to Victor). "I'm going my own way, " he declares before departing.

QEX then cuts to the chemist's shop, where Quatermass, Lomax and Best investigate Victor's break-in. It is established that the chemist is dazed but still alive, having merely sustained a blow to the head after slipping. Discovering traces of Victor's mixture, the chemist insists that it would "be highly poisonous," to which Briscoe suggests it might have "been needed to perform some essential function in a...biochemical change...some further change..." Fullalove shoulders his way into the shop, striking a tentative alliance with Quatermass that is maintained through the teleplay's conclusion. A subsequent dialogue in Lomax's office cements their relationship, where Briscoe persists in his theory that Victor's chemical solution was a catalyst for further transformation. Lomax mobilizes an extensive search in a prescribed radius from the chemist's, and the camera zooms into Lomax's map, specifically St. James Park, the location of the following scene.

The Quatermass Conception

None of this appears in the Hammer film, which cuts from Victor's fatal assault on the chemist to Lomax's home, where a teatime shave is interrupted by a telephoned report of the chemist's shop break-in. Lomax meets Quatermass and Briscoe at the pharmacy. Briscoe's study of the chemist's shattered stock suggests that Victor prepared and ingested an unknown chemical solution. "I have a very sick feeling it was something to speed up the change going on inside him," Briscoe postulates. When Quatermass offers that Carroon had no knowledge of chemistry, Briscoe implies what is made explicit in the teleplay: that the absorbed astronaut Charles Greene knew chemistry. The depleted corpse of the chemist is found stuffed into a pantry, after which **QX** moves directly to a night shot of Victor collapsing, while picking his way through the shipyards, trembling in terrible agony. This shot fades into morning and is followed by Victor's meeting with the little girl, after which Lomax is notified of the encounter. After calling for a city-wide search, Lomax blusters, "Where's he getting food? That's what I'd like to know"—and the film cuts to a close shot of a caged lion at the London Zoo.

The parallels between the two versions of Victor's nocturnal feedings—staged in the film at the London Zoo, in the teleplay at St. James Park's Duck Island bird reserve—are fairly close, save for the species and the magnitude of Victor's horrible appetite. The teleplay, however, leads into this sequence with some rather insipid cooing between two teenage lovers (John Stone and Christie Humphrey; inspiration for the couple who open the Hammer film?) until the Park Keeper sends them home.

In the teleplay, *two* glimpses of Victor's advanced condition on Duck Island frame an inconsequential exchange between Lomax and Best at Scotland Yard (no doubt scripted and orchestrated to permit the makeup change for Lamont during the live broadcast). In the first (quoting Kneale's script), "there is a rustling among the undergrowth. Heavy strained breathing...then through the leaves crawls the soaked figure of Carroon. He is half-naked, dragging himself along on his stomach. He lies for a moment, panting. What can be seen of his skin is dark grey, with raised, gnarled patches. His right arm trails...at the sound [of Big Ben striking] Carroon looks about...as if searching for some deeper shelter. He starts to move again, and as he does so swings his right arm up—a shapeless mass as big as a bush!"

The second glimpse is similar to that seen in the film version: "In close shot is a mass of undergrowth which is all in gentle, swaying motion. It consists of small leaves with patches of a firmer, moss-like variety. Very, very slowly an eye opens among the leaves, as if someone is looking through. It moves forward. A second eye can be seen, dead and twisted. The mossy foliage comes forward with them. The effect is not unlike the 'Green Man' of mythology. As it move slowly, shapelessly out of shot, the bird-cries rise in sudden, shrill alarm..." The focal reference in this shot to Victor's recognizably human eye is emulated in the feature version, and indeed provides the *only* link between the character of Victor and the tentacled mass revealed at the film's climax, properly emphasized with a closeup of a humanoid orb staring out from the creature's undulating folds.

There are minor variables in the teleplay and Hammer film between Victor's feeding at the zoo/bird reserve and the conclusion of Chapter Five, when the BBC producer (Gordon Jackson)—monitoring the live documentary broadcast from Westminster Abbey—spots the Thing (in "the arches of the triforium, high above Poet's corner" in QEX, and slithering atop a restoration scaffold in the film). In both versions, the producer gasps, "It must be twenty feet across!"

In the teleplay, Quatermass and Lomax commiserate over newspaper headlines containing Paterson's anti-Quatermass declarations, before they are summoned to Duck Island to analyze the bird-strewn wake of Victor's feast. In both versions, it is Briscoe who discovers a still-living fragment of the Thing wriggling in the underbrush, though in the film he discovers it at the end of a trail of glistening residue. After Quatermass and Lomax order the zoo closed until further notice, the film's parallel zoo scene is protracted long enough for us to catch Quatermass' hilarious dismissal of the zookeeper's query.

"What killed the animals?"

"You'd better say natural causes for now," Quatermass replies.

As visitors are turned away at the gate, the camera strays from the dispersing queues to follow an unseen slime trail across the brick walkway leading away from the zoo. In the film, the visual shorthand of the slime trail is used twice again—when Quatermass, Briscoe, and Lomax investi-

The Quatermass Conception

gate the sighting at the brick wall, and once more to indicate the creature's moss-like creeping up Westminster Abbey's outer wall.

The sequence in the research facility lab as Quatermass and Briscoe study the incubated growth of the Thing-fragment is similar in both versions, with the significant exclusion of Judith from **QX**. Guest and Landau reasonably condenses the sequence's narrative impact by incorporating information from the teleplay's sixth and final chapter, particularly the "feeding" of the fragment ("...twelve minutes and every animal completely absorbed except one," Briscoe notes; in the teleplay, animals and vegetation are fed to the glob) and its implications ("It's tripled its size in an hour," Quatermass exclaims. "This is only a fragment of the main organism. If the same thing is happening to him at the same rate of speed—").[66]

Lomax's teleplay interview with an intoxicated local (Wilfred Brambell) who has seen a shape "'igh up on [a] wall" is revised to provide one of the film's most amusing character bits, with Rosie (Thora Hird), a middle-aged lady lush, reporting a similar sighting to a police desk sergeant. Rosie's description is a little more specific than Brambell's ("a creepy-crawly...somethin' enormous...crawlin' up on a wall..."). This is followed in **QX** by two newly invented sequences: a phone conversation between Lomax and Quatermass, which prompts them to visit the wall with Briscoe and two policemen in tow, beginning with the slime trail and ending with Lomax sending out a warning to London police.

Both versions share the laboratory scene in which Quatermass and Briscoe discover that the Victor-fragment has matured into a reproductive phase, spouting clustered sporangia zones, each capable of generating hundreds of thousands of infectious spores. The Hammer sequence has the engorged glob smashing through its incubator and dying, presumably of hunger, just as it is about to consume a cage filled with laboratory mice.

---

[66] This sequence, the further growth of the contained blob fragment within the lab, and all that follows involving the transformed Carroon were imitated and expanded upon in subsequent 1950s 'blob' movies, prominent among them **SPACE MASTER X-7, THE BLOB** (both 1958) and **CALTIKI—IL MOSTRO IMMORTALE / CALTIKI—THE IMMORTAL MONSTER** (1959). There were ample literary precursors in the pulp era, including Anthony M. Rud's "Ooze" (*Weird Tales*, March 1923), Joseph Payne Brennan's "Slime" (*Weird Tales*, March 1953), etc., and countless successors, including Stephen King's "The Raft" (*Gallery*, November 1982), etc.

Briscoe, finding it inert on the lab floor, tells Quatermass, "If it had lived to complete this reproductive cycle this room would have been a jungle of living tendrils."

The impending threat sufficiently explained for its dramatic purposes, QX now races to its conclusion. Lomax calls for a massive mobilization of civil defense and military forces.[67] A montage of military might concludes at Westminster Abbey, as the BBC documentary broadcast begins. In the film, the broadcast is ominously interrupted by an unresponsive camera, which leads to the discovery of a dead technician. The producer orders the broadcast to proceed despite Lomax's orders to halt, culminating in the on-camera revelation of the Thing Victor has become.

QEX, on the other hand, arrives at the Abbey via a short sequence at Victoria Station, where a young policeman is reporting fallen stonework at the Abbey. Remembering the drunk's claim that the shape had climbed "'igh up on [a] wall," Lomax decides to investigate. At this point, the teleplay joins the BBC broadcast, affording more screentime to the nervous, camera-shy architect Sir Vernon Dodds (John Kidd) who hosts the live-broadcast documentary.

Lost upon the feature film is the teleplay's witty framing of its apocalyptic climax within a fictionalized live BBC broadcast—which must have raised at least a few hairs for late-tuning or uninformed viewers. Kneale's model, of course, was Orson Welles' infamous Oct. 30, 1938 radio dramatization of H.G. Wells' THE WAR OF THE WORLDS. BBC's publicity and onscreen warnings prior to the TV broadcast, coupled with the immediate popularity and widespread public awareness of the QEX serial, effectively neutralized any possibilities of mass hysteria. Besides, the Brits

---

[67] This aspect of 1950s sf films would become a fixture, with the spectacle of many productions utterly dependent upon such footage of escalating military movement. My late friend writer Steve Perry lovingly called many 1950s sf films "mobilization movies" and delighted in those that lavished excessive screentime on such footage, whether stock footage (as in **INVADERS FROM MARS, THE DEADLY MANTIS**, etc.) or specially-created special effects sequences (as in the Toho Studios Japanese sf and monster films, in which Eiji Tsuburaya's effects team would set extraordinarily inventive miniatures into constant motion, as in the prolonged effects climax of 地球防衛軍 / **CHIKYU BOEIGUN / THE MYSTERIANS**, 1957/1960). Nigel Kneale not only despised such formula: he actively subverted it in QUATERMASS II, wherein whenever there is military mobilization, it is inevitably mobilized against innocent citizens, a manifestation of covert invasion, government infiltration, assassination, and the collapse of civilized order.

The Quatermass Conception

had already proved during World War II that they could handle *real* invasions with more grace and solidarity than Americans hand been able to bear on a completely imaginary one! Undoubtedly most viewers, recalling the panic which Welles' broadcast had aroused in the States, savored the audacity of Kneale's conceit.[68]

CHAPTER SIX: "STATE OF EMERGENCY"

Condensed In QX to 6m 27s.

While it's true that "Val Guest's direction show[ed] a combination of American expertise and British sensitivity reflecting his American publicist background,"[69] the blend falters in the film's perfunctory climax, in which Guest intercuts dull military mobilization montages with compelling glimpses of the Thing (designed by Les Bowie), which Quatermass decides to electrocute before it can scatter its spores. The ensuing operation efficiently terminates the imminence of apocalypse in an unexceptional flurry of sparks, flames, and roasted monster meat. That said, the climax is effective, and many who saw the film at an impressionable age have the Carroon creature's writhing form burned into their gray matter.

Though both film and teleplay shared a certain technical ingenuity, QEX easily outstripped the Hammer production in terms of conceptual ingenuity. Kneale's insistence that his original finale was "better than just electrocuting [the Thing] by putting a lot of voltage into some girders on which it had unfortunately sat," is borne out by his published teleplay. Hammer's electrocution solution, in fact, was inspired by the teleplay's final laboratory sequence (early in Chapter Six), where the growing

[68] The same would not be true almost four decades later, when the BBC broadcast of Stephen Volk and Lesley Manning's GHOSTWATCH (October 31, 1992) prompted public complaints and considerable outrage. Rich Lawden's documentary GHOSTWATCH: BEHIND THE CURTAINS (2012) and companion book of the same title (2013, available at http://www.lulu.com/shop/rich-lawden/ghost-watch-behind-the-curtains/paperback/product-21256963.html) offers a comprehensive overview of every aspect of the production, broadcast, and all that followed in its wake. Per author Volk's happy admission, Nigel Kneale, more than Orson Welles, was Volk's primary inspiration for the teleplay, which he'd originally conceived as the final episode of a six-part serial.

[69] John Baxter, SCIENCE FICTION IN THE CINEMA (Paperback Library edition, 1970), pg. 95.

WE ARE THE MARTIANS

Victor-fragment is electrocuted once it outlives its research value. When Briscoe suggests that the same method might be used against what Victor is becoming, Quatermass replies, "It isn't sealed helplessly in an oven like that. And you're forgetting something else... We're going to meet intelligence. Still at least partly... human."

Kneale's original Quatermass had already spelled out why the more ruthlessly efficient Hammer Films finale simply wouldn't work. Furthermore, Kneale's conception of the Carroon-composite-thing was more convincing and complex an organism than that of the film version. Bluntly put, Kneale counted on and engaged the intelligence of his audience, where Hammer, Guest and Landau banked on their ignorance and impatience.

Kneale's monster grows far beyond the "twenty feet across" calculated by the BBC producer in Chapter Five's final movement. Almost the entirety of Chapter Six dramatizes the implacable growth of the Thing (to use Kneale's scripted word) as it approaches reproductive gestation and the expulsion of its spores, which Quatermass has already assessed in the lab as possessing "irresistible virulence." While there is an unfortunate *deux ex machina* offhandedness to Peterson's self-sacrifice during Chapter Six—he recklessly volunteers to venture into the Abbey basement chambers, in order to atone for his abuses against, and re-ally himself with, Quatermass—the sequence is crucial in its revelation that the Thing has "penetrated the [flooring] stonework—creeping down there like the roots of a plant while we thought it was inactive!" With the Thing's penetration into the Abbey's very foundation, any conventional means of destruction are rendered useless.

Quatermass' solution—to appeal to the latent humanity within Victor and urge the thing he's become to an act of self-destruction—is realized in QEX with considerable power; every thematic element of the narrative reinforces its impact. Unlike Donlevy in Guest's film, Tate's Quatermass has by this time only strengthened his bonds with Judith, Briscoe, Lomax, and associates, as well as earning the cooperative alliance of Fullalove. The firm bonds in the teleplay between Quatermass and his team are tested and potently *reinforced* by the finale; even the intrusive military presence has no option but to cooperate with their resolute solidarity.

The Quatermass Conception

Quatermass' final appeal to Victor is further amplified by Judith's last-minute idea to replay the wire-recording of the three astronaut's voices, a maneuver that successfully stirs their vestigial claim on the creature which has consumed them, destroying it from within. We accept this climax because Victor—himself an integral member of Quatermass' circle—has, throughout the course of six episodes, so heroically asserted his own humanity against the infectious transformation. Victor's struggle implicitly culminates in his choice of the Abbey for his last stand—"the temple of God" harboring a perverted "temple of the spirit" in a final desperate search for redemption. Paterson's reckless self-sacrifice is another personal bid for redemption, demonstrably reaffirming the severed bonds between Quatermass and his associates and foreshadowing the self-sacrifices that conclude Kneale's narrative.[70]

All of these elements are eloquently articulated with a minimum of sermonizing. Judith urges Quatermass to publicly deal with the growing panic with an evocation of common dignity, "so that [the populace] can face it—at least with understanding. Don't let it overtake them like the beasts and the plants and—" Quatermass conveys the essentials of the situation over television, concluding with, "If the worst should happen...I ask for your...forgiveness." But the remorse he confides to Fullalove is fleeting, giving way to resolve. His appeal to the Thing is initially directed to the original components of its conglomerated intellect: "We worked together for achievement. This is the time, [Greene]...this will be the achievement...Reichenheim, this is no longer the unexpected. When the conditions are known, action can be taken..." He urges Victor to move beyond his fear, galvanizing their reawakening consciousnesses crying, "You are not to submit!...You will overcome this evil. Without you, it cannot exist upon the earth...It can only exist through your

---

[70] In terms of the immediate post-WWII, Cold War context of the teleplay, this arguably is the meat of Kneale's central Conservative metaphor, or the metaphor as it might have been read by Conservative viewers (and the BBC), though that's likely not as Kneale intended it to be understood: only by appealing to the spiritual inner strength of the selfless British scientist/soldier/citizen—in the eleventh hour, against desperate odds, rallying their inherent Britishness (including the loyalty of Reichenheim to his adopted nation) against the deforming transformation wrought by malignant "outside" contagion to reject that irreversibly terrible change—can Quatermass save the planet. Thus, by convincing the Carroon-creature to autodestruct, Quatermass ensures its redemption, and his own, and preserves Britain, and thus the world.

WE ARE THE MARTIANS

submission. With all your power and mine joined to yours...you must dissever from it...send it out of earthly existence! You—as men—must die!"

Kneale wrote the teleplay's climax with actor Reginald Tate specifically in mind.

"I knew he could do it," Kneale explained to interviewer Bill Warren. "In fact, I hadn't written the last episode when they started showing the first, so nobody knew what it was going to be. Particularly when I saw the way he was playing in the early episodes, I wrote it directly for him, and he did it superbly well. He had to appear almost quasi-religious. He has to appeal to the last human vestige in the monster, which he believed was there, to will itself to death, until it all came disintegrating and fluttering down. It worked, and I think it was a much more moving ending, a thing you don't always get in science fiction."[71]

Given the brusque insensitivity of Donlevy's Quatermass, one can only imagine Donlevy relentlessly badgering the last vestiges of the tortured Victor into committing suicide. By no stretch of the imagination could anyone accept him appealing to the creature's sublimated humanity and coaxing into a heroic act of self-sacrifice to save Mankind. Since American producer Robert Lippert had required Donlevy's participation as a prerequisite to the coproduction with Hammer, perhaps we should give Richard Landau and director Val Guest's adaptation more credit for their pragmatism. Recognizing the screen persona and limitations of their lead actor, and the essential transformation of the character of Quatermass that casting necessarily imposed, Guest and Landau's no-nonsense stripping-down of Kneale's final chapter makes absolute dramatic and aesthetic sense. It's a colder, more calculated finale, but let's face it: Kneale's television Quatermass had been supplanted completely by an American "outsider," Donlevy, as completely as Carroon had been by the alien transformation—or, perhaps, as the Cold War had already transformed Britain and its former Allies. It's a steely, dark future foreseen in **QX**, but one arguably truer to its time than that which Kneale and Cartier envisioned in QEX.

[71] Kneale, interview by Warren, Ibid., pg. 35

The Quatermass Conception

In the film's coda, Marsh asks Quatermass, "Is there anything I can do, sir?" Quatermass replies, "Yes, I'm going to need some help... going to start again." The resolute, unrepentant scientist then exits Westminster Abbey and marches off into the night, a shot which dissolves to the next rocket lifting off without fanfare. Just as Guest's Quatermass embodies the iron-willed determination of the archetypal 1950's scientific hero distilled to its promethean essential, we can also see in him the blueprint for Hammer's forthcoming Baron Frankenstein—forever responding to his experimental failures with the grim determination to try, try again... forever, if necessary and, if need be, at the cost of many human lives.

There were issues. Every episode of the BBC serial ran slightly over its designated time slot; antiquated cameras compromised the quality of the broadcast image throughout; the failure of a studio microphone resulted in a break in transmission of the fateful final episode, which as a result ran six minutes over schedule. Plans to telerecord each episode onto 35mm film were abandoned after the kinescoping of only the first two episodes, which survive as the earliest record of live serialized British drama.

Still, a reported 3.4 million viewers watched the first episode, growing to 5 million viewers for the climactic sixth chapter (some of whom reportedly thought the serial's finale was spoiled by the technical glitch and

WE ARE THE MARTIANS

broadcast interruption); Hammer Films website historian Robert Simpson called THE QUATERMASS EXPERIMENT "event television, emptying the streets and pubs for the six weeks of its duration."[72]

The popularity of THE QUATERMASS EXPERIMENT led to Kneale's QUATERMASS II, which the BBC broadcast in six live installments between October 22 and November 26, 1955. Reginald Tate was signed to reprise his starring role but, tragically, Kneale's favorite Quatermass interpreter died shortly before rehearsals began. He was replaced by John Robinson. Q2 was also produced as a Hammer film, the first scripted by Nigel Kneale, once again directed by Val Guest and starring Brian Donlevy. This film — released in the US as **ENEMY FROM SPACE** — is widely considered the best of the Hammer Quatermass series. It was not until 1967, when his 1959 BBC serial QUATERMASS AND THE PIT was also filmed by Hammer, that Nigel Kneale had the satisfaction of seeing *his* Quatermass — a dedicated, admittedly egotistical and self-obsessed benevolent scientist, intolerant of the authoritarian obstacles strewn in the path of truth — transposed to the big screen in the person of Scottish actor Andrew Kier. Kneale brought an end to his most famous character in Piers Haggard's QUATERMASS / **THE QUATERMASS CONCLUSION** (1979), a four-part miniseries which starred John Mills as an aging, disillusioned Quatermass.

By this time, Val Guest's steely, abrasive Quatermass had long since served his higher purpose, paving the way from the black-and-white realm of science-fiction *noir* into the Technicolor Victorian laboratories of the new Hammer Gothic. Peter Cushing's cold-blooded Baron Frankenstein pursued scientific knowledge at any cost well into the 1970s, attaining the dispassionate opacity of Donlevy's Quatermass in Terence Fisher's **FRANKENSTEIN CREATED WOMAN** (1967).

Back in the 1980s, late friend, journalist, and devoted genre scholar Bill Kelley once posited to me, in conversation, that Quatermass was the first of a trio of Hammer leads whose stature was determined solely by their ability to make decisions and act upon them, regardless of the consequences to others. Brian Donlevy's Quatermass, embodied the first

---

[72] Simpson quoted in BBC's obituary for Nigel Kneale, "Quatermass Creator Dies, Aged 84," *BBC News Online*, November 1, 2006, archived at http://news.bbc.co.uk/2/hi/entertainment/6105578.stm

The Quatermass Conception

Hammer phase of the fading American star as hero; Peter Cushing's Baron Frankenstein embodied the ascending Hammer star as anti-hero; and Christopher Lee's Duc le Richleau in **THE DEVIL RIDES OUT** (1967; US: **THE DEVIL'S BRIDE**) was the Hammer hero transcendent, coincidentally ringing the death knell for the studio's commercial reign over the horror genre. The decisive charisma and commanding personality of each figure allowed them to mobilize and manipulate all, even fleeting, acquaintances into becoming accomplices to their higher needs.

Sharing Bill's perceptions in an earlier version of this essay that saw print in *Video Watchdog* in 1992, no one could foresee how accurate that assessment would remain over two decades later. Politicians and authorities steamroll over and/or actively sideline and bury science when it is inconvenient to their own (usually mercantile) goals. Quatermass, in any of his pre-1970 incarnations, would hardly stand for such abuses of power. Are we in an age ruled by those whose charisma and commanding personalities allow them to mobilize and manipulate all to become accomplices to their "higher needs," or is it just me?

In tandem with the New Conservatism sweeping western nations — arguably mirroring, in many ways, the Conservative government of England in 1951-1964 — there seems to be constant talk of a new Quatermass.

Nigel Kneale himself approved of two of these — the first, a screenplay for a proposed 1993 remake of THE QUATERMASS EXPERIMENT written by ALIEN co-author/co-creator Dan O'Bannon, which Kneale reportedly read and approved.[73] A year before his death (on October 29, 2006), Kneale was a consultant for BBC Four's *TV on Trial* earnest but ill-fated live broadcast remake of THE QUATERMASS EXPERIMENT (April 2, 2005), the first live BBC drama produced in two decades. Adapted "and brought up-to-date"[74] by BBC Fictionlab head Richard Fell and directed by Sam Miller, the well-intentioned revamp/condensation of Kneale's original serial into a 97 minute production simply didn't gel, retaining

---

[73] Andy Murray, *Into the Unknown: The Fantastic Life of Nigel Kneale* (Headpress, 2006), pp. 182-184.

[74] "BBC Four to Produce a Live Broacast of the Sci-Fi Classic, The Quatermass Experiment," BBC Press Office, March 3, 2005, archived at http://www.bbc.co.uk/pressoffice/pressreleases/stories/2005/03_march/03/quatermass.shtml

some of the strengths and urgency of Kneale's characters and concepts while keeping the Carroon transformation and creature offscreen—a decision that decidedly undercut the power of the teleplay—and relocating the climax to the Tate Modern art gallery instead of Westminster Abbey. Kneale and Cartier's original, and Val Guest and Richard Landau's Hammer adaptation, had captured something essential of their era; in hindsight, only actor David Tennant's role as Dr. Briscoe (Tennant's about-to-be-announced winning of the lead in the next season of *Doctor Who* slyly acknowledged in one line) and the inadvertent overlay of a BBC News item (citing the simultaneous coverage of the death of Pope John Paul II over on BBC News 24) stand as signposts of this production's time and place.

It was an interesting experiment, "... *an operation designed to discover some unknown truth. It is also a risk...*" The risk was self-evident, but there were precious few "truths" to be found, save the attempted, admirable in-and-of itself fidelity to the spirit (sans broadcast time to embody the particulars) of Kneale's and Cartier's original. After screening the production via DVD (DD Home Entertainment, October 2005), I could only sadly wish anew that we could somehow see more than just the surviving kinescope of first episode of the original 1953 serial.

Or is it just me?

In January 2015, a BBC Radio 2 interview with Simon Oaks, CEO of the newest incarnation of Hammer Films, revealed that Hammer was planning on producing a brand-new Quatermass series for television.

The thing is: do we need Quatermass in the 21st century? Kneale himself long ago bade farewell to his most famous character with the mournful threnody QUATERMASS / **THE QUATERMASS CONCLU-SION**. It was, in its way, a brutal farewell, devoid of much that made Quatermass Quatermass, but that was the point, wasn't it? By the close of the 1970s, in Kneale's view, Quatermass was too old and broken to buck the times, and the youth of that decade were flocking to New Age ideals Kneale found worthy only of despair. Kneale looked around him and reflected all that spelled out the sorrowful demise of his once-beloved professor. A recent restoration of that teleplay on Blu-Ray has helped restore a luster it never enjoyed (even among aficionados) in its day, but

The Quatermass Conception

the new praise heaped upon the resurrection does beg the question: do we need a new Quatermass?

I see and hear the echoes of Kneale everywhere—in the nooks and crannies and Devil's Bridge of Y GWYLL aka HINTERLAND, in Charlie Brooker's debut BLACK MIRROR, installment "The National Anthem," in journalist Linda Moulton Howe's incredulous interview in the documentary MIRAGE MEN—and I know, for a fact, it isn't just me hearing these echoes, seeing these ripples, making these connections.

Still, somewhere in these cool and often cruel shadows, the warm spirit of Nigel Kneale's original Quatermass lingers, waiting to be recognized and seen—

—and, perhaps, to be reborn.

©2015 Stephen R. Bissette, all rights reserved; deepest appreciation to Neil Snowdon, special thanks to Tim and Donna Lucas, and thanks to Tim Paxton, Bill Kelley, Stanley Wiater, John Garbarino, Tony Timpone, Michael H. Price, Bill Warren, Richard Halegua, Brad Stevens, Jonathan Stover, Chad Lee Carter, and to Luke Healy (for tutoring me on some basics that helped resurrect earlier versions of this article) and to my favorite fellow traveler in the Nigel Kneale theme park, Joseph A. Citro. An earlier version and subsequent portions of this essay originally saw print in *Video Watchdog* #12 (July/August 1992, pp. 32-47, which benefitted enormously from editor Tim Lucas' input and edit) and *Monster!* (Vol. 4, #8, August, 2014, pp. 56-68).

Photo © Kerr-Kneale Productions Ltd

A Conversation with Judith Kerr

Neil Snowdon

*J*UDITH KERR IS THE ACCLAIMED THE AUTHOR AND ILLUSTRATOR *of* THE TIGER WHO CAME TO TEA, MOG, *and* WHEN HITLER STOLE PINK RABBIT. *Born in Germany in 1924, she left with her family in 1933, fearful because her father—influential theatre critic, Alfred Kerr— had openly criticized the Nazis. She worked for the Red Cross during the Second World War, helping wounded soldiers, and later won a scholarship to study at the central School Of Arts & Crafts. She married Nigel Kneale in 1954. They remained married until his death in 2006. In 2012 Judith was awarded the Order Of The British Empire (OBE) for "Services To Children's Literature and Holocaust education".*

We met at the offices of her agent, Stephen Durbridge, in London to discuss the book that you are now holding, when in its infancy. Judith was warm, generous and utterly charming. I was flustered, nervous and sweating. I can't speak for Judith's impression of me, but from my perspective, our meeting was an absolute delight…

NS: *One of the first things I'd like to ask is when you met?*

JK: We met by chance at the BBC, because I was teaching art at a school across the road and a woman I met at a friend's house said "why don't you

We Are The Martians

come across the road and have lunch with me in the canteen", and Tom sat down at the table, and that was it really.

NS: *So, you weren't working there at the time?*

JK: No, no, not at all. I did afterwards because it was better than teaching.

NS: *As a profession or in terms of the pay?*

JK: As a profession. They wanted me to work full time, and I'd never done that. Tom suggested that I read the slush pile and, as I can read rubbish in three languages, I got the job.

I ended up writing stuff because of learning so much from Tom, I wrote a six part adaptation of HUNTINGTOWER.

NS: *Television was still a very young medium at the time—*

JK: Oh, it was wonderful. Because nobody interfered with anything. You just...the thing was written, very often, mostly, was put on soon afterwards, and there was the director—who was also the producer—and the cast, and one assistant and the cameraman, and that was it. And everybody helped. I mean, Tom did the special effects for the first Quatermass; we did them together[75], and it was wonderful. We had to be there every time it went out; everything was live of course and the first Quatermass—the first episode just surprised them; the second episode cleared the pubs and everything. Suddenly, there was nobody who wasn't watching. It was quite incredible.

And Tom, although he had already won the Somerset Maugham Prize; short stories don't actually make one very famous or make one very much money. With this, suddenly, over night, he was famous. Everybody wanted him to write for them and we got married on the strength of it.

[75] When the people charged with creating the special effects for THE QUATERMASS EXPERI-MENT balked at this particular task – there was no SFX department at that time – Nigel and Judith created the effect themselves by gluing plant roots to gardening gloves until they were unrecognisable, then donning the gloves and pushing their hands through a photographic enlargement of Westminster Abbey, and 'wiggling' their fingers to make the roots move like tentacles.

154

NS: *It must have been an incredibly exciting period to be working in television. As I understand it,* THE QUATERMASS EXPERIMENT *was written quite quickly, to fill a gap in the schedule—*

JK: It wasn't to fill a gap. They wanted him to write a serial, and he said 'why don't we make it Science Fiction'. He wasn't a Science Fiction writer, but he just thought it would make a change from all the sort of "drawing room" things that went on...

I found his diary the other day. He wrote the first episode in a week. The second episode he did in four days. The third episode he did over the weekend, and after that he had to go out filming with Rudy [Cartier] so I don't know how long it took him to write the rest, but he was still writing the last episode, when the first episode went out. I mean he knew exactly what was going to happen, he just hadn't put it down yet.

NS: *My impression is that he seems to have been a very quick writer.*

JK: Yes, what he used to do was, he used to spend quite a long time thinking about things. And quite often he made furniture while he was doing that. And then when he reached the point where he *had* to write...I was always afraid that he wouldn't finish the window seat or whatever it was *before* he got to the point where he had to stop.

But then he wrote at tremendous speed. He couldn't stop, and he would write six episodes in one go. He wouldn't stop and he was almost ill at the end of it. But he couldn't stop...

NS: *There's a story—it may be apocryphal—about him writing the adaptation of* THE WOMAN IN BLACK *in ten days and his agent at the time, telling him not to send it in, that the production company would think he'd rushed it or something.*

JK: (laughing) Yes, that's right! He spent a long time planning, and knew exactly what he was going to do.

NS: *I wonder what it was then that drew him to TV as a medium—he'd*

We Are The Martians

worked in theatre, and won prizes for his fiction by then—

JK: He loved it.

It was partly practical, because after he got the Somerset Maugham Award they immediately wanted him to write a novel, and he didn't want to write a novel. And it's a travelling scholarship, a travelling prize. So he went off on his travels and came back thinking that he would be rich, or a bit rich, and found of course he wasn't at all because short stories don't sell. So he was casting about for a job of sorts, he had been an actor—he started as an actor—and he went back to RADA to ask them if they had any advice and they said "well there's this man who's just taken over in television called Michael Barry, why don't you go and see him?" He was from RADA, or he'd been at RADA or had taught at RADA or something. And so he went and saw Michael, who gave him a job, but hadn't really got a job for him, so they paid him out of the petty cash, to just fix things, to adapt stage plays for television which was more or less all they had at that time and which usually meant—where it said in the programme "the following spring" you put in a picture of daffodils –it wasn't very much to do. And then he did everything. He wrote dialogue for vegetable puppets, which had been abandoned by their creator, for a children's programme. I think it was voiced mostly, by the Carry On team, and Tom himself played the onion, and they all sent it up like mad...

So, he did everything, and there was a man who wrote a weekly thing for children, called—I think—SPOT. And this was somebody who animated stuff in his bathroom and he'd do one a week about this thing called SPOT, about various drawings and things. And Tom used to write this on Thursday and the man would film it in his bathroom on Friday and it went out on Saturday I think.

NS: *It seems like such a wonderful period for being so hands on and so cross collaborative.*

JK: It was, it was wonderful. And you know, as you went out [of the studios] you'd say to the man who let you in, the man who watched you go in, "Any calls?" [no one could be contacted while a show was going out

A Conversation with Judith Kerr

live]. And I remember that we went out with Rudy after NINETEEN EIGHTY FOUR and Rudy just said "Any calls?" and the man nearly killed him, because it had been such a row!

NS: *Of course! There were questions raised in parliament about it, people found it so shocking...*

JK: Yes, there was a discussion in Parliament about whether they should allow it to go out the second time—they always put them out on Sunday and then they did another performance on Thursday, because it was live—and there was this argument about whether or not it would be alright to put this out again. A woman was claimed to have died while watching it, but then it turned out that she was also wrapping Christmas presents and doing the ironing and they didn't think her attention was entirely on the television after all.[76]

NS: *It sounds like Tom had a very good relationship with the BBC at that point.*

JK: He had a very good relationship with the BBC for a long time, in spite of the fact that they didn't pay him for Quatermass [THE QUATERMASS EXPERIMENT when it sold to Hammer], because he was on the staff and they reckoned it belonged to them, having always said before that it wouldn't matter. He didn't mind that much at the time, we were getting married you know...

NS: *That relationship with the BBC obviously changed over time.*

JK: It was fine until—I forget over what—it may have been over THE BIG BIG GIGGLE, I'm not quite sure, but they didn't want to do it and I think Tom probably then spoke to ITV, I'm not sure...

NS: *I understand there was some back and forth regarding the final Quatermass, which had been planned much earlier originally, at the BBC.*

---

[76] Nigel was also quoted as having said that word got back from the Palace, that the Queen had rather enjoyed NINETEEN EIGHTY FOUR, after which all the parliamentary furore went away.

WE ARE THE MARTIANS

JK: There were problems about that. It was all very unlucky. I think the original director's brother was killed . . . I mean, we saw the first shots and we knew it was not going to work, it was one of those. Bits of it worked; the people underground worked.

NS: *It's flawed, but I do think there's still an overall power to it, I think most of Tom's work does, it always comes through — even with the Hammer Quatermass films, where I know he wasn't happy with Donlevy at all, the writing still comes through.*

JK: Well, at least the second and third he wrote himself. The first one was unbelievable . . .

NS: *The quality of the writing, and the mood of Tom's work always come through though, there's always something you can put a finger on that says or feels like Tom's writing.*

JK: He was very good.

NS: *And were you writing at the same time?*

JK: No, no, what I did at the BBC . . . there was a man called Donald Wilson, who went on and did the FORSYTHE SAGA, he took over the script unit and suddenly, I think there simply weren't enough people who knew anything about television, because it was growing at such a pace, and he suggested that I could become a writer. And of course, I'd learned so much from Tom, and it was just an adaptation . . . so I did that, and then I had our daughter. After that I didn't want to go back to television, because deadlines are impossible when you have children anyway, and Tom was so much better at it than I was anyway.

I'm not really a writer. I draw things, that's what I've always done. I went to art school, but I can just write enough you know, to go with the pictures. So I did picture books. And that was lovely, because we were both working at home and doing different things, which I think is essential for people. I don't know how Kingsley Amis and Elizabeth Jane Howard managed.

A Conversation with Judith Kerr

They were married for a while, and there was some theory that they each read to each other what they had written that day. In which case, I don't know how they lasted as long as they did.

NS: *Well, they didn't last at the end of the day...*

JK: No, they didn't!

NS: *Do you have a sense of Tom's... legacy, for want of a better word. The influence that he's had?*

JK: Oh, enormously. I think he was, and he thought himself, probably better at construction than almost anyone else. And I certainly learned that from him. I think Matthew [Matthew Kneale, son of Judith and Nigel, and author ENGLISH PASSENGERS] did as well. You're with a writer, you're going to pick things up, besides, he was so funny.

NS: *He's not always acknowledged for his way with comedy, but he had an unerring ability to write a funny line or character so that it still fit inside the drama without undermining it. Mark Gatiss says that Nigel invented popular drama for television with THE QUATERMASS EXPERIMENT. It set the standard. And it's so far ahead of anything else on the landscape at the time.*

JK: Well, he and Rudy got on so well because Tom wanted to do difficult things and Rudy was prepared to do them. It was great fun being with him. I find other widows... and I'm surrounded by widows, who are all very nice, and they talk about their husbands and they say something like "Oh, Richard would say..." so and so. I never knew what Tom was going to say. It was always a surprise.

NS: *It seems to me that in those early days of Television, it was a little closer to theatre, in spirit at least, the way people were working together as a small tight team...*

JK: It was very like theatre, in the sense that you got a reaction immedi-

WE ARE THE MARTIANS

ately. It was a wonderful time. A terribly exciting time. Now it's all at arms length of course, but at that time it was live. They did that idiot version [of THE QUATERMASS EXPERIMENT], do you remember? And it under ran by 20minutes. And all they did was blackouts between scenes, which was crazy. Whereas the interesting thing about that was that the camera—there'd be two people have a conversation and the camera would be on one, who would be asking very meaningful questions of the other… meanwhile the other man would be having a change and was *racing* across the set and then sitting just in time in the other chair as the camera went to him and he gave his reply. So they would cut from one scene straight into another *in action*. It was like that.

NS: *Were the originals done at Alexandra palace?*

JK: Yes, the cameras were fixed to the floor and the picture was upside down and right to left!

The thing I liked very much about the first Quatermass was—because we all had to help for the special effects—there was this "thing", this vegetation that appeared in West Minster Abbey, and Tom and I made the "thing", the wiggly "thing", but there was a very nice, very good actor called Duncan Lamont[77] who played the astronaut who went up into space and came back; and of course, once he'd turned into a vegetable, he no longer had a job! But he still felt so much in touch with it that he used to come in and when it came to the last bit when the vegetables had grown huge and were just branches they'd brought in and they had to move on cue—because they were reacting to Quatermass—Tom and I, and Duncan Lamont, all huddled under these twigs and sort of moved them, when they had to move…so Duncan Lamont was still playing the part!

NS: *It seems like—if one were to write a biography of Nigel—then in order to do it justice, you would be looking at not just Nigel's career, but the real birth of the medium of television in terms of the excitement of pushing it and*

[77] Lamont later played the drill operator in the Hammer film of QUATERMASS AND THE PIT.

A Conversation with Judith Kerr

seeing what the medium could do, and inventing it, there and then on the spot...

JK: Yes, the only thing is that Tom did a lot of other stuff that was very good, and sometimes even better. I think THE PIT is as good as anything he ever did, but you have THE YEAR OF THE SEX OLYMPICS which is extraordinary and THE ROAD... one that I like, that he never thought he got quite right, THE WINE OF INDIA, that's incredibly relevant now, what with stem cell research and so on.[78]

NS: *Am I right in thinking you worked together on an adaptation of* WHEN HITLER STOLE PINK RABBIT, *for German television?*

JK: It was never made.

I think there's a very good chance now of the BBC doing PINK RABBIT. I think the Germans also say they're making a film.

I can't find Nigel's script anywhere. It was very good I remember, though no one wanted to use it in the end. We worked together in as much as we talked about it a great deal, but he wrote it alone. He was much better than I. Anything I do in writing I learned from him.

NS: *You've said that he was a great structuralist...*

JK: Yes, which is the main thing. If you have that you can do anything. And you see he was so fast...

He'd think for weeks then write it fast and he'd be ill at the end of it.

He wrote this television adaptation of THE WOMAN IN BLACK and his agents said you can't hand it in, they'll think you haven't worked hard enough on it. So he had to keep hold of it for another ten days. I'm the opposite, I'm very slow.

But it was Tom who taught me about it [writing].

---

[78] In the year 2050, advances in medicine have resulted in a need for population control. People reaching the age of 100 must submit to a government controlled euthanasia program. The story centers on a 100-year old couple who must now make plans for their funeral. —imdb.com/title/tt0214305/plot-summary by Mike Konczewski

I remember when we were at the BBC. I was just reading scripts at the time, and a man called Donald Wilson, who later did the Forsythe Saga, was brought in as head of the script unit. I had started by reading the slush pile. And I think they were suddenly so overwhelmed with work, and I think there weren't many people who understood about television, so he decided I should become a script writer. Knowing that Tom would fix anything that went wrong, because Tom had written QUATERMASS by then, so Mrs. Quatermass was quite safe!

And so I wrote this six part adaptation of HUNTING TOWER, with terrible difficulty, never having written anything like that before. And I remember thinking about 'how do you do this?' and talking to Tom and asking him "How, if you've got to make a certain point in a scene, how do you get to that point? Do you just have a conversation and somehow sort of bring it in?" And he said, "no you plan for it. You know that you're going towards it." Which is such an obvious thing, but you know, I had to be told.

You know what he used to do, when I first knew him and before, and he was doing all these odd jobs for television. They used to get these terrible plays, which I later read. And in those days, they *had* to respond to them. And so he used to send them fake plays. One of his favourite things he used to put in, was "And his plan is going according to plan"! And the stage direction: "They talk for a while." And he used to get these very polite letters back saying "Very interesting". He used to just write really terrible plays for a laugh!

NS: *He seems to have been a man of great humour. But rather unfortunately he seems to be remembered as somewhat more curmudgeonly, which is not at all the impression I get from talking to you. And of course one of the most striking things about his writing is the humanism of it, the touches of character humour that always said to me that he liked people. Liked life.*

JK: Well, this is it; I fell in love with him because he made me laugh so.

NS: *And of course in things like* **FIRST MEN IN THE MOON** *that was to the fore. I'm thinking about the first scenes of the film, which are Nigel's*

A Conversation with Judith Kerr

invention, in which the first manned mission to the moon (and this was shot before there had been one) lands, ready to plant a UN flag, only to find a British Flag waiting for them, which is so delightfully funny and really sets the tone for the whole film.

JK: (clapping her hands and laughing) Oh yes, I loved that! I mean, that's wonderful.

I mean he just used to make me laugh so much!

And he'd think of things that... Well, I suppose he was just a total original. I remember we used to sit in the BBC canteen and look at all the people there and try to imagine, if they had tails, what sort of tails would they have. That was typical, the sort of mad, Tom idea. Because in those days it was very democratic and everybody ate there, from the head of the BBC downwards. Of course, it was a different world.

NS: *My impression was that, given that Tom knew how good he was at certain things — he absolutely knew how good he was at structure — he therefore perhaps didn't take so kindly to the way production in TV changed, the increased interference and so on. As I say, I think there's an impression that he was a little curmudgeonly, but in talking to people who knew him, that's not the way he comes across.*

JK: Well, in the last years of course... he wasn't getting enough blood to the brain. Which is why, when he thought of a good idea for another Quatermass, a sort of PRE-Quatermass, he couldn't write it.

NS: *Was that the Berlin setting [mentioned in Quatermass Memoirs] with the Olympics?*

JK: Yes. In those last years, he would say "I used to love words, and I can't remember them". And the other thing of course, which was a huge thing in his life, though he didn't talk about it was... when he was a little boy, they lived in Lancashire and of course they never saw the sun in those days, because of the industrial smog. And then one day it was a nice day and they went to the seaside. And it was a fine day. And Tom was two years

WE ARE THE MARTIANS

old and got dreadfully sunburned and got sand in it. And as a result of that he couldn't be in the sun. He always wore his hat because he couldn't be in the sun, and he wore gloves in the summer because he was terribly ill then . . . but people didn't know about the sun. And I think when he was eight they suddenly realised. I think he was on a school outing, and he was on a bus, and he sat by the window and the sun was coming right in and he got terribly ill, huge temperature, like a burn. Nobody knew what it was in those days. People used to rush and sit in the sun whenever they could, so it was very difficult for him . . .

Then during the war, a lot of soldiers got it in the desert. It was called "sandburn" I think. And then a little more was known about it. Somebody made up a mixture for him which was some kind of sun block, or sun cream . . . but in those days it was something unheard of.

It was a very sad thing for him. I mean, it was quite manageable, we knew about it. If we sat outside a restaurant we'd find a table that was half sun and half shade. But particularly when he was younger and travelling, it . . . in a way I suppose it was a blessing; he wanted to get in the air force and fly during the war, and would have been very good at it, and probably would have been killed in the 1940, when they were all killed those young boys. Of course, they wouldn't touch him, wouldn't take him. So I think he minded about that, of course he did. He used to say "The sun and I are enemies".

He didn't go in for self pity at all. Also—I know lots of things don't get made, but being ahead of his time, he was unlucky—I mean, this business about CROW[79] was nothing to do with him but so very disappointing.

And another film . . .

NS: CREATURE FROM THE BLACK LAGOON?

JK: No, I don't think he minded about that one so much. It was one which

---

[79] CROW was a long time passion project of Nigel's, factually based, about Manx Slaver Hugh Crow. He wrote it first as a series, then later as a feature and finally as a play. It evidently meant a great deal to him. The series version was commission by Lew Grade for ITV. Apparently Lord Grade had a falling out with the set designer, who wanted to spend more money than Lord Grade was willing. When the designer wouldn't back down, Grade cancelled it.

A Conversation with Judith Kerr

was actually about to be made in Spain. We were about to go out there... BRAVE NEW WORLD! With Jack Cardiff as director.

Anyway, we were ready to go out there. I think they'd found us a flat, and even a nursery for Tacy, the children were only little at the time. The director was already out there and he rang up to say "They're selling the cars!" They'd gone bust! But that's what films are like.

But it would have been a good one.

NS: *My feeling was always that the changes in television production meant it became a little bit more like the Hollywood studio system where their respect for the written word was. . . less. And for anyone who had achieved the amount that Tom had, and had the talent that Tom had, that would have been enormously frustrating.*

JK: Well, yes that's just the way it was. I'm very conscious of it because if you're doing picture books, the worst thing that can happen is that they print it badly, which can be absolutely maddening, if you've spent a year or whatever doing these drawings. But they don't usually get cancelled.

I don't know. I think the sun thing... was hard for him. Nowadays nobody would care a hoot! It would be so easy!

But it was difficult for him. There were things he couldn't do, and he would have loved to have done, like my son did and travel all over the world, which he did. He got the Somerset Maugham Award he went all over the place, he went all over Italy with his brother, Bryan, who was in Rome, he got the Rome Prize when Tom got the Somerset Maugham, which involved travel. He went to Germany and all sorts of things. I imagine though he probably did it in the winter or in early spring.

Before we were married, after Quatermass, we did go to Italy, and it was fine. We went all over the place, because he wanted to show me all the places that he'd been to with Bryan, because I didn't know it. We just had to be a bit careful you know, not rush out inot the middle of the sun. But it made a huge difference.

The last four years, when he wasn't well, I always thought it was just him, he was just himself, but just had odd moments. But the Doctor says no, he wasn't getting enough blood to the brain, but he was alright with me, nearly all the time—got a bit confused sometimes, but...

He had heart trouble at that time. No, I mean he made everybody laugh. He was 84 when he died, possibly a *bit* curmudgeonly, but then I think one's *allowed*!

NS: *To be perfectly honest, I think a lot of it is a result of their being relatively little documentation of his career and the production history of the things he made, but of what there is—a LOT of it is about his less than satisfactory experience working on* **HALLOWEEN III**. *It must have been immensely annoying to him, given that he removed his name from the film (at some cost to himself) because he felt the film was so bad, and yet he was linked with it in almost every article and review ever written "Based on a script by Nigel Kneale".*

JK: Did they?
I don't think he minded.

NS: *He's on record in interviews being quite harsh about the film.*

JK: It was a rotten film. But it hadn't been...
I don't think he was *terribly* upset about it, he thought it was very funny.
But one of the things that happened was, he thought a long time about taking his name off it, because of course it meant losing quite a lot of money. And then he thought "you can't leave it on this terrible film", and so he did. And in order to do that in those days, you had to send a telegram. And the way you sent it through was that you telephoned it through—you phoned a telegraph agency or something—and so he rang up this agency and dictated his telegram and the man who was taking it down, he sounded like a youth, said "John Carpenter!? Oh I love him!" which Tom thought was terribly funny.

NS: *It seems that Tom was not a man to suffer fools gladly.*

JK: Well, he wanted things to be good. I'm reckoned to be a very gentle

A Conversation with Judith Kerr

person, I think I am ... but if they don't print my stuff properly, I get very fierce. Because you *love* the stuff. It's your life. You make it as good as you can. You work and work to get it right. And you *know* when it's right. And if people start messing with it, you get cross.

I suppose ... all the Quatermass things, at the BBC, he never got paid what he should have—and I know Stephen [Durbridge, Kneale's agent] killed himself to try and sort it out but the BBC said as he'd written the first one in staff time, it therefore belonged to them, despite having *always* let him have it when it was a lesser thing, but because suddenly there was money there ...

And then the people who made the films they went bust and one man who wasn't a film-maker at all, he bought what was left of it. Stephen got it sorted so that the BBC would do something in partnership because there were lots of people wanted to remake the Quatermass films, big American companies and so on—and then it turned out that this man who had bought up what was left of it, had sold all sort of rights he didn't have, to all sorts of film companies, so it had become insoluable. Stephen worked and worked at it, he tried to get the rights back and, on the one hand the BBC had held on to the rights, and on the other this man had sold all sorts of film rights that he didn't have, so all sorts of film companies had claims to some aspect of them, which was useless to them. So he did have a certain amount of bad luck financially, but you know we've got this house. We bought this house with one film script. But I don't know what other screenwriters are like. Not getting things made seems the nature of the thing.

Perhaps ...

But when a talent of Kneale's calibre doesn't get to make **CROW, LORD OF THE FLIES, A BRAVE NEW WORLD, CREATURE FROM THE BLACK LAGOON, THE MAN WITH THE X-RAY EYES, THE BIG BIG GIGGLE,** *and no doubt many more ... I think it's the audience who really lose out.*

ON NIGEL KNEALE

Ramsey Campbell

I FIRST ENCOUNTERED NIGEL KNEALE WHEN I WAS NINE YEARS old—a rumour of his work, at any rate. A fellow pupil at Ryebank, my primary school, came in one morning eager to share the spectacle he'd seen last night on television. Sixty years later I still recall my shock at being told that some people were trapped in a factory by monsters, who then stuffed some of their victims into a pipe, from which—as my informant revelled in conveying—blood began to drip. I confess that I didn't entirely believe him; could you ever really see such a thing on television? I had little means of checking, since we didn't have a set at home, and so the image was stored in my mind as something I never expected to see. Who knows how an actual viewing would have affected me so young? The BBC Light Programme's radio serial *Journey Into Space* was already haunting my sleep, not least with the Martian mantra "Orders must be obeyed without question at all times." How disconcerted I was in later years to discover that the Martian and his minions, not to mention sundry other characters, came of David Jacobs putting on yet another voice.

At nine I had a curious and often erroneous view of the world, and at eleven too. That was when I first came upon Kneale by name, in Groff and Lucy Conklin's anthology *The Supernatural Reader,* and convinced myself that the title of his tale was pronounced Minnyewkay or

WE ARE THE MARTIANS

Minnyewkey if not Minnookey or Meenookey (I forget which I settled on). Much more to the point, the story stayed with me after dark for quite a few nights after I read it, especially the way the supernatural didn't simply invade the mundane but made use of familiar everyday items as uncanny tools. Kneale would have disapproved of my reading it so young, I gather, just as he felt his television work oughtn't to be watched by children. Myself, I think many of us who love the field start by reading books or watching films that might be considered unsuitable, and who knows whether he did as a child?

I came to Quatermass in my early teens, but only in book form. Penguin Books published the scripts of all three television serials. I assume someone felt that these scripts, like the Penguin editions of Tennessee Williams and other playwrights' work, could be read for pleasure as well as watched or performed. I certainly found them as readable and compelling as a good science fiction novel (some of which they rather resemble in terms of spare quick compelling prose, and I'm also put in mind of Ira Levin's *Rosemary's Baby*, a horror novel told very largely through dialogue). I have a persistent sense of having read the names of some of the episodes earlier than that—in a newspaper listing, perhaps, if not the *Radio Times*—and finding them ominously evocative: "The Bolts", "The Mark", "The Food", "The Coming"...For me often a title is all it takes.

The X certificate the first film celebrated with its British title (*The Quatermass Xperiment*) barred anybody under sixteen, or at least unable to feign the age, from seeing it on its original release, and I didn't catch it or its sequel until 1961. By then, sadly, I'd had problems with coming late in my life (or so it felt) to horror films with which I was already somewhat familiar. Since I was twelve I'd been coughing up my half a crown for *Famous Monsters of Filmland*, which meant that I knew quite a few of the classics far too much by heart—key shots and lines of dialogue as well— by the time I actually saw them. (One that suffered grievously was Browning's *Dracula*, which I could never engage with until I had the shining revelation of the recent Blu-ray release.) I was delighted, however, to find that having read the Quatermass scripts robbed the films of none of their power. The opening bars of James Bernard's score for *Xperiment*— a score almost as stark and radical as Bernard Herrmann's *Psycho* music—sets the tone for an uncommonly urgent piece of filmmaking, in which the script drives unstoppably forwards and delivers some genuine shocks along with much suspense and inventiveness. It's worth noting that the notion of film recovered from the crashed spaceship influenced Mario Bava in *Caltiki*, which borrows several elements from the first two Quatermass films (and that the use of fictitious recovered footage then extends through *Cannibal Holocaust* to *The Blair Witch Project* and beyond).

The headlong pace of *Xperiment* does leave behind some of Kneale's observation of his minor characters—bits of mundane behaviour that he rightly felt distinguished his narratives from most science fiction films, situating them in the everyday, following on from the likes of "Minuke" and from the seminal example of H. G. Wells. On the other hand, his exemplary sense of structure survives intact, and is as crucial to the effect of his best work as Lovecraft's was to his. He develops it in *Quatermass II*, where the narrative progresses through a series of revelations, each larger and more disquieting than the last. At fifteen I finally came face to face with the monsters that used their victims to block the pipe, and learned why. Among other things, the factory episode is a remarkable metaphor for the exploitation of labour.

Here I should confess to pinching from Kneale. His juxtapositions of the alien with the familiar may have influenced my stuff, though I was more aware that Fritz Leiber's forties fiction did, and there's one unmistakeable instance. At the very end of 1961 I wrote to August Derleth as follows:

"I have an idea for another story, which might conceivably reach novel length if I ever get to work on it. It'd deal with the Starkweather-Moore expedition mentioned in the MOUNTAINS OF MADNESS—could you tell me if it was ever actually said to be an American expedition? I don't have access to a copy at present, but I hope it wasn't another Miskatonic-sponsored expedition) into the same regions as the former party. They discover a dome-shaped metal object at the center of a zone of extreme cold. Meanwhile, at the same time in England, a number of people in the Severn area are apparently infected with some unknown virus, which subjects them to catalepsy and involuntary actions of a seemingly meaningless type. When they begin to converge on an uninhabited area near Brichester, it becomes evident that they are under some sort of hypnotic control from an unknown source. When the Starkweather-Moore party return to England after various disturbing experiences, a few of the scientists in the group visit the area where the hypnotized men have gathered. By now the men are engaged in activity, while some of them have procured guns and are actually shooting at anybody who approaches the region—even planes which the army has patrolling overhead! There seems to be no way to restrain them short of opening fire on them, since they have even got gas-masks which they still owned from the last war—thus ruling out the use of tear-gas—and as what they are doing with materials taken from a local building site seems harmless—even meaningless—the police have merely evacuated surrounding habitations and cordoned off the area, keeping the planes patrolling in case of new developments. The scientists are taken up in one of the planes for a view of what the men are building—and are startled considerably. For what is taking shape, 100 feet high, in the concrete from the building site below is a replica of the dome in the center of the ice at the Pole . . . The story continues from there and I think I might be able to make something of it."

I never did, and I suspect Kneale's admirers would have readily spotted the source if I had.

Did any of them deduce that X *The Unknown* had been proposed as a Quatermass sequel? It would have fallen between the first two Quatermass films, but Kneale vetoed the proposal. No doubt he would have been as unhappy with Dean Jagger as he was with Brian Donleavy, though both give perfectly creditable performances (admittedly, in terms of the narratives, American without explanation). Indeed, in *Danse Macabre* Stephen King enthuses at length over Donleavy's portrayal of the scientist, finding it fruitfully ambiguous. Like the two Kneale films, X brings the amorphously monstrous into everyday British settings. If it illuminates those less than Kneale's scripts did and is relatively short of cumulative revelations, Jimmy Sangster nevertheless does a creditable job. Quatermass wasn't the only model for this magpie screenwriter; in *The Brides of Dracula* he

On Nigel Kneale

would borrow a scene with a padlocked coffin from M. R. James, and in his screen treatment for X he describes the menace as "a dark seething putrid mass writhing with corruption and hideous rottenness giving off unctuous oily bubbles". I imagine some of my readers will recognise how much this resembles a line in Arthur Machen's "Novel of the White Powder".

I celebrated my age of majority (the year of it, anyway) with *Quatermass and the Pit*, at last on the big screen. I thought then that it was Kneale's filmic masterpiece, and I still do. It's the most elaborate and most fully developed of his structures, built up in a series of glimpses of the truth, each giving way to something larger and more terrible beyond them. The soldier who dismisses the disinterred alien relics as a failed Nazi plot to undermine morale is just one of many masterstrokes I can't imagine from anyone but Kneale. On the other hand, Quatermass's famous final declaration that "We are the Martians" surely echoes Gerald Kersh's 1954 short story "Men Without Bones" (in which the discovery of an apparently extraterrestrial species leads to the revelation that "Those boneless things are men. We are Martians!") I do also find echoes of Lovecraft, specifically *At The Mountains Of Madness*, which it resembles both in its construction and in the idea that the human race was created by aliens (though Kneale hadn't read his predecessor: he seems to have acknowledged few of those except for M. R. James). The script is fine enough to survive one dire special effect—the vision of the marching Martians, whose rudimentary nature even filming out of focus can't disguise. (Decades later they were topped by the wonderfully comical Bruno Mattei and his swarming rats, which seem to have been created the same way.) And the role of Barbara Judd might have been written for the splendid Barbara Shelley, who perfects the portrayal of transformation she first displayed in *Cat Girl*, a bizarre British bid to marry Monogram monstrousness (that obligatory beast in the cellar!) to a Val Lewton theme.

1972 brought *The Stone Tape*, which is for me the final work of his creative peak. Like *Quatermass and the Pit* (and also some of Lovecraft's later tales and Richard Matheson's *I Am Legend*) it reimagines the supernatural in scientific terms without by any means dispelling the sense of dread. Indeed, that's a structural element: in both films the apparently

WE ARE THE MARTIANS

supernatural is rationalised only to lead to further terrors. Again, the special effects may most kindly be described as basic, but the intellectual power of Kneale's concepts lends them a real sense of disquiet. I'd call the film the culmination of an approach that Kneale made very much his own.

Few of us could keep up that splendid standard. *The Quatermass Conclusion* is more curmudgeonly than visionary, and the development of its themes is thin compared with its predecessors. Admittedly it took several years to see production, but even if it had been filmed earlier it might have seemed painfully dated. *The Woman in Black* is a fine adaptation of a good book, and less eager to chuck in extra shocks than the Hammer version, though Susan Hill reportedly disliked it and blocked a later release. *Stanley and the Women* solves the problem of Kingsley Amis's first-person narrative (in which the late Harry Harrison maintained that all the female characters were aspects of Elizabeth Jane Howard) by siding with the women, presumably on the basis that Stanley's vision is misogynistically warped. The adaptation earned Kneale considerable praise from Amis, himself a Quatermass admirer.

I'm afraid I was disappointed in *Beasts* at the time, and rewatching the various episodes has failed to change my mind; they feel overlong for their ideas or else for their development. Despite the changes made to Kneale's script (which, according to Dennis Etchison, was originally more anti-Irish than the film), I persist in finding *Halloween III: Season of the Witch* stimulating in the manner of his best work. Yes, some of the violence is unnecessary, especially the drill scene (why would such a strong assailant need a weapon at all, other than to vary the gruesomeness?), but the film benefits from the play of ideas that informed Kneale's greatest achievements, and I assume its use of Stonehenge derives from an abandoned element of *The Quatermass Conclusion* (which was originally to use that location).

What of his continuing influence? John Carpenter acknowledged it, of course, by writing *Prince of Darkness* as Martin Quatermass. Though Kneale was peeved by the tribute, it's appropriate, since the film celebrates the play of multiple ideas as wittily as Kneale's own work. No such overt admission can be found in *Poltergeist*, though Spielberg's film (or, if you will, Hooper's) plays like an extended adaptation of "Minuke". My good friend John Llewellyn Probert pointed out while we were watching *Network* recently that Paddy Chayevsky's vision was anticipated by Kneale in the comparably acerbic *Year of the Sex Olympics*, another black satire on television by a television writer. James Herbert regarded some of his early work (especially *The Fog*) as continuing Kneale's tradition, and Steve King seems to have learned from him, but by far the most inventive inheritor of Kneale's conceptual prodigiousness is Kim Newman—look for the traces yourself. And the things from Kneale's Pit live on: Hob's Lane looms ominously in the *Zombie Apocalypse* trilogy created by Steve Jones.

Let me end on two personal notes, as if the rest of this has been anything but personal. Given how much Kneale deplored the early *Doctor Who* for scaring children, I imagine that he may have been offended to find his tale "The Pond" in *The Gruesome Book*. I bought it from his agent without establishing that the anthology was aimed at children—at the time I didn't realise that Kneale might be unhappy about this. No doubt he wouldn't have cared for the ambition my Glaswegian editor proposed: she wanted me to collect tales that would turn the reader's troosers broon. I felt I was putting together an anthology of the kind of tale that I'd read as a child, but now it would be pitched to that readership. I never heard that the publisher received any complaints.

So how would Kneale have liked to be remembered? Not as a horror writer, certainly. "Jesus Christ!" he remarked to Andy Murray. "To want to be thought of like that I find, well, horrific!" Might he prefer to be feted for science fiction? Perhaps not, to judge by his description of the 1979 Worldcon in Brighton, where he said he'd been "surrounded by loonies" who "all go there in depressingly large quantities and dress up as fairies or bogeys or werewolves." I have to admit I didn't, though I was there, along with Fritz Leiber, Kneale's predecessor in fantastic urban horror, and many other professionals. Still, Kneale "hated them and couldn't wait to get out. That gave me a desire to show them up, show how awful they are" (which led to his television serial *Kinvig*).

I'd read none of these comments at the turn of the century, when the Horror Writers Association asked me and other recent recipients of the Lifetime Award to recommend candidates for it. Would I have named

WE ARE THE MARTIANS

him if I'd been aware of his views? I believe I would. He was at the top of my list, and at least one other member of the informal jury (the late Charles L. Grant) agreed. I've no idea what Kneale's reaction to receiving the award may have been, but I'm glad he got it. It's remarkable how many writers, despite ranging widely across genres, come to be remembered only for their work in the fantastic. I suspect that Kneale will continue to be celebrated for his science fiction and, yes, horror. His best work is incomparable and deserves a place high in the pantheon.

THE QUATERMASS LEGACY
A Personal Reflection On Kneale And His Influence

David Pirie

QUATERMASS. THE NAME IS NOT MERELY A CODE FOR ALL horror fans. It is also (and this is remarkable) *still* vaguely familiar to young people. And yet nothing new has come out of it in thirty six years. And that last hurrah — in itself very much a delayed tail-end — was made before even Margaret Thatcher ruled Britain.

Of course there is constant talk of a Quatermass revival. A few years back Hugh Laurie was the favoured name but anyone making the attempt faces a tangle of contractual problems within the late writer's estate that seem somehow appropriate since Kneale never wanted anyone else to do it. And he had a point. It will be a lot easier to find an actor to play Quatermass than to find a plot that gets anywhere near his creator's originality.

Kneale's achievements look increasingly epic as time goes on. Without him, would there even have been a British horror revival? Probably not, for Hammer only turned to horror because of his success with THE QUATERMASS EXPERIMENT and they even tried to get him to give them copyright in the character. I loved Kneale's typical response to this: 'I was actually approached by them (Hammer) and asked if they could use the character of Professor Quatermass. I said 'No you can't it's mine.' They were funny people.'

As this remark shows Nigel Kneale (known to his friends as Tom) was his own man and not given to any sort of compromise. He was in his way a visionary and I could never forget being exposed to that vision in my first year at primary school, when QUATERMASS 2 was broadcast at 8.00 every Saturday night. There was no watershed in those days, just a warning that the show was not 'for those of nervous disposition' which might be considered a pretty major understatement. For there were elements of QUATERMASS 2 that could not pass the UK film censor even as an 'X' certificate (16 and over) when Hammer filmed it years later.

And aspects of it today, yes even in the GAME OF THRONES era, would give most TV producers pause. When was the last time you saw a contemporary thriller set in the UK in which men are reduced to human pulp to block a pipe or a family with very young children on a holiday outing to the seaside are slaughtered at close quarters by men with machine guns? (OK the actual execution was only heard but all else was

The Quatermass Legacy

shown). Now in the same slot you will see The National Lottery! It is measure of Kneale's wild genius that he took us miles outside the normal boundaries.

And not, by the way, for reasons of pure sensationalism. Not for a minute. This was subversive genre fiction with a capital S, far more so than its predecessor THE QUATERMASS EXPERIMENT. Kneale was not a political writer in the narrow sense, but he hated the stifling autocratic Tory Britain of the 50s with its complacency and secrecy. So the serial was specifically designed to use the classic alien theme of possession to express these views in a knife edge suspense thriller as full of sardonic wit as it was full of terror.

The show was prophetic too: only months after it appeared the truth about the deadly Windscale nuclear reactor fire of 1957 was suppressed on direct orders of then Prime Minister Harold Macmillan and — with cows visibly dying in the fields — even meteorological records were altered to pretend that the radioactivity had not been spread. The fire itself was directly related to the fact the reactor was secretly doubling as an H bomb

WE ARE THE MARTIANS

factory. Here is the UK QUATERMASS 2 chronicles—a place of criminal lies—and it does so via a wonderful central conceit: that a government populated by faceless (and brainwashed) bureaucrats is breeding vicious poison as a new atmosphere for aliens under the pretence of making 'synthetic food'. It always struck me as beautifully apposite that the 'plant at Winnerden Flats' appears, from the script's geography, to be fairly near Windscale. And its 'pressure domes' housing poisonous monsters resemble nuclear reactors more than anything else.

All of this made QUATERMASS 2 a Kafkaesque nightmare with a hard kernel of truth. By comparison Kneale's other masterpiece QUATERMASS AND THE PIT was more concerned with religion and anthropology while QUATERMASS/THE QUATERMASS CONCLUSION was a slight misfire, commenting on the hippie era but, thanks to the BBC's timidity, arriving far too late. Its packaging on ITV was also for me too anodyne to pack Kneale's usual punch.

The first three Quatermass serials, though, are the real deal and as a child not surprisingly I found QUATERMASS 2 a revelation. There are poetic fairy- tale aspects to its first episode that hooked me utterly: the idea of roads that lead nowhere, government notices that warn of forbidden zones, massed dark figures on the skyline, miles of threatening yet deserted countryside and the magical if menacing 'plant' viewed from far away. It also strongly conveyed the notion, fascinating to any child, that authority might be both dull and evil. Seen at a time when children were expected to watch boring patriotic war films and so much young programming was utterly patronizing–how to build boats with matchsticks–it was just what I needed.

As a result I recall with incredible vividness the viewing of each episode in our family sitting-room, sometimes alone, sometimes with my sisters (my parents were to their great credit highly positive about the whole experience but watched only intermittently, being out or busy). And I was stunned too by the incredibly spooky episode titles, which haunt me still. 'The Destroyers', 'The Frenzy', 'The Coming', The Food', 'The Mark', 'The Bolts'. At school on Monday I could talk of nothing else and I think I would date the start of any capacity to invent that I have from those Saturday night viewings.

The Quatermass Legacy

But it would be more than twenty years before I met their creator. It happened while I was at Time Out and, for the first time in a while, the Hammer film of **QUATERMASS II** was shown on TV. For some reason I was in favour with a Radio 4 arts show at the time and they actually agreed with my suggestion we should do an item about the screening and interview Kneale.

He was suffering from a bad cold and, looking back, I suspect such interviews were quite a chore for him. But the bonus was we had to go to his house to record it and I talked to him in the end-of terrace home overlooking Barnes common where he had lived and worked for quite a while.

No doubt the cold did not help but I recall that, when we first got there, he expressed amazement we were bothering to cover 'that thing on TV' (the Hammer **QUATERMASS II**) at all. It was not as well known then as it is now that Kneale had strong views about the first two Hammer films, even though he had co-written the script of QUATERMASS II. In particular he absolutely loathed the casting of Bryan Donlevy as Quatermass.

When I first saw the film years after its release I was not worried by Donlevy because (though clearly cast for the US market) I could not consciously recall ever seeing the actor before and he seemed passable as a determined and stubborn Canadian scientist. But in retrospect I can imagine the sheer horror Kneale must have felt at the thought of an actor who had played gangland bosses, tough cowboys and illiterate hoodlums masquerading as his beloved Professor. Quatermass, after all, was clearly a bit of an alter ego for Kneale, the scientist expressed Kneale's own views and explored his own fears. He was also an unlikely, almost anti-heroic, figure representing rationality and dogged determination in a baffling universe. Donlevy would have seemed to Kneale like a mockery of all this and he took it personally.

That was understandable but still I think an over-reaction. For, when suitably edited, Donlevy's rugged energy works well enough in the film, combining with James Bernard's remarkable nerve-jangling crescendo of strings to evoke a tone of muted hysteria. On this first encounter with Kneale I noted his criticism but made it clear that for me the material still shone and after that he settled down to talk, in a fascinating way, about how he had seen England change for the worse in the 50s, the spread of secrecy, the nuclear culture, the government installations and no go areas which seemed to spring up overnight. By the end he had relaxed completely and talked with some excitement about his current project the BEASTS anthology (covered elsewhere). I left him to nurse his cold, now well aware that the refreshing thing about Kneale, unlike other screenwriters, was that he was quite prepared to speak his mind.

It was also obvious that his mental outlook was coloured by a bracing and uncompromising pessimism. My book A HERITAGE OF HORROR was, I guess, among the first to analyse Kneale's work and also to ruminate on the cold war paranoid themes of the 1950s. **QUATERMASS II** fell into this category, one of the masterpieces of the genre. But I was fascinated to find that Kneale quarreled with the whole notion. He argued the adjective 'paranoid', was unfair as a description of the period because the times were so dangerous and the possibility of nuclear war so real. I was, he said, failing to understand that in the 50s people had seriously begun to wonder if they would ever see the 60s at all and they had excellent grounds for doing so. With crisis after crisis and two opposing nuclear powers armed to the teeth how could they have felt otherwise?

The Quatermass Legacy

Being an optimist, looking at the period, I don't necessarily agree. But who cares when it shaped such a phenomenal vision? The notion of nuclear apocalypse clearly haunted Kneale and reappeared again and again in scripts like THE ROAD and THE CREATURE (filmed as **THE ABOMINABLE SNOWMAN**) to amazing effect. He was a visionary, but a very dark one. Producers were often amazed by his ability to think way outside the box as in the breathtakingly prophetic YEAR OF THE SEX OLYMPICS. But sometimes his predictions proved wrong. In the last Quatermass (and in the fascinating 1996 QUATERMASS MEMOIRS on Radio 3) London becomes a semi-derelict no go zone with massive crime and mercenary police ('paycops'). Here was surely the weakest of Kneale's dystopian visions since what actually happened to London was almost exactly the opposite.

Sometime in the 1980s the National Film Theatre got round to a season celebrating Kneale's collaboration with the great TV director Rudolph Cartier, an emigre from Hitler's Germany (his mother died in the Holocaust) who had directed much of Kneale's finest work including the first three Quatermass serials and many of the single dramas. Cartier proved an extraordinarily imaginative film-making partner for Kneale, adding a touch of realism and also expressionism. The two worked very closely, so closely that in QUATERMASS 2 Kneale voiced the slightly sinister recaps at the start of each episode and is also heard over the loud-speakers at the plant.

There was a party to celebrate the NFT season and here I met Kneale for the second time and we talked about THE STONE TAPE and why at that point it had never been repeated by the BBC. He told me that a junior BBC exec had been delegated to watch it in order to see if it was appropriate for a repeat. The man had come back to report that it was not worth the trouble and Kneale made no attempt to hide his fury. At this point in the conversation something slightly unexpected happened, which has stuck in my mind. Someone appeared at our side, ignored Kneale, the guest of honour and started complimenting me on my first TV film RAINY DAY WOMEN which had just come out. I was a bit stunned. Grateful of course, but it just felt so weird to be suddenly talking about RAINY DAY WOMEN at a celebration for (and right in front of) the man

183

who had inspired it. Yet I couldn't say anything without sounding false and I have a memory of Kneale standing a little bemused as the party moved on.

You could say I was over-reacting but the truth was Kneale *had* inspired my first ever production. Of course it was not about aliens from outer space (though it is about imminent invasion) but, while writing it, I had been haunted by the idea of reproducing the tension and menace in an isolated and threatened rural community that had first electrified me when watching QUATERMASS 2. In RAINY DAY WOMEN's opening sequence I had even tried to recapture some of the feeling of the journey of Quatermass and Dillon (renamed Marsh in the Hammer film) as they travel down unmapped roads to Winnerden Flats. I had Truman (Charles Dance) driving deep into the isolated rural wilds of 1940s England at a time when maps were forbidden, petrol was rationed and signposts deliberately turned. I could hardly however explain any of this to Kneale and I didn't try.

But, as things turned out, (and it's the reason I recount such a trivial incident) the chance did come. It happened at our third and last meeting many years later in 1999 when a weekend school was organized in Cardiff to honour Kneale and show much of his work. The organizers were anxious to import some writers who had been influenced by him and the two chosen were myself and horror writer (of **GOTHIC** and GHOST WATCH and many others) Stephen Volk.

I was given a slot to explain to him and the assembled guests how he'd influenced me. This time I did not hesitate. I talked of that amazing viewing experience I had as a child. I explained how it struck so many chords, not least because there were two secret installations near my town in Scotland, with barbed wire and scary warning notices as well as (though we did not know it then) a hidden top secret bunker from which the cold war could be run. The bunker had been disguised as an ordinary isolated cottage though it was actually made of metal! My father, who fished the river nearby, once even pointed the lonely place out to me as a child and told me he thought there was something very strange about it!

I had also secured a movie print of RAINY DAY WOMEN and now I showed him on the big screen the opening ten minutes and pointed out the parallels with the start of QUATERMASS 2.

The Quatermass Legacy

He saw it at once and was, I like to think, slightly amazed. The rest of the session and those that followed were highly memorable and, by the time he left, his whole manner to me had changed. It was gentle and warm, very different from how I had ever seen him. Close to the end of the session many asked Kneale why he had not written an autobiography. It turned out he had no interest in the idea at all. He still had scripts he wanted to write. But alas his last show, an episode of KAVANAGH QC had already aired two years earlier. Nobody knew that at the time. I hoped there would be far more. But I did at least feel as I left that at last I had done what I wanted to do when we first met. Explain to him how much his work had meant, honour the debt. It was a good feeling.

Mark Gatiss, who writes the foreword to this book, paid a very welcome tribute to Kneale after his death, emphasising that he was among the first rank of British television writers, but had been overlooked in favour of the Alan Bleasdales and Alan Bennetts and Dennis Potters. He pointed out this was largely to do with a kind of snobbery in the UK about fantasy and science fiction.

I strongly agree. In terms of TV and film there has always been a tendency for realism and issue-based drama (and also sometimes comedy) to get serious attention here and for fantasy and suspense and mystery to go unheralded. There are almost certainly major historical and cultural roots for this, which run far deeper than any minor prejudice. They may well connect to the whole British documentary tradition, to our tabloid and newspaper culture and (in terms of comedy) to music hall and theatre.

Of course Gatiss was writing in 2006 and it would be nice to think the recent acceptance of quality genre shows to which he has contributed like DOCTOR WHO and SHERLOCK imply a change. But I don't think I will be truly convinced until another 'Quatermass', comes along and starts winning awards. There are, however, good reasons for optimism: we have come a long way since Hitchcock was dismissed as a shock merchant and Hammer was reviled.

As to Kneale, he may not have generated the same mountain of newspaper copy or awards as a Dennis Potter. But there is another way of looking at this. People may admire Potter's work but they don't on the

We Are The Martians

whole seek to emulate it. And fashions fade. In contrast, it is almost impossible to overestimate the impact Kneale had on the whole horror, fantasy and thriller genres. Hundreds of other writers took his work on board, film after film betrayed his influence. A whole generation of top US directors and writers sang their admiration.

It is as if in movies, TV and books, genre progresses through a series of metaphorical prison walls. Inferior and derivative work merely scratches the surface, some not even that. But the giants—the geniuses and serious innovators—smash the walls down before our eyes, allowing whole new narratives to be born. And the myths that result from this are with us forever, a PETER PAN, a DRACULA, a QUATERMASS. Kneale was such a giant and he transformed our world.

CREEPING UNKNOWN PT 1

The Lesser Known Kneale

Kim Newman

KIM NEWMAN IS THE CRITIC THAT OTHER FILM CRITICS GO TO, *to check their facts.*

A Contributing Editor to Sight & Sound *and* Empire Magazine, *he is the author of* NIGHTMARE MOVIES, BFI Classics *texts on* **CAT PEOPLE** *and* **QUATERMASS AND THE PIT**, *and a book on* Doctor Who *for the* BFI Television Classics *series.*

Novelist, Broadcaster and Semi Professional Kazoo player, Kim also has a lifelong relationship with the work of Nigel Kneale: the Ray Harryhausen movie **FIRST MEN IN THE MOON**, *directed by Nathan Juran and scripted by Kneale (from the book by H.G. Wells) was the first film that Kim ever saw in a cinema. One might therefore legitimately claim that the subsequent direction of Kim's life was—at least in part—Kneale's fault. Kim has appeared in numerous documentaries and DVD/BluRay extras talking about Kneale and his work, and in 2001 accompanied him on the commentary track for the BFI DVD release of* THE STONE TAPE.

Here, Kim offers us something about the less seen, less available, but no less important titles from the canon of Nigel Kneale.

WE ARE THE MARTIANS

WUTHERING HEIGHTS (1962)

In 1953, BBC producer Rudolph Cartier had Nigel Kneale do a rush job adapting Emily Bronte's novel for a live TV production starring Richard Todd and Yvonne Mitchell. In May 1962, Cartier dusted off the script and remounted it with a sexier cast, though Kneale oddly goes uncredited on screen or in the *Radio Times* listing (in the 1960s, several Kneale BBC adaptation jobs were similarly remade — notably his version of 1984).

Confined to the interiors of Wuthering Heights (grim) and the Grange (luxurious), with a single token against-a-cyclorama moor scene, this studio drama has to take Yorkshire scenery on trust, but focuses intently on the character interplay. Unlike many adaptors, Kneale opens with an unambiguous supernatural element: Lockwood (Ronald Howard), the new owner of the Grange, has to stay at the Heights thanks to a blizzard and is put in Cathy's old room, where the scratching of a tree at the window segues into Cathy's ghost's calling and a glimpse of the cold, dead, clutching girl. It's also a rare adaptation which stresses that the heroine is just as demented in her own way as Heathcliff (played by Keith Michell), and keeps highlighting incidental cruelties to illuminate the central tragic relationship. Of course, Bloom (as Cathy) is the biggest star here so there must have been an incentive to make a showpiece for her, and she is mercurially fascinating in a part too often played as simply pretty and vapid. Cathy is a wild spirit even when seduced by the ways of gentlefolk, capriciously loving and cruel by turns, while Keith Michell (later a UK TV star as Henry VIII) makes a finely glowering, intelligent Heathcliff, seething at the wrongs done to him and pitiless in taking revenge on the deserving and undeserving alike.

This is a production which has to have contact-free stage-fighting for many of the physical confrontations, but makes up for it with savagery in the dialogue (much of it high-flown gothic straight from the book)...when he has admitted that he has only married her for the "loathing", Isabella (June Thorburn) begs Heathcliff to strangle her, but he breaks off while she can still draw breath and coldly tells her he wants to draw out the torture as long as possible. Edgar Linton, who David Niven said was the most wretched role in English literature, is played by a pre-

UNCLE David McCallum with an elaborate hydrocephalic hairdo and an infuriatingly genteel manner—but even he turns nasty, calling in servants with guns to turf the troublemaker out of his house. Patrick Troughton, the second Doctor Who, takes the role of Hindley, the alcoholic and abusive brother who is usually made out to be the villain of the piece, and delivers a splendidly terrified, gutless, brutal and doomed reading of the part.

Kneale was always good at rum old country folk, and there's wonderful hypocritical viciousness from Frank Crawshaw as the Bible-reading servant who is rude to everyone, and—in a strong set-piece—makes a great show at sneering at poor Isabella's attempts to make porridge. Much of the narrative falls to Ellen (Jean Anderson, who has the most consistent accent), the sympathetic servant who explains the ghost story to Lockwood. It rattles through the plot, highlighting scenes of characters clutching each other with love or hate, but a few snippets seem to be missing from the surviving master tape—Cathy's death takes place in an ellipsis around a reel change, when only a few crucial seconds gone astray make a difference to the impact of the piece. WUTHERING HEIGHTS still gets redone for television or cinema every few years, so that versions jostle with each other for attention—because it's studio-based drama, this can't rely on the landscape the way most adaptations do, but that forces it to come to grips with Bronte's cast of demented, doomed characters.

"THE CRUNCH" (STUDIO 64: "THE CRUNCH") (1964)

Though the bulk of his TV work before the mid-1970s was for the BBC, Nigel Kneale wrote this hour-long suspense piece for ATV's STUDIO 64 series of one-off plays. It has resonances with his other work (not least Anthony Bushell of QUATERMASS AND THE PIT back in uniform as another army officer bristling unhelpfully behind sandbags at the site of a crisis in London) and again manages to distil an extraordinarily complex, multi-layered drama into a tight, thoughtful piece.

In a strangely-empty terrace as an irritating constant beeping of massed car-horns assaults the ears, a milkman (Cyril Renison) tries to deliver to the shabby house that serves as the Embassy of the independent Republic of Makang, a former island colony, and is beaten up and thrown down the front stairs, his smashed bottles revealing a listening device he has failed to plant. Pulling back behind the lines, we find we're in a siege situation and Prime Minister Goddard (Harry Andrews) is being pressured by Mr Ken (Maxwell Shaw), the Makangese ambassador, to pay several hundred million pounds in reparation for all the tin mined from the island over the century it was part of the Empire.

In Kneale's usual manner, evidence is brought in—from puzzled artisans and a safe-cracker dying of radiation poisoning, solicited by various experts on weapons and politics—which forces the PM to believe the Makangese have built a small nuclear weapon in the basement of the Embassy and have the will to set it off at midnight if the demands aren't met. A wonderfully subtle moment comes when the bland, reassuring boffin (John Gabriel) assures the PM that what the enemy have doesn't even really count as a bomb ("more a small thermo-nuclear device")— only to squash momentary hope by stating that it could still go off and level London. The army, represented by a harassed general (Bushell) and a gung ho captain (Peter Bowles) who is all for blacking up and storming the building, urge action, but Goddard parlays with the Ambassador— who makes a dignified, persuasive case against Britain and for the native culture which has been overwritten—and decides he has to make a deal. However, Ken is himself nagged to extreme measures, by tortured-to-the-point of madness premier Jimson (Wolfe Morris), who always intended to destroy London rather than take the money. With Jimson locked into the vault, Ken—a master of "the dark path", a fakir-style discipline built on ignoring pain—volunteers to confront him, knowing he can take twenty-five bullets in the chest (which he does, bloodily enough for Peckinpah) and distract the maniac momentarily so the bomb can be switched off.

The addition of a mystic, fantastical element is suprisingly potent, drawing on an aspect of "Makangese" culture the British have supposedly wiped out (Jimson is also a practitioner of 'the dark path') along with the native names, dress and tableware the Ambassador resumes when he has the upper hand. Kneale is masterly when it comes to detail, building a whole backstory for his invented island and giving even walk-on characters depth: an old colonial soak (Carl Bernard), who fled Makang on

Creeping Unknown PT 1

Independence Day and is terrified of Jimson, suggests in a single inter-rupted line ("I was with a young—") that he is one of those pederast beachcombers who drifted to the ends of Empire to have access to the native boys. Morris, a Kneale regular from THE CREATURE to "Buddyboy", was often cast in "ethnic" roles in the 1960s: his semi-Asiatic features work well in the context of an imaginary Eastern country, and if he is the only player to go over the top it's probably inevitable given the kind of lunatic Jimson is supposed to be. Maxwell Shaw, a familiar bit-player who seldom rose to leading parts, gets the role of his career as the enigmatic, civilised, desperate Ambassador. Also in the cast: Hira Talfrey (**THE CURSE OF THE WEREWOLF**) as the Ambassador's wife and thir-teen-year-old Olivia Hussey as one of the Ambassador's daughters.

Long thought lost, this play was rediscovered in the archive and screened at the BFI Southbank in 2006.

1984 (1965)

In 1954, BBC television transmitted an adaptation of George Orwell's novel NINETEEN EIGHTY-FOUR, adapted by Nigel Kneale, produced (which, in the TV terms of the time, also means directed) by Rudolph Cartier and starring Peter Cushing, Andre Morell and Yvonne Mitchell. This production remains famous, for the controversy raised by its horrific (though not, it seems, politcal) content, and as an early example of serious science fiction on television. As it happens, the book had been adapted a year earlier for American television's STUDIO ONE anthology, with Eddie Albert, Lorne Greene and Norma Crane.[80] One of the reasons the '54 1984 is so well-remembered is that it was broadcast at a time when the UK only had one television channel, which meant owners of television sets tended to watch anything—including programs they would (and did) avoid when given the choice after ITV (known for decades as 'the other side') started. The debate this raised within the BBC led in 1965 to the launch of BBC2, conceived as a home for programs the corporation

---

[80] This 1984 is available on DVD in the STUDIO ONE ANTHOLOGY box set along with the orig-inal TV version of 12 ANGRY MEN and other interesting, ambitious productions.

WE ARE THE MARTIANS

deemed more adult, esoteric or experimental. If you didn't like it or made your head hurt, you could turn back to THE BLACK AND WHITE MINSTREL SHOW or THE MAN FROM UNCLE on BBC1.[81] Just after BBC2 launched, it had an Orwell Season, consisting of documentaries, talks and three adaptations broadcast in the *Theatre 625* anthology slot. The climax of the 'World of George Orwell' strand was a redo of Kneale's 1984, broadcast on November 28, 1965.

Long thought lost, this 1984 was among the trove of BBC-TV productions found last year in the US Library of Congress, and was shown at the BFI Southbank in a season of these rediscoveries. Sadly, a brief section of the second reel was damaged—the section deals with the growing relationship between Winston Smith and Julia. When I interviewed Nigel Kneale in the 1990s, he was fairly dismissive of the second 1984 and gave the impression that it was a simple restaging of his 1954 script, though he remained impressed by Joseph O'Conor's interpretation of the role of the torturer O'Brien as "a fallen priest".[81] Actually, his script was worked over quite thoroughly, bringing in elements of the novel omitted the first time, and changing the emphases. Directed by Christopher Morahan (**ALL NEAT IN BLACK STOCKINGS, CLOCKWISE, PAPER MASK**), who had also done "Keep the Aspidistra Flying" and "Coming Up for Air" for THEATRE 625, the remake is forced to lower the ages of Winston (David Buck) and Julia (Jane Merrow). With only nineteen years 'til 1984, this had to be done so the characters would have only a dim memory of life before "the Revolution". This, not incidentally, makes it a story of youth protest rather than an intellectual rebellion against the state. Buck and Merrow are sexier than Cushing and Mitchell and vaguer in their beliefs. They even seem naively dangerous when they go along with the suggestion that throwing sulphuric acid in a child's face would be acceptable if it advanced the cause. Kneale was cynical about youth culture (see the Planet People of QUATERMASS) and, understandably but intriguingly,

---

[81] Now, a channel would get more complaints if it put out THE BLACK AND WHITE MINSTREL SHOW than if it broadcast **A SERBIAN FILM** uncut before the watershed.

[82] In the 1956 1984, O'Brien is renamed O'Connor because Edmond O'Brien was cast as Winston Smith; now, he's O'Brien again and played by an O'Conor – whose slight, amiable Irish accent makes the terrifying speeches all the chillier.

Creeping Unknown PT 1

had come to dislike the *performances* of Buck and Merrow when what I suspect he really disliked were the *characters* they played (which he had written). Both leads strike me as rather good, given that everyone who plays the parts has to cope with the fact that the novel (written by a man with severe, terminal health issues) is so despairing that its hero and heroine are tentative rebels at best, utterly crushed by the climax (it wasn't until I saw this adaptation that I noticed how the gin-soaked, broken Winston of the last scene prefigures Nicolas Roeg's **THE MAN WHO FELL TO EARTH**).

Morahan didn't have to stage the whole thing live, and apparently had bigger, more elaborate sets—but this feels more claustrophobic than the 1954 production. No matter how grim they might be, dystopiae are all satiric—highlighting contemporary horrors by exaggerated extrapolation. The 1945 version is relentlessly grim, but the 1965 is moving towards the horror-comedy vision of the future Kneale would advance in THE YEAR OF THE SEX OLYMPICS and WINE OF INDIA (which is, tragically, lost). On its first publication, NINETEEN EIGHTY-FOUR was often read as a simple indictment of Stalinism (or fascism), which must have irritated Orwell no end, and 1950s adaptations (Michael Anderson directed the 1956 film with Edmond O'Brien looking like Tony Hancock as Winston and Jan Sterling as the most glamorous member of the Anti-Sex League ever) could be sold as anti-communist propaganda. By the mid-60s, that aspect had faded and Orwell's warning about the incipient totalitarianism of all governments (inspired, in part, by working for the BBC during WWII) was more apparent. This production opens with an atomic war in the (then) near-future, even making a reference to **DR STRANGELOVE** (casualties figured in megadeaths), to explain how the world of Big Brother comes about. To acknowledge the space age, Britain is no longer Airstrip One but Pad One (as in launch-pad, not crash-pad). In tune with the 1960s, there's an emphasis on the state's involvement in the creation of junk culture, with a manufactured pop song (a trivial lyric with a military band beat—truly horrible) running through the show like a virus (prefiguring Peter Watkin's 1967 **PRIVILEGE**) and Julia toiling over a computer device that manufactures pornographic novels for the proles which are distributed

WE ARE THE MARTIANS

in plain wrappers to encourage the idea that they are illegal (and thus taking attention away from any actually subversive literature out there).[83] By 1965, the world of 1984 was starting to seem comic—a process that would pay off with Terry Gilliam's **BRAZIL**—and there's even an attempt to read the Two Minutes Hate as a sort of officially-sanctioned comedy, with Goldstein (Vernon Dobtcheff) bleating like a sheep during his anti-BB speech.

In all versions, even the compromised 1956 film, the horrible details tell. The omnipresent televisions, with grilles to prevent damage. The unappetising food and "Victory gin". The crowded jail cells like waiting rooms (the spectacularly emaciated William Lyon Brown is disturbing as the starved arrestee). A pre-**RAILWAY CHILDREN** Sally Thompsett is venomous as a spiteful junior spy, blaming the sink clogged up with her hair on saboteurs and informing on her pathetically devoted-to-the-state father (Norman Chappell). O'Conor is gentle and unfailingly polite as the manipulative spokesman for the state, who entraps Winston and Julia into joining "the Brotherhood" and then punishes them for it, getting a chill from Orwell's most-remembered speeches ("if you want a picture of the future, imagine a boot stamping on a human face forever"). The illusion of "the Brotherhood", an underground group essentially made up by the state as a threat and a temptation, is another innovation of this adaptation (perhaps a dig at 1960s radicalism), as is the stress on the probability that the state is behind the missile attacks on London that perpetuate the myth of an unending war and keep everyone cowed under emergency regulations which will never go away. The torture scenes have an antiseptic feel, with men in white coats continually checking on the victim's health to see if the process can go further.[84] Kneale said that no version of NINETEEN EIGHTY-FOUR managed to make Room 101 properly the worst thing in the world because on camera rats tend to look adorable rather than hideous, but Buck—like Cushing—manages an upsetting simulation of extreme phobia (Winston's explanatory speech about why he hates rats is

[83] Orwell's idea of porn, incidentally, sounds like Mickey Spillane, but was obviously inspired by James Hadley Chase (he wrote an essay attacking NO ORCHIDS FOR MISS BLANDISH).
[84] The sound effects of the electric-crucifixion device are a futuristic radiophonic whine heard often on DOCTOR WHO.

Buck's best scene). Also in the large cast are Cyril Shaps as the chess-playing Newspeak dictionary compiler and John Garrie as the antiques shop proprietor—surrounding Buck (the handsome young lead of **THE MUMMY'S SHROUD**) and Merrow (of **NIGHT OF THE BIG HEAT**) with older, craggier character actors like these only serves to make them seem younger.

Footage survives from a LATE NIGHT LINE-UP special on the production, which fascinatingly brings together participants in the 1954 and 1965 productions for polite debate (Mitchell cites the then-recent introduction of traffic wardens as a step towards Big Brother). Morahan, put on the spot, suspects this will be the last production of 1984, unable to conceive the obvious notion which would be hit on by Mike Radford of making a 1984 in 1984. Now, of course, Big Brother has come to connotate another brand of junk pop culture, closer to the vision of Kneale's YEAR OF THE SEX OLYMPICS. For all his terror of television and use of it as an instrument of oppression, Orwell was a radio man and didn't understand the new medium which would periodically reissue his warning (the 1984 of 1984 was a Film on 4 production). Kneale was a TV man, and saw how much more insidious the medium could be as a means of social control and eroding human values.

PHENOMENA BADLY OBSERVED AND WRONGLY EXPLAINED

Quatermass, The Pit, and Me

John Llewellyn Probert

SCIENCE HAS ALWAYS PLAYED AN IMPORTANT PART IN MY LIFE, both professional and otherwise. From that very first chemistry set my parents bought me for Christmas, through school and university to my career in the medical profession, gaining extra degrees and doctorates in biochemistry and molecular science along the way, science and I have become familiar bedfellows. I have drunk deep of the well of scientific knowledge, mostly voluntarily, sometimes out of necessity to pass exams. I have even contributed to the vast body of existing scientific literature that exists out there, with papers published in peer-reviewed journals on subjects as diverse as bladder cancer pharmacogenetics and the employment of magnetic resonance imaging in urological surgery. In my spare time I have delighted in the originality and creativity of the genre we call science-fiction, and my library contains everything from the so-called hard SF of Gregory Benford to works by Philip K Dick, Alfred Bester and many more.

Before I encountered any of those, however, and when a career in the sciences was still a twinkle in the eye of a small boy who found the life cycle of insects one of the most fascinating things he knew about in his limited world, there was just eight year old me and a Hammer film called **QUATERMASS AND THE PIT**. I know I was eight because now, through the miracle of the BBC genome, I have been able to look back and see that my very first exposure to this classic of science fiction was on Monday the 10th of November 1975. Little did I know that the film I settled down to watch in the absence of my parents would have such a profound effect on me, or that I would be writing about it forty years later.

And on the first occasion, I didn't even get to see the entire film. I can't remember exactly why, but my parents turned up at the point where Sladden (Duncan Lamont) imagines himself to be one of the Martian horde and is running through the back streets of London near Hobbs Lane, pursued by pots and pans and eventually falling to the ground in a graveyard, only for it to start undulating beneath him. My parents asked me what I was watching and when I replied, they nodded and my mother said "Oh yes, Andre Morrell — he was the best." I had no idea what she was on about as I was pretty sure the chap playing Quatermass in this was

Andrew Kier as Prof. Bernard Quatermass

called Andrew Keir—at least according to the *Radio Times*. But that slight confusion was nothing compared to the fact that I was, at that point, ordered off to bed.

It is hard to explain now what an effect it can have on an eight year old wildly overimaginative child to be only shown half of something like **QUATERMASS AND THE PIT**. What were those giant grasshopper things? Where had that spaceship come from? Why were there skeletons of primitive man in it? Why had people in the abandoned houses across the street seen things described as 'hideous dwarves'? My imagination ran riot. I could not have been hooked on science fiction more effectively if it had been planned that way. I recently rewatched the Hammer version for the umpteenth time, and I defy anyone who is unfamiliar with the film to be able to guess the outcome from the first thirty minutes of delicate laying down of its fabulously ambitious and complex, but never confusing, plot.

But back to 1975, a time when there was no means of recording a television screening, no VHS tapes and only minimal access to Super 8 versions of popular films. My school friends proved useless as no-one had been allowed to stay up and watch the film, and so it was that I found myself resigned to having to wait until it was shown again. It was, half a lifetime later (ie four years) as the second half of a double bill in BBC2's 'Masters of Terror' season in the summer of 1979. To say I was blown away by watching the full film would be an understatement, and the full impact of its storyline was further cemented by Arrow paperbacks issuing reprints of Nigel Kneale's first three Quatermass serials. These had originally been published by Penguin in 1960, but were all being reissued to tie in with the broadcasting of the ITV series QUATERMASS. Oh, and if you want an idea of how popular Nigel Kneale and his character were at the time, FIFTY SHADES OF GREY has nothing on the number of posters, promotions and sheer numbers of copies of the paperback novelisation of that fourth series that could be found everywhere. Even the local Abergavenny branch of Woolworths must have boasted a dump bin filled with fifty copies.

I'm digressing but I hope not too much. I hastily grabbed the new updated versions of THE QUATERMASS EXPERIMENT, QUATER-

MASS II and QUATERMASS AND THE PIT, all illustrated with stills from the original BBC productions, and sat down to read the Pit first.

I very much suspect it was the first time I had ever read a 'grown up' book from start to finish without a pause. I remember the occasion well because it was a Sunday and my mother got tired of calling me down to lunch. Eventually she came up to check in case I was unwell. By the time I had finished the book I was not just well, I felt infinitely better than I ever had. My life had been enriched in ways it was difficult to explain, even to myself. I just knew things would never be the same again. Many fans of film and literature become so because of a similar epiphanic moment, that point where you realise what you have just read or seen is not just words on a page or sprocket holes running through a projector, but something that has had the power to completely change the way you feel about art and life in general. It changes your outlook, it changes the way you view things and, if you're young enough, it can influence exactly what you plan to do with those precious years that lie ahead. I've given it much careful thought over the years and can say with confidence that, more than any other work of art, **QUATERMASS AND THE PIT** made me the man I am today. Its influence on me was complex and nothing but positive. The plot made me want to be a scientist, and the quality of Kneale's writing made me want to be an author. When I told the Careers Officer at school I was going to be a surgeon and write plays in my spare time I was rewarded with a weary nod and a piece of paper sent to my parents that said something along the lines of 'He can probably do whatever he wants. Just be careful he doesn't burn himself out'.

It's interesting that in **QUATERMASS AND THE PIT** the character I identified most with was not Bernard Quatermass at all, but anthropologist Dr Roney (Cec Linder in the TV series, James Donald in the film) and the moment Kneale's story spoke to me more than any other was close to the end, when London is in chaos and Quatermass and Roney take shelter in a pub. "Can't you feel it?" says Quatermass of the hive mentality straining to control him, to drive him to kill those who are different. Roney rewards him with a blank stare. He has no idea what Quatermass is talking about.

I grew up in a Welsh town to very proudly Welsh parents, and grand-

Phenomena Badly Observed and Wrongly Explained

James Donald as Prof. Roney with Quatermass (Andrew Kier)

parents, and their Welsh friends. It is difficult to be brought up in such an environment when you feel little or no sense of identity to the place the rest of your family would, it seem, happily die for if it came to it. Worst of all I had absolutely no interest in rugby, the country's national sport and followed with such a passion that the mere mention of such a lack of interest brought nothing but disdain and querulous looks, as if they were wondering which psychiatrist I should be sent to. It sounds funny to see it written down now, but when I was eight years old it was awful. I would be forced to sit and watch rugby matches on a Saturday afternoon because, my Dad would explain, I wanted to be able to talk about it in school on Monday, didn't I? Otherwise everyone would think I was strange. I would become a social outcast, a pariah. The fact that I actually spent Mondays as I spent all the rest of the week, sitting in the corner of the schoolyard with a book, or talking to friends even less socially competent than I was about the latest episode of DOCTOR WHO or BLAKE'S SEVEN was not something that could ever be entertained as a viable excuse.

And so I hope you can understand that when I saw Dr Roney's blank stare as Quatermass asked him if he could feel the thrusting, surging, instinctual drive to go with the crowd, to be like all the others, not because it was a choice but because if you thought there was a choice you just weren't One Of Them, how much that meant to me, and how much it helped me cope with that difficult period of our lives we call Having To Put Up With Almost Everyone In School. It was okay. It was finally okay, because Nigel Kneale had told me it was. It wasn't my fault I couldn't fit in, it was because, as Quatermass says, 'perhaps some are immune'. Dr Roney dies at the end of the story, saving the earth from a five million year old Martian demon. A noble and heroic act that also did not escape my attention.

There's a line in **QUATERMASS AND THE PIT** that sums up the appeal of much of Kneale's fiction for me, in fact I consider it important enough to have used it as the title of this essay. Just after the scene when I was originally sent to bed, of Sladden lying on rippling graveyard gravel, Quatermass and Barbara Judd (Barbara Shelley) take Sladden into the church vestry, accompanied by a vicar (Thomas Heathcote). While musing for an explanation of what might be going on (and we the audience certainly have no idea, even by now), Quatermass says "I suppose it's possible for ghosts to be phenomena that were badly observed and wrongly explained." A little later in the same scene the vicar responds to Quatermass's theorising with disdain, using the dialogue "Science? To explain it all away?" only for the professor to quickly reply that, on the contrary, he agrees with him. There are several important things going on in this scene, not the least of which is the fascinating attempt to consolidate science and religion when the popular cinema of the time tended to side with one element or the other, although the success of Hammer Films' most enduring characters has often been cited as a meeting of the two worlds—Frankenstein being a scientist in an essentially superstitious world, whereas Dracula seemed able to thrive more as that series of films went on because of a pronounced lack of religion in the world he inhabited.

I have always considered myself lucky in how I was introduced to the world of horror cinema, namely through those marvellous Hammer horror films of the late 1950s and early 1960s. Mixed in with them was a generous helping of movies from studios such as Amicus and Tigon. After a wondrous smorgasbord of such cinema, how could I be anything but hooked?

Phenomena Badly Observed and Wrongly Explained

I also consider myself lucky now that my very first encounter with Nigel Kneale's scientist was through that 1975 screening of Hammer's **QUATERMASS AND THE PIT**. A couple of years later I saw the Hammer version of **THE QUATERMASS EXPERIMENT**, on 22nd July 1978. This time I didn't like Quatermass at all, or rather Brian Donlevy's interpretation of him, but then neither did Mr Kneale, who described the performance as that of 'a bawling bully.' Mr Donlevy has come in for a lot of criticism over the years for this and the sequel, **QUATERMASS 2**, but to be honest I don't think we can blame an actor who was used to playing the heavy in Westerns. He was no more equipped to play a troubled professor than Christopher Lee might have been able to play Frodo Baggins, and it's the chaps at Hammer, desperate for an American name for their posters, who are probably more to blame here.

Don't get me wrong—I liked **THE QUATERMASS EXPERIMENT** a lot, and I still do. I love Richard Wordsworth as Victor Carroon, I love all the British character actors (including a tiny Jane Asher, of whom more in a moment, who gets to do a 'Frankenstein' scene with Carroon) and I even love the creepy crawly monster slurping its way around Westminster Abbey as it gets ready to reproduce. The irony of vast and inappropriate alien sexual activity taking place in a building representative of the repression of such an act was hopefully not lost on audience members of the time. But I didn't like Quatermass. In fact I couldn't even understand Quatermass that well, Mr Donlevy's mumblings all the more congruous amongst the clipped accents of trained British actors. I even had to ask my Dad (who was watching with me this time) what the final line was, even though the rocket taking off over the end credits made it obvious. It took me years (and years!) to eventually catch up with **QUATERMASS 2**. By then I was prepared, of course, and Donlevy's repeat performance in the role didn't grate quite so much.

So let's get back to good old Andrew Keir's Quatermass and that line of his about badly observed and poorly explained phenomena. One of the things I have always admired about Kneale's work is how his stories often have scientists delving into the mysteries of the unexplained, and actually coming up with an answer that is far more terrifying, and sometimes even less rational, than what had originally been perceived by superstition.

WE ARE THE MARTIANS

In THE STONE TAPE (1972) a corporate team of engineers and scientists move into a huge old house with the intention of using it as their base while they work on inventing a new recording medium. When Jill Greeley (Jane Asher) witnesses the ghost of a chambermaid in an empty room the theory is postulated that perhaps the stone of the building's walls might act as the medium they've been looking for, whilst also providing a handy explanation for why ghosts exist. Kneale gives us another quote to rival 'phenomena badly observed' with a line by hard-edged rationalist Peter Brock (Michael Bryant) who tries to rationalise supernatural activity as "a mass of data . . . waiting for a correct interpretation." There's also an excellent, and scientific explanation, for why ghosts don't show up on recording media—we ourselves are the receivers for the information being presented to us. There is something in the human brain capable of picking up 'psychic' vibrations that technology is still in too crude a state to appreciate.

"Let's dispel with the word haunting," Brock says a little later, "it gets in the way." He then goes on to ask the assembled group if any of them are religious, but no-one gets the chance to reply.

Kneale gives us a rather different picture of scientists here compared to the more restrained technical team we see in **QUATERMASS AND THE PIT**, and I suspect it is no accident that one of the opening scenes depicts them as a gang of lads persecuting a 'Martian'—one of their number dressed up in true period DOCTOR WHO costume style as an alien. They literally enter a world of ancient horror when the room designated to store their computers is revealed. Rotting, mouldy and built from damp stone, it is nothing like the 'modern' (for 1972) interiors we have been exposed to in the opening scenes. Despite the obvious age of the building, that first look at the room is still a shock.

In **QUATERMASS AND THE PIT** it is Dr Roney's insensitivity to his 'heritage' that enables him to save the world. In THE STONE TAPE, it is the insensitivity of most of the group that ultimately leads to Kneale's ancient evil to flourish by causing the tape to be wiped. When publican Alan (Michael Graham-Cox) is asked to stand in the haunted room (he has been regaling Bryant and Asher in the pub with tales of visiting the then-deserted house when he was a boy) he cannot bear it and actually ends up crawling out. "He's the sane one," says Jill, the most sensitive to the haunting, "we're the freaks." Significantly, by the end of THE STONE TAPE it is Jill who has succumbed to whatever lives in the room, even though she is the one who has been most aware of the danger there.

So just like in **QUATERMASS AND THE PIT** we have scientists who are 'immune' to perhaps some deep-bred 'protective' instinct to preserve their kind. However here, Kneale almost seems to be suggesting that, rather than lead to the salvation of humanity, the lack of this will actually lead to to the world's undoing?

In his 1964 television play THE ROAD, we are introduced to Sir Timothy Hassall (James Maxwell) an eighteenth century amateur ghost hunter who plans to use a new technique he has developed himself in order to investigate a stretch of country road where the ghosts of Boadacea's army are rumoured to come thundering through at regular intervals. With him is Gideon Cobb (John Phillips) who is visiting from London and has great faith in this new thing known as science. At the climax, the assembled team get to hear the ghostly manifestation, and so do we. But quite brilliantly both parties interpret what they are witnessing entirely differently. Despite all the scientific 'advances' of the year 1775, they are no substitute for a further three hundred years of hindsight and experience.

I came across both THE STONE TAPE and THE ROAD much later in life (and on the same BFI DVD, with the script for the long-wiped THE ROAD included as a pdf extra). Another of Kneale's scientists whom I encountered at a much younger age, however, was Leo Raymount (played by Patrick Magee), the animal experimenter of 'What Big Eyes'. This was one of six television plays Kneale wrote for ITV under the collective title BEASTS. I'm still not sure quite how I was allowed to stay up and watch these on their original 1976 broadcast as I would only have been about nine years old, but somehow I did. I remember the 'Baby' and 'During Barty's Party' episodes scared me to the point of mortification, but 'What Big Eyes' had its fair share of scares, too. Amateur mad scientist Raymount is obsessed with the concept of lycanthropy, and has taken to inoculating himself with a self-created 'Grandma Vaccine' he has distilled from the spinal fluid and macerated brain extracts of Romanian timber wolves. Michael Kitchen is Bob Curry, the RSPCA officer investigating the

WE ARE THE MARTIANS

supplier of the wolves, and his findings lead him to Raymount's pet shop, which he runs with the aid of his daughter, Florence (Madge Ryan). In a seedy bedroom-cum-study crammed with books and papers, and presided over by a still of Oliver Reed in full makeup from Hammer's **CURSE OF THE WEREWOLF**, Raymount explains his crackpot theories regarding DNA memory to a disbelieving Curry. Magee's intense performance culminates in the demonstration of his back room laboratory, complete with restraining straps for when he needs to harvest his samples. The episode ends with Magee dead, presumably as a result of his self-experimentation, but not before he has treated us to a glorious lecture demonstration before an audience of his imaginary peers, culminating in his intended transformation as the ultimate illustration of his theories. Do scientists dream of being able to present their theoretical work in such a way? Certainly I was only able to appreciate this part of Kneale's script when I was finally able to catch up with BEASTS. Now older and wiser, and established in my chosen career as a urological surgeon, Magee's final monologue merely served to remind me of the now-infamous story of one of my colleagues who was instrumental in the pioneering of research into the treatment of erectile dysfunction, otherwise known as impotence. This colleague was invited to present his work at what is considered the most prestigious annual meeting of the specialty in the world. Perhaps unsurprisingly this meeting took place in the USA.

With a mixture of panache and eccentricity that has since become the stuff of legend, my colleague presented his research findings to a large audience of eminent American surgeons and then, to finish off, he announced that he had injected himself with his test drug twenty minutes prior to the presentation. He then pulled down his trousers and his underpants and displayed to the rather shocked audience the proud results of his research endeavours. Now that's how to give a guest lecture. I should probably add here that I have never attempted to emulate this particular individual.

Network's double disc region 2 DVD set of BEASTS gives you all six stories, and as an added bonus we get a programme called 'Murrain' as an extra. 'Murrain' is another hour-long (with adverts) television play, written by Kneale as one of seven stories shown in the series AGAINST THE

CROWD (1975). Kneale's contribution tells the story of young country vet Alan Crich (David Simeon) who, when asked to treat the pigs of farmer Beeley (Bernard Lee) finds the inhabitants of the desolate, isolated country village he has been called to convinced that the animal deaths, and other occurrences, are all down to local 'witch' Mrs Clemson (Una Brandon-Jones). While not exactly a scientist, Crich certainly has a scientific training and background, and Kneale uses his character as the voice of reason in the land of the superstitious. Our sympathies are clearly intended to lie both with Crich and Mrs Clemson, but Kneale attempts to pull the rug from under his viewers with the final scene, where there is the suggestion that the villagers' fears aren't that unfounded after all. The programme ends there, which is a shame, as a STONE TAPE-type investigation of Mrs Clemson's possible powers might have produced an even more interesting drama than the one we have been left with!

Let's finish as I began, with Quatermass. Nigel Kneale wrote his fourth Quatermass adventure in the early 1970s, but it didn't get filmed until later in the decade, this time by Euston Films who had enjoyed considerable success with THE SWEENEY (and virtually revolutionised the television police drama after years of glamorous ITC adventures like THE PERSUADERS and JASON KING). The drama was eventually filmed in 1978 and it's forthcoming broadcast on ITV (in four episodes) was much heralded with posters and the previously mentioned novelisation. Then it all went pear-shaped in the form of a strike at ITV that caused a full-scale blackout of the channel beginning on the 10th August 1979 and lasting for eleven weeks. I was eleven at the time and I remember it well. ITV's regular listings magazine the TV Times kept going for a couple of redundant weeks and then ceased publication for a while. Someone at ITV (at least in our region) tried to keep the home fires burning by broadcasting movies. I don't think they knew how to operate the pan-and-scan machine, however, because I remember this being the first time I had seen films on our tiny family television in widescreen. It was also something of a novelty to watch something on ITV and not have it interrupted by adverts. There was no rhyme or reason as to what was shown, and often films were shown repeatedly—I certainly remember **THE DIRTY DOZEN** being shown several times.

The strike was resolved and broadcasting restored on Wednesday 24th October. The first episode of QUATERMASS was shown at 9pm. Unfortunately the TV Times wasn't yet up and running again and many newspapers were behind as well, which meant that an awful lot of people missed that episode because no-one knew it was on. I remember stumbling across it halfway through and guessing (from all the advance publicity) what it was.

QUATERMASS does some things well and some things not so well. It's an interesting depiction of a Britain on the verge of social breakdown, even if the gangs who besiege our hero are probably a bit too well spoken to be believable. More than anything nowadays, it comes across as being written by a man who was a bit fed up with much of the society that was around him at the time he was writing it. You can almost imagine him grumbling 'bloody hippies' as he tapped away at his typewriter (although Kneale actually envisioned his 'Planet People' as punks rather than peace-loving). Quatermass is less a noble, thoughtful, contemplative scientist in this one and more a desperate old man. In fact he admits as much in the first episode, saying all he cares about is finding his grand-daughter. It's a rather depressing story with a grim outcome.

Far more satisfactory from my own point of view was THE QUATER-MASS MEMOIRS, the five-part radio serial broadcast on Radio 3 in 1996. I was in America doing research at the University of Pittsburgh at the time, and so my Dad recorded them for me and sent them over. So it was that I was able to listen to Andrew Kier, my favourite Quatermass, reminiscing over the character's life, as I was writing up the results of my own doctorate thesis in molecular biology. I had gone from an eight year old boy wide-eyed at the concept of Martians beneath a London Underground station to a twenty nine year old man completing research in bladder cancers as part of my training to become a surgeon.

And Quatermass had been with me all the way.

Thanks Nigel.

UNDER THE INFLUENCE
Kneale's Dramatic Legacy

Maura McHugh

I DIDN'T WATCH ANY OF NIGEL KNEALE'S TELEVISION PLAYS OR films when they were first aired, so I have no anecdotes to relate of hiding behind pillows or discussing his latest scary story with my pals in the schoolyard. I wasn't around for much of Kneale's career, and growing up in the West of Ireland I missed a whole swathe of British TV due to the simple fact that we couldn't receive the channels on our side of the country until I was in my early teens. My love for anything sf, fantasy, or horror had been fixed early in my childhood so I'd have gone to any lengths to watch spooky or strange television. What I didn't realise, until I encountered Kneale's work later in my adulthood, was that in a way I had always been watching his work, through the resonance of those who influenced him, and the following response from his contemporaries and successors in the field.

In my twenties I had the fortunate experience of watching **APOCA-LYPSE NOW** (1979), for the first time, in an art house cinema. Through happenstance I'd never seen any of the poor versions of the film that had been knocking about on late-night television or on video at the time. It was an overwhelming, astonishing experience, the kind that marks you and

WE ARE THE MARTIANS

remains in your memory. What I also recognised, as I left the cinema somewhat dazed, was that a gap in my cinematic literacy had been filled. I had seen homages to parts of the film many times without the corresponding layer of insight. I also understood that the echoing response to the original signal will never be as pure or as strong as that first creative beat. Over time I came to further appreciate that Francis Coppola's nightmarish look into the insanity of war was also part of a chain of influences, including Joseph Conrad's novella, HEART OF DARKNESS.

Truly original creative work is about refinement and synthesis—taking the multitude of influences and filtering them through a narrow lens: such as an insight about a generation of people, a novel approach to an old concept, or the examination of a philosophical question.

As writers are fond of saying: *ideas are easy, but stories are hard.* Wrangling a concept into a well-executed and compelling narrative is the difficult trick of fashioning memorable work. Kneale was an innovator during the genesis of a new art form in Britain, but he was also someone who built upon existing ideas and reflected the preoccupations of his era.

It's easy to forget that Kneale started by studying to be an actor, and after giving that up turned to working as a jobbing writer. Like many people, he shaped his career by the pragmatic desire for a steady pay check. Despite his initial success as a short story writer, he understood he could hardly make a living this way.[85] He entered broadcasting by reading, and later writing for radio, before his foray into television.

Although BBC television began broadcasting in 1932, it ceased operating during war time, and sales of television sets only slowly began to rise after 1950. The British television network had not even been properly established across the UK until the decision to broadcast the coronation of Queen Elizabeth II was taken in 1952. Then the outer territories, such as Scotland and Northern Ireland, were quickly hooked up. This also escalated the purchase, and rental, of television sets for the event in June 1953, and the adoption of this form of entertainment into the homes of ordinary people.[86]

---

[85] 'The Magic Word here is Paradox', Jack Kibble-White interviews Nigel Kneale.
[86] 'Why Elizabeth II's 1953 Coronation is the day that changed television', Joe Moran, Radio Times: 02 June 2013.

Prior to that radio was King of the British airwaves. Going to the Pictures was the favourite excursion, and if you were lucky to live in a city there was theatre, concerts, music halls, and galleries, otherwise it was local dances, newspapers, journals, magazines, comic books, and gossip for popular culture.

Television remained the brash upstart in the eyes of the British people, and the BBC itself, and the full range of its abilities had not been properly tested when Kneale was hired as a television script writer in 1951. Kneale himself claimed never to have watched television before he began working for the broadcaster.[87] He also had a poor opinion of the teleplays the BBC was producing: it favoured straightforward adaptations of existing theatrical productions with little camera movement resulting in a rather static affair.[88]

At this important juncture point Kneale met Rudolph Cartier, an Austrian producer/director who had worked in Berlin's UFA studios prior to the war. With Cartier Kneale was able to test his talent for writing television, as well as the medium's capacity for captivating an audience. It was one of those rare, collaborative relationships for which most writers and directors yearn. Luckily for Kneale and Cartier the stars aligned correctly, and the *Quatermass* serials were born, among other projects.

Kneale's quintessential British boffin, Professor Bernard Quatermass, continues a lineage of fictional investigative scientists, and forges an important link in what would become a stalwart character in television. Kneale was drawing upon an archetype established by the likes of Mary Shelley's Dr. Frankenstein, HG Wells' Dr. Moreau, Fritz Lang & Thea von Harbou's Rotwang, and Alex Raymond's Dr. Alexis Zarkov. Plus, within horror literature there existed the trope of the occult investigator, who was often also a scientist, such as Sheridan Le Fanu's Dr. Hesselius, Bram Stoker's Dr. Abraham Van Helsing, Algernon Blackwood's Dr. John Silence, and William Hope Hodgson's Thomas Carnacki. And always the great presence: Sir Arthur Conan Doyle's deductive sleuth, Sherlock Holmes.

---

[87] 'The Magic Word here is Paradox', Jack Kibble-White interviews Nigel Kneale.
[88] *idem*

WE ARE THE MARTIANS

During Kneale's formative years science fiction stories were rising in popularity through literature, comic book stories, and film and radio serials. Wells himself was a regular broadcaster for the BBC on matters of science and culture, and had adapted his story THE SHAPE OF THINGS TO COME into a landmark science fiction film in 1936. The strategic importance of scientific developments had been dramatically played out across the battlefields of the global arena during World War II, culminating with the explosive start of the nuclear age and the cold war.

Scientists in these stories didn't remain in labs to cook up formulas and gadgets, they were out in the world engaged in saving (or destroying) it through solving puzzles and facing possible catastrophe. Quatermass was less incoherent mad scientist, and more rounded humanist, who relied on facts but kept an open mind. He had a healthy scepticism for the military and idiotic bureaucracy, but worked well with others and cared for his teammates. In this way Quatermass evolved the scientist-hero in science fiction drama into a more nuanced character.

The critic Susan Sontag noted that much of the interest of science fiction films is not about science, but about disaster, and 'the aesthetics of destruction'.[89] The cinematic science fiction tradition places primacy on spectacle and big budget effects, where the audience can (safely) experience annihilation first-hand. Yet, in television the tradition favours characters, and the potential to explore ideas with more time and latitude.

The intimacy of the television screen (small in the 1950s), and its presence in the homes of people, did not have to be a code word for "cosy", which is the kind of drama that Kneale, and Cartier, loathed. Together they created stories that exploited the close connection offered by television to the viewers, while pondering big ideas powered through exciting, well-paced drama. Television at this point might not be best suited to sweeping vistas, but through careful cutting between cameras during live screenings, and the use of close-ups on agonised expressions, the dramas could sweep up the audience in its spell.

Initially, even the BBC couldn't telerecord its own stories, which were broadcast live, and home recording by the audience was decades away.

[89] 'The Imagination of Disaster' by Susan Sontag, Against Interpretation and Other Essays, Picador, 1961, p 213.

Under the Influence

You either had to be present and watch, or miss the show entirely. It was a medium of the moment, and only those who witnessed it could be part of the conversation about its impact. In this way it possessed the *frisson* of live theatre. This also meant television required rehearsals, good writing, and fine acting to engage people. Kneale and Cartier drew upon these factors to generate drama for an audience primed for something new.

Kneale had two strong impulses in his genre work: a horror sensibility, and an exacting scientific inquiry. He often married these two facets successfully, which gave his stories a distinctive complexity. Horror is an internal gaze, dwelling upon the fears within, while science fiction is an outward questing and engagement with ideas. QUATERMASS AND THE PIT (December 1958–January 1959), for example, has elements of the occult and folklore horror mixed in with its careful cataloguing of the remains of an ancient spaceship discovered in a London building site, and how it affects modern people. Memories of the past are dredged up and replayed, but no amount of scientific understanding can stop its renewed assault upon our lives. You can only explode the device that attempts to divide people upon the lines of difference.

Kneale's adaptation of George Orwell's NINETEEN EIGHTY-FOUR (1954), with its minimalist sets, and depiction of extreme emotional states and awful torture remains a gripping and compulsive drama today. Technically a dystopian science fiction story, it has the claustrophobia of a horror story, where the worst fate possible occurs: the utter perversion of the self. Thought, the very essence of a person, is twisted inside the mind of the man so that it betrays him. This intense adaptation, which provoked questions in parliament after its first broadcast, no doubt ensured that Orwell's prescient story kept its prestige as a remarkable warning about the potential dissolution of people's rights and agency under totalitarian states.

Many of the themes sweeping through Kneale's work are classic post-war anxieties: fear of infection, and conversion to the alien cause. In THE QUATERMASS EXPERIMENT (1953) and QUATERMASS II (1955) the threat comes to Earth from beyond. In the former it is the professor's quest into the heavens that results in the taint returning to Earth, and the potential for sublimation to an alien lifeform. In the latter humans are converted into mind-controlled zombies by a gas contained in meteorites, and those who are changed begin a conspiracy of subversion among the highest ranks of the British military in order to create a habitat fit for the new alien overlords.

These storylines were part of a cultural zeitgeist that spawned similar ideas in cinema, such as **THE THING FROM ANOTHER WORLD** (1951), and **INVASION OF THE BODY SNATCHERS** (1956), both of which have been remade many times in various media. What makes Kneale's versions so memorable is a bedrock of British pragmatism underlying the high concept ideas—someone has to offer tea and biscuits (or whisky, or gin) to soothe jangled nerves, dig out the muck around buried artefacts, or build the alien base. Although, it's never Quatermass or his educated chums who do the manual labour.

Kneale's final excursion with the Professor, simply called QUATERMASS (1979), was a four-part serial broadcast on ITV (and also a shorter version intended for theatrical release called **THE QUATERMASS CONCLUSION**). It was a combination of previous themes infused with the 1970s unease caused by oil shortages and widespread strikes, instilling a worry that the world was crumbling. The alien threat comes from without, but it is provoked by an ancient signal buried deep within the earth under stone circles, which are activated by the presence of groups of hippie youth congregating at the monuments. In this lawless world even English television studios—bastions of genteel artistes—are beset by violent gangs.

The gritty, pessimistic tone of the 1970s pervades the series, which is part of the rise of science fiction cinema—often with dystopian visions— which dominated the decade. Examples of the gamut of stories that were popular at the box office includes two **PLANET OF THE APES** movies, **A CLOCKWORK ORANGE** (1971), **THE ANDROMEDA STRAIN** (1971), **OMEGA MAN** (1971), **SOYLENT GREEN** (1973), **LOGAN'S RUN** (1976), **CLOSE ENCOUNTERS OF THE THIRD KIND** (1977), the remake of **INVASION OF THE BODY SNATCHERS** (1978), **MAD MAX** (1979), and **ALIEN** (1979). Plus **ASSAULT ON PRECINCT 13** (1976) for that dash of stylised gang violence.

In his last outing Quatermass is depicted at his most human: much

Under the Influence

older, and preoccupied only with recovering his lost granddaughter, Hettie. His sense of his mortality has readjusted his priorities.

When he witnesses the coupling of an American and Soviet space station as a PR stunt to distract a decaying world he bursts out with an anguished rant:

> "What we're looking at here is a wedding. A symbolic wedding between a corrupt democracy and a monstrous tyranny. Two superpowers, full of diseases: political diseases, economic diseases, social diseases, and their infections are too strong for us, a small country. When we catch them we die. We're dying now. And they *mock* us with that thing? Well, their diseases are in there too. It can't live."

As ever Quatermass is spot on, and the whole endeavour collapses once the first alien strike occurs.

This series is muddled, and there's an unpleasant suspicion of the young, who are depicted as spurning science in favour of nonsense. One of them screeches, "Stop trying to know things!" They are directly opposed to everything in which Quatermass believes: solving problems through rational deduction. They are all mad instinct and rejection of systems, thus most of them are destroyed in the 'lovely lightning'.

It's the older generation who have made do during World War II who go back to work and save the young from their trance magnetism for the alien hotspots. Yet Quatermass only achieves his goal with the aid of his granddaughter, which is a hint at a potential bridge between the generations. But unlike her scientist mother who appeared in QUATERMASS II, she is part of the youth movement that has spurned rationality.

A similar examination of the intersection between science and superstition is evident in the one-hour story, "Murrain", which Kneale wrote for ITV in 1975 as part of its AGAINST THE CROWD series. The story revolves around a stand-off between the educated vet, Alan Crich, and the ill-kempt farmers who are searching for the source of a mysterious illness killing their pigs, and affecting one boy. They seize upon the idea that it's being caused by the elderly, squinting Mrs. Clemson, and ask the vet to participate in some anti-witch magic.

WE ARE THE MARTIANS

Repelled by the outlandish suggestions, Crich refuses, and tries to befriend Clemson. Kneale strikes just the right note in the story, showing how poverty and ill-education result in dangerous notions, especially those directed at women, and how even the most sensible of people can be swayed to irrational, murderous solutions. The story is written so that it can be read either as the triumph of magic or the dangers of stress on the heart, and it's up to the viewer to decide.

Crich yells, at one point, "We change the rules for better rules. But, we don't go back!" It might as well have been the rallying cry of Quatermass.

Kneale's six-episode series for ITV the following year called BEASTS is a fantastic array of stories on a loose theme. One story, "Baby", is also concerned with witchcraft. The young, pregnant housewife Jo discovered a mummified piglet in a jar buried in her wall of her newly-converted farmhouse. This brings a new strain to her difficult marriage to egotistical bullying husband Peter, who is also a vet, and dismissive of any female hysteria. As Jo becomes more fearful and alienated in her isolated home, she succumbs to a terrible vision of monstrous motherhood. The middle class couple in "During Barty's Party" realise they are besieged by a plague of poison-resistant "super-rats" (never seen but chillingly evoked through sound), but that doesn't save them from their onslaught. Kneale gives us a proper mad scientist in "What Big Eyes", but his experiments and theories about an ancient connection between humans and wolves don't pan out except in the imagination of his daughter. A grieving, unstable father runs amuck when he connects too strongly to the chthonic energy of a mask in "The Dummy" — his mind was not in a fit state to control that old power.

In a great deal of Kneale's stories, even the adaptations of other work, his preoccupation with maintaining an organised mind in the face of apparently unnatural forces crops up again and again. Even in his work which is outright horror, such as **THE WITCHES** (1966) and THE WOMAN IN BLACK (1989).

THE WITCHES (based on the novel THE DEVIL'S OWN, by Peter Curtis/Norah Lofts) is a Hammer Films production which would pass the most difficult Bechdel Test with flying colours: women take all the main roles, and are not much occupied with what men are doing. Even though the story is essentially about a witch's attempt to become young again, she

Under the Influence

treats the study of magic as a system that can be cracked, and airily dismisses Satan himself a "dark force". Magic is her mechanism to take over the body of a young woman, thus giving her sharp intellect the extra time on Earth so she can improve it. Her's is not the pursuit of youth for vanity, but for knowledge. But like some Kneale characters who tangle with ancient powers, she comes a cropper.

For THE WOMAN IN BLACK adaptation (original book by Susan Hill) Kneale was writing for television again, and the story is paced sedately to start. The figure of the Woman in black is both ordinary and eerie at the same time, which gives her sudden, shrieking attack so much force when it happens quite late into the story. The silence of the locals on the subject of the ghost is wise, for to invoke the hidden menace is to court disaster. It's like the posters in QUATERMASS II warning the locals about the need for secrecy, or the villagers in **THE WITCHES** who keep their occult leanings quiet. Wilful Ignorance might be the enemy of those who wish to solve mysteries, but those who delve for understanding might not survive the answers.

Arthur Kidd, the solicitor digging up the past in THE WOMAN IN BLACK, sorts through piles of documents and phonograph recordings to understand what's causing the appearance of the phantom woman. He makes a distinct connection between the artificial recordings and the replayed ghostly memory of the fateful crash in the marsh that triggered the haunting. In this way Kneale harkens back to THE STONE TAPE (1972), his ITV original play which is a forensic examination of an instance of haunting, depicting how a tragic event can become etched into the very walls of a building.

For both the computer programmer Jill Greeley in THE STONE TAPE and Kidd in THE WOMAN IN BLACK, understanding the past and its inhuman malevolence does not free them from its influence. Instead they are dragged down into the depths with it.

One of the obvious inheritors of Kneale's body of work is the American television series THE X-FILES (1993-2002), which was also inspired by weird story serials such as ALFRED HITCHCOCK PRESENTS, THE TWILIGHT ZONE, THE OUTER LIMITS, NIGHT GALLERY, TALES FROM THE DARKSIDE, TALES FROM THE CRYPT, and KOLCHAK:

WE ARE THE MARTIANS

THE NIGHT STALKER. The popular television show featured FBI special agents Fox Mulder and Dana Scully who are the only investigators in a department considered an embarrassment by most officials: they examine the FBI's unsolved cases (the X-Files) that appear to present paranormal underpinnings. Like Quatermass they are both embedded in, and embattled by, their own organisation.

Scully is the scientist, sceptical and exact, who reins in Mulder's explicit belief in strange phenomena, and especially the government conspiracy to cover up alien contact, which Mulder believes he witnessed as a child. Scully is the obvious continuation of Quatermass, along with the realisation that the boffin needs a counterpart, someone who will provoke questions for the scientific answers, and will provide a bit of humour. What's interesting about this pairing is that the obvious match to the scientist would be a more muscular, active agent (which happens later when Mulder is replaced with special agent John Doggett). Mulder lacks the usual macho aggression typical of this type of character. He's thoughtful and unafraid to listen to Scully. Scully is a trained agent and no fainting damsel when in action, and Mulder has elements of scepticism when the balance in their dynamic shifts.

THE X-FILES episodes that were most successful were when it got the balance of horrific trappings and scientific inquiry right, much like Kneale's work. There is a genuine alien threat that is infiltrating the highest offices (per QUATERMASS II), but there also more ordinary terrors to explain. At its best the series represents an amalgamation of Kneale's interests exhibited in his *Quatermass* series, THE STONE TAPE, and BEASTS.

A short-lived American television series called THRESHOLD (2005-2006) was one of the true inheritors of THE X-FILES and the Quatermass-type character, for not only were the characters part of a secret government task force who were investigating alien first contact, but most of them are scientists. Similar again to QUATERMASS II the alien "signal" that has infected people turns them into carriers, who are intent on spreading the contagion to prepare the way for a hostile takeover. The fear of being converted to an alien mindset is one of the principal worries exhibited in the series. But this is post-9/11 American television, which is

218

Under the Influence

coping with the realisation that infiltration of the country by enemy forces is very much possible — as if all the "red scare" bogeyman tales of the 1950s and 1960s had turned out to be real, and infiltrators are indeed living among us.

Following on from this was the TV series FRINGE (2008-2013), which involves yet another division of the FBI (called Fringe), updated so that it's also under the supervision of Homeland Security. It's a series living with the aftermath of 9/11, since the twin towers themselves are used as an important visual landmark for the plot. Special Agent Olivia Dunham works with "mad scientist" Walter Bishop (who has suffered a mental breakdown), with the help of Walter's son John, to track down those who are experimenting illegally with cutting-edge fringe science. Over the five seasons it unfolds that there is a threat of invasion from without, but this time it's from a competing alternate timeline, and the control of the Observers: who are actually future humans. As with many Kneale stories within our race lies the seeds of our destruction. The series is very focused on forensics and science as the solution to all the problems, with a great deal of time spent in the division's base, which is also a laboratory. Yet, science is also the cause of the problems in the first place, with researchers making catastrophic blunders — often originating from selfish, emotional decisions.

During this period a significant change in the always-popular television detective procedural saw an adjustment in viewers' expectations of how ordinary, criminal mysteries are investigated and resolved. The huge popularity of CSI in all its incarnations, has helped this style of story dominate. The boffin, or boffins, is an integral part of every team, and they come in a huge variety of shapes and sizes, such as the cool forensic pathologist Professor Sam Ryan in SILENT WITNESS, goth forensic scientist Abby Sciuto in NCIS, the geeky technical analyst Penelope Garcia in CRIMINAL MINDS, forensic anthropologist Dr. Temperance Brennan in BONES, medical examiner Dr. Maura Isles in RIZZOLI & ISLES, and computer specialist Amir Arison in THE BLACKLIST — the list could go on. They all work with their more active partners, but their input is vital to solving the case. We now expect science to be fundamental to the illumination of every mystery, straightforward or alien.

Towards the end of Kneale's career there was a change in focus away from television drama onto the cinematic spectacle, with television becoming the less prestigious form of entertainment. While there was always worthy drama being made on television during the following period, this trend has reversed dramatically in the past two decades with the proliferation of formulaic, blockbuster cinema, and the increase in brilliantly written 'event' television. Often these are special mini-series, where the emphasis is on the vision of a writer/creator, such as HANNIBAL in the USA, ORPHAN BLACK in Canada, or UTOPIA or in the UK.

With the advent of the Internet, and the increase of an always-on global audience, there has been a strange re-emergence of television as theatre. For a younger generation there a premium placed on watching the show as it airs, and broadcasting a stream of live observations upon the story as it is unfolds. People throughout the world watch television together, as if the walls between them are invisible. Companies with little history of broadcasting are commissioning original, popular dramas that can be downloaded in one big gulp, to be discussed online instantly.

Technology has advanced so that our lives are becoming increasingly science fictional, where everyone has access to a virtual version of James Bond's Q, and our governments are privy to every signal we emit. "We are the Martians", indeed. All memory and communication is digitised for broadcast to everyone. These days people attack each other virtually prompted by online chatter, determined to eradicate those who are different as part of a new Wild Hunt. Occasionally, it even spills into real world violence.

In this fashion, the circle has turned again so that Kneale's legacy of well-conceived, well-acted television that must be watched on the night, has returned, but in slightly altered form. Science continues to explain and imperil us, but as the Kneale rationalist character would attest, that tricky enterprise just might lead us towards redemption, rather than the obscure future roughly sketched by superstitious belief.

Under the Influence

BIBLIOGRAPHY

Abbott, Stacey & Jowett, Lorna, *TV Horror: Investigating the Dark Side of the Small Screen*. I.B. Tauris, 2012.

Cook, John R. & Wright, Peter, *British Science Fiction Television: A Hitchhiker's Guide*. I.B. Tauris, 2006.

Kibble-White, Jack, 'The Magic Word here is Paradox'.

Moran, Joe, 'Why Elizabeth II's 1953 Coronation is the day that changed television', *Radio Times*: 02 June 2013.

Pixley, Andrew, 'Nigel Kneale — Behind the Dark Door'.

Sontag, Susan, 'The Imagination of Disaster', *Against Interpretation and Other Essays*. Picador, 1961.

Thumim, Janet, *Small Screens, Big Ideas: Television in the 1950s*. I. B. Tauris, 2001.

A Conversation with Joe Dante

Neil Snowdon

JOE DANTE IS ONE OF THE GREAT HEROES OF AMERICAN CINEMA. *His highly subversive, wildly entertaining movies, are unique in the Hollywood landscape: cine-literate, politically aware, and scathingly satirical. His films will make you laugh, they'll make you feel, they'll make you think.* **THE HOWLING, GREMLINS, GREMLINS 2, EXPLORERS, INNERSPACE, THE BURBS, MATINEE, THE HOME-COMING, THE HOLE** . . . *it's an extraordinary filmography.*

Joe is also one of Hollywood's great advocates for cinema history. His encyclopaedic knowledge is on display in all his movies, and at his website: trailersfromhell.com

No conversation with Joe can ever stay entirely on topic, nor would you want it to. The "Man Who Knows Too Much" must take a tangent now and then, but when he does you learn something. About movies, their making, and their history. Sit back and listen . . .

NS: *What was your first exposure to Kneale's work? How old were you and what kind of an impact did it have?*

JD: I think the first thing I must have seen was **QUATERMASS 2**, which

WE ARE THE MARTIANS

was called **ENEMY FROM SPACE** here, and it was a double bill with some other movie I can't remember, it was the second feature, and I found it really electrifying. I just thought it was a very intense and unusual movie. And I was not aware of the TV series, wasn't aware of the prior picture. It was 1957, so I guess I was eleven years old. I was probably more aware of the Hammer connection than I was the Nigel connection—or Tom as he liked to be called—and that led me backward into learning a little bit more about the movies and who made them.

When you're a kid you have a tendency to just sort of let it all wash over you, you don't pay much attention to the credits or anything like that, but I'd already reached a point where I was getting pretty serious about figuring out who was doing what in movies.

In the old days we didn't have the internet, we didn't have wikipedia, we didn't have any of that stuff we couldn't just look up somebody's credits. You had to go to the library. And even then it was pretty difficult to figure out where you would look to get credits for writers and directors and things. But I managed to figure it out and of course his name started appearing on more films that were a little higher profile, like **FIRST MEN IN THE MOON**, and it was quite obvious that he was somebody to be reckoned with, and then of course I found out about the published work, the TV scripts, THE YEAR OF THE SEX OLYMPICS and all that, and as I went into college I became quite a fan of his work. I used to read John Wyndham and all the other British Sci-Fi guys too, but there was something about the way Kneale approached his projects, and I was particularly taken with his penchant for co-mingling Science Fiction and Celtic Mythology and History and all that. So by the time I got to see **QUATER-MASS AND THE PIT**, it was a pretty revelatory movie. There just weren't any other movies around—outside of maybe 2001—that were doing that kind of speculative writing. I mean, the idea that where we came from and 'We are the Martians' and all that, was pretty heady stuff.

NS: *That was the one that really broke it open for me. I saw* **QUATER-MASS AND THE PIT** *because it was another Hammer movie—I'd been watching the Dracula and Frankenstein movies by then, but* **QUATER-MASS AND THE PIT** *was the first movie to really scare me with an idea.*

A Conversation with Joe Dante

JD: Which is a pretty remarkable thing when you think about the period, and you think about the way that these pictures were generally approached. In America it was called **FIVE MILLION YEARS TO EARTH**, because there was no Quatermass connection at all in American culture. So it went out on a double bill with **THE VIKING QUEEN**, and I saw it at a fleapit theatre in Philidelphia, it was probably a year or two old by the time that I saw it, and I was just blown away by it. I just thought "how come nobody knows about this picture?!"

NS: *And what were the reactions of the audiences you saw those movies with?*

JD: You gotta remember a lot of these pictures were seen either as Saturday matinees, early on, or in Grindhouses. When I went to Philipelphia there were a lot of theatres still standing from the forties, including one called the 'News Theatre' that had a square screen and originally ran newsreels all night for people who came off their shifts at the munitions place. So they would run scope movies and you would see the middle of the picture and the rest of it was on the wall because they never bothered to change the screen.

These were places were, basically, drunks went to sleep. And so they were fairly dangerous places, but that's where all the movies that I wanted to see were playing.

There was another theatre called "The Family", which was a tripple-bill theatre right in the shadow of City Hall in Philidelphia, and it was the one theatre where you didn't go into the bathroom. You didn't go downstairs. You just held it! Because there were stories about people not coming back from the bathroom! And I saw some amazing events there. I saw somebody get knifed during a screening of Mario Bava's **THE WHIP AND THE BODY**, and I just, I moved . . .

The great thing about the place was that they would never turn the lights on, and it was a 24 hour theatre. So, they would only clean it if somebody threw up, and they would do it while the movie was on. So, whatever happened, you could still see the rest of the movie if you just changed seats. Sometimes you would have to change seats several times

WE ARE THE MARTIANS

during a picture depending on who was sitting next to you. But that's really the kind of places that I saw most of these pictures, so for me to report on the audience reaction, other than loud snoring...I don't think I can do that!

NS: *That's fine! That's really interesting! They're relatively atypical movies for the time, especially* **QUATERMASS 2** *I guess—*

JD: They played a lot of drive-ins. A black and white picture like **QUATERMASS 2** was a picture that would be available on a flat rental for very little money, for years after its release, until the prints wore out. So it would just be like "oh, throw that one in, that'll be the third feature". They used to call that "the clearance movie". That was the one that was supposed to get all the people to drive out of the drive in before it was over so that people could go home. "The Chaser" that's what they called them. Nonetheless sometimes that was the best movie.

NS: *It's such a big difference to the way they would have screened here in the UK, especially because of the TV connection. The series were huge over here.*

JD: It was an event. But here it was just a relic of something we didn't really know anything about. Each movie was considered as a separate piece. None of them were called Quatermass, they all had different titles.

NS: *And so things like* **THE ABOMINABLE SNOWMAN** *would have played in exactly the same way?*

JD: Well, **THE ABOMINABLE SNOWMAN** has the lowest brow trailer in America. I have a website called Trailers From Hell. If you watch the trailer for **ABOMINABLE SNOWMAN**—click the button and watch it without the commentary—it is the most annoying and condescending trailer that I have maybe ever seen. They obviously thought this was a real piece of shit, and of course it's a fantastic movie. It's one of the best British pictures of the 50's.

226

A Conversation with Joe Dante

NS: *It's great to hear you say that. I really think it's a fantastic film, and not at all well known, even within the Kneale cannon. It's really underrated. Perhaps because the title conjures up something a little hokey. But it's a really wonderful human drama.*

JD: It is, and the majority of treatments of the abominable snowman have really been pretty junky. It's like zombie movies were, y'know, "It's low budget it's junk", and now who would have ever thought that zombie movies would now be like this mainstream, big budget, **WORLD WAR Z** kind of movie. When I was a kid zombie movies were like the lowest of the low.

NS: *O f course there are rumours that the current incarnation of Hammer Films are planning a remake.*

JD: I don't think it's a very good idea actually, because it started as a TV play and the good thing about the movie was that they did have all that great footage from the Pyrenees, so it's a fairly expansive looking movie, and I just don't know that you could cast it as well as that picture is cast.

NS: *I don't know what Nigel would have thought, but from what I can gather in speaking to his wife, he really didn't like the idea of people remaking things from his work.*

JD: At the time he wasn't keen on the movies either. I think he was almost always happier with the TV versions. I found that he had quite a blind spot about Val Guest. I think that in retrospect, Val Guest is emerging as one of the most interesting British directors of his period, and Tom was always kind of dismissive because it wasn't exactly the way that he wrote it, which it couldn't be because they were all serials, they were long and they had to be compressed. And he did the compressing .

NS: *His ability to compress his work was incredible, if you look at* **QUATER-MASS 2** *and* **QUATERMASS AND THE PIT***, they don't lose a thing in terms of impact. If anything they seem almost more potent for it.*

JD: Yeah, I mean, I kept telling him that he was underestimating the value of those movies. But they just didn't meet his high standards. And he did have high standards.

NS: *He had very high standards; very exacting standards. I think he may have come around a little to the second of the Val Guest Quatermass movies—for all he still despised Brian Donlevy in the title role. He appeared on a commentary track for one of the* **QUATERMASS** 2 *dvd releases.*

JD: Dennis Bartok at the American Cinematheque set up a screening of my print of **THE DAY THE EARTH CAUGHT FIRE**, while Val was still with us, and it was quite an event, because the movie hadn't been seen in many years and it was very hard to find and I happened to find a 35mm print. And so, after it was over, not only did it get a standing ovation, but some 20 year old girl told Val that it was the best movie she'd ever seen.

NS: *Val had this incredible energy to his work, he was a really good visual director whose films always had a lot of pace. I'm always surprised that Nigel didn't have a better relationship with him, because actually he seemed to bring a very similar style and set of skills to the movies that Rudolf Cartier had in TV and with whom Kneale had a very fruitful partnership early on.*

JD: I don't think Tom ever got over the loss of Rudy Cartier. I think he thought that nobody else could fill his shoes.

NS: *From what I've read, and from talking to Judith, I know they were really very close, personally and professionally. They were a great partnership. Of course, he did work outside the genre as well with* **LOOK BACK IN ANGER** *and* **THE ENTERTAINER** *and so on.*

JD: Most of those were adaptations I believe.

NS: *They were—John Osbourne and others, and of course with some of the unmade projects. He wrote an adaptation of Aldous Huxley's* **A BRAVE NEW WORLD**, *which was to have been directed by Jack Cardiff, but which went bust days before they were due to begin shooting.*

A Conversation with Joe Dante

JD: These things do happen unfortunately. But I wonder where that script is now. Didn't I just read that Spielberg wants to remake it or something?

NS: *He also did an adaptation of William Golding's* LORD OF THE FLIES—

JD: Really? The one that Peter Brook eventually did?

NS: *Yeah. Nigel's version would have deviated further from the book, he planned to put girls in it as well as boys.*

JD: Wow. Well, that's more commercial.

NS: *You mentioned earlier* **FIRST MEN IN THE MOON,** *that movie would have screened a lot more widely in the US.*

JD: That was a big movie. The Harryhausen movies used to get a big advertising push from Columbia, so that picture played a lot of places. Whether it was ultimately successful financially, I don't know but it was a 'couldn't miss it' movie, it was everywhere.

NS: *It seems like one of the more underrated of the Harryhausen movies these days. People don't talk about it as much, I think. Although Twilight Time put it out on BluRay recently in the States.*

JD: Yeah, it's just come out in the States, but I think that—for some reason—in the rotation, the later Sinbad movies are more well known. They're not as good, needless to say, but I think because it was a period picture, that may have hurt it.

NS: *I've always thought it was one of the best scripts that Harryhausen ever had.*

JD: It was. That and **JASON AND THE ARGONAUTS** I think are the two best scripts he ever had. But in the advertising, they really shied away from pointing out the period. And the picture starts with modern astronauts, so there's a lot of that in the trailer. I don't know what the story is, but it was

WE ARE THE MARTIANS

an odd one-off that didn't have the impact that some of the other Harryhausen pictures did.

NS: *But it's one that you obviously like quite a lot.*

JD: Yeah. But a little Lionel Jeffries goes a long way with me, and there's a *lot* of Lionel Jeffries in that movie, doing his Lionel Jeffries thing. Which is okay for a while . . . but no, it's a great movie.

NS: *It's relatively unusual in terms of the films made from his scripts—of course we can't speak for the unmade, and maybe there's a sense that we never got to see all his facets as a writer because of those scripts that never got made. He's seen as quite a serious writer and a serious man. But he had a real facility for humour.*

JD: I think he did. There's a lot of great satire in THE YEAR OF THE SEX OLYMPICS and some of the other things. It's funny that he isn't better known here in the US. I assume he's better known in Britain.

NS: *He is better known here, but not as well as you would hope or expect. I can say his name—even to people within the genre, some of the authors I approached for this book for instance—and quite a number of them said, 'I know the name, but I've never seen anything by him'. That was genuinely shocking to me.*

JD: Well, dying is a bad career move.

NS: *I remain shocked though that, considering his influence, not just on the genre, but on the medium of TV itself—he really did pretty much invent TV drama as we know it here in the UK. Taking it from something very theatrical and stage bound and making it more cinematic with THE QUATERMASS EXPERIMENT, which was the first TV drama to be a national event, it really did empty the pubs when it was showing . . .*

JD: And don't forget 1984 which was also a tremendous cultural event.

A Conversation with Joe Dante

NS: *His TV work never really screened in the US at all, did it?*

JD: No, we never got to see the TV stuff until probably in the late 70's or early 80's when home video came in and these smaller companies like Sinister Cinema would put out kinescopes of whatever was still existing, because a lot of that stuff doesn't exist anymore. But that really became the purview of people who already knew the movies, which isn't a large group of people. So we would be compelled to go back and look at the videos and see the difference. See how much more complicated the TV stories were compared to what was done with the movies, make all the comparisons etc, but that's a very film buff kind of thing, and in general most people are completely unfamiliar with the television work here.

NS: *But you had managed to catch up with some of his past work via the scripts that were published?*

JD: Yeah. And also the other movies he had done that weren't horror movies, I was quite aware of that and who he was and I was reading the published scripts and things, so I got a good idea of who he was and he became one of my favourite writers. And then, when I actually got to meet him, it was quite amazing. We were...I guess it was after **GREMLINS** maybe...I can't remember. I was at Warner Bros and my friend Jon Davison was working at Orion which used to be American International, and somebody came up with the idea of remaking **THE MAN WITH THE X-RAY EYES**, and Tom did, I think, two treatments for us on it, which was quite different than the story of the original film. It really just used the title. And we got a little traction from the people at Orion, but I think ultimately they just decided that wasn't what they wanted to do, and we never really moved any further than that.

NS: *From what I gather of his working methods, he wrote really fast...*

JD: He was *very* fast. He was very fast and if you had notes for him, he would get them back the same day.

NS: *I'm trying to imagine what a Nigel Kneale version of* **THE MAN**

WITH THE X-RAY EYES *might have been ... it sounds like we missed out on something that could have been an amazing film.*

JD: He took it in a more metaphysical direction. Not that there isn't a metaphysical aspect to the original movie, but he decided to expand on that. And I think that must have been what scared them off. If he had just synopsised the same movie and handed it in, they probably would have said "Oh, okay!", y'know, because that's what they knew. But when you give them something that's off-beat that's like "I don't know do we really wanna do that? With this *British* guy?"

NS: *So, in the early days of video, you were managing to catch up with some of the TV work through the likes of Sinister Cinema. Is that when you managed to see things like* THE YEAR OF THE SEX OLYMPICS *and* THE STONE TAPE?

JD: I've seen THE STONE TAPE. I've never seen THE YEAR OF THE SEX OLYMPICS. I have the script, but I've never seen it, no.

NS: *You mentioned working with Nigel on* **MAN WITH THE X-RAY EYES,** *I was just coming to your having worked with him. You were attached to* **HALLOWEEN III** *for a while, and I believe it was your suggestion that they approach Nigel to write it. Did you meet with him for that?*

JD: Oh yes! I met him frequently, we would go out to dinner. We would go to a place called Dharma Greg, which was a Middle Eastern restaurant where you had to eat with your hands. He seemed to like it for some reason. And he would hold forth, in his way. Sometimes a little negatively, about certain people, or projects, or things, or whatever ... but he was always fascinating to listen to.

NS: *But you hadn't met him at the time you suggested him to John Carpenter as someone who could maybe write that movie.*

JD: No, I had not met him then. I just thought that he would be great for it because John said that he didn't want to do **HALLOWEEN 2** again. But

A Conversation with Joe Dante

he had this other idea, and as soon as I heard the kernal of the idea—and I was supposed to direct it at that time—I said, "we should get Nigel Kneale". And of course, John was a big fan, but it hadn't occurred to him that Tom might be available or interested or want to do it. So, that went forward and then I took the job on the TWILIGHT ZONE movie, because it was a real job as opposed to this maybe job, and John went on ahead and I guess Tom turned in what he turned in and John futzed around with it, a little too much maybe for Tom's comfort, and he ended up taking his name off it.

NS: *That's quite a big deal, to take your name off a project like that.*

JD: It is. It effects your residuals. It's a ballsy thing to do, but certainly when you see the movie you can see his influence in the picture. And Tom suggested Dan O'Herlihy to play that part, which was perfect I thought. All those scenes with Dan O'Herlihy I think you can really see Tom in them. But all the scenes with the secondary characters seem kinda like filler.

NS: *I can see why he wanted to distance himself from it, because it's very much not...*

JD: Up to his standard. Let's face it.

NS: *Do you remember much about that script? Did you see his finished draft?*

JD: I think I was gone by then...this all happened very quickly. I was offered **TWILIGHT ZONE: THE MOVIE** out of the blue, and it was actually happening and it was sort of barrelling forward, and it was a bigger deal than a sequel to another picture. This was THE TWILIGHT ZONE movie! And the other three directors were big directors—except that George [Miller] wasn't a big director then, but nor was I. But we turned that to our advantage.

NS: *Then later there was* **THE CREATURE FROM THE BLACK**

We Are The Martians

LAGOON *that John Landis was planning to remake, with himself as producer and Jack Arnold (director of the original movie) returning as director. As I understand it, you also had some involvement with that?*

JD: Yes. **CREATURE FROM THE BLACK LAGOON** was a project... in Jack Arnold's later years, in a rare case of studio largesse, Universal was really very good to him. Because he'd been there for a long time. He'd spent most of his career at Universal. And when he lost his leg to... whatever he lost his leg to, I can't remember what disease it was... they kept him on. And they seriously intended, I think, to make this sequel to/remake of **THE CREATURE FROM THE BLACK LAGOON**, with him directing. I was the back-up director in case he couldn't go up the hill or go under water or whatever it was that he wasn't going to be able to do. I was there to step in if needed. And that fell apart for reasons that I really was not that privvy to, but I know that the script that Tom wrote had extra monsters in it, for some reason. It wasn't just about the creature from the black lagoon, there was another monster as well. And I know that he and Jack had a lot of issues about what should be in the script and what shouldn't be in the script. I don't know that that was a happy pairing. And then when ultimately the whole thing went south, the studio has spent— over the years since then—probably *millions* of dollars on treatments and scripts for **THE CREATURE FROM THE BLACK LAGOON**, none of which have ever panned out. Now it's up to a point where, in order to make the picture, there's so much money into it already that it's almost not worth it. Because so much money has already been expended on nothing that they can use. And then the other question of course is the design of the costume, which has become very iconic, and they wanted to change it quite a bit and I think the fans were not happy about that. It just became kind of a hot potato and didn't happen for a while.

But that was not uncommon at Universal. I had a remake of **THE MUMMY** that was supposed happen for a number of years. It was a contemporary remake of the picture, and it was canned because the studio decided it should be a period picture "like the first mummy movie". Which of course was *not* a period picture, it just looks like one *now* because it was the nineteen thirties *then*.

A Conversation with Joe Dante

So then they spent more money over the next several years on different writers and different directors trying to come up with another Mummy franchise movie, and they finally ended up with the one they did with Stephen Sommers, which is sort of a **RAIDERS OF THE LOST ARK** take on it. And they did a bunch of those, and made some money, and now they're apparently rebooting it again. But nothing about the creature. I haven't heard anything about **CREATURE FROM THE BLACK LAGOON**.

I don't think Tom's script was ever published. But John Landis might have one, because he was ostensibly the producer of that.

NS: *Do you remember reading that script?*

JD: Oh yeah.

NS: *Did it feel like it worked?*

JD: No. It felt like it was just...not working.

NS: *It was an unusual pairing. In that Nigel was always quite dismissive of the 'Bug Eyed Monster' approach to Horror and Science Fiction...*

JD: Which was why I was surprised that his take on it was less metaphysical than his other stuff. I don't know how much of that was writing to orders, y'know "this is what we want", and he was already into it and so he would give them what they wanted. There are connections, there are things in the script, discussions about the Devonian age and where we all come from and those kind of discussions. But it was basically a monster movie, and not a particularly distinctive one. That's why I think he would be dismissive of it.

NS: *That's a shame. Because it was such an unusual pairing, there seemed to be a lot of potential there. It made me think about* **THE ABOMINABLE SNOWMAN** *and whether it might have gone in that sort of direction.*

JD: I don't think they would have let him do what he did with **THE**

WE ARE THE MARTIANS

ABOMINABLE SNOWMAN. I just don't think that would be what they wanted.

NS: *You mentioned that you spent a certain amount of time with him, that you had dinner and met up on a number of occasions. What was your impression of him as a person, not just as a writer?*

JD: I found him a big, garroulous guy, who had his intimidating side, but I liked him. I was just so much of a fan that he could have ordered me around dismissively and it would have been okay with me, but he didn't do that.

NS: *What did you think where his real strengths as a screenwriter? He had a very good sense of his own abilities I think. He knew what he could do. He knew how good he was.*

JD: He was very good with plot, he was very good with structure, and the standard attributes of a good screenwriter. But he also had a different take, a slightly off-beat take, on all these... sometimes *mundane* projects he was involved with. And sometimes it worked, and sometimes you get to a picture like **THE DEVIL'S OWN** (aka **THE WITCHES**) where it just doesn't work. You can see how it's *supposed* to work. But for a variety of reasons, some of which may not even have to do with the script, it just doesn't work. But I think everybody has that.

NS: *Do you have any particular favourites of his work, now that you've pretty much caught up with all his stuff?*

JD: Well, needless to say, I'm partial to the ones I first saw, because I was so impressed with them. I didn't see the original Quatermass picture until much later, but I really admired it's newsreel like quality. All three Quatermass pitcures are pretty high on my list, although I wish that the Roy Ward Baker one [**QUATERMASS AND THE PIT**] had been a little less brightly lit. It's just so high key. And Arthur Grant was a good DP, but for some reason it's just so over lit that it doesn't have the gravitas, visually,

A Conversation with Joe Dante

that it would need to match what the story is. But script-wise, it's the best of all of them I think.

NS: *That's interesting. I never really thought of it that way — in part because it was the first Quatermass movie that I ever saw, and Andrew Kier has such gravitas as an actor in the role, but you're absolutely right that the visual scheme doesn't quite match it. As you mention on the Optimum BluRay, it's a mark of how well written the movie is that it also over comes one of the single worst special effects ever committed to film.*

JD: The cleansing of the Martian hives . . . it's unfortunate. It would have been better to not show it at all!

NS: *Especially considering that it looked a lot better in the TV version, where they had even less budget as well!*

JD: The design of the aliens in the TV version was better. They're much more complicated and insectoid. I mean these guys looked all smoothed out and like they're carved in stone or something. Whereas the originals are all rotting, and have little pieces that stick out, like a combination of a frog and an insect or something and they were really cool, but for some reason the movie didn't go with that design.

They did manage to do the final special effect well. I mean, it's a cheap movie and there are a lot of effects in there. The whole town falling apart and the big apparition in the sky and all that kind of stuff; I mean all that stuff was done for like a dollar ninety-eight, so I think they probably ran out of money before they got to the Martian war scene.

NS: *And really, it holds up so well as a movie, it's still so effective.*

JD: It's still a good movie, and it's very well acted.

NS: *It's a great cast. Kier and Barabara Shelley, and James Donaldson . . .*

JD: And the other guy, Julian Glover, the bad guy. They're just all great. Maybe it's not even that it's so well acted, but it's so well *cast*. I mean everybody is absolutely perfect for the parts they play.

WE ARE THE MARTIANS

NS: *I agree. For all that Kneale was partial to earlier actors from TV in the role, Andrew Kier is my Quatermass.*

JD: Well, he looks like he was born to the part. And I used to listen to the tirades about Brian Donlevy all the time, but of course, to my American eyes I never saw anything wrong with that casting, because I didn't know the character. I didn't know who he was supposed to be. And his gruff, no nonsense, take charge kind of "get out of my way approach" worked well in those two pictures I thought. So, we used to talk about that. We would have spirited discussions about those two Quatermass pictures.

NS: *You mentioned having caught up with* THE STONE TAPE *now, what did you think of that when you saw it?*

JD: Oh, I thought it was terrific.

NS: *It's one of the ones that I do think that — if done right — could be an interesting remake. But the fear would be that somebody would tamper with it too much.*

JD: In today's market . . . I think it would have to be done for television, as an episode of BLACK MIRROR or something.

NS: *It seems to me — rather unfortunately — that Nigel has been . . . certainly not forgotten, but he's appallingly underappreciated. What do you think is his legacy to the genre?*

JD: I think his legacy has become, sadly, more of a cult legacy than a general one. Those of us in the business who love these kind of movies, and love this kind of material, revere him. How far that has travelled outside our circles however, is open to question.

NS: *The influence is certainly there all through TV, even if it's not acknowledged or not overtly referenced as much. To a greater or lesser degree there would be no* DOCTOR WHO *without him, without Quatermass as a predecessor . . . there'd certainly be hardly any stories from the John Pertwee*

A Conversation with Joe Dante

era of DOCTOR WHO *without him! But considering the way he changed television, he still doesn't seem to be held in such high esteem over here as one of our Great Dramatists.*

JD: I think that's because of the remoteness of early television. There are all these stories over here about David Letterman — he's a talk show guy — and he's going off tonight, it's his last show. And they're all talking about what a genius he is and how he revolutionised late night television. But what they leave out is that...there was another guy called Steve Allen in the 50's who did all of that stuff live on television and no one knows. Nobody remembers him. And when they do their stories about Letterman, about how this was all such imaginative new television...the people who are writing it are younger, too young to remember that this all was based on something else. And I think you get the same thing in today's writing about the genre, which is that — if it's before a certain period it's really not that well known.

NS: *I think as well there's a sense over here that, for all he should be held up as one of our great dramatists for television, along with Dennis Potter, or David Mercer or whoever...*

JD: Well some of that might be a little bit of genre snobbery.

NS: *Exactly. I think it is precisely because some of his greatest successes were within genre, that he isn't thought of in the same league, even though he revolutionised TV drama in the UK with* THE QUATERMASS EXPERI-MENT. *Hammer were already having some success before they adapted his dramas for the cinema but...*

JD: No, they basically...that was the movie that really put them on the map. Frankenstein was even bigger, but that was the one that gave them their new direction. Because they'd been chugging along making these sort of unremarkable melodramas for years. And this was something new. It was also tied in with the 'X' rating, so they managed to make quite a splash theatrically with this thing, and also it had been a TV phenomenon so it was like they couldn't lose. If they did it well.

WE ARE THE MARTIANS

NS: *And though Nigel wasn't happy, it really turned out pretty well. I think it helped that that was one of the ones where they really got the right director for the material. You're absolutely right about Val Guest being integral to those early successes.*

What I hope with this book is that—inevitably it's going to appeal to the people who already like him—but I'm trying to keep it open and accessible to people who might not have come across him yet. Young genre fans who perhaps haven't encountered his work yet, so that we might be able to encourage them to go look at it, to experience his work.

JD: That's why I started *Trailers From Hell,* was to try to get people— young people—to be interested in movies that they really otherwise don't have any connection with. I mean, anything that happened before they were born is certainly ancient history to them. Oddly enough my generation, things that happened before we were born were very interesting to us. We saw all those 1930's horror movies that all were made before we were born, and they were a revelation. We thought they were great! And there was a whole fan culture starting up that was basically just people our age. Which is, I think, one of the reasons that the genre which was so disrespected when I was a kid, has now become so mainstream. Because so many of us ended up making movies, and decisions about what movies get made, and invading pop culture so that all this stuff now, it's not beyond the pale anymore.

NS: *It worries me too. We're of different generations, but certainly when I was growing up here in the UK, TV was showing an enormous amount of old stuff.*

JD: It was also cheaper to show that stuff.

NS: *It meant that I was exposed to Johnny Weismuller Tarzan movies, Basil Rathbone as Sherlock Holmes, Ray Harryhausen, Charlie Chan,* **KING OF THE ROCKET MEN**...

JD: But none of that is the case now. There's no place to go to see those things. And so that little piece of culture exists in the fervent minds of a

240

A Conversation with Joe Dante

dwindling few. And I think that's true not just of this genre but *all* old movies and *all* old books, and old everything, is that it has its niche fans, but in the general market place, in the world of 'Reality Television' and the crap that people watch and they options they have...the *millions* of options that we never had...I mean we could either go to the movies, or put on a record or listen to the radio, that was about it. And now there's a zillion things that they can do, and even new movies are only a part of that. But old movies are *really* remote from them and that's one of the reasons I think it's imperative to write books like this one, so this stuff doesn't get lost.

BRIEF ENCOUNTER

Stephen Laws

THIS IS A TRUE STORY.

I was on my way to the offices of my then publisher, Hodder and Stoughton, on Euston Road in London—and it had been a long train journey from my home in Newcastle upon Tyne. However, long train journeys are never a problem for me; in truth, I rather look forward to them since they're not only a good opportunity for uninterrupted reading, but also to do some writing. On the latter point, I always feel somehow more creative. The fact that the train is rollicking through the countryside at great speed while words are appearing from my fingers, gives me a strange psychological 'kick'—in the sense that if I've reached a difficult point, or words will not come, I can look up and out of the carriage window on yet another, new, flash-by landscape and think: *Yes, I'm getting somewhere*... Then I'm loosened up and the words are coming again. One of my most pleasurable and productive long train journeys was from Newcastle to Cornwall on a research trip for my novel FEROCITY, watching the sun go down on the East Coast of England on my way to a real-life encounter with the mysterious Beast of Bodmin Moor—but that's another story, and do you see how easily I can commit the writer's sin of digression?

As well as delivering a manuscript to Hodder and Stoughton (this being pre-internet days), I had brought a paperback book that I'd had for years but had not actually read yet. It was Nigel Kneale's novelisation of his TV mini-series QUATERMASS starring John Mills. As I say, this was a long while after the transmission. So why then had I not read it, given that Nigel Kneale is one of my two greatest inspirations? (The other is Richard Matheson). Well, the answer to that question is the fact that I'd been attuned since childhood to a sort-of Nigel Kneale 'radar'. Everything that he wrote, every television or newspaper/magazine interview that appeared was instantly 'flagged' by that radar, and I was alert to the possibility that something new, exciting and deeply scary might be on its way from this extraordinarily gifted writer. (Elsewhere in this collection, others will be writing not only about the Quatermass phenomenon but other wonderful material such as his adaptation of George Orwell's NINETEEN EIGHTY-FOUR for the BBC, his stand alone plays like THE ROAD, THE STONE TAPE and THE YEAR OF THE SEX OLYMPICS; look how prophetic the latter was in anticipating 'reality TV'!, the BEASTS television series—and I'm also hoping that someone will have written about what seems now to be a 'lost' television play that affected and moved me profoundly and is in great need of proper reappraisal: BAM, POW, ZAPP!)[90] So it shouldn't be a surprise that I was aware of Kneale's frustrations associated with what eventually became the John Mills QUATERMASS (retitled **THE QUATERMASS CONCLUSION** when edited to feature length.)

Devouring genre magazines and fan publications, I'd learned that the project had struggled from Kneale's first incarnation at the hands of various broadcast 'developers'. (I recall that first drafts involved 'things in the sewers'. Wow. Bring it on, Nigel.) After revisions that seemed to deeply frustrate Kneale, the television series appeared; by which time, elements that had then been fresh and contemporary (the hippie theme of the 'Planet People' cult, for example) now seemed, well, a little 'dated'. Also, there was a suggestion somewhere (I can't recall the provenance) that not only were there elements of unhappiness with the casting of John Mills as

---

[90] Though the recording is now 'lost', the script may exist in Kneale's archives, and we hope to be able to cover it in a future volume (ed).

Brief Encounter

'Quatermass' but also that the actor himself was not happy with the part. Tie that in with what I can only describe as my reverence for the role as essayed by Andre Morell in QUATERMASS AND THE PIT (others in this collection will no doubt praise Reginald Tate equally as highly in the original series)—and you can imagine why I'd delayed reading the novelisation for so long, since it was a transcription of what was eventually broadcast rather than Kneale's original vision, and I therefore already had some disappointment.

So then—my own work on the aforementioned journey to Hodder and Stoughton has been going so well that I haven't begun to read the paperback, and on arrival at Kings Cross station I pack away my papers and put the paperback into my overcoat pocket. Onwards to Euston Road after a further short trip on the London Underground. It's a bright, chilly day and I'm looking forward to my meeting with Humphrey Price—one of the best, most incisive and 'on the ball' editors with whom it's been my pleasure to work. There's a cold wind now and up ahead is a figure walking in my direction—also with a briefcase, a long overcoat, head down and wearing a large felt hat, the brim of which he's holding on to because of the wind. There is no one else here on this stretch of Euston Road. Just me, heading towards my publisher's offices—and this gentleman now heading towards me.

And as that figure draws near, I am utterly astonished to recognise him.

It is Nigel Kneale.

I know, I know—you're saying to yourself: *Is he really expecting me to believe that after this build up, he really came face to face with the great man himself?*

Yes I am.

Because it's absolutely true.

What on earth do I do? Do I stop him—this writer who has so inspired me, but whom I've never met—introduce myself and tell him how much his work means to me? I know, by all accounts, that he has a reputation for being irascible at times. And even if I have caught him on a good day and he's prepared to be accosted by a stranger—how will I come across? How will I be able to validate my own credentials as an admiring writer and not some weirdo? If he keeps his head down, shrugging off my approach as if I was asking for a hand-out—what then?

"Excuse me, Mr Kneale. I'm a horror novelist, and I'm one of your biggest fans..."

No!

"Excuse me, Mr Kneale. I'm a horror novelist, and to prove it..." (*Throws open briefcase to reveal new manuscript*). "I'm also one of your biggest fans."

No, no!

I know! The paperback in my pocket. The John Mills QUATERMASS.

"Excuse me, Mr Kneale. I'm so sorry to bother you—but I wonder if you might sign this paperback? I've admired your work ever since I saw episodes of QUATERMASS AND THE PIT when I was a boy..."

No, no, no!

Now I recall Kneale getting very angry at someone who, like me, had been allowed by his parents to stay up late to watch that series, only to be sent to bed because it was too terrifying. Kneale was angered that parents had allowed such a thing, because this was (then) adults only entertainment with a pre-transmission announcer's warning that the programme might 'not be suitable viewing for persons with a nervous disposition'. What am I going to do? We're about to draw level now, and the moment will be lost if I don't do *something*!

My ultimate decision is suddenly instinctive rather than considered, and I startle myself by hearing my own voice say:

"Nigel! What a surprise."

Mr Kneale has clearly been deep in thought as he walks, and is now very startled when he looks up at me.

"I hadn't realised that you were in town," I continue. "What a nice surprise."

I hold out my hand.

In what seems to be a daze between his own deeply focussed thoughts(until now, that is) and the appearance of a stranger who seems to know him, Mr Kneale warily holds out his hand—I drop my briefcase on the ground, and I take it, shaking vigorously now with both of mine.

"Stephen Laws," I say—feigning some concern that he might *possibly* have forgotten someone whom he's previously met (not) and may have some regard for (but doesn't know me from Adam).

There's a tentative softening of his puzzled features, but he's still not sure and I'm still pumping his hand.

"Screenwriting seminar at the BBC this April," I continue (I know he was there, even though he doesn't do a lot of these things now. I also know that he enjoyed it, despite his strained relationship with the BBC these days.) "You were so helpful in the advice you gave me," I lie (although his writing 'advice' is something that I've lapped up over the years—just not at this seminar).

"And you're . . . ?" Nigel's somehow looking for a further clue, but I have to play this hand with confidence, so I say: "I'm on my way to Hodder and Stoughton to deliver my latest manuscript, and a meeting with my editor."

Nigel's searching my eyes.

"Humphrey Price? You may know him? One of the best editors I've ever had."

"Oh, *Humphrey*. Of course, yes . . ."

And now my biggest gambit in this conversation: "Have you got much time?" I venture. "I've got an hour before I meet Humphrey, and I did promise to return the favour last time you bought me a drink." There's a pub, yards away. "Maybe a little early, but a coffee perhaps, with a nip of brandy? A nice bracer?"

I've now politely disconnected our hands and Nigel, still trying to focus, looks at his watch. Then at the pub.

Then at me.

And says: "Stephen?"

"Yes, Stephen Laws."

"Of course, of course. Just a quick one then."

Yes!

So we repair to the pub, the name of which I still can't remember. Perhaps, like some pub in Brigadoon, it's no longer there? Vanished after this magical moment.

And in the course of that magical hour, I'm able to 'remind' Nigel of the novels I've written, my so-called reputation, my debt to his own work—

We Are The Martians

which he brusquely brushes aside, insisting that my work is intrinsically *my* work and not dependant on other inspirations, including his own — and, of course, since I know Nigel's work inside-out, I'm able to convince him how serious I am about my love of his writing and truly how inspirational it has been. He doesn't even get annoyed when I say that my parents allowed me to stay up late as a boy to watch QUATERMASS AND THE PIT. Naturally, my business card ends up in Nigel's wallet to replace the one that he couldn't find (ahem) with a promise to stay in touch, and since — of course — we are both very busy with other appointments to meet, we duly depart after the allotted hour to go our separate ways after a firm handshake and an understanding that this stranger is indeed a horror novelist whose work has been very much inspired by this astonishing Manxman and with absolutely no guilt or shame on my part that I have managed to pull off such a serious confidence trick.

So there you go.

My personal encounter with Nigel Kneale.

As I told you at the beginning, this is a true story.

Face to face with Nigel Kneale on the Euston Road.

Wow.

How astonishing is that?

Unbelieveable.

And true — like I say — true.

Up to a point.

Perhaps not one hundred percent true.

Maybe not fifty percent true.

But true. Oh yes, true.

Sort of.

I *did* come face to face with Nigel Kneale on the Euston Road, London; exactly as I've described it, right up to the line that reads: '*We're about to draw level now, and the moment will be lost if I don't do something!*'

Up until then, all true. But, I'm afraid, far from doing 'something' — I did nothing.

I couldn't find a thing to say; couldn't bring myself to accost him, couldn't reach into my pocket and pull out that paperback. Instead, he passed by my left shoulder and kept on walking, head down. I turned to

Brief Encounter

watch him go, still lost in his thoughts and all I could think was: "I can't believe it... I can't *believe* it!"

I turned and trudged up the road to my appointment with Humphrey. He couldn't believe it either.

I never got to meet Nigel Kneale and now, having been asked to write this article, I do wish I'd tried harder, been braver. It's important, I think, at some stage that we should let the people we admire know just how much we admire them. Even if they may have a reputation for not suffering fools gladly. This fool failed missed his chance to do so.

However—I was given a chance some years ago to have something published that speaks of my debt to Nigel Kneale and I'd like to thank Steve Jones and Kim Newman for permission to reproduce the following article, written by yours truly in 1988 for their excellent HORROR: BEST 100 BOOKS, and now reproduced here in its entirety. One hundred practitioners of the genre were asked to write about a favourite book, and I chose the Penguin edition of Nigel Kneale's published screenplay for QUATERMASS AND THE PIT. I haven't been tempted to update it, since every word I wrote back then is as true now as it was then. I hope that it makes up for my somewhat less than factual encounter with the great man himself on that cold London street so many years ago.

QUATERMASS AND THE PIT

While digging the foundations for an office block, London workmen discover a five-million-year-old spacecraft, complete with mummified Martians. Professor Bernard Quatermass, of the British Experimental Rocket Group, and archaeologist Dr Matthew Roney are among the boffins called in. Their investigations uncover a history of demonic manifestatation and lead them to make some frightening conclusions about the nature of humanity. The third of Kneale's four Quatermass television serials was transmitted by the BBC in six episodes in 1959, with Andre Morell in the lead role, first published as a book in 1960, and adapted for the cinema by Hammer Films in 1967 (US title: **FIVE MILLION MILES TO EARTH**), *with Andrew Keir. In its various incarnations, it remains one of the most influential works of modern horror, leaving trace effects in movies like Tobe Hooper's* **LIFE**

FORCE *and John Carpenter's* **PRINCE OF DARKNESS** *and books like Stephen King's* THE TOMMYKNOCKERS. *The other Quatermass serials are* THE QUATERMASS EXPERIMENT, *1953 (filmed 1955, US title:* **THE CREEPING UNKNOWN**; *script published 1959),* **QUATERMASS II**, *1955 (filmed 1957, US title:* **ENEMY FROM SPACE**; *script published 1960) and* QUATERMASS, *1980 (theatrical title:* **THE QUATERMASS CONCLUSION**; *novel published 1979).*

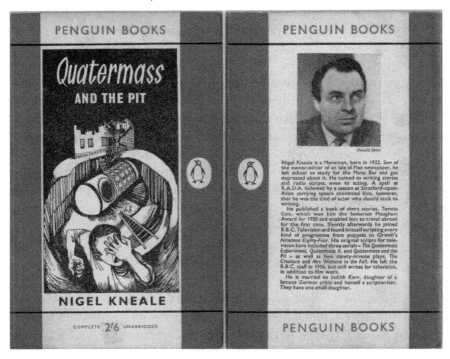

When is a book not a book? Answer: when it's a screenplay. More specifically, a television series in six parts entitled QUATERMASS AND THE PIT, written by Nigel Kneale and broadcast to genuinely alarmed and enthralled English viewers in 1959. When asked to cite a favourite or influential 'book', it may seem to be an anomaly to opt for a screenplay. But there are a number of reasons: ultimately the skill of Kneale's writing and his ability to play on subconscious dreads. Analysis of his writing nearly thirty years later still gives clues to any writer wishing to tap into the

Brief Encounter

vein of 'supernatural terror' with any effect. As a seven-year-old back in 1959 I begged my father for the privilege of staying up late to watch QUATERMASS AND THE PIT. Under extreme pressure and with reservations, I was allowed to do so. Unfortunately, I was often despatched to bed after becoming too spooked. (Hell, even Trevor Duncan's background music was enough to make me hide behind the settee.) So my initial viewing was very fragmentary, Later, my childhood frustration at not really understanding why the series was so frightening drove me to the public library where I discovered to my delight that Penguin Books had published all of the Quatermass screenplays by Kneale. I devoured THE PIT, reading it inside-out until the bizarre and fascinating premise — that the Martians were on Earth five million years ago and left their consciousness subconsciously implanted in mankind — was crystal clear.

Fantastic in the true sense of the word? Yes, of course. But written in such a down to earth way as to be extraordinarily convincing, with incident building upon incident, clue upon clue. The most original aspect of Kneale's story is the fact that the hobgoblin-like Martians of antiquity are in actuality the hobgoblins and demons from the race memory of our mythical, superstitious past. As Quatermass says, "Could it be that ghosts and the like were simply phenomena wrongly observed?" Quatermass' investigation ensues, resulting in the most effective build-up of unease and eeriness, until the climactic sequence where the Devil himself towers over the city in a glowing protoplasm of unearthly light. Only gradually does the full import of Kneale's title make its mark. QUATERMASS AND THE PIT not only refers to the clay pit in which the cylinder is found, but more specifically to The Pit of Hell itself.

One of the key elements behind the success of Kneale's premise is his depiction of a British no-nonsense sense of propriety. The characters themselves have difficulty in accepting the situation. But as traditional eerie goings-on are introduced into this modern (1959) situation and the characters are forced by the weight of evidence to accept the terrifying implications, so does the reader/viewer (subject to a slight mental wavelength adjustment from 1988 to 1959). Reader/viewer empathy with these realistic characters is strong, with a resultant 'suspension of disbelief'.

THE PIT had a profound effect on me. The echo of its cosmic terror,

I'm sure, was one of the reasons that I strove to be a writer in the vein of terror fiction. As a screenplay, the story unfolds via dialogue and action. The mood is created by an escalation of gradual discovery and the growing suspicion that something long dormant and deeply disturbing is on the verge of reawakening. The more Quatermass investigates, the greater the underlying fear that his human probing and 'interference' in things perhaps better left alone will resurrect some terrifying threat from the past. By necessity, there is no lavish, descriptive prose; no long and detailed examination of the way people are thinking. This is, after all, a screen-play—not a novel. Everything stems from the realistic quality of dialogue, the character interaction and the fascinating investigative structure of the story. Reading the screenplay without direct recourse to the visuals makes one aware of just how much the reader's imagination is being harnessed by Kneale's dark hints. This has been a useful benchmark for me in my own writing. Likewise, the need to establish a realistic setting with believable characters before introducing supernatural elements.

Another extremely important aspect to QUATERMASS AND THE PIT is the fact that it achieves its effects without any reliance on traditional horror motifs or blood'n'splatter (not that this would have been acceptable by the BBC in 1959 anyway). The keynote of Kneale's work here is 'terror' in its pure sense, a trademark which also applies to his writing for the BEASTS TV series and THE STONE TAPE in the 1970's.

QUATERMASS AND THE PIT had a tremendous effect back in the '50s and it's easy to dismiss it now as a product of its time, dated and over-taken within the genre. But in a trend of ever increasingly visceral 'horror' in the 1980's, an examination of Kneale's writing and the way he achieves his effects gives some very valuable guidelines on how to weave a story that will really frighten people. If Kneale's THE QUATERMASS EXPERI-MENT was 'man into monster' and QUATERMASS II was 'monster into man', then QUATERMASS AND THE PIT could be summarised as 'man was the monster all along'. And it's this last theme which surfaces in some of the best horror fiction being written today. As Quatermass discovers, the worst demons are those which hide in the deepest recesses of the human mind'.

ADAPTATION AND ANGER, OR:
The Nigel Kneale/John Osborne Synthesis

Richard Harland Smith

THE FACT THAT NIGEL KNEALE WROTE THE SCREENPLAY FOR Tony Richardson's 1959 film adaptation of the John Osborne stage play LOOK BACK IN ANGER has been relegated in most of the pertinent texts to the status of footnote. In THE CINEMA OF TONY RICHARDSON: ESSAYS AND INTERVIEWS, Kneale's name pops up just three times. Reference to Kneale is relegated to the appendices of JOHN OSBORNE: A CASEBOOK, and in the published diaries of LOOK BACK IN ANGER star Richard Burton, as well as in Michael Munn's 2014 biography of the actor, Kneale's name is conspicuous in its absence. Among those who prize Kneale's achievements in the realms of science fiction and the fantastic, his LOOK BACK IN ANGER adaptation merits the equivalent of a critical flyover—credit noted, at a distance. Andy Murray's trim but informative INTO THE UNKNOWN: THE FANTASTIC LIFE OF NIGEL KNEALE devotes a half dozen paragraphs to **LOOK BACK IN ANGER**, tucking them in between more generous coverage of Kneale's 1955 BBC telefilm THE CREATURE (adapted for the cinema by Hammer Film Productions in 1957 as **THE ABOM-INABLE SNOWMAN**) and the 1959 miniseries QUATERMASS AND

253

WE ARE THE MARTIANS

THE PIT (remade by Hammer for the big screen in 1967). In the first decade after his death, Kneale seems caught between two worlds: lauded by genre aficionados who express little interest in his tonier accomplishments while paid lip service by the art house crowd for his contributions to the British New Wave before being dismissed from the party like a member of the wait staff.

The professional marriage of Kneale and John Osborne was one of convenience. Osborne's LOOK BACK IN ANGER was the first of a run of plays that redirected British theatre from the mundane to the topical. Some have gone as far as to say that LOOK BACK IN ANGER saved British theatre but before the English Stage Company's groundbreaking 1956 production could achieve that end, it first had to be saved—by television. Osborne's incendiary drama, now widely recognized as a seminal text in the new wave of British plays and films that emerged a decade after the end of World War II—the first shot across the bow of British complacency and social inequity—was a box office disappointment at the time of its premiere in May 1956 and a magnet for critical contumely. Arbiters of the public taste had been savage in their disdain for this "kitchen sink" polemic, the polar opposite of a well-made drawing room comedy, which had the temerity to lay its action entirely within the attic bed-sit of a working class couple scratching out a subsistence living in a dreary Midlands city. "Unspeakably dirty and squalid," crowed the drama critic for the British Broadcasting Corporation—and he only meant the set dressing. (Legend has it that the sight of an ironing board, center stage at curtain up, elicited gasps from the opening night crowd at the Royal Court Theatre.) The dialogue, the ideas. and the outbursts of the play's 27 year-old author were branded "putrid bosh" by the *Evening News* and "prolix and ugly" by the *Guardian*. Having weathered two failures already, the newly-founded ESC was looking at another lost cause.

LOOK BACK IN ANGER did have its champions. Dissenting views came early on from the *Daily Express* and the *Financial Times* but the critical tide was turned by Harold Hobson at the *Sunday Times* and Kenneth Tynan of *The Observer*—paradoxically, the sort of posh "Sundays" that Osborne had derided through the mouthpiece of his vituperative anti-hero, Jimmy Porter (played at the ESC by Kenneth Haigh). The good

Adaption and Anger, Or . . .

press gave Osborne, ESC founder George Devine, and LOOK BACK IN ANGER's director Tony Richardson renewed hope but there remained empty seats at the Royal Court. What helped change the course of things was the intercession of the British Broadcasting Corporation, where Richardson had begun as a trainee director straight out of Oxford before moving forward as a freelancer committed to changing up the cozy stock-in-trade of Great Britain's (then) only television network. (In addition to mounting a jazz documentary, Richardson had staged a live TV adaptation of Shakespeare's OTHELLO starring gay African-American folk singer Gordon Heath, whose sexual preference could have, in 1955, sent him to prison.) In July 1956, Osborne went on television to discuss LOOK BACK IN ANGER as a guest on the BBC current affairs program PANORAMA; that October, the Corporation was persuaded to truck three cameras to the Royal Court to broadcast a 20-minute except from LOOK BACK IN ANGER; favorable response to this broadcast led to a Granada Television-produced restaging a month later, taped at the Manchester studio of BBC rival ITV with Richard Pasco subbing for Kenneth Haigh as Jimmy.

With TV ownership on the rise in Great Britain after the 1953 coronation of Queen Elizabeth II (broadcast by the BBC live from Westminster Abbey), the televised LOOK BACK IN ANGER brought the play in particular and theatre in general to those not ordinarily predisposed to visiting the West End. (Also influential was the publication of Osborne's script in book form, a boon for those who wanted to savor and quote Jimmy Porter's incendiary jeremiads, and the play's popularity with provincial theatre companies.) Osborne's message, his pointed attack on British middle class complacency and the custodial clutch of the Lord Chamberlain (who had retained, since the Licensing Act of 1737, veto power within the British theatre world to maintain "the preservation of good manners") appealed to the young, who flocked to the Lyric Theatre, where LOOK BACK IN ANGER had been moved to accommodate its following. In 1957, the play transferred to Broadway with Richardson at the helm and most of the principal cast (Haigh, Alan Bates, Mary Ure) in place. Recognized by the New York Critics Circle as the best foreign play of the season, the production ran for a year and was nominated for a 1958 Tony Award as Best Play. A film version was inevitable and well before the Broadway production loaded out of New York's John Golden Theatre pre-production was under way.

Produced by Canadian Harry Saltzman, who with future business partner Albert Broccoli would soon roll the dice on film adaptations of the spy novels of British writer Ian Fleming, Richardson's feature cinema adaptation of **LOOK BACK IN ANGER** was meant to capitalize on the tumult that had so shaken the British theatre and, by extension, British society. Having learned never to bother with half measures, Saltzman insisted on a big name for the role of Jimmy Porter and brokered the enthusiastic commitment of Richard Burton, who was keen to break away from his Hollywood assignments and even accepted a reduced fee to play the part. (There was very little financial risk on the part of Burton, who purportedly had £1,000,000 squirreled away in a Swiss bank account, out of reach of the British inland revenue service.) With actress Mary Ure (by then, Mrs. John Osborne) brought back in the role of Jimmy's long-suffering wife Alison and the other roles doled out to Gary Raymond (as Jimmy's pal and business partner Cliff) and Claire Bloom (as comely plot catalyst Helena Charles). Though Osborne resisted the notion of having the play "opened up" for the cinema, of having the plot played out in various locations rather than being restricted to the womblike/tomblike attic location of the ESC production, he was relieved to have the job fobbed off on another writer. Enter Nigel Kneale.

Kneale had been a jobbing writer at the BBC since 1951, having forfeited a literary career (to which he seemed pointed with his receipt of the 1950 Somerset Maugham Award for fiction) for one in television. Known as an adaptation man, Kneale had proven himself a dab hand at distilling a novel, short story, or theatre piece into commanding telly. In 1952, he had adapted an obscure Anton Chekhov tale as the television drama CURTAIN DOWN, directed by Tony Richardson for the BBC's WEDNESDAY THEATRE show and starring English Stage Company president George Devine. A year later, Kneale and producer Rudolph Cartier had changed the course of British television with the original miniseries THE QUATERMASS EXPERIMENT. Commissioned to fill a six week gap in summer programming, a time when the majority of

Adaption and Anger, Or...

TV license holders were expected to be on their holidays, THE QUATERMASS EXPERIMENT drew an audience of five million viewers. A rejoinder to American science fiction epics that demonized science and lionized the military (Kneale deplored the Howard Hawks-produced **THE THING FROM ANOTHER WORLD**), THE QUATERMASS EXPERIMENT focused for the most part not on its monster-on-the-loose (an astronaut who has returned to Earth from deep space as the host for an alien entity) but on its boffin hero—rocket scientist Bernard Quatermass—the only man in all of England with the intelligence t o understand what is happening and the know-how to stop it. It was Kenneth Tynan's inspiration to tap Kneale for the job of adapting LOOK BACK IN ANGER, though likely it was Kneale's efficiency and afford-ability that won him the job more than the scope of his startling narrative vision.

Bernard Quatermass seems, at first pass, the antithesis of Jimmy Porter—cool where Porter is boiling, compassionate where Porter is cruel, clubbable where Porter is on the outside looking in; while Jimmy Porter is indeed an angry young man stewing in his resentful juices, the elder Quatermass has aged beyond any anger that might once have taken hold of him, though he retains possession of an admirable temper to which he is willing to give rein when stymied by institutional intractability (invariably personified by the governmental seat in Whitehall, and a War Office that seeks to weaponize every scientific breakthrough). Yet despite holding a well-earned place among the nation's higher men, Quatermass often finds himself—in THE QUATERMASS EXPERIMENT and two televised follow-ups, QUARTERMASS II (1955) and QUATER-MASS AND THE PIT (1959)—on the poor side of town, where disaster often puts him in the company of the hoi polloi, the working class—the punters, whom he must ultimately protect from some unimaginable evil and the complacency of a bureaucracy over-focused on appearance and orthodoxy. In the first serial, an experimental rocket launched on Quatermass' watch returns to Earth and crashes in Wimbledon, shearing off the façade of a terraced house not dissimilar from the Midlands dump in which Jimmy and Alison Porter are domiciled in LOOK BACK IN ANGER. As the upended rocket steams in eerie silence where it fell, the

WE ARE THE MARTIANS

sundered building stands with its humble living quarters revealed. The crash site fills with assorted Cockneys, someone's mongrel dog yelps, and a baby cries.

The baby is the unexpected touch, its bothersome wailing so unlike anything British TV watchers would have seen on CAFÉ CONTINENTAL or THE GOOD OLD DAYS. The unseen infant cannot help but bring to mind, for those viewing the serial from the far side of history, the unborn child at the heart of LOOK BACK IN ANGER—the issue of Jimmy Porter, whose unforeseen conception drives him away from Alison and whose death in utero brings the pair back together. Conceived in different conditions, for different reasons, under vastly different circumstances, and by writers who could not have differed more completely from one another in temperament and outlook, THE QUATERMASS EXPERIMENT and LOOK BACK IN ANGER share several points of disarming commonality. (It bears remembering that the serial's original title was BRING SOMETHING BACK.) Both works begin in close quarters that compress living, eating, and sleeping spaces into a single unit: LOOK BACK IN ANGER opens with Jimmy, Alison and their friend Cliff pressed in together on a lazy Sunday (lazy because the pubs are closed, by order of the Lord Chamberlain) in their shabby attic and THE QUATERMASS EXPERIMENT with three astronauts (offscreen but foregrounded in the dialogue) in an experimental rocket that has veered off course. When the craft plummets to Earth, Quatermass describes the insidiously tight cockpit to an investigating policeman with words that would do as well for the Porter garret ("You can call it snug or abominably cramped, whichever you like.") and which bear an attitude of impatience that would apply just as aptly to Jimmy Porter.

Kneale's changes to Osborne's LOOK BACK IN ANGER script were minimal, though there is the occasional line (Jimmy refers derisively to Alison's toffee-nosed brother Nigel as "the Platitude from Outer Space") that seems positively Knealean. Kneale's tack with the adaptation was not to mess with Osborne's speechifying but to move indoor scenes outside, to connect the playwright's insights into the private lives of disenfranchised Britons with their public environs (e.g., the market where Jimmy and Cliff run a sweets stall, the mixed race jazz club that Jimmy haunts, the local pub), and to stage scenes to which the play's dialogue had merely referred. The adaptation also opened up Osborne's four-hander to an assortment of minor characters, the very sort of regular folk that Kneale enjoyed folding into his Quatermass stories: the laborers, the publicans, the pensioners, the salariat, the hospital staff. (Kneale borrows a trick from THE QUATERMASS EXPERIMENT and sets a scene for LOOK BACK IN ANGER inside a cinema during a matinee.) Kneale also added the character of an Indian immigrant whose presence as a vendor in the marketplace drives the locals to racially-motivated acts of sabotage. Jimmy's outraged (one might even say heartbroken) response is in sympathy with Kneale's thoughts about British colonialization and racial intolerance in QUATERMASS AND THE PIT and his belated wrap-up QUATERMASS (1979), where the professor quips about "pulling down the natives" and a colleague replies "That's what we were for—pulling down the natives. Our own."

Kneale's adaptation of LOOK BACK IN ANGER begins not in the Porter attic, as Osborne had intended, but in a jazz club, where Jimmy jams soulfully before heading home. His solitary passage on foot through the darkened and empty streets of his patch is a visual echo of monster-in-the-making Victor Caroon's lonely perambulations in THE QUATERMASS EXPERIMENT as he attempts to elude all who would exercise dominion over him. Both journeys have a metaphoric currency, representing as they do different but allied takes on Great Britain's post-colonial journey-to-self. Caroon and Jimmy Porter are walking amalgams: Caroon having assumed/consumed the essence of his fellow astronauts and Jimmy the everyman of his generation, the voice of a nation embroiled in a crisis of identity. Both stories conclude with an appeal to basic humanity: while Quatermass implores the now monstrous Caroon to tap into his vestigial humanity in order to do the right thing (which is to say, commit suicide and ankle the impending alien takeover), LOOK BACK IN ANGER ends with Alison opening her heart to Jimmy and in so doing breaking his. It's interesting that Kneale red-penciled Alison's line from the play "Don't you see? I'm in the mud at last!" given that he would go from LOOK BACK IN ANGER to QUATERMASS AND THE PIT, in which the discovery of a Martian spacecraft dug out of the mud of a postwar housing development gives way to a parable about racial denial and the fragility of identity.

It would be unforgivably glib to say that THE QUATERMASS EXPERIMENT and LOOK BACK IN ANGER are companion pieces in any literal way; if the same writer were not linked to both, the titles would rarely, if ever, be discussed in the same breath. It is the name of Nigel Kneale that forces the association and encourages cross referencing, the intertextual experience of which is not unrewarding. Though Kneale and John Osborne were very different writers, with very different takes on British life and very different personalities to boot (though both suffered from childhood rheumatic fever and in later life traded repertory acting for the writing life), THE QUATERMASS EXPERIMENT and LOOK BACK IN ANGER chronicle postwar British life with equal acuity. That Osborne's angle is through a prism of contempt while Kneale's is the more objective, less pained perspective (his father was, after all, a journalist) does not mitigate the fact that both works gave voice to a nation undergoing turbulent transformation, that both were an expression of a new generation whose anguished birth cries helped drown out the death rattle of the old Edwardian order. The kinship of the Quatermass films to the so-called kitchen sink school of socially-driven, class-centered British dramas (following LOOK BACK IN ANGER, Jack Clayton's ROOM AT THE TOP, Karel Reisz's SATURDAY NIGHT AND SUNDAY MORNING, Lindsay Anderson's THIS SPORTING LIFE, and Tony Richardson's A TASTE OF HONEY, based on Shelagh Delaney's influential 1958 stage play) argues for the symbiosis of high and low art, whose camps should comingle more often than they do.

THE PROMISED END

Nigel Kneale's lost masterpiece—THE ROAD

Jonathan Rigby

"*THROUGH SWIRLING DUST, IT CAN BE SEEN THAT THE INCAN-descent hull has almost gone...sublimated into the monstrous shape that hangs above the pit. A shimmering form bursts rhythmically into a blinding glare. It extends upwards for a hundred feet or more, and its outline is defined. It recalls that of the Martian bodies...a terrible horned thing!*"

By 1963 four years had elapsed since this apocalyptic image formed the climax to 'Hob', the final instalment of Nigel Kneale's QUATERMASS AND THE PIT. In the interim, two of his 1953 scripts—for GOLDEN RAIN and WUTHERING HEIGHTS—had been submitted to BBC remakes in 1959 and 1962 respectively. Otherwise Kneale was engrossed in the screenplays for **LOOK BACK IN ANGER**, **THE ENTERTAINER** and **HMS DEFIANT**, as well as refashioning the six episodes of QUATERMASS AND THE PIT into a proposed feature for Hammer Film Productions. But with a belated return to the BBC in September 1963 came a long overdue recurrence of apocalyptic imagery, imagery lent greater weight by the previous year's Cuban Missile Crisis.

THE ROAD accordingly went out at 9.00 pm on Sunday the 29th; a taut and unnerving 55 minutes, it must have sat oddly in a schedule that

WE ARE THE MARTIANS

placed THE BLACK AND WHITE MINSTREL SHOW and US import PERRY MASON directly before it and a MONITOR profile of choreographer Gillian Lynne directly after it. Yet viewers had been forewarned. That week's *Radio Times*, with David Frost and the THAT WAS THE WEEK THAT WAS ensemble pictured on the front cover, contained a brief note to the effect that "This *First Night* story by Nigel Kneale—of Quatermass fame—is set in 1770." The mere reference to Quatermass should have been warning enough. But Kneale himself contributed a written introduction that asked the provocative question "Do ghosts and science belong together in the same play?" The equally provocative answer? "They do in this one." Then came Kneale's statement of the conundrum that had triggered the project in the first place. "Today science holds all humanity in a death grip," he wrote. "Yet only 200 years ago it scarcely existed."

How to top, or at any rate equal, that terrifying image of the horned Devil hovering over London? Kneale did so by proffering no literal 'image' whatever, instead conjuring the most appalling spectacle of all—what Shakespeare called "the promised end"—through the use of sound. He'd made major demands on the BBC sound department before; the paranormal phenomena of QUATERMASS AND THE PIT, for example, had involved plenty of sonic disturbances. (Indeed, the published script, which I read avidly at about the age of 12, introduced me to the splendid but sadly neglected word 'crepitation'.) But THE ROAD would present the biggest challenge of all, calling for a crescendo of screaming panic arising from "the worst, most frantic traffic jam of all time" and leading inexorably to "the colossal sound of a thermonuclear blast wave, sweeping outwards from the point of impact, [which] thunders out and spreads and fades."

Yet the play was set in 1770, a time, as Kneale put it, when science "scarcely existed." To build up to his climactic reversal—a reversal too profoundly shattering to label with the trite phrase 'twist ending'—Kneale crafted a gripping and beautifully written evocation of the late 18th century and created two contrasting characters who "between them," he later explained, "possess the strands of thinking that will lead to some of the horrors of our own time."

262

The *Sunday Telegraph's* estimate of the finished product—"as obsessive, well-argued and worrying as all the best science fiction aims to be"—no doubt gratified and exasperated Kneale in equal measure. When the script came to be published in 1976 alongside two more recent works, THE YEAR OF THE SEX OLYMPICS and THE STONE TAPE, he introduced all three with a by-then customary denial that his plays were intended as science fiction. "My primary interest," he insisted, "was in the characters, in developing them as real people. In each case they were faced with some extraordinary situation, of course, but they had first to be brought alive and rendered actable. THE ROAD," he added, "is a ghost story set in the 18th century and I have tried to place its characters firmly there, in the Age of Reason." Indeed, here was Kneale's first stroke of genius in conceiving THE ROAD. What better setting for an outburst of the ungovernable and irrational than an era priding itself on enlightenment and progress?

In 1770, Horace Walpole's prototype Gothic novel THE CASTLE OF OTRANTO had been in print for six years, signalling a return to atavism that would eventually exchange the Enlightenment for the Romantic movement. Appropriately then, in THE ROAD Kneale offers an early warning of the undercurrents that will finally destroy his protagonists' intellectual complacency, beginning the play with a tableau that trades unashamedly on Gothic conventions. We have the dusky October twilight, the crooked tree branches, the owl hooting at a distance, the frightened young man isolated in a woodland clearing. "His eyes search the darkening trees," Kneale elaborates. "His hands are working feverishly to bind two sticks together with strands of grass, into the rough shape of a cross."

Then Kneale introduces a strange, disconcerting detail of his own—a group of workmen among the trees, connecting them together by means of tautened ropes, and another man decorating the ropes with "metallic oddments" such as "old bells, jangling bits of harness and chain, scrap from a rural forge." Lukey Chase is a manservant of the local squire and is clearly involved in some arcane outdoor experiment. "Any tricky lad come boltin' through 'ere tonight," he points out, "he'll set this lot off an' we'll have him." The first two sound effects—a couple of contributions from the hooting owl—have already been joined by "the familiar sound" of a

WE ARE THE MARTIANS

barking dog. Now a rat chimes in with "a tiny squeal a short distance away in the darkening undergrowth." Lukey is unfazed. "Killin' early tonight, that owl," he says to the cowering young man.

It's a brilliant opening, establishing a climate of workaday weirdness with the deftest of strokes. And pretty rapidly we're apprised of what's actually going on. Sam—the quavering youth—is the latest to experience the frightening sonic eruptions for which this patch of woodland has long been notorious. "I was laid on the ground an' I could feel it startin' to shake," he says. "An' the noises come nearer, a-roarin' and a-rattlin' like naught I ever did hear...Yelling and screeching. And footsteps running... under the ground I was lyin' on!" (This line, like many things in THE ROAD, irresistibly recalls Kneale's previous blending of science and the supernatural, QUATERMASS AND THE PIT—specifically the moment when the possessed drill operator Sladden flings himself down outside a church and the ground ripples uncontrollably beneath him.) The local squire, Sir Timothy Hassall, theorises that the disturbances are an echo of "some great catastrophic event...an event of such spiritual force that it somehow imprinted itself on the very landscape." The flight of Boadicea's army from the Romans is posited as a likely cause; whatever the truth may be, Sir Timothy is convinced that "There is something here worth probing with all the means we have!"

In his *Radio Times* piece, Kneale neatly contextualised the sensitive and somewhat fussy Sir Timothy. "From being the hunting-ground of charlatans," he explained, science "had become the domain of gentlemen amateurs, who called it natural philosophy. They converted libraries and outhouses into laboratories where they might tinker with crucibles and gas jars. Sir Timothy Hassall, rural squire and self-taught natural philosopher, is one such. He is fascinated by the search for new knowledge. He strives for a humility in the face of fact that would do credit to a scientist of our own time. But he is a prisoner of his age. He seeks knowledge at random, even in such suspect areas as the supernatural." Reassessing the play in 1976, Kneale noted, more bluntly, that Sir Timothy's "meek and insatiable curiosity makes him the prototype of the socially irresponsible scientist."

"Hassall's Law: Man can never move back." Living under this precept,

The Promised End

Sir Timothy has at his command various items that go well beyond the "crucibles and gas jars" referred to above. Pride of place goes to "a crude electroscope in an ornamented case. Some of its internal parts are made of small bones, and it is topped with a mummified cat's head with whiskers." The squire's young wife Lavinia—who herself watches his procedures with the lofty amusement of a pampered cat—calls this contraption 'pussy'. For Sir Timothy, however, it's no joke; the whiskers "may provide additional attraction for electrical fluid." The whole procedure is reductively described by a conceited London visitor as "a new proof for the existence of hobgoblins"—another line providing a distinct echo of QUATERMASS AND THE PIT.

The London visitor—invited along, somewhat to her husband's irritation, by Lavinia—is Sir Timothy's opposite, "a sub-Johnsonian iconoclast of the London coffee houses" called Gideon Cobb. Just as the purity of the proto-scientist is coloured by superstition, so the Enlightenment demagogue "has a great and glittering vision, larger by far than his own nature, of how the world should go." Again, Kneale's coy hint in his 1963 introduction was made far more explicit in its 1976 counterpart. "The idealist," he wrote plainly, "is also a sensual bigot."

Indeed, we first meet him as he wolfs down his pudding at the local tavern—a steak pie, washed down with plenty of coffee, having been first on the menu. "Coffee is the element I float in, madam, be it exquisite or vile," he tells Lavinia. "I chart my way through the flavours like the great whale in his sea." The dialogue in THE ROAD may occasionally smack of pastiche Sheridan, but there's no doubt that it's at least as flavourful as Cobb's coffee and also eminently speakable, the kind of thing actors love to get their tongues around. And Cobb is a larger-than-life figure whose feet-of-clay contradictions would be a gift to any performer.

He speaks eloquently of a perfectible future, most notably in a speech that will acquire baleful significance at the end of the play: "The great steam pumps we see now are going to have a million descendants. In a hundred years—in two, certainly—machines will do all the world's fetching and carrying. They'll be more obedient, loyal and industrious than any slaves in history. They'll carry men through the air and over the seas. They'll sow and reap for us, water the deserts, melt the polar snows..." Yet he continues to patronise his own slave, a highly intelligent Jamaican manservant called Jethro. "Jethro's an experiment," he pronounces loftily. "On the whole, he works." (When Sir Timothy wonders at Cobb's disrespectful attitude, he replies, "You might as sensibly ask me to respect him for the silver buckles I've put upon him.") He also blandly dismisses Sir Timothy's helpers as yokels, scoffs at Sam's supposed illiteracy with "If you'd only learned your ABC!" and even seems poised to enter into an opportunist affair with the bored and rootless Lavinia.

Sadly, the female roles in THE ROAD, though certainly playable, are by no means as fleshed out as Cobb and Sir Timothy. Lavinia is the standard-issue jaded aristocrat who is titillated by the metropolitan Cobb purely because he seems to confirm her view of Sir Timothy as a provincial dullard. (Her language in response to Cobb's idealist rhetoric is decidedly sexual, notably her rhapsodic cry of "I want to feel history sweeping me away like a great warm tide!" She appears not to notice her husband's quiet but rapier-sharp demolition of Cobb's Golden Age posturings: "He denounces fantasy only to set up another one.") The other female role, 18-year-old Tetsy, is the landlord's daughter and keen to defend her beau, Sam, from accusations that he's a credulous fantasist who has experienced no weird phenomena whatsoever. She later fulfils the mediumistic Barbara Judd role from QUATERMASS AND THE PIT, experiencing those weird phenomena herself but through vision as well as sound. "Like a lightnin' flash, I seen it!" she stammers. "There wasn't no trees, but a huge, wide road—an' things movin'..." Despite juicy moments such as this, the Barbara Judd role wouldn't assume centre stage until being converted, nine years later, into THE STONE TAPE's Jill Greeley.

As Sir Timothy's woodland investigation gets under way, Kneale is careful to intersperse the gathering omens with some light humour. Hoist by his own petard, the natural philosopher trips over the carefully wrought jingle-bells contraption and is left "spluttering in the leaf mould." His means of conjuring Boadicea's slaughtered army are quaintly absurd, too—"amateurishly occult," as Kneale puts it. For scene-setting purposes, various prop swords and shields are hung among the trees, together with a horse's skull and, above it, a human one wearing a plumed Roman helmet. Lavinia confirms Cobb's suspicion that these items were had from a troupe of strolling players. "They passed in the spring," she says, "playing *Julius Caesar.*"

Yet in the midst of all this, brilliantly planted by Kneale, comes an authentic chill. Sir Timothy's speculations about "animal-magnetic fluids" being left behind in the area—"As if part of the vital spirits of the people there had been torn away under the dreadful pressure of fear and death"— cause Tetsy to spook the gathered workmen with a panicked cry of "Part of their souls!" Here, Cobb's way with easy humour, normally employed in sneering terms at Sir Timothy's expense, does a smooth job of rescuing the situation. "I think the squire means something more—more chemical than souls," he reassures them. "Besides, Queen Boadicea may be officially doubted to have had any. She was a pagan."

Despite this intervention, Cobb persists in humiliating Sir Timothy in argument, and as a result the 'understanding' between Cobb and Lavinia almost finds expression. With exemplary timing, however, this tremulous moment is rudely cut off by the first of the night's sonic disturbances—"a mere blink of sound, shrill and gone in a moment." Yet to those with the right kind of sensitivity the sound clearly brings with it an image, too. "I seen the road!" whispers Tetsy in mortal terror. And Cobb too; he puts it down to "a touch of dyspepsia" but his chalk-white face belies this attempt at bravado. That the pathological debunker should be sensitive to paranormal manifestations is, of course, Kneale's crowning irony. Better still, Cobb's visible discomfiture gives Jethro (previously referred to by his master as "that damned cannibal") the opportunity to express some home truths: "Mr Cobb, you have a great mind, but there are too many things in it you won't admit—troubling, odd, hid-away, mean things—even in yourself." These human frailties, Jethro astutely observes, "will rise up and spoil your grand design."

After this the sounds go on, increasing in intensity, terrifying the women and workmen, initiating a mass stampede, and engulfing the formerly cocksure Cobb "in a wave of demoralisation." Now, though, as Kneale points out, "for the first time it is possible to read some meaning into them. Nothing that Cobb can understand, as his expression shows—but to listeners of two centuries later, the sounds would be hideously significant." The sounds comprise throbbing air-attack sirens, the "metallic crunches"

WE ARE THE MARTIANS

of a huge traffic jam and multiple pile-up, a Babel of panicked voices (mostly car-bound parents trying to protect their small children), and finally "a thunderous nuclear roar." Cobb is horrified by what he sees, clapping his hands over his eyes "as if to crush the eyeballs and destroy the sight in them." Tetsy, the other 'seer', has a heart attack and dies. Sir Timothy, traumatised too but desperate to know what they saw, gets no satisfaction from Cobb, whose "face has curiously collapsed" and who ends the play with "a low howl of utter despair."

On this note THE ROAD fades out. Of course, Kneale makes no attempt to resolve the contest between his archetypal protagonists; his attitude sensibly adheres to the Shakespearean formula "a plague on both your houses." He clearly knew that his 'haunting from the future' climax would stagger his audiences quite sufficiently, without recourse to a pat philosophical resolution—and there's much anecdotal evidence to suggest that contemporary viewers were indeed shattered by the experience. Merely on the page, Kneale's detailed description of the future apocalypse has extraordinary power, leaving the reader emotionally drained and, yes, shattered.

Sadly, 'on the page' is all we have. THE ROAD was seen just once on that Sunday evening in September 1963 and later wiped. Can we see James Maxwell (Sir Timothy), John Phillips (Cobb), Ann Bell (Lavinia), Meg Ritchie (Tetsy), Rodney Bewes (Sam) and Clifton Jones (Jethro) giving life to Kneale's all-important characters in Christopher Morahan's production? We cannot. By the same token, we'll never hear the ingenious sound effects devised by Brian Hodgson of the BBC Radiophonic Workshop, effects that were recorded, according to Kneale biographer Andy Murray, in the concrete yard of Morahan's alma mater, Highgate School.

That the BBC's policy of wiping apparently 'worthless' programmes was short-sighted cultural vandalism of the worst kind hardly needs reiterating here. Kneale himself accepted the situation with a characteristically jaded shoulder-shrug. But, to show that others weren't quite so philosophical, I'll just add a personal reminiscence of the Canadian director Alvin Rakoff, who did so much important work in the early days of British television. Talking to me in October 2006, he made it clear that the destruction of so

The Promised End

many of his productions still—well, 'rankled' seems an inadequate word, given the molten indignation that obviously remained very much alive. Videotape was expensive, of course, and it was the 1970s snooker programme POT BLACK that was recorded over much of the junked material, he told me. "And do you know who was responsible for this?" he added with rising disgust. "Gerald Savory." Having identified the BBC's 1970s Head of Plays, Rakoff moved on to what was obviously, for him, the ironic final straw: "And he was a *playwright!*"

As a footnote to this grievous loss, it's worth noting that THE ROAD was also produced by Patrick Barton for the ABV-2 station in Melbourne; transmitted on 17 June 1964, this version, too, seems not to have survived. And the play has twice been mooted for a 21st century remake. In 2002 Mark Gatiss visited Kneale at his home in Barnes with a proposal to disinter the script and mount a new production. In the wake of 9/11, Kneale realised that the play's relevance was back at full strength; once so firmly wedded to the 'brink of destruction' horror of the Cuban Missile Crisis, it had now acquired fresh impetus because, as Kneale put it, "The world has become so dangerous again."

Pursuing the project, Gatiss faced the standard round of corporate niggling; there were worries, for example, that the dialogue was dated, presumably coming from executives who'd failed to notice the play's 18th century setting. (Kneale's frequent use of the word 'frikkened' for 'frightened' was a particular sore point.) But the production seemed likely to go ahead—until, that is, Kneale watched the Fiction Lab production SURREALISSIMO on 2 March 2002. This play about Salvador Dalí was the drama centrepiece for the opening night of BBC Four and came from several of the people due to be involved in THE ROAD; indeed, Gatiss had an acting role in it. And Kneale loathed it. Suddenly, the deal was off. "I discovered that this was a pattern many had experienced over the years," Gatiss later pointed out.

A few years later the team that produced BBC Four's live remake of THE QUATERMASS EXPERIMENT considered THE ROAD for revival too, but abandoned the idea because it hadn't been a live broadcast in its original incarnation. Given that live transmission was no longer, as it had been in 1953, a necessity, Kneale felt the idea of performing either play

We Are The Martians

live was an absurdity, and his decidedly low opinion of the premise extended to the finished product when THE QUATERMASS EXPERIMENT finally went out on 2 April 2005. So the idea of resurrecting THE ROAD is unlikely to have come to fruition even if the production team had decided to go for it.

These near-misses leave the door open, however, for a new version of THE ROAD at some time in the future. Poignant and stunningly powerful, it's one of Kneale's key works and certainly deserves it.

A Conversation with Mark Gatiss

Neil Snowdon

MARK GATISS IS AN ACTOR, COMEDIAN, SCREENWRITER, *director, novelist and, not surprisingly, one of the busiest men in television. Best known for his work as part of* THE LEAGUE OF GENTLEMEN, DOCTOR WHO *("The Unquiet Dead", "The Idiots Lantern", "Victory Of The Daleks", "Cold War", "The crimson Horror", "Robot Of Sherwood" and "Sleep No More") and* SHERLOCK *(co-creator with Steven Moffat and writer of "The Great Game", "The Hounds Of Baskerville", "The Empty Hearse", and co-writer of "The Abominable Bride"), he can currently be seen on screens playing Tycho Nestoris in* A GAME OF THRONES.

Busy he might well be—put his name in the search engine of your choice if you want to see just how extraordinarily prolific he is—but Mark is also one of the nicest men in television and one of the most vocal supporters of the work of Nigel Kneale, and it's importance in the history of Film and Television. We spoke by phone and had a ball...

NS: *Do you remember when you first came across Nigel's work?*

MG: I can remember it distinctly. It was **QUATERMASS 2**, the movie. I have weirdly vivid memories of the night I saw it. These days you can prob-

271

WE ARE THE MARTIANS

ably track down the transmission, but I think I was about 7 or 8. I remember it because my cousin, who lived with us, had a date with this guy whose name was Stuart Blenkinsop—I'll always remember his name—and he had big platform shoes, but the bottoms had worn away and where he walked, there were columns of dried mud that fell off his shoes. And that was the evening I watched **QUATERMASS 2**. That image, plus the creatures thrashing about in the dome at the end, somehow fused in my mind.

But I suppose I was aware of the name Quatermass from my family. So when BEASTS was shown in 1976, I was very aware that it was by "the Quatermass Man", and I was terribly, terribly excited. I've never tracked this down precisely, but I'm certain that the first one to show in my region—Tyne Tees—was "During Barty's Party". That's how I remember it. And I was utterly petrified. So, I had an awareness of the fact that BEASTS was from the mind of Nigel Kneale, and I loved the series. It had a sort of sweaty intensity that really scared me. it ticked all my boxes really.

And then, I think a short time after that, I remember **QUATERMASS AND THE PIT** being on while I was at school and it being the talk of the playground obviously. Then I seem to have some memory of talking to my family about it, and them saying traditionally, about how terrified they were and it emptying the pubs and all that sort of thing.

But the thing that made the crucial difference was the '79 QUATERMASS, and the scripts coming out. I remember buying all of those. I was very aware of him as a phenomenon there I suppose, and I was very keen to spend my pocket money buying those three scripts for THE QUATERMASS EXPERIMENT, QUATERMASS II, and THE PIT then the novelization of the Mills one, because I was aware of him as a writer, I suppose.

NS: *Being aware of him as a 'phenomenon', his name was obviously still very well known at that point.*

MG: Well, I remember reading the introductions to those books, I was just glancing at them the other day, and there's something so charming about the fact that he says "my wife and I celebrated our Silver Wedding" which

A Conversation with Mark Gatiss

was only twenty five years later on from THE QUATERMASS EXPERI-MENT—it feels like no time at all! And all these things where he's kept the spelling of computer with an 'o' (ie 'computor') as a period touch. But I was always interested to see him in the behind the scenes stuff. One of my bibles was actually a Target book, THE MAKING OF DOCTOR WHO because I was just so interested in how things were done. I learned so much from the credits of programmes, as we all did I think in those days, and I was keen to know more about what the difference was between a director, a producer or a script editor, or such like. I suppose all these things came together around that time: a huge interest in Science Fiction and Fantasy, and the name of Nigel Kneale being predominant. Roughly around that time as well, I would see his name invoked by people as a god! And it was a perpetual thing in reading interviews with various DOCTOR WHO alumni, particularly script editors. Essentially, every time a script editor joined DOCTOR WHO they would try to get Nigel Kneale to write for it and he would tell them to fuck off!.

So I quickly became aware that he was "the Daddy".

NS: *I didn't see BEASTS until the Network DVD release, I was born in '77—*

MG: Child! I'm hanging up now!

NS: *But I found—and I was in my thirties when I saw it—it really, really got under my skin. And the ones that stick for me...I'd been led up to "Baby" by having lots of people tell me about it, and I really liked it, but I found that some of the others, stuck with me more, perhaps because I wasn't as expectant, so they felt more like discoveries for me, and therefore made a greater impact.*

MG: Well that's often the way isn't it. I found when I watched them again–and this was a long time before the Network ones, I got some very ropey bootlegs–but "Buddy Boy", which I remember not liking, *really* got under my skin. It's *queasy*. The whole series is queasy, but that one...I can remember watching it go out and there was an atmosphere about it...I

WE ARE THE MARTIANS

mean it's astonishing to think that was essentially the slot that now might have BENIDORM or something. It was a midweek ITV slot. It's wonderful! It's so dark and strange and the idea of pitching a series like that, "I want to do six one off television plays, tangentially about animals." But what they are is...something strange and wonderful. "What Big Eyes", for example: what an incredible piece of work that is.

NS: *Of all of them, it's that and "Murrain"—which isn't part of the series proper, I know—but "What Big Eyes", I just can't get that one out of me. The performances, because it's essentially a three hander, there's essentially nothing to be seen on screen that's scary, it's all about what they say and how they say it.*

MG: Patrick Magee makes it feel very Becket-like, of course, but there's something indefinably Kneale there too!. When I watched it again, when Michael Kitchen goes to pull the cloth off Magee's face you actually think for a minute, you *really* think he'll have changed into a wolf. That is a scary moment you can't quite quantify. Because you're thinking "he can't have changed". They can't have done a quick change—in fact you can still see him breathing, even when he's died. But somehow it casts such a spell, it's a sort of jump moment. It's brilliant really.

NS: *It's astonishing. And one of the things I've been bringing up in talking to people about it, is how well...he seems to understand the medium intrinsically from the word go. But one of the things that BEASTS shows me is that, because he keeps them very limited a lot of the time in terms of settings—they really could be redone as stage plays—is how incredibly well he writes for actors. And obviously he had a background as an actor so that might be why, but the way that he locates the entirety of the drama within the characters and lets the actors play it...I can't quite get my head around how he does what he does!*

MG: Well, he was simply brilliant wasn't he? And there's a wonderful example in that, there's a brilliant bit of exposition when Gerald James is on the phone talking someone's cat down from a tree and at the same time

A Conversation with Mark Gatiss

he's telling Michael Kitchen all the exposition about the pet shop and Patrick Magee's character, and it's terrific. So simple. It's just an info-dump, but he's doing it in the course of a charming phone call to someone whose cat's stuck up a tree. Then something like "During Barty's Party", the way that the husband who is the dominant character, becomes the submissive character, is so deftly handled you almost don't quite notice until it's happened. Again, less is more. The stuff you could do with the sound! It's a psychodrama with two people. It's a wonderful idea, and he was just full of them.

For me, and I know for Jeremy [Dyson], my favourite thing about his work is his incredible ear for very light-touch scary dialogue. There are turns of phrase, you know in "Baby", when that elderly builder says "Thing like that, it'd have been suckled." I mean, the picture it paints is so horrible, with just a couple of words. There's a bit in QUATERMASS II which I've always cherished—in the TV version—when they're talking to the old man in the pub and he says "I used to court a girl from Winnerden Flats"... It's just a window into a past. That old woman who touches him and says "you have a kind face"... it's very moving, and so spare, and so simple. And then my absolute all time favourite, one of the best pieces of dialogue ever written, which is in THE WOMAN IN BLACK, when Adrian Rawlins drops his folio stuff on the train and Bernard Hepton says "I couldn't help but notice you're involved in the Drablow Estate" and he says "Yes, I'm going for the funeral".

"Oh. Eel Marsh House."

"Yes. I expected I'll be in and out of there quite a bit."

And Hepton says quietly—"Do you now..."

That's the work of a master. With the most deft touch of his pen he conjures a world of terror. It's just so effective. And one of the scariest things in it! Just the implicit threat: "Do you now...?" Horrible!

NS: *It's says awful lot again, I think about the humanity of him and of his work, in that the characters are so rich, and warm, even the smallest of them, and it is phrases like that, that really linger. But he also saw himself as a real structuralist. When you're talking about that sequence in THE WOMAN IN BLACK... I've not seen the script for that, but I would lay*

WE ARE THE MARTIANS

money on the fact that it is laid out in such a way that it will play to that specific beat.

MG: Yes, I'm sure it is.

NS: *It's very carefully structred writing, carefully structured dialogue, but it feels very natural, quite casual almost and completely chilling not by what it does overtly, but by what it implies.*

MG: Here's another one: "The figure was small he said, like a monkey or a dwarf."

NS: *That really shouldn't be as scary as all that, but it is...*

MG: It really is.

The thing is—and I find this absolutely fascinating—his last work for Central etc, even then, the episode of KAVANAGH QC is called "Ancient History", and the absolute seam of gold that runs through his work is this uncanny link to the past, and a glorious, agile way of conjuring it up. Which weirdly reminds me of M.R. James who had a similar gift for ventriloquising dialogue from the past. The dialogue in THE ROAD is terrific. It feels authentic to the 18th Century. And those extracts from old books in the Westminster Abbey archive in QUATERMASS AND THE PIT, are written so well that you feel like those are proper written records about the charcoal fellers and things like that. Then just a little hint— "The figure was small, like a monkey or a dwarf. It crossed the room and passed through the wall." You feel like you could just stumble across that in an authentic book.

NS: *It's not overdone either, as you say it's almost off-hand. It sounds common place in a sense...*

I recently read the Folio Society M.R. James collection that Nigel edited and wrote an introduction for. One of the most interesting things about it for me, is that... James is often just depicted as a dry, stuffy, sexually repressed academic. But what Nigel gets from him, is the humanity of the man. His warmth. What he focuses on is the man, in a way that I've never seen him depicted before, and in a way that seems uniquely Tom. It says a lot I think that his prime directive, his prime response to James, is not the obvious. Not the expected. He just sees him from a different angle.

As far as I can tell it seems like it was James and H.G. Wells who were the big influences on him in literary terms.

MG: For someone who hated the cult of the personality, they were his big heroes, I think that's very clear.

Wells was a visionary, who was very like Kneale, I think. And James was an acknowledged master of the form . . . I think Nigel said somewhere "All my stories are ghost stories". And I think that's sort of true really. There's an element of a haunted past or something like that about them.

NS: *I think the way that he uses things like the books in the Westminster Abbey Archive in PIT are very Jamesian touches.*

MG: Exactly, James used to actually fake documents for fun and enjoy colleagues authenticating them before telling them he'd made them up! One of his best stories, which has never been done [for TV], is one called "Martin's Close", which is entirely made up of transcripts of Judge Jefferies trials. It's all made up, but it's completely convincing. And you get the personality of the judge from . . . it's all dialogue really . . . but it's an unusual case, where someone has been accused of murder and the victim won't stay dead! It's wonderfully written. James and Kneale shared a real gift for getting the sense of the past, and getting the speech patterns, so that they feel convincing. It just *feels* right and that's half the battle really.

NS: *It's interesting that you mention James faking things for his colleagues. Something that Judith mentioned to me last time I met her—in the early days of the drama department at the BBC, they really would read everything that came in, because they needed scripts and this was the early days of the medium, so they had to give feedback on it. And apparently Tom spent quite a lot of time just dashing off scripts that were bad by design, just to get the readers reports that were terribly polite about all these awful pieces of* *writing, with all the worst kind of script writing mistakes you can imagine. And it was just his way of having a joke with them! He actually seems a much funnier man than I think he gets credit for.*

MG: Well, I met him, as you know, with a view to remaking THE ROAD. I'd heard so many stories about how curmudgeonly he was, and he was, on that day, delightful. I asked him all the questions I'd ever wanted to ask. How he came to write THE WOMAN IN BLACK. Whether Andre Morell would have reprised his Quatermass if the fourth story had been made when originally planned. I gave him THE LEAGUE OF GENTLEMEN and he gave me his DVD of THE STONE TAPE. It was a charming and fascinating afternoon and I remember how lovely and courteous he and Judith were. And then what happened, subsequently, was that he sort of conformed to what we'd heard before, there was a sort of backlash. That seems like the way he was with people for years. People would get quite close and then he'd just sort of snarl at them. But I didn't experience it personally. In person he was delightful and funny, and everything you'd want. I think I did express how much I thought he was a genius, but of course, he didn't want any of that.

I remember talking to Andrew Pixley about a mini season of Kneale's stuff which was organised in Wales. It was meant to show the breadth of his TV work, not just the sci-fi. They were going to show his excellent adaptation of JANE EYRE along with lots of other rare gems. It was all planned. Then at the last minute Kneale said, "No, put QUATERMASS AND THE PIT on". And he made them change it. He seemed to weirdly lose confidence in some of his other stuff. It seems so contradictory, in that he didn't want people to beat their way to his door saying "You are the Master". But if people failed to give him proper acknowledgement, he was furious!

NS: *That's certainly my impression as to why he might have fallen out with television production as it went on, as things changed from the initial days with Rudolph Cartier, where they really were in control of everything.*

MG: Well, it's all about control isn't it? I know from my own experiences,

A Conversation with Mark Gatiss

that's the most important thing if you have a vision, and it's great if you collaborate with people who share your vision and that you trust, but if you suddenly find yourself in a situation with people whose opinions you don't respect, it's deadly. I'm sure that must have happened to him.

NS: *I think so. And increasingly as time went on, that seems to have been the case. He was aware of how good he was—he wasn't falsely modest about his ability—and that with his track record, he really shouldn't have to explain that.*

MG: Yes, but you know, in a way that's the history of us all. I read a wonderful story the other day about Shelley Winters who, in her latter days, when she had to go and read for things, she'd be very polite and sit down and they'd ask her to read and she'd just get this carrier bag out and put her two Oscars on the table and say "They read for me". Never worked again, but she kept her self respect!

NS: *I think this pervasive idea that he was curmudgeonly, is interesting. I did bring it up with Judith, and she seemed fairly perplexed by it. When was it that you met him? Was it during the last years of his life?*

MG: It was—I can tell you precisely or you can help me—it was somewhere between September 11th 2001 and the beginning of BBC4, which I think may have been the beginning of the next year.

I know that we talked about 9/11, which wasn't that much before, because he was saying that he had thought THE ROAD might be a bit dated, but suddenly felt that it was very relevant again. And then the guy who was going to direct THE ROAD if it had happened—Richard Curzon Smith—directed the first drama on BBC4, which was about Salvador Dali and was called SURREALISIMO. Nigel rang Richard up after that went out, and he hated it. And Richard got the brunt of it. I remember him ringing me up that night and saying "I think I've just experienced the other side of Nigel Kneale". In the end the whole thing never happened, but it was somewhere between those two dates, that I met him. I went down to Barnes for tea...

WE ARE THE MARTIANS

NS: *Likewise, the last time I met with Judith was out that their house, we were discussing the script for* THE BIG, BIG GIGGLE...

MG: Another prescient piece. I remember when—a few years ago—there really was a suicide craze, in Wales. I remember thinking about that play. Nigel Kneale's tombstone should have just read 'I told you so'.

NS: *It does feel that way a lot of the time*... THE BIG, BIG GIGGLE *has the teenagers using what he calls 'transistor-talkies'. So they're playing music and talking to each other through these handheld devices. This is 1965!*
But to go back a bit—I've gotten a little off track—at the time when you first encountered Kneale at 7 or 8 were you already watching other Hammer movies?

MG: Oh yes.

NS: *It must have really stood out then. Certainly that was my experience, having watched* **DRACULA** *and* **CURSE OF FRANKENSTEIN** *that when I came across* **QUATERMASS AND THE PIT** *thinking it would be just another Hammer, and it blew my mind wide open.*

MG: It's an interesting thing of course, because the two Donlevy films are very charming, particularly **THE QUATERMASS EXPERIMENT** is a wonderful piece of work. Richard Wordsworth's performance is astonishing. It's Karloff like. It's like the film didn't expect him to do that! He's amazing. And obviously, Donlevey is stiff and bleary and just points his raincoat at people. Kneale hated him, and that's why he refused permission for Hammer to make **THE PIT** for so long. But obviously, there is an alternative universe in which there is a 1960, black and white version of **QUATERMASS AND THE PIT** with Brian Donlevey, something I entertain in my lighter moments!
Still, he held off for ten years and then, the version that we eventually got is so much more literate and... low key, really, than most of Hammer's output. It's a terrific film. Andrew Kier is wonderful.
I can remember, in a way, as a child, being disappointed that there

A Conversation with Mark Gatiss

wasn't a Martian invasion. Because that's what you want when you're that age. But that's the point! You don't appreciate the same things, and it's only years later that you come to see how subtle and clever that script is. It's been said before, but he absolutely invented so much of what we now consider the staples of Science Fiction and Fantasy writing. And particularly with THE PIT, the whole idea of an ancient invasion, and black magic actually beginning in ancient science and the image of the devil... DOCTOR WHO completely ripped it off for a Jon Pertwee story called "The Daemons". And I think he saw that and wasn't very pleased, but no one had done that before! And at a stroke he comes up with all this amazing stuff... a five million year old invasion! And then the central idea of THE ROAD, of a backwards haunting is so bloody clever. He just had loads and loads of these wonderful ideas. He always used to protest that he wasn't a Science Fiction writer, that he used it as a vehicle for his ideas, and it's true to an extent, but he also—along the way—created so much of the form that we take for granted today.

NS: *It's astonishing because, as you've been quoted saying, he pretty much invented popular television, or popular drama...*

MG: Yes. I mean, he did, didn't he? Television was this brand new medium, stopped by the war. When it came back it was so dull and worthy. And then in the middle of it, like a rocket, lands this horror serial. No wonder it caused such an impact. In retrospect, though, it's not just because it was different, it's because it was good. What we have of it is terrific, particularly Reginald Tate [original Quatermass actor] I think Kneale had his finger on the pulse. And he and Rudy Cartier wanted to properly shake things up, and it worked in spades really.

NS: *What's interesting to me is the way he seemed to understand the medium without having done an awful lot of work in it before that. From what I gather in talking to Judith he was there doing odd bits and pieces of writing and rewriting, getting paid out of petty cash a lot of the time, so he maybe picked a lot up as he went along, learning how to fix things, by seeing what was wrong.*

We Are The Martians

MG: It's an interesting combination of things isn't it: he started as an actor, then won the Somerset Maugham Prize which I think brought him to the attention of the BBC, but, as you say, he's one of those people who just got it. I suppose, every now and then when there is some kind of new form—and it doesn't happen very often because they tend to be big things like Cinema or Television—people get it very quickly. Sometimes...you can look at early sound film and there are actors in it who are marooned from the silent era, or from the stage. Then, suddenly, in the middle of it, there's a Star, who just gets how to do film acting from the beginning, and their performance doesn't date. Other people around them are being very stagey and shouty, and they're totally naturalistic. I think in a similar way, he just grasped what television could do, and how to do it with limited resources.

Everything you were saying is absolutely true, about pouring his energy in to the dialogue; in to containable scenes...I mean, NINETEEN EIGHTY FOUR...but I'm forgetting again! I have to do everything backwards! It's like Nigel Kneale, it's all ancient history! I'm forgetting again that actually, the chronology for me would have gone: **QUATERMASS 2, QUATERMASS AND THE PIT**—the movie—then BEASTS, then the repeat of NINETEEN EIGHTY FOUR. 1977 I think. I can remember peddling home on my bike like a mad thing to get back in time to watch NINETEEN EIGHTY FOUR. Maybe it was the 50th Anniversary? TV started in 1927, so I think it was something like that TV 50 it was called, or something like that, but they did loads of things, including a repeat of NINETEEN EIGHTY FOUR, and I remember being knocked out by how good it was. There was nothing, sort of, stiff about it. It was still frightening, and again that sort of queasy quality to it. But I can remember being very struck by Peter Cushing and Andre Morrell and Donald Pleasance, but also by how contained it was, how clever it was to make a big novel like that work live, in a series of very contained scenes.

NS: *One of the things that strikes me about the TV work and the fact that it was live, and obviously increasingly with* QUATERMASS II *and* THE PIT *more pre-filmed location sequences, but still, the hand off for those is remarkable, because it must have needed perfect timing really.*

A Conversation with Mark Gatiss

MG: You know that bit near the beginning of THE PIT? Where Doctor Roney reveals the statue: "He wasn't very tall, but he walked like a man." Fanfare of music. The camera dashes in, it cuts to the Gentlemen's Club, where three members of the press are saying "I'm not sure about this Roney". It cuts between them and then suddenly it's on Roney. The reason there are three shots on those people before is because Cec Linder wasn't there — he was running over from the other set, all the way round!

NS: *That's one of the things Judith talked to me about, she talks about those early days of television with incredible vividness and fondness as well, and she was explaining to me that the producer was usually the director as well at the time and there were very few people on the set, but that she and Tom generally were. And one of the things she was telling me was that they'd be shooting two men sitting at a bar having a conversation and you'd have one of them in shot talking to the other guy, who happened to be in the previous scene and is now racing across the studio — probably getting changed along the way — in order to sit down in the seat, in time for them to cut to him to get his line or reaction ... but in the mean time the first actor is doing his lines to an empty stool.*

MG: When I was in the remake of THE QUATERMASS EXPERIMENT it was remarkably unchanged, it was the same sort of thing. But I have to say that we had more of a support network. We had people pushing us around and stuff like that. Whereas I think the scale of it ... doing something like QUATERMASS AND THE PIT live, is breathtaking. The fact that it looks as good as it does is really amazing. And doing brilliant things like, they couldn't dig down, so they simply raised the walls, so the hole appeared to be going deeper, and they were actually pushing things further up. It's so clever.

NS: *It's remarkably clever, and I think that when you talk about NINE-TEEN EIGHTY FOUR ... I mean, the first Quatermass was really the first drama to be that kind of cultural event and have that kind of impact, emptying the pubs and so on. But then, with NINETEEN EIGHTY FOUR, you've got another first, in that it's the first time that a drama was discussed* *in Parliament, with regard to whether they should even be allowed to have a second performance, given the impact of the first. It was that shocking to some people. That powerful.*

MG: Absolutely. Just amazing. And as with so much he did, game changing. It's the first time. He is, in every sense, a pioneer I think.

NS: *There's a lovely thing that Judith told me as well, about Duncan Lamont, who played Victor Caroon in the TV version of* THE QUATERMASS EXPERIMENT. *Obviously at a certain point the character has mutated to become a vegetable mass all over Westminster Abbey, at which point Lamont no longer has a job. He's not needed as an actor. But apparently, he was so invested in it that . . . there's a certain point where Quatermass is talking to the vegetation, appealing to whatever humanity is left within. And the only thing on screen for him to react to, were these large branches to represent root systems and tendrils, which were being wiggled around to suggest that it was alive, and so Lamont was on set with Tom and Judith, off camera, and while Quatermass was talking, they were the ones moving the branches, because Lamont wanted still to be part of his character, still acting it right to the end. It's such a lovely story that says so much to me about the way that they were making things at the time.*

MG: There's a homemade quality to it. But it's exciting still to think that those people were in that tiny studio at Ally Pally, and what they were doing.

I'm not going to promise, because I have to make sure they still exist, but in 1993 a friend and I interviewed Isabel Dean, Monica Grey, Dominic Lefaux, and at least a couple of others who were in EXPERIMENT and QUARTERMASS II, and I think the tapes still exist. If you want them, you're very welcome to have them.

But I remember, we showed them the existing episodes, and they were all very proud of it. I remember Isabel Dean talking very fondly about Duncan Lamont, and they all had very vivid memories of it. And I suppose particularly by the time it got to QUATERMASS II because EXPERI-

A Conversation with Mark Gatiss

MENT had been such a smash they were kind of aware of being in Quatermass and what its cultural reach was.

NS: *It seems like things were a little closer to the theatrical experience back then in terms of the production, where there was a more tightly knit group of people working closely together to make it happen.*

MG: I think that's absolutely true. In many respects TV is still the same as it was then but I think they had a floor manager who was much closer to a stage manager and it was much more like a theatrical troupe, and they rehearsed and rehearsed and rehearsed, which you never get to do in TV anymore. The cliché of the time is that it was just filmed theatre. And one of the key things that Kneale and Cartier brought to it was to bust that open by doing things that were wildly ambitious. But there's still a very clever understanding of what a scene requires. The fact that, as you say, a lot of his later stuff, you could put them on stage, because he knew about the power of those kind of scenes. It's one of the reasons that something like I, CLAUDIUS still stands up so well, is that they're actually very long scenes, they're ten of fifteen minute theatrical scenes, and they have a real power because everyone involved gets their teeth in to it. They're not just cutting constantly.

NS: *Given everything we've talked about, about just how important he is to the formation of the idea of what modern popular drama is and how TV works, why is it do you think, that his name isn't so well remembered? That the work isn't as well known? I was interested to hear you say his name did still have as much cache when BEASTS was coming on. That's not the case now. I can't say his name and guarantee that whoever I'm talking to will know who he is.*

MG: He's a prophet without honour. Which I think is, sadly, his ultimate destiny. I'm not being pretentious about this, but to people who know, he is the best. He is it.

There was obviously a time when his name carried the same clout. I tried to get him a BAFTA. I spoke to some people and lobbied saying 'He

285

WE ARE THE MARTIANS

is absolutely up there with Potter, and Alan Plater, and Alan Bleasdale' and all these people whose names are bandied about all the time. I remember the chairman of BAFTA writing to me saying 'you're absolutely right, it's ridiculous', but it never happened. It was basically his death that robbed us of it, although he probably wouldn't have accepted the award! But I suppose, really, in this country TV writers rarely get that sort of name recognition. And I suppose as time goes by, people forget. They'll remember Quatermass as a name, they'll remember certain things, but then part of both his appeal and his problem — a word I hesitate to use, but I suppose a problem in terms of perception — is, that his stuff was not easy, and as we have crept ever closer to a world in which the "Tittupy Bumpity Show" is actually a part of the schedule, I think people remember less and less, what someone like Nigel Kneale used to represent: which was fierce intelligence and integrity.

I had a meeting with BBC 2 around the time we were trying to get THE ROAD done and, it was a two part brief. THE ROAD remake and I wanted to get them to commission Nigel Kneale to write a *new* TV play. To me it was a no-brainer: I want to know what this man thinks is going to happen next, because he's always right... and he's a fucking genius, excuse my language.

And they... there was a lot of 'mmmmm-mmm-mmmm', humming and hawing. And essentially the argument was: anyone who came from the age before the remote control was effectively dead. And so again, it never happened. And it's a tragedy, because even if he'd written a draft, even if he was interested... but unfortunately everyone's destiny — it'll happen to me, it'll happen to Steve Moffat, it'll happen to us all — people forget. Suddenly you're too old. You're not hot, and it doesn't matter what you want to write, if the parade's moved on it's moved on. That's the way it goes. It's not right, and it's very sad that in a lot of other forms like in music or painting, it doesn't matter at all. I mean, obviously fashions change, but I think there's something particularly brutal about film and television in terms of how they regard the age of people. And whereas you should be looking at these people as pioneers and wanting to know what they have to say now, what people tend to do is to look at them as if they're museum pieces. I mean, I don't think it's an accident at all that the main thread of

A Conversation with Mark Gatiss

THE QUATERMASS CONCLUSION is about old people triumphing over the young. And he wasn't even that old then!

NS: *He really wasn't. I was talking about this with Tim Lucas who's writing about Kneale's prose fiction, including the QUATERMASS novel, and he was saying that he'd realised suddenly that Kneale was younger when he wrote that than Tim is now, and that he couldn't quite get over it. To him — and I agree with him — somehow Nigel was always an 'older man'.*

MG: I think that's true. I think perhaps he was an old soul. It's partly that curmudgeonly thing again, there's something quite reactionary about THE QUATERMASS CONCLUSION, but I understand it more now than I did then. I understand that feeling, especially when you go in to a meeting with a twelve year old. And the thing is — I know this for a fact because he showed me a letter which he'd received around the time he first fell out with the BBC, and I remember him saying... it was essentially a list of things... it's everything that's still wrong with the BBC! It's always been very bad at nurturing its talent. It's always been very bad at saying thank you. It's always been very bad at the most basic things, but there was one particular bit, I remember him saying "This is not a million miles from the sort of thing that Hitler used to say." I can't quite remember the details, but that's really stuck in my mind. But I think he was endlessly disappointed with the level of people who he worked with. Not all the time, obviously. There were certain people like Cartier and Christopher Morahan whom he worked with repeatedly, and then there were some times where I think he just thought he was surrounded by idiots, which he probably was. One of the reasons that he hated Hammer; they made admittedly very successful and thrilling and brilliant films, I think, but undoubtedly cruder and rather 'dumbed down' versions, of incredibly literate texts.

But some of the people he had absolutely no time for and you can understand it, because he had integrity and, as I say, fierce intelligence. He didn't want to see things transmogrified into popcorn fodder, which is why so many of his plays, which we really only know from references, THE WINE OF INDIA and so on, they're ideas plays that perhaps didn't

WE ARE THE MARTIANS

have the reach of a popular serial like THE QUATERMASS EXPERI-MENT, but that was where his heart really lay I think. Trying to express these ideas and say something. That's all any artist is really trying to do, and it's increasingly rare and difficult in the modern age of TV or Film, to do that, because people aren't interested in ideas, they're interested in money.

NS: *That "reactionary" sense that people talk about from* QUATERMASS CONCLUSION, *in reading* THE BIG, BIG GIGGLE, *which could prob-ably be interpreted in a similar way in terms of the way he depicts youth cults etc. Nonetheless seemed as much to be about him railing against what he sees as a similar "idiocy". Of people not thinking things through, but also the idea that there seemed to be an escapist sense to their thinking—in* CONCLUSION *it's quite literal, they want to escape the planet—without really interrogating it. The idea that they are/were throwing away what they have instead of engaging with it.*

MG: I think, particularly with THE QUATERMASS CONCLUSION, and I think it's a fascinating piece of work, I think it's wonderful. But you can't divorce it from the fact that it was originally written in the 60's. And weirdly, it was much criticised for being dated, because the Planet people were so obviously a hippy thing, but actually now they look much more like 'Crusties'! I think it's an accidental bit of prophecy, because he didn't sort of think that it would happen again, but they looked much more like the people who go to Glastonbury than they do like hippies—or at least, Glastonbury of the 80's before it became so much more commercial and mainstream. But I'm sure the original intention, the original feeling was—and he was only an early middle age man—but a feeling of helplessness, of puzzlement at what young people were doing. And it is reactionary, but it was probably written post Manson, so the 60's dream had already gone sour, and in a way that's the sort of thing he's talking about there. I mean, I don't know if there is a copy of the original version...

NS: *It may be there amongst his papers. At some point I'll have to organise an extended holiday to just dig through them now that I have access...*

MG: I'll come with you!

Do you have the radio play he did "You Must Listen"?

NS: *No.*

MG: I've got it somewhere. I think it's the basis of THE STONE TAPE…

NS: *Which brings that full circle in way, since Peter Strickland [director of* BERBERIAN SOUND STUDIO *and* THE DUKE OF BURGUNDY] *is now directing a radio version of* THE STONE TAPE.

MG: It's from the late forties I think, and it contains the germ of the idea that I think became THE STONE TAPE.

One of the things I did ask him in my mopping up of all the things I'd ever wanted to ask Nigel Kneale was whether, if QUATERMASS CONCLUSION had happened in '70, and had replaced DOCTOR WHO as was the intention, would he have cast Andre Morrell again, and he said yes, which made me happy.

NS: *Going back again to that 'reactionary' idea, there's something interesting in that still, whatever else he's reacting against, Quatermass sacrifices himself in order for life to continue on earth. So, whatever else, there's still a spark of hope or belief that this can be better.*

MG: You hit upon an interesting thing here, because I'm always being asked to bring things back—oddly enough, a Nigel Kneale nod there—which I don't want to do, despite being associated with two of the great 'bring backs' of recent times, but the problem is it's very hard to get new things off the ground, and whenever people talk about rebooting Quatermass—and Hammer have talked about it forever, and I think Red Productions might actually be doing it—but the problem is that Quatermass is not a format. Quatermass is Nigel Kneale. So, what is the character of Quatermass? He's a widower. He's troubled. He has a kind face. He has integrity. He ultimately sacrifices himself, but he's not a character in that way. It's a thing, it's a form, Quatermass is just Nigel Kneale's ideas. So he's

WE ARE THE MARTIANS

different—accidentally, he's a different person/actor every time he's appeared, and he's, I suppose, in a sense, the author's mouth piece, rather than a set of characteristics. You just can't format Quatermass—though people will try—but, it's Kneale, isn't it?

Hammer did commission Nigel's son, Matthew Kneale to write a new Quatermass, as a novel, in the hope that it might then become something else. I don't know how far it might have got, but Simon Oakes the CEO of Hammer told me that they did that.

NS: *That would be fantastic. They obviously approached some real literary names for their novels, and Matthew won the Booker Prize for* ENGLISH PASSENGERS. *I've never heard anything about that, so perhaps it didn't get very far, but I'd love to think we might see that some day...*

You've been trying to mount a remake of THE ROAD *from Kneale's original script for quite some time now. Given that the BBC wiped the tapes of that one, how did you first come across it?*

MG: I bought that privately printed script book, but where I found it I cannot remember. It was a second hand book shop somewhere, I just remember falling on it.

I think I remember seeing THE STONE TAPE when it was first on, but I can't quite work out if that's true anymore, or if I've just overlaid it with other memories of watching it later. But I remember reading it, and YEAR OF THE SEX OLYMPICS which I found a bit baffling, but THE ROAD I thought was astonishing. Then I found out it was wiped, and then, I was very involved with Fictionlab, which was the drama studio thing, beginning of BBC4, because of the Dali thing, and Quatermass which was two or three years later, where they worked heavily with Nigel Kneale on the script. And he was very begrudging because it was the only one where the BBC had the rights not him, so I think he wanted to be involved rather than not be involved, but I convened a meeting with the controller and pitched the idea of Kneale writing a new play and a remake of THE ROAD and they went for the possible remake of THE ROAD and that's why we went to see him. It occurred to me that it was eminently doable being an early 60's TV play, that the budget constraints of BBC4 would

A Conversation with Mark Gatiss

actually suit it, and with very little work it could just be done again, because it's a wonderful idea. As I say, the dialogue and the characterisation of the Squire and the coffee house intellectual are all gorgeous, but the central idea is so clever, of a backwards haunting. It's so spooky and prescient. I just remember reading when it says something in the stage direction like 'The sound is mysterious and the people are terrified, but it makes perfect sense to us. It is the sound of the siren.' I just remember the hairs on the back of my neck standing up and thinking "wow, that's brilliant". And it is brilliant. I'd still like to do it, even though I don't want to bring things back, but some things which are lost, you should try to bring back, and that's one of them.

NS: *It's too good not to. When you met with him did you talk about how you might rework it, or were you planning to do it pretty much as is/was?*

MG: I was keen on keeping it as was, as much as possible. I seem to remember the BBC thought it needed more work, and definitely one of the sticking points was that he wasn't prepared to collaborate with anyone, and I think that was kind of what killed it in the end. But I don't think it does need much work. It's really just about making it doable, but it's shootable as it is really. It's wonderful.

There are two arguments really. You could sort of try to recreate it absolutely as it was, and having done AN ADVENTURE IN SPACE AND TIME, using original Marconi cameras, you could actually make it look like it did in 1963 if you wanted to . . .

Or, you could say this is still very relevant and you could make it sumptuously, and modern, but still basically from the same script.

NS: *We've probably covered it by now, but what do you think is Kneale's legacy?*

MG: Well, certainly he's a prophet without honour . . . but not completely. He did essentially invent popular television with Quatermass and his legacy remains with us. Also what remains are his preoccupations, and the things that haunted him . . . and so many of them have come true.

I remember when BIG BROTHER started, Patrick Stewart was the only person I think I read saying 'Does no one remember THE YEAR OF THE SEX OLYMPICS!? This is it!' And the fact that he not only predicted, essentially, BIG BROTHER, but also SURVIVOR at the same time! Strand them on a desert island and watch them 24 hours a day. And then introduce a killer on the island... I mean, how far are we really from that kind of dystopia? So I think it's great that we... that any of us... do still remember him, because most TV writers don't get remembered.

The BFI have always been huge supporters of him. I don't know how long it's been since they did anything like it, but they're doing the complete Dennis Potter at the moment, and they've always been very loyal to Nigel Kneale. I think it would be fantastic to have a complete season of what exists I think, and maybe rehearsed readings of lost things and all kinds of stuff.

He's one of the Greatest TV writers we've ever had, and I think as an individual talent, possibly one of the most imaginative, audacious and challenging writers this country's ever produced.

COOL THE AUDIENCE, COOL THE WORLD
Media, Mind Control and the Modern Family in THE YEAR OF THE SEX OLYMPICS

Kier-La Janisse

"**I** HAVE BEEN WRITING TELEVISION PLAYS FOR ABOUT SEVEN YEARS," Nigel Kneale wrote in a 1959 article for *Sight and Sound*. "An interesting time to be close to the thing, as it included the phase of its most rapid growth in this country, from a social joke to a social problem. The 9-inch 'goggle box' has expanded to the 21-inch Home Screen."[91]

Although Kneale would come to be known primarily as a television writer, his teleplay THE YEAR OF THE SEX OLYMPICS (1968) was the only original work in which he would directly address the medium of television itself (if you don't count his ill-fated script for **HALLOWEEN III**). But an interest in the processes and effects of broadcasting would colour his career throughout, from his radio play "You Must Listen" in 1952 to his celebrated 1954 adaptation of George Orwell's NINETEEN EIGHTY-FOUR and THE STONE TAPE in 1971. The aforementioned statement by Kneale in *Sight and Sound* — in an article specifically addressing what he sees as a dangerous reliance on the "intimacy" implied by the television

---

[91] Kneale, Nigel. "Not Quite So Intimate" in Sight and Sound Spring 1959 Pg 86-88

screen's domesticated size — not only refers to different perceptions of what the television screen *means*, but what its inevitable increase in size implies for society as a whole.

He refers to the television as a "goggle box" — a common enough colloquial term in 1950s Britain, but one which is also the name of a current reality television show whose participants and constituents alike fulfill Kneale's satirical predictions while likely ignorant of the cultural precedents for this now-ubiquitous programming format. THE YEAR OF THE SEX OLYMPICS has commonly been cited as eerily prescient concerning the rise of reality television. But when Kneale wrote SEX OLYMPICS he was tapping into shifts in televisual architectonics in the late 60s, and also anticipated how this new media would come to centre on the family unit as a microcosmic reflection of larger anxieties.

MINING MEDIA

The haunted phone line of Kneale's radio play "You Must Listen" (September 16, 1952), in which a dead woman's voice manifests on a phone line installed in an office, imploring "I want to hear you and talk to you, only that...you must listen"[92] — was one of Kneale's many explorations of different forms of broadcasting and "crossed wires" or "infected" channels (1972's THE STONE TAPE probably being his most lingering example of this). He famously adapted George Orwell's *1984* for the BBC (broadcast December 12, 1954), anchoring the term "big brother" in the vernacular and self-reflexively introducing the notion of a totalitarian state that monitored its constituents through CCTV surveillance. *1984* was a controversial broadcast that, while receiving almost unanimously favourable critical reviews, was followed by a smattering of lurid headlines implying a negative reaction among the populace — most notably from tabloid paper *The Daily Express*, who insinuated that a housewife had died of shock while watching it.[93] The teleplay was even a catalyst

[92] Murray, Andy. *Into the Unknown: The Futuristic Life of Nigel Kneale*. Headpress, London 2006. Pg. 25
[93] Wake, Oliver. "Nineteen Eight Four (1954): Myth Versus Reality" http://www.britishtelevision-drama.org.uk/?p=4722

Cool the Audience, Cool the World

prompting motions for Parliamentary debate on the level of sadism in BBC programming, although such a debate never made it to the House of Commons despite media reports to the contrary.[94]

Many of Kneale's stories are set in the present, interacting with an archaic past; his first original work set in the future was 1965's THE BIG, BIG GIGGLE, about a suicide fad among the youth culture, featuring early LSD references, fictional would-be smartphones and "an unethical talk-show host stirring up trouble for ratings".[95] Though they went as far as location scouting, the script was never produced due to its controversial subject matter and budgetary concerns (still, one can't help but think that the idea made its way to Don Sharp, the director of 1973's PSYCHOMANIA). Kneale was older than the baby boomer generation and not a fan of psychedelia (though as Andy Murray points out in his 2006 book INTO THE UNKNOWN, the flower power kids were certainly fans of Kneale),[96] but he was aware of how close this new counterculture was to that depicted in THE BIG, BIG GIGGLE. Since the teleplay was never produced, he returned to its themes of a future society run headlong into hedonism in his next TV play, THE YEAR OF THE SEX OLYMPICS.

MEDIA AND CLASS

THE YEAR OF THE SEX OLYMPICS was broadcast as part of the anthology series THEATRE 625 (which had also featured a less-successful 1965 remake of Kneale's adaptation of Orwell's 1984) on July 29th, 1968 and repeated on PLAY FOR TODAY in March 1970. Originally produced in vivid colour, the teleplay only survives in a black and white version—presumably kinescoped—due to the BBC's long-running tradition of wiping video tapes for re-use. The film, directed by theatre director Michael Elliott, was a critical success and Kneale was purportedly pleased with it.

---

[94] For a comprehensive analysis of the reaction to Kneale's 1984, see http://www.britishtelevision-drama.org.uk/?p=4722

[95] Newman, Kim. Facebook comment July 28, 2014.

[96] Murray, Andy. *Into the Unknown: The Futuristic Life of Nigel Kneale*. Headpress, London 2006. Pg. 98

The film takes place in an enclosed space station-like community known as "Output" whose population is divided into "High Drives"—those supposedly endowed with higher intelligence, analytical skills, ambition and wit—and "Low Drives", who are seen as pathetic plebians who must be constantly entertained with a slew of inane game shows to avoid them procreating and thus increasing the Low Drive population. The most popular TV show on Output is "Sportsex", a show that involves various levels of sexual competition, the culmination of which is the "Sex Olympics".

Nat Mender (Tony Vogel) is the showrunner for SportSex while his ex-girlfriend Deanie (Suzanne Neve)—45 couplings previous, according to his new dish, Misch, the infantilized host of SportSex (played by Vickery Turner, who would marry cult icon Warren Oates within the year)—works on "The Hungry Angry Show", which consists of grunting contestants throwing food at each other. The two are brought back together when Deanie calls him to say that the child they had together (who has subsequently been raised in a mass nursery away from her parents) has been ill.

It becomes clear that the two had shared a special bond, and that Nat responds to her with more depth than he reserves for the shallow Misch. The two share a number of conversations about the alleged social and intellectual chasm between High Drive and Low Drive citizens. In particular, Nat often wonders what purpose the Low Drives serve, why they are there, and why the High Drives spend so much of their time strategizing about how to keep the Low Drives entertained and passive. "Put 'em off food, put 'em off sex," he muses. "Still 200 of 'em to each of us in Output, getting their babies done at 15 and then just sit til burnout. Most of 'em got no work to do . . . just sit. Dead by 35."

The High Drives all live on Output, which appears as sort of a floating ecosystem full of screens, both for watching and monitoring, while the Low Drives live "out there" in some unspecified place, herded in groups to sit in front of the screens all day, every day. From SportSex to the Hungry Angry Show, there is a nonstop queue of mindless television shows designed to keep them watching. Ironically, Channel 4's current TV show GOGGLEBOX has its participants doing just that: in circuitous fashion, it is a show that depicts people watching television so that we can watch them watching.

THE UBIQUITOUS SCREEN

By definition, dystopian science fiction depicts totalitarian societies that tout themselves as utopian—and it is precisely this disfigurement of utopian ideals that renders them dystopian. And one of the key images of dystopian science fiction is the looming screen, which broadcasts the propaganda of these seemingly omnipotent forces. This predates the advent of television, as depicted in early dystopian novels like H.G. Wells WHEN THE SLEEPER AWAKES (1910—although first serialized in 1898-1903—in which huge screens called "Babble Machines" broadcast misinformation), Yevgeny Yamyatin's WE (1924, the influence for George Orwell's NINETEEN EIGHTY-FOUR and arguable Aldous Huxley's BRAVE NEW WORLD) and films like Fritz Lang's **METROPOLIS**. While television was established in the UK and Europe much earlier than in the US (they were available to consumers as early as the 1920s, the BBC

WE ARE THE MARTIANS

was broadcasting regularly by 1936 and by 1939 James Joyce had depicted a trash TV show in FINNEGAN'S WAKE and there were already 19,000 televisions in British homes),[97] the proliferation of television in the 1950s and the massive technological shift that followed in the wake of Sputnik in October 1957 would see this motif become a defining staple of cinematic depictions of a world gone wrong. Dystopia and new media have often travelled hand in hand.

This notion of screen ubiquity and screen size is interesting given the context of Kneale's SEX OLYMPICS teleplay. It was broadcast on July 29, 1968, the summer after the most successful World's Fair of the 20th century, Expo 67 in Montreal, had unveiled the world's largest number of media screens in history. As scholars Janine Marchessault and Monika Kin Gagnon have noted, the experiments of Expo 67—which not only included the multiplication of screens, variations in screen shape and dimension, but also elevated the screen to something architectronic in itself—"lend much insight to the aesthetics and phenomenologies of contemporary media."[98] Expo's use of screens defied the totalitarian associations the screen had adopted from nearly a century of science fiction. "Expo's image of the screen, on the contrary, was not that of a closed circuit," writes Marchessault, "but one of open, intercultural connectivities located in an excess of visual media."[99]

If Expo 67 was a utopian vision, the world of SEX OLYMPICS is its dystopian double. According to Donald Theall, the media screens of Expo celebrated "Man as communicator." Ironic then, that in SEX OLYMPICS, man's primary means of communication—language—has been primitivized. Articles and conjunctions are absent, the language hovers somewhere in an eternal present, without clear definition of the passage of time. This feeling is reinforced by the interiority of Output as an architecturally dense mass of screens and showrooms (an effect that belies the

---

[97] Fordham, Finn. "Early Television and Joyce's Finnegan's Wake: New Technology and Flawed Power" in *Broadcasting in the Modernist Era* eds. Matthew Feldman, Henry Mead and Erik Tonning, A&C Black, 2014. Pg 40
[98] Gagnon, Monika Kin and Janine Marchessault. *Reimagining Cinema: Film at Expo 67*. McGill-Queens University Press, Montreal 2014. Pg 6
[99] Marchessault, Janine. "Citerama: Expo as Media City" in *Reimagining Cinema: Film at Expo 67*. Eds. Monika Kin Gagnon and Janine Marchessault. McGill-Queens University Press, Montreal 2014. Pg. 87

relatively few sets utilized in the production). SEX OLYMPICS presented a cold future, while tapping into the image bank of 60s counterculture — including male fashions recalling the ponytailed tunic-and-tights look personified by Paul Revere and the Raiders' Mark Lindsay or Jack Nicholson in Richard Rush's PSYCH-OUT.

APATHY CONTROL

But while mining some familiar visual design, it is interesting that Kneale's dystopia is not utilitarian. Instead Output aims to breed passivity and sloth; it dissuades the forming of individual opinion, but not for the purpose of a mindlessly busy, constructive society. Instead it is their collective leisure that would be disturbed by any kind of drama or "tension." Trash TV is used to keep the lower classes submissive, or in the film's unique jargon, "cozy and comfy." In the Sex Olympics, contestants have sex live onscreen in an attempt to make sex so banal that the libidos of the lower classes are diminished and the population thus kept under control. Unlike traditional censors who believe that exposure to sex leads to an increase in deviant behavior, SEX OLYMPICS was prescient in predicting a nation of voyeurs, of people content to watch. "Sex is not to do," barks Nat, "Sex is to watch!"

When Deanie's new boyfriend Kin Hodder (Martin Potter of **GOODBYE GEMINI** and **SATYRICON**) accosts Nat, hoping Deanie's old flame can get him a job on SportSex, Nat spurns his desperation. But Hodder gets Nat's attention when he shows him paintings he has made in secret—dark, grotesque images that came from a tortured imagination. Nat recognizes that Hodder's emotionalism is dangerous, but he finds himself drawn to this illicit artwork all the same. When Hodder manages to flash one of his unsanctioned images onscreen during ArtSex, the audience is visibly upset—even Nat experiences feelings he can't name, largely because society has rid itself of most of its nuanced words out of longtime disuse. Nat goes to his superior, the coordinator Ugo Priest (Rossiter), hoping he may be able to tell Nat some "old days" words that may help him describe the feelings the paintings gave him; on Output, only older coordinators like Ugo Priest remember things from the "old days". The loss of language in Sex Olympics is also nod to real-life fears that the rise of television would make people illiterate.

Ugo Priest describes how in their strategy to curb Low Drive population expansion, they developed "Apathy Control". "That's what the world

needed," he offers. "Just a big HALT. No more progress... the world needs a rest."

This also ties in with fears of the time surrounding the rapid advancement of technology—a notion that would later be promulgated memorably in Alvin Toffler's best-selling book, FUTURE SHOCK (1970). "The symptoms of Future Shock are with us now," touted the book's logline. "This book can help us survive our collision with tomorrow." Reflecting Ugo Priest's sentiments, Toffler asserted that humankind was suffering from information overload. But when scientific progress was halted on Output, it was not in favour of moral progress; instead, they are just biding time in a spiritually vacuous existence, losing their humanity along with their language.

SEX OLYMPICS' method of controlling the masses through television is also key in Cronenberg's **VIDEODROME** (although in a much seedier setting) and would become a staple social pacifier in real life through the explosion of daytime talk shows, live trials like THE PEOPLE'S COURT and, most importantly, Reality Television.

REALITY TELEVISION

"When lived at one remove—via a TV screen—the two most powerful forces acting on Mankind, sex and death, are reduced to being nothing more than light entertainment," wrote Andy Murray in INTO THE UNKNOWN.[100] With SEX OLYMPICS, Murray says that Kneale wanted to explore the boredom that comes with total permissiveness.

But boredom is not enough—even Ugo Priest concedes that the audience "needs to laugh." It's healthy and "above all—safe!" The entertainment factor has to continue to evolve as boredom sets in. When the unusually angst-ridden, artistically-driven Kin Hodder has an accident while trying to share his artwork to the SportSex audience and falls to his death on live television, the viewers react with excitement and "boffo" laughter. But Nat questions what drives people to laugh. He notices that his fellow crew members on Sportsex seem to laugh at the misfortune of

[100] Murray, Andy. Into the Unknown: The Futuristic Life of Nigel Kneale. Headpress, London 2006. Pg 100

others, or in the absence of outright misfortune, at people who are "old or fat." As Hodder lays limp and bloody on the SportSex floor and the low drive audience erupts with laughter, Nat is shocked. "They're laughing because he's dead!" he gasps. "No," says Ugo Priest, "it's because *they're* not." A similar event occurs in Brian DePalma's **PHANTOM OF THE PARADISE** (1974) when the character of Beef (Gerritt Graham) is accidentally electrocuted onstage; the audience's enthrallment with the spectacle prompts a deliberate shift in the concert hall's programming mandate. The ultimate goal in **PHANTOM OF THE PARADISE** may not be population control, but as the nefarious puppetmaster character Swan (Paul Williams) exclaims: "An assassination live on television? *That's* entertainment!"

Ugo Priest explains that in the "old days" life was unpredictable, you never knew what was going to happen. Lasar Opie (Brian Cox), an ambitious young SportSex staffer, suggests that maybe people miss this unpredictability, even though they don't necessarily want to experience it themselves. But perhaps they could handle experiencing it vicariously. Which leads Nat to propose a crazy idea for a new "unpredictable" type of television program—*reality* television.

With Nat and Deanie volunteering themselves as guinea pigs (with their estranged daughter Kenton in tow) and Opie asserting himself as the new showrunner, the studio creates "The Live Life Show", which will feature a real family placed on a deserted island "out there" away from the safety and comfort of Output, left to survive independently by living off the land. But the "unpredictable" nature of reality TV also has to be controlled and manipulated, otherwise they risk boring the audience again. So the studio places a psychopath on the island, and in good Hitchcockian fashion, the audience is in on it but the subjects are not.

In the dystopian world of SEX OLYMPICS, instead of expanding man's world, the media overload shrinks it tighter inward—even on the comparatively "open" space of the island, which is transformed into an enclosed space by the CCTV cameras. This aligns with Janine Marchessault's assertion that the use of the screen in 1960s science fiction "marked a fundamental shift in the popular imaginary toward understanding simul-

Cool the Audience, Cool the World

taneity as space to be controlled."[101] Interestingly, the island exteriors were shot on Kneale's birthplace, the Isle of Man, which had served as a temporary internment camp for ethnic residents and refugees during WWII.[102]

There is a mixture of surveillance and voyeurism at work in how The Live Life Show is created and interacted with by its audience. Voyeurism is a more passive means of gratification, while surveillance implies a motive with more dangerous, rippling consequences; the watcher is waiting for someone to trip up. Talking about Orwell's NINETEEN EIGHTY-FOUR in the SF:UK television series episode "Big Brother Goes Hardcore", Kim Newman says, "I suppose what Orwell didn't realize is that there would be bored security guards rather than frighteningly efficient secret police out there, and that the worst that would happen was not that the thought police would come and get you, but that you having sex in a lift would be sold to a television show."

In The Live Life Show, the subjects know they are being watched. Nat and Deanie have volunteered to be subjects in the pioneering program — but they don't know that there are machinations behind the scenes that affect their 'reality.' Drama is being created by the show's executives, much as it is by their real-life counterparts today.

But while an important precedent, THE YEAR OF THE SEX OLYMPICS did not invent the concept of reality television; Allen Funt premiered CANDID CAMERA in 1949, after a year of hosting its radio incarnation, THE CANDID MICROPHONE.

Allen Funt knew that manipulation was key. As Fred Nadis has pointed out in his essay "Citizen Funt: Surveillance as Cold War Entertainment," before Funt had even established CANDID CAMERA as a TV show, he "left behind the role of silent eavesdropper and took on the role of dramatic provocateur."[103] Nadis likens the CANDID CAMERA audience to "a peeping tom, engaged in fun that paralleled government surveil-

---

[101] Marchessault, Janine. "Citerama: Expo as Media City" in *Reimagining Cinema: Film at Expo 67*. Eds. Monika Kin Gagnon and Janine Marchessault. McGill-Queens University Press, Montreal 2014. Pg. 89
[102] Murray, Andy. *Into the Unknown: the Futuristic Life of Nigel Kneale*. Headpress, London 2006, Pg 11
[103] Nadis, Fred. "Citizen Funt: Surveillance as Cold War Entertainment" in *The Tube Has Spoken: Reality TV and History*. Julie Anne Tadeo and Ken Dvorak, Eds. The University Press of Kentucky, Lexington, 2010. Pg 14

WE ARE THE MARTIANS

lance and censorship."[104] This again connects to Brian DePalma, whose 1974 film **SISTERS** opens on a television game show called "Peeping Tom," wherein the audience gets to watch an oblivious CANDID CAMERA-style 'victim' faced with moral decisions when they think no one is watching.

While CANDID CAMERA seems like proto-reality TV fluff, there was an experiment at work; Funt was very concerned about how people were so easily susceptible to pressures to conform (Michael Almereyda's 2015 film **THE EXPERIMENTER** even dramatizes Stanley Milgram — of the controversial 1961 Milgram electric shock experiment — enjoying Funt's show). CANDID CAMERA was predated by the rise of the hidden camera at the turn of the 20th century, and it, in turn, predated Direct Cinema and Cinema Verite, both types of "observational" cinema. "Funt intentionally gave his footage the feeling of a wiretap or surveillance film, "says Nadis. "He insisted on a stripped-down aesthetic for his show."[105] Likewise, on *The Live Life Show*, Nat and Deanie's time on the island is filmed in a primitive fashion, in contrast to the glitter and deliberate production design of the SportSex and ArtSex shows (and even the Hungry Angry Show), as though limited access to refined aesthetics more easily conveys a sense of reality. As Alexandra Heller-Nicholas has noted in her studies of found footage horror films, handheld cameras, bad sound and clunky editing are often seen as "badges of truth."

THE MODERN FAMILY

When Nat, Deanie and Kenton are deposited on the island, wrapped in bulky parkas and given a primitive stone cabin to shield them from the blasting wind, they are provided very few supplies and only basic instructions as to how to build a fire or hunt animals for food. The foreignness of having to survive on their own is at first enough to keep viewers of *The Life*

[104] Nadis, Fred. "Citizen Funt: Surveillance as Cold War Entertainment" in *The Tube Has Spoken: Reality TV and History*. Julie Anne Tadeo and Ken Dvorak, Eds. The University Press of Kentucky, Lexington, 2010. Pg 21

[105] Nadis, Fred. "Citizen Funt: Surveillance as Cold War Entertainment" in *The Tube Has Spoken: Reality TV and History*. Julie Anne Tadeo and Ken Dvorak, Eds. The University Press of Kentucky, Lexington, 2010. Pg 21

Life Show glued to the screen. The raw nature of real life—watching people have tedious conversations, struggling to keep warm or witnessing their reaction to seeing a sheep for the first time—is in itself exotic to the Low Drive population. The three of them have never even lived together as a family unit before, and so the show is as much about their developing relationship as it is about the trials they will undergo in the days to come.

It's fitting then, that as with Kneale's depiction of *The Live Life Show*, the first reality television shows were about families.

In 1974, the same year that DePalma's equally prescient **PHANTOM OF THE PARADISE** was released, BBC1 debuted THE FAMILY. THE FAMILY was a 12-part documentary series inspired by the success of its American counterpart, PBS' AN AMERICAN FAMILY, a year earlier. Producer Paul Watson and director Franc Roddam (the latter not yet known as the director of **QUADROPHENIA**) chose a working class family from Reading as their subjects, both as a response to the upper middle class family depicted in AN AMERICAN FAMILY, and to "make a film about the kind of people who never got on to television."[106] This emphasis on "regular people" aligned with the mandates of many filmmakers of the time, both in England and abroad—including Peter Watkins, the directors working within the structure of the National Film Board of Canada's "Challenge for Change" program and even children's programming like WGBH Boston's ZOOM, that put the show's writing in the hands of kids. Accessibility of the media to all was a hallmark of the era right through the mid-80s when public access television was at its height among emerging and amateur filmmakers. Likewise, the BBC was exploring public access TV at the same time (such as with unfiltered shows like OPEN DOOR, 1973-1983 and even later specials like the teenage diary IN BED WITH CHRIS NEEDHAM, 1992), with a focus on giving television access to marginalized communities.

Like CANDID CAMERA, THE FAMILY boasted mini-microphones and lightweight, non-intrusive technology that would further enable the 'realness' to transpire. While scholar Su Holmes has cited the BBC's MAN

---

[106] Watson, Paul. qtd. in "The Family's Margaret Wilkins, First Lady of Reality TV, is Dead" by Paul Revoir in the *Daily Mail*, August 19, 2008. http://www.dailymail.co.uk/news/article-1047125/The-Familys-Margaret-Wilkins-lady-reality-TV-dead.html

WE ARE THE MARTIANS

ALIVE television series (1965-1982) as an important precedent for THE FAMILY, the obvious difference is that MAN ALIVE is not strictly observational, nor does it transgress the boundaries of privacy — this transgression is key in any discussion of what constitutes "Reality TV", and is the primary issue that opens the first episode of THE FAMILY, as the family in question, The Wilkinses, sit round the breakfast table discussing their decision to open up their lives to being filmed candidly 24/7.

As Holmes writes: "THE FAMILY provoked debate about questions of privacy and television's role in mediating, and often reshaping, the boundary between public and private."[107] A big difference between the Wilkinses and the family in SEX OLYMPICS is that the Wilkinses had real-time contact with their viewers, or their "fanbase." During and after filming, they had to interact with the public (many of whom had no choice but to appear on camera with them) and were aware of their fame. The public admired their ability to remain "down to earth" in spite of this notoriety, and this tension between "being famous" and "being normal" was a big appeal of the show. However, the parents divorced a year after the show ended, citing the intrusive filming as a causal factor.

As we know from several decades of reality television focused on families like THE OSBORNES to former child actors Kim and Kyle Richards on THE REAL HOUSEWIVES OF BEVERLY HILLS — there is no such thing as unmediated reality when there is a camera in the room. In THE YEAR OF THE SEX OLYMPICS, Nat believes that by removing himself and his family from the society on Output and its inherent class divisions (especially considering his own daughter has been deemed "slow"), they can have a normal life and bond as a family through their own self-reliance. But he is foolish to believe that their reality will not be manipulated by external forces, most notably the showrunners who need to keep the Low Drives entertained.

When the daughter succumbs to illness and dies, the two parents bury her and despair sets in — but it's only going to get much, much worse for them given the violent stranger that the showrunners have placed on the

---

[107] Holmes, Su. "The Television Audience Cannot Be Expected to Bear Too Much Reality: The Family and Reality TV" in *The Tube Has Spoken: Reality TV and History*. Julie Anne Tadeo and Ken Dvorak, Eds. The University Press of Kentucky, Lexington, 2010. Pg. 102

Cool the Audience, Cool the World

island with them. Meanwhile those back in the studio are having a ball watching Nat and Deanie crumble onscreen. "I was right," boasts Opie. "The audience can take tension—even want it. Sadness, worry, pain, fright... I was right."

Contrary to the dehumanized coldness of Output, Nat and Deanie's distorted expressions of pain and despair are a "human" spectacle that is fascinating to the Low Drive viewers. Reality television continues to proliferate precisely because of this schadenfreude—and our continual interaction with various forms of media—especially today's social media—places us in a destructive cycle of watching and being watched as we all consent to live in public.

In the 21st century our lives are still consumed by screens, but unlike Kneale's predictions that our screens would all be cinema-sized, and that "the 'intimacy' idea will only be of antiquarian interest, like the tiny screens that produced it,"[108] instead the screens we spend the most time interacting with get smaller and smaller. While the image of the atomic family gathered around the television set may have faded from reality decades ago, these mini-screens—iphones, tablets—have us more isolated than ever, even as we attempt to connect to everything all at once. This shift, and the anxieties surrounding it, mirrors the developments in telecommunications in the 1980s that saw single family phone lines replaced by individual phone lines for the kids. Then too, parents were concerned that individual phone lines for teenagers were a threat to the integrity of the family. While Expo 67's use of screen size, shape and multiplicity asserted the utopian ideal of a global family connected by a vast mediascape that could be absorbed collectively, the compactness and portability of today's screens has changed the purpose of the screen from a means of shared experience to an individual (and often oblivious) experience. Unlike the population of SEX OLYMPICS, when we watch, we watch alone.

"I don't like the term 'Science Fiction'," Kneale wrote in that long-ago *Sight and Sound* article, "but if we're going to bandy it about, it could be applied just as well to the world we live in."

---

[108] Kneale, Nigel. "Not Quite So Intimate" in *Sight and Sound* Spring 1959 Pg 86-88

THE STONE TAPE

Nigel Kneale

PUSHING THE DOOR HE UNLOCKED

GHOSTWATCH and THE STONE TAPE

Stephen Volk

CHRISTMAS DAY, 1972. THE WORLD TURNS, IN BLUE AND BEIGE. The distinctive and comforting BBC logo. But what is about to follow will be anything but comforting. I watch eagerly as the title card fades up. Not particularly dramatic: THE STONE TAPE.

I have no idea it will change my life forever.

As a teenager just beginning to take baby steps into writing myself (carbon paper, portable typewriter, Tippex), I'm excited not only because ghost stories on TV are rare as hen's teeth even then, but because of the expectation that goes with the writer's name, famous for spooking the nation with the Quatermass serials I was too young to watch but my father has told me emptied the pubs and gave people nightmares.

I hardly blink as the play (disappointingly on video, not film) gets off to an innocuous start. ("No creaky gates. No rattling chains..." Michael Parkinson would say after a re-vamped BBC ident twenty years later...) An old house, yes, but no gothic lighting. It's daylight, in fact, and the characters arriving are scientists. Modern scientists. No frock coats. No crucifixes unloaded with the equipment in this Yuletide ghost story. Because in this scenario, at the outset it was clear the gloom of the supernatural was going to be put under the glare of science, of technology, of present-day analysis—of us.

Inspired by his visit to a BBC research and development unit in a Victorian house in Kingswood, Surrey, Nigel Kneale's THE STONE TAPE came to embody the juxtaposition of science and superstition that was to become, if it wasn't already, the writer's trademark. This intoxicating dichotomy lit a fuse in my young mind and was to inform my future career as a screenwriter. But more than anything else, he and it showed me that genre work—horror, science fiction—needn't be the stuff of childish "B" movies and thus to be ashamed of, but could in fact, with the proper integrity of intention, be thematically original, multi-layered, witty and populated by characters who were as naturalistic, compelling and finely drawn as they were in the most acceptable, social realist dramas on the box. This was no less than a revelation.

As a result I no longer struggled with the idea of working in a field of storytelling derided by those who little understood it, and criticised historically for base and puerile motives. THE STONE TAPE gave me the evidence (and pluck) to stick to my guns, and to the genre I innately loved. To hell with the critical establishment and their prejudices: I was going to write horror for TV—my only aim now was to do it as well as he did.

Ultimately (and now I consider it a noble cause), I wanted to scare the pants off people, but also, like Kneale, give them something to think about in the process. What's more, like him, I'd bring it into their homes. Their place of safety. To their comfy armchairs. Via the medium they trusted.

I've often recounted how, nigh-on twenty years later, I pitched GHOST-WATCH to a BBC drama producer in her office and how she reacted to the idea of "a Hallowe'en special from a haunted house that we pretend is a live broadcast" with slack-jawed glee. Obviously the format bore comparison to Orson Welles' infamous radio production of WAR OF THE WORLDS, but I confess paramount in my mind as I realised that this would have to be recorded on video to capture the verisimilitude of an O.B. transmission was: "Could I pull off something as chilling, as smart, as effective and as memorable as THE STONE TAPE was when I was younger?

Pushing the Door He Unlocked

Kneale's hallmark was intelligence and thematic brilliance. (Paul Schrader says you don't know you have a film until you have a theme and the metaphor for the theme — Kneale did this time and again, seemingly as easily as falling off a log.)

His writing didn't condescend to genre, in fact often seemed to skirt around it, sniffing at it suspiciously, but (unusually, and perhaps uniquely) his visionary SF dramas were as well-wrought, considered and "grown-up" as any regular PLAY FOR TODAY. And far more challenging and innovative than most of them. His not-so-abominable snowman in his television play THE CREATURE (with its ultra-Kneale archetype of the abhorrent human "creature" or "beast": the brash and insensitive American) — eschews a scare ending for one of alarming depth and wisdom, just as Quatermass rejected Buck Rogers derring-do for tense, gritty post-war realism while reflecting upon the actual space race as an existential idea (or ideal), but one fraught with the dread of potential hubris, with the thought that we were courting not progress but a malevolent self-willed destruction. Something that via thrills and suspense nevertheless subtly examined what it means to be human — as all great writing should.

Perhaps in aspiring to the same goals, my references to Kneale abound in GHOSTWATCH. It couldn't be any other way.

At the outset, in both, we have technology descending on a location, full of boyish drive and intent but also an air of smugness. In both cases what is implied by their ebullient confidence is pride coming before a fall, preparing the audience for tragedy, which, as Arthur Miller put it, is when the chickens come home to roost — in spite of the most up to date gizmos money can buy. In GHOSTWATCH as in THE STONE TAPE the protagonists will be dabbling with things left well alone. But isn't that what science always does in order to facilitate progress? And while we want and need progress, isn't there a part of us fears what we might discover, what price might have to be paid for added convenience, more pleasure, less suffering? Has centuries of religious indoctrination brainwashed us into thinking that some things are unknowable, and to question that is a kind of blasphemy? And what better time for blasphemy than Halloween?

We knew all along that Halloween was the ideal date for GHOST-WATCH to be transmitted. Not only was it eminently plausible that the

WE ARE THE MARTIANS

BBC would schedule a "live" ghost hunt on that day in the calendar above all others, but also it gave us "permission" to perform an outlandish trick on the British public. A trick and treat on Halloween being not only just about acceptable, but *de rigeur* on the night when dark forces were believed to hold sway. That belief in itself was the superstitious bedrock and baseline that gave our premise credibility.

But Halloween provided another delicious Kneale connection.

Though he took his name off it, he wrote an early draft of **HALLOWEEN III**, in which children were affected by an insidious TV commercial in the run up to the Celtic festival of Samhain. In my own Halloween horror show, the programme *itself* was what was insidious, the psychological effect on children all too real—(it was quoted in the British Journal of Medicine as being the first television programme to cause Post-Traumatic Stress Disorder in children—*gulp*!). But Kneale's creepy earworm of a TV jingle, primed like a terrorist time bomb, had its parallels in GHOSTWATCH's many asides to televisual banality—the cheesy graphics, the phone-in desk, the vox pops ("We want to hear *your* ghost stories . . ."), and the earnest nodding of on-the-spot interviewers.

Early in THE STONE TAPE there is a light-hearted moment when a man is dressed up in an alien costume. This is Kneale's way of saying, "Don't expect Quatermass from me this time. You are not going to get rubber mask monsters here. You are in for something different." And he dismisses it in a gag. I consciously used the same exact moment for the same reason in GHOSTWATCH when Craig Charles pops out of the kitchen closet to give a cheap jump-scare to Sarah Greene (using that word again: "Beast"). It told the viewer we were well aware of cheap horror tactics and were not above playing them for spoof value, but at the same time upping the ante for the coming fall, paving the way for the more insidious and "real" scares to come when the *actual* mask is ripped away.

Sometimes life takes its lead from art, and it's a mark of Kneale's prescience that his one-off drama defined the "Stone Tape theory", one bandied about to this day by parapsychologists and the public alike. This is the appealing (if not scientifically robust) proposition, first postulated by Thomas Charles Lethbridge in 1961, that, under certain conditions, stone

Pushing the Door He Unlocked

can act like a magnetic tape recording, preserving past events as depicted in the (fictional) programme of the same name. (By a weird coincidence, only yesterday, a clergyman in Chester Cathedral who was helping us during the filming of MIDWINTER OF THE SPIRIT, when asked if the building was haunted, and telling us that he heard disembodied footsteps when he was alone at night, said the cathedral was built on sandstone with sandstone walls *"and they say sandstone can retain the past like a tape recorder."*) One explanation for poltergeist activity ("May be our poltergeist, eh, Dr Pascoe?") is that it is due to disturbances in electromagnetic energy created by geological features underground: the nature of a location directly affecting certain individuals' behaviour. We are, after all, electrochemical beings. The glorious conceit of Kneale's play elaborates on such thoughts, postulating that as one peels away layer after layer of the past, you are left with—what?

This chilling notion resurfaces in GHOSTWATCH when Dr Lin Pascoe, our parapsychologist "expert", talks to a baffled Michael Parkinson about "the onion skin", making a direct allusion to THE STONE TAPE in positing that layer upon layer of people have lived and died in that place and in some realm we can neither perceive nor detect as human beings, still exist there. (In GHOSTWATCH there's child molester Raymond Tunstall and before him Victorian "baby farmer" Mother Seddons; in THE STONE TAPE the Victorian maid is erased to expose a powerful, malevolent earlier entity, the "tape" finally recorded over with Jane Asher's final screams.) Through such ideas, though never on the nose, Kneale hints at a subtextual stripping away of civilisation and a return to the primal, the pre-human, even pre-life. Darkness made real. The literal unknown. Technology as a gateway, not by way of rockets to deep space but in this case, and in GHOSTWATCH's case, to the deep past.

Which brings us to another trope GHOSTWATCH shares with THE STONE TAPE, and, to an extent, with Professor Bernard Quatermass. The Cassandra-like scientist forced up against a brick wall, arguing against narrow-minded officials set in their view, whether the military's stiff-collared jobsworth Breen, or dour Barnsley TV anchorman Michael Parkinson. The lesson from Kneale (and from me) is pretty clear: the person in authority often doesn't know what's going on, let alone what's

We Are The Martians

best. And there's nothing more frightening than the person in charge being out of control.

Also, I realised recently that I duplicated his chilling use of a nursery rhyme: lilting innocence implying a coming ritual of invocation. In the final QUATERMASS serial, set against a megalithic stone circle, it went:

Huffity, puffity, Ringstone Round,
If you lose your hat it will never be found,
So pull your britches right up to your chin,
And fasten your cloak with a bright new pin ...

The use of the word "ring" alone evokes memories of "Ring o' Rosies", the seemingly cheerful ditty which we all know is underpinned by symbolic memories of the Black Death. In GHOSTWATCH, I recalled another such superficially innocent-sounding lullaby similarly using the word "round" to imply a circular path, perhaps magical (intoned both by Pipes, the ghost, and Michael Parkinson in demonic voice mode at the fade out):

Round and round the garden
Like a teddy bear
One step, two step,
Tickle under there ...

A tickle being an intimate gesture between parent and child—but what if it isn't? And what if "Atishoo" means Death?

Folklorist Dr Jacqueline Simpson says of Kneale's lyrics (made up for the Quatermass programme, though based on the stress patterns of "Cottleston Pie" from the Winnie the Pooh books): "Obviously, 'Huffity Puffity Ringstone Round' refers to the traditional idea that if you run around your local circle so many times at such and such a time of day or year the devil will appear." In other words, a variation of running widdershins round the kirk. But in her expert opinion the rhyme has no antecedents in folk tradition. It is simply Kneale's brilliance. And I had not even realised until I compared the two that "Round and round the garden" also sounded, out loud, like an incantation.

Pushing the Door He Unlocked

The incantation having worked, at the end of GHOSTWATCH we are at the point of chaos. The Lord of Misrule has won. Pipes is in the pipes — being "piped" into our homes, as deeply desired and deeply reviled as most TV fodder. The ghost, our hideous unearthed memory, is in control of what we see and what we feel. We have conjured him and we are abandoned as terror reaches its height. No end credits — or at least that would have been my preference: as it was, the BBC bottled out. Which may have been just as well, given the furore that exploded in the tabloids over the coming days and weeks. I wanted to leave on a note of trauma, loss, confusion — just like the devastation at end of Hammer's **QUATERMASS AND THE PIT**, where the titles run over Andrew Keir sitting in the Blitz-like rubble, the Martian demon defeated but the world beaten to a pulp. *No, you can't end it there.* But they did. And I wanted a similar effect at the end of my own programme. But I wanted the TV audience to be complicit in the outcome too.

Our desire (our invocation) created "Pipes", just as the essence of the Martians was inside us waiting to erupt. We, as Kneale almost always conveys, are the problem. And the carapace that protects society from panic and fear is wafer-thin. But the desire for chaos is the fulfilment of a sense of anxiety. Only by destruction can fear end.

According to Alexandra Heller-Nicholas in *Supernatural Studies* (Vol 2; Issue 1, Winter 2015): "Dr Pascoe comprehends that the GHOSTWATCH broadcast has provided a way to disperse and condense supernatural energy across the United Kingdom" and this sums up my indebtedness to Kneale in the conceptualization of the project. It's a transparently Knealean concept, and I'm not ashamed to admit it.

By now it will hopefully be apparent that I've learned many things from his craft and genius — but nothing so profoundly as his recurrent theme of the tug-of-war clash between scientific and pagan forces, the fundamental tussle between a bright new gleaming future and the lingering gloom of the past; the quest to know and be enlightened, or to succumb to the enigmatic, animalistic forces of the unknown and unwanted.

Often I think that behind his stories Kneale is pleading with Humanity to adopt a trace of humility. Or at least curb its obscene arrogance in placing Mankind at the centre of the universe, and our present-day selves as the pinnacle of all that has been achieved in the past: another delusion.

The craggy Quatermass, looking like a bearded Old Testament prophet in the sixties movie (or Father Shandor, vampire slayer, to be exact), faces netherworld devils albeit in science-fiction drag, while the communications boffins in THE STONE TAPE (based on actual BBC technicians) come to apply their machines to that most ubiquitous of supernatural entities, ghosts. Some of his other work has modernity combating ancient wisdom (or foolishness), as in "Murrain" or the Euston Films QUATERMASS with John Mills, where the aged and frail old school prof is up against a neo-pagan hippy cult blissed-out in their holy wish to contact aliens via the mechanism of ancient technology — Stonehenge by any other name.

I was all too aware of this rich seam running throughout Kneale's work when I devised and wrote my ITV show AFTERLIFE, featuring as its two main characters a sceptical psychologist and a psychic medium (a "sensitive" like THE STONE TAPE's Jane Asher character), played by Andrew Lincoln and Lesley Sharp respectively: symbolic opposites, constantly at loggerheads yet eventually finding a level of respect and oneness, albeit finally as one of them faces death.

Curiously (if you'll forgive the diversion) in the late 1980s I was asked to come in on a TV drama series developed from "an idea by Nigel Kneale" and naturally I jumped at the chance.

It was called PUSH THE DARK DOOR — and before you get excited, no, it never got produced. The intriguing concept (pre X-FILES) concerned a disparate group of investigators brought together by a rich billionaire to investigate cases of the supernatural in a general quest for the rich man, who was dying, to know whether life after death existed or not. I was involved in coming up with future storylines alongside fellow screenwriter Arthur Ellis (the off-beat writer of A TURNIP HEAD'S GUIDE TO ALAN PARKER) but the first storyline was written by Kneale himself. The plot involved a haunted flat in a tower block, the location of which coincided, historically, with a pagan site. I have to say my own story ideas weren't very good looking back on them, and word came from the producer that the great man thought they were awful. Ah, well ... Anyway, it died a death. Perhaps deservedly so.

Pushing the Door He Unlocked

But my point is, even that aborted project, to my mind, betrays Kneale's most fertile recurring preoccupation — our attempts as human beings to apply our perhaps hopeless rational thinking to the irrational, if that can even be possible. This produces a delicious tension which I believe — and I think he did too — is a contradiction at the core of the human character (and one I chose the dramatise in AFTERLIFE). Our left brain, our logic, seeks to explore and understand but our right brain, our emotion, fears what might be waiting for us. The desire, as Freud would say, and the repression of the desire. (Though I'm sure Kneale would baulk at anyone discussing his entertainments in psychoanalytical terms.)

Nevertheless, for the reasons given above, his themes permeate and resonate even in an industry, television, in which being a journeyman (better, a yes-man) is sometimes prized above all else. In the hallowed halls of broadcasting where, as I know to my cost, a writer's work can at best be embraced, interpreted and changed by countless others: but at worst, mangled and shown a death by a thousand "improvements".

It is often said that latterly he became curmudgeonly (notably bitter in his response to flattering homages to his name in John Carpenter's **PRINCE OF DARKNESS**), yet I can sympathise with someone who reached the stage where his new ideas weren't as eagerly green-lit by commissioning editors as they once were, and instead of being celebrated as an original and unique voice — far less a national treasure — he was expected to swallow his creative ambitions and turn in decent but unremarkable scripts for KAVANAGH QC or the historical drama SHARPE. A respectful, if ignominious, fading light on an astonishing career. But I am positive that while he was beavering on these jobs-for-hire his drawers were full to overflowing with unproduced screenplays that the Powers That Were deemed "not quite what we are looking for". Luckily, in a business that records over its past all too swiftly, he has a presence in the onion layers of television history, with THE QUATERMASS EXPERIMENT mentioned on the timeline on the walls of BAFTA headquarters, as indeed is GHOSTWATCH for 1992 — while said commissioners are rightly forgotten. It seemed cruel, even then, that while people of my generation were venerating his output as seminal classics, our hero was cast into the wilderness, even before the age of "age-ism".

However, I am eternally grateful I was able to pay tribute personally to the legend shortly before he died. At a special screening, I think in Cheltenham, David Pirie (whose outstanding TV film RAINY DAY WOMAN starring Charles Dance had been directly inspired by QUATERMASS II) was first on his feet to give "Tom" a standing ovation. I was second. The rest of the audience immediately followed. Characteristically, Kneale affected embarrassment at being subjected to such a heartfelt accolade. To hell with that—it needed to be done. And I think I detected a tear in his eye as he gently motioned us to sit back down.

But my *real* tribute to him, without doubt, was GHOSTWATCH.

It was created, quite literally, in form and content, as a direct result of the impact of seeing THE STONE TAPE on a small screen in the corner of the sitting room of my parents' house in Pontypridd, South Wales, aged seventeen, any thoughts of being a professional television writer a dim and distant fantasy.

I increasingly see that, in so many ways, my story of media technology descending to tackle paranormal forces, and failing, was my way of paying respect to the Master. Not by a standing ovation or a fan letter, but by writing something new that built on what had gone before. Something that I hoped would thrill and terrify people in the way I had been thrilled and terrified by ninety minutes of videotape twenty years earlier.

He pushed the dark door, so that the rest of us might follow.

It's a cliché that we stand on the shoulders of giants, and a truism that readers become writers, but TV viewers become writers too. Images and scenes as well as books become part of our shared lives, our creative souls. Fictional characters and dramatic ideas live after death and percolate within us, and the best of us leave traces in the DNA of the culture.

I can only say that if Michael Bryant, Iain Cuthbertson and the other scientists in THE STONE TAPE were to peel away the "onion skin" layers of my screenwriting, especially that notorious BBC TV "hoax" that caused sleepless nights on Halloween 1992, I'm pretty sure that the ghosts they would uncover would be themselves.

BEASTS
An Overview

Mark Morris

WHEN, IN THE MID-1970S, NIGEL KNEALE'S IDEA FOR A fourth Quatermass serial was rejected by the BBC, the writer decided to cast his net further afield. He turned to the commercial channels, and for the producer Nicholas Palmer he wrote a play called AGAINST THE CROWD: "Murrain" (sometimes referred to simply as "Murrain"), which was produced and transmitted by ATV in 1975. The play was an intelligent, successful drama about the possibility of witchcraft in rural England, and during its production Palmer and Kneale discussed ideas for a six-episode supernatural anthology series, all the stories of which would have a common theme or link. After some debate it was decided that each play should focus on some kind of animal or creature, but to avoid duplication of mood or content each should approach the subject from a different direction. Kneale remembered: "The aim was to make them as different as possible: one comedy, one horror, one straight drama, one mystery...all sorts."

The result was BEASTS, transmitted by the ITV network in the Autumn of 1976. Though the six episodes are not as clearly delineated in terms of mood as Kneale suggests they were intended to be, they are nevertheless all unique in terms of the thematic approach taken towards their individual subjects, and remain six of the most powerful, witty, frightening and often poignant hours of TV horror ever committed to screen.

Although the scheduling of the series varied from region to region, the intended and most common running order saw BEASTS kicking off on the evening of 16th October 1976 with—in my region—"Special Offer". To all intents and purposes a low budget, British re-make of Brian de Palma's recent hit movie, **CARRIE**, "Special Offer" tells the story of Noreen, a downtrodden employee in a shoddy, back street supermarket. Like every other episode in the series, "Special Offer" relies for its impact on committed performances from a small but universally superb cast, each member of which seems to relish Kneale's characteristically meaty and vigorous dialogue. Noreen herself, the focus of this episode, is magnificently portrayed by a very young Pauline Quirke, and it is interesting to note that Quirke's character (unlike Sissy Spacek who had portrayed Carrie in de Palma's film) matches Carrie White's description in Stephen King's original novel to a tee.

Grotesque and dim-witted on the surface, Noreen is, in fact, a far more complex character than she originally appears. Never entirely likeable, she is nonetheless achingly sympathetic. As the episode opens, she is building a display tower of baked bean tins, only to be ridiculed by the store manager, the young and fiercely ambitious Mr Grimley (Geoffrey Bateman). Noreen seems unaffected by her boss's bullying sarcasm, but within seconds a number of tins shift in the display basket she is standing beside and a display card depicting the store mascot, a crudely-rendered cartoon of a cute, yellow, squirrel-like creature named Briteway Billy, falls from its display stand. A few minutes later another store employee is puzzled to see a tin of baked beans rolling towards her along the aisle. Her puzzlement increases when the tin halts for several seconds, then resumes rolling. She picks the tin up, momentarily disturbed, then shrugs and places it in the display basket. Innocuous events, but they are the first eerie indications that the "beast" has been unleashed...

Little by little the bizarre events become more pronounced. A jar of coffee flies from the checkout counter to smash on the floor; packets of

bacon are found shredded in the refrigerated foods section; a scuttling sound precedes a row of tins cascading from a shelf. The supermarket staff are frightened and bewildered, but to the viewing audience it is evident that these incidents are directly linked to Noreen. Whenever Mr Grimley makes her the butt of one of his scathing put-downs or flirts with glamorous checkout girl, Linda (Shirley Cheriton), another mishap occurs.

It is Noreen herself who mentions seeing "an animal", which she claims is responsible for the increasingly chaotic events. However, when she is vague about its shape and colour, Mr Grimley mockingly suggests that Briteway Billy is running amok in the store. Noreen snorts with laughter, but latches on to the suggestion eagerly. The supernatural manifestation of her repressed emotions now has a name and a personality, and as such renders her free of both responsibility and inhibition. Now, when frozen food explodes out of the freezer or a stream of urine appears to arc from behind tins on a shelf (in reality a bottle of washing up liquid disgorging its contents), Noreen playfully chides, "Naughty Billy." As the chaos ensues she becomes more aware and assertive.

To the viewing audience it is obvious that she has a dawning, though child-like, sense of her own wild power. Her character — initially lovesick, naïve, hesitant, pathetic and almost pathologically defensive (a classic victim in other words) — becomes darker, more knowing. Simply because she is the underdog, we still care about her, but we fear her now too. Kneale further toys with our sympathies, even suggesting they may be misplaced, by giving us indications that Noreen's power will corrupt her just as readily as Mr Grimley's far more limited power of authority has corrupted him (or, more likely, simply given him leave to indulge his brutish personality with impunity). When warehouseman Mickey (Herbert Norville), who has previously shown Noreen only friendship and understanding, is clearing up after one of "Billy's" attacks, she disdainfully tosses an apple core into his path.

It is evident from the snippets of background information we are given that Noreen has had a tough life (her father is dead, her mother is "sick a lot"), but before the appearance of "Billy" there is the suggestion that she has been almost ennobled by her plight, that her previous inability to fight back means she is as vulnerable as a child, and therefore touched by innocence. This is what makes Noreen both an appealing and a tragic character. Like Carrie White we understand her pain and we want everything to turn out all right for her. The tragedy is that the only way she can make this happen is to become as ruthless as the world around her. At the end of Part One she drives Linda screaming from the store with a display of telekinetic power. When Mr Grimley turns he sees Noreen standing motionless in the aisle, wearing a knowing, self-satisfied expression that, for the viewing audience, is both chilling and saddening to witness.

Part Two opens with the arrival of the avuncular Mr Liversedge (Wensley Pithey) from head office. His is the voice of reason and understanding. He talks to Mr Grimley, who tells him that, despite vague sightings of an "animal" in the store, he is certain that Noreen is involved in the disturbances. When Mr Liversedge asks him what evidence he has of this, Grimley admits that it is "just a feeling". Though underplayed here, this becomes a running theme in BEASTS. Throughout the six stories, certain of Kneale's characters feel a sense of presentiment or foreboding, a sense that something terrible is just around the corner. This, of course, is a dramatic device, designed to play on the apprehension of the audience, but it is also indicative of the vibrant and instinctive nature of the characters that Kneale has been renowned for creating throughout his career.

A touching scene ensues when Mr Liversedge takes Noreen to the café across the road where he can speak to her away from the bustle and tension of the store. "How do you like your coffee?" he asks her. Noreen is wary, uncertain, and our collective heart goes out to her; she is obviously not used to being treated with courtesy and respect. Hesitantly she responds, "Oh ... I *do* like it." When Mr Liversedge gently asks her opinion of what's been going on, she becomes tongue-tied. Again she is not accustomed to the notion that someone actually wants to hear what she has to say.

Later, back at the store, Mr Liversedge openly doubts what she has told him about Briteway Billy being responsible for the devastation. Instantly Noreen becomes distressed. "He's here now," she wails and begins to call Billy by name, looking up as though evoking a malevolent spirit. The results are spectacular: tins and packets fly off shelves, milk bottles, cereal

WE ARE THE MARTIANS

packets and lights explode. Noreen watches, enraptured, then as though speaking to an errant child, says, "Oh, Billy, that's naughty."

Now acting as the voice of the audience, Mr Liversedge explains to Grimley exactly what's going on. He tells him that the incidents are the work of a poltergeist, though modifies the statement to explain what the audience has known for some time—that the destruction is the physical manifestation of Noreen's pent-up emotions. He further proffers the theory that Noreen is doing it because of love.

"Huh?" says Grimley.

"She's in love with you," replies Mr Liversedge in exasperation.

Grimley looks horrified, his callous, insensitive character encapsulated in the riposte, "Well . . . that's sick!"

Mr Liversedge tells Grimley that the solution to the problem is simple. "Be kind to her," he says. "Just kind, that's all."

The next day, however, a buxom, brassy brunette appears in the store asking about the job vacated by Linda. As Grimley begins to flirt with her, Noreen straightens up, the familiar brooding, blank-eyed expression crossing her face. She begins to call for Billy, and as the staff flee in terror the inevitable happens. Eventually only Noreen is left, sugar and cornflakes flying around her, glee on her face. Despite Mr Liversedge's advice, Grimley dismisses her, but the following day "Billy" is back. A tin flies from a shelf, smashing the window, and the staff see Noreen in the café across the street, gazing at them, trance-like.

Once again Mr Liversedge speaks to her, this time gently confronting her with her power.

"I don't know what you mean," she says.

"I think you do," he replies. "What you call Billy . . ."

Mr Liversedge leaves, leaving Grimley alone in the store. Expressing herself in the only way she knows how, Noreen begins to make items leap from the shelves. Enraged, Grimley rushes out and confronts her, grabs her hand and drags her into the shop, demanding that she admit she is causing it all, describing her as "a mad, foul horror." A second later what appear to be the entire contents of the store erupt towards him. He is buried in an avalanche of tins and packets, rendered unconscious. When it is over, Noreen kneels beside him and tenderly begins to brush the debris from his shattered body. When Mr Liversedge arrives after Grimley has been carried out on a stretcher, Noreen looks up and says dreamily, "He loved me really. He took me by the hand."

It is an achingly sad and poignant ending to a tragic episode. Noreen has not benefited from her power and is unlikely to do so in the future. The simple white titles displayed on a silent black screen at the end emphasise the funereal, downbeat atmosphere of the episode, though in fact this is not a factor unique to this story. Only "Buddyboy", the third episode of BEASTS, contains incidental music. This may well have been a budgetary rather than an artistic decision, but Kneale turns it to his advantage. In the absence of music, each episode employs the use of various unsettling sound effects to evoke an atmosphere of dread. This is perhaps most prominently utilised in the second "officially" transmitted episode, "During Barty's Party".

Kneale himself regarded this episode as the most effective of the six. "What was interesting to me," he said, "was it was like making THE BIRDS with no birds. In this case it was rats with no rats. The rats were purely sound, you never saw one, and it was only through the superb acting of the two principals that the thing worked. It was entirely in their minds and their eyes."

The two principals in question are Elizabeth Sellars and Anthony Bate as Angela and Roger Truscott. They are indeed superb in their roles as a well-off, middle-aged husband and wife whose isolated country house is besieged by an unseen swarm of voracious, super-intelligent rats. The only other characters in this episode are heard but not seen, chief amongst them Barty Wills, an excruciatingly chirpy local radio DJ, who is amused by stories of "king-sized meeces" rampaging around the home counties. Only when Angie's fear and desperation get through to him later in the episode, after she has called him up to tell him that she and Roger are trapped in their house, does he become more human. Tragically, however, he mis-hears their name as "Prescott" and the rats gnaw through the telephone cables, cutting them off, just as Angela is about to give him their address.

With only two actors, one location and very limited special effects (unlike "Special Offer", which is by far the most effects-laden episode of

WE ARE THE MARTIANS

the series), "During Barty's Party" has the flavour of a stage play adapted for television. This, though, is its strength rather than its weakness. Almost from the moment when Angie awakens from a nightmare-haunted snooze, agitated without knowing why (another example of a Kneale character overwhelmed by a sense of foreboding), we share her jittery sense of claustrophobia and entrapment. Fearful of the silence, or of what might invade it, she puts on a bouncy, cheerful pop song (Lulu's "Shout") and turns the volume up loud. Throughout this episode, perhaps more than any other, Kneale uses not only sound, but the *juxtaposition* of sounds to convey contrast, and more especially to emphasise the intrusion of the terrifying into the cosy mundanity of everyday life. The comedy *boing* of bedsprings during Barty's radio broadcast, for instance, is offset against the scrabbling of rats beneath the floorboards, and later the joyous, laughing voices of their off-screen neighbours arriving home after a day out are chillingly drowned by the shrill, crazed squealing of the attacking rats, a sound which is itself then heightened still further by the hideous, dying screams of those same neighbours being devoured alive.

Another reason why the episode is so successful is because Kneale has written his characters in such a way that they are never static. Roger and Angela's individual reactions to what is happening to them are wildly different, and in fact their very characters transform and eventually swap places as the crisis develops. At the beginning Angela is depicted as nervous and neurotic. Among other things she is scared of getting old, of being alone and abandoned. When she tries to express her nebulous fears to Roger he is wearily dismissive.

"It's like the fuse box, the gypsies, that business over the barbed wire," he tells her. "It's a kind of indulgence."

He himself, though steadfast and sensible, is pompous and smug—not uncaring of his wife, but patronising towards her. He *seems* practical too. When Angie tells him they've got a rat, he tells her to set the dog on it—but, ominously, the dog has disappeared. When the rat begins to scratch, he stamps on the floor and it stops. "That's all it takes," he says confidently.

This, however, is one problem that not only refuses to go away, but which worsens with each passing minute. Roger responds by getting angry,

then furious, then childishly unreasonable—until, by the end of Part One, after Angie has realised with horror that the rats beneath the floorboards are actually following their footsteps, he loses it completely, becoming hysterical and helpless, like a frightened child.

As the second half opens it is Angie who begins to adopt the role of the sensible, practical one. The suggestion is both that she is gaining strength from her husband's weakness and is sparked into action, even invigorated in a way, by the fact that her tenebrous anxieties have finally become tangible. As Roger, faced with a situation out of his control, falls apart, it is left to Angie to try to find solutions to their increasingly hopeless predicament. Her efforts are in vain, however. Each time it appears that help may be at hand, the rats prove to be one step ahead of them.

The Truscotts' growing desperation throughout this latter part of the episode is harrowing to witness. When it becomes evident not only that the rats have cut off their link to Barty Wills, but that Barty has mis-heard their surname, they scream at the radio with such full-blooded panic that we fully share their frantic futility. Similarly, Roger's hysterical screaming of his wife's name when the rats chew through the power cables and the

We Are The Martians

Truscotts are plunged into darkness is a gut-wrenching moment of absolute primal terror. As he clings to the banister, hyperventilating, it is Angie who gets the lantern and the portable radio, who encourages him to don a thick coat and a fencing mask in the hope that the garments will protect them from rat bites. She suggests making a break for the car, but the door to the garage is rattling, the wood splintering as the rats gnaw their way through. When their neighbours are despatched—the scene made all the more harrowing by focusing solely on the utter horror on the Truscotts' faces—they have no option but to flee upstairs, screaming in terror. The episode ends with a close-up of the portable radio sitting on a shelf, which is shaking with the sheer force of the countless rat bodies swarming into the house. Barty Wills is still babbling his banalities, but his voice grows fainter as the hideous, crazed squealing of the rats rises to a crescendo...

Many of Kneale's stories are cautionary tales about mankind's hubristic attitude towards his environment and "During Barty's Party" is a case in point. He reminds us often that despite our millennia of progress and evolution, despite all our technological advancements, civilisation is a

Beasts

sham, a flimsy veil that Mother Nature can rip away at a moment's notice. He suggests that we would do well to remember and respect the fact that there are stronger and more ancient forces than our own on this planet.

The third episode, "Buddyboy", is the strangest and yet in some ways the most earthy of the series. As mentioned earlier, this is the only episode to feature an opening theme and incidental music, which immediately lends it a particular flavour all of its own. The music, a kind of synthesised seascape—the kind of thing we might play to lull ourselves to sleep, albeit with an added edginess, and intercut with sinister, ghostly dolphin cries—plays over the opening titles, which themselves appear over stock footage of dolphins skimming through the waves.

The contrast between seeing these beautiful creatures in their natural habitat and the dank, run-down, abandoned dolphinarium we are subsequently confronted with is stark and jarring. Instantly, even before a word has been spoken, the theme of the episode has been established. This is a story about exploitation, and more specifically about exploitation by man (as opposed to woman) kind. It is man as parasite, feeding off the misery of his fellow creatures. Again this is a common theme of Kneale's (the final episode of BEASTS, 'The Dummy', explores the subject from a different angle). Watching "Buddyboy" you get the opinion that Kneale does not like his fellow humans very much—or at the very least that he is of the opinion that the scum always rises to the surface.

The episode opens with the dolphinarium's owner, Mr Hubbard (Wolfe Morris), showing a potential buyer around the building. The potential buyer is Dave (Martin Shaw), owner of a porn cinema called the Peek-a-Boo Club, who has ambitions to turn the dolphinarium into something similar on a larger scale, something with "class," which he defines as "red plush, fur...maybe sell hamburgers". Mr Hubbard is sweaty, bug-eyed with nervousness. Dave is arrogant, ruthless, hard-nosed and manipulative. He quickly realises that Hubbard is running scared of someone or something and knows that he can use the man's fear to his advantage. Hubbard is eager to sell—which is precisely why Dave keeps him dangling. He knows that he can play Hubbard along, can keep turning the screw tighter and tighter until the owner of the building becomes so desperate that he will accept whatever Dave is prepared to offer.

329

WE ARE THE MARTIANS

It is poetic justice in a way. Hubbard himself has earned a very lucrative living from exploitation and manipulation, but is now washed up, an old and feeble animal in a very savage jungle. His health is shot to pieces. He is haunted by his past—not least, we soon discover, by the spirit (whether real or imagined) of the eponymous dolphin, Buddyboy.

Buddyboy, he tells Dave, had "exceptional intelligence." He was the star of the show, all the visitors loved him, but "he tried to take over...I hated the bastard...I had to show him." He claims that Buddyboy had a "death wish", that one day he decided simply to die, but the insinuation is that somehow Hubbard was responsible for the animal's death. He is haunted by Buddyboy's ghostly chirruping cry, but whether it is simply in his mind, a manifestation of his guilt and paranoia, is never made clear.

Later Dave, too, hears the sound, but by this time it has been established that he is simply Hubbard rejuvenated, cut from the same cloth, destined to follow in the man's footsteps. During the initial viewing of the building, the men hear a sound and discover a girl, Lucy (Pamela Moiseiwitsch), an ex-employee at the dolphinarium, who has been living rough. Hubbard is enraged to find her there, but Dave saves her from the man's wrath, takes her back to his club and gives her a meal.

"You're like him," Lucy says.

"Like Hubbard?" Dave replies, unconvinced.

"You will be."

Lucy is fey and innocent, child-like and tractable. She dresses in greens and blues, which is suggestive of the sea, of the dolphins themselves. In fact, she is more dolphin than human in many ways. "I hate people," she says. She adored the dolphins, though. "They know and they feel and they understand...they love each other," she tells Dave. The dolphins are presented as noble, beautiful, intelligent creatures. Speaking to Hubbard, Dave says of them, "You said they never turned vicious? Funny that. That's where they're different from us."

After Hubbard has fled with the pittance that Dave has deigned to pay him for the dolphinarium, Dave inherits Hubbard's flat and his belongings, thus becoming almost indistinguishable from the man he has replaced. And just as Hubbard owned Buddyboy, so Dave now owns Lucy. Naively she thinks he loves her, but he tells her, "I used you to get him rattled."

When his henchman, Jimmy, arrives at the flat with two prostitutes, Dave argues with him and beats him up before throwing him out. Brimming with his own power, he then takes Lucy almost as forcefully, and barely even notices when she simply lies pliantly beneath him, her face blank. Afterwards she reaches out to him for a little tenderness, but the only way he shows his appreciation of her is by expressing his desire to get her to star in a film he can show in his club: "give the customers a treat... spread it around a bit." Realising what she has allowed herself to become, Lucy goes into the bathroom and calls softly for Buddyboy (an echo of the equally naïve and damaged Noreen's evocation of Billy in "Special Offer"). Later, when Dave goes to see why she is taking so long, he finds her drowned in the bath—and instantly hears Buddyboy's ghostly, chirruping cry. Just as Hubbard destroyed Buddyboy, so Dave has destroyed Lucy. The cycle is complete, and the only consolation is that at least the abusers and exploiters are seemingly destined to be haunted by their sins.

In my opinion the fourth episode, "Baby", is one of the most frightening hours of television ever made. It is certainly the most traditional horror

We Are The Martians

story of the series, dealing as it does with an area of farmland blighted by an ancient curse. Peter and Jo Gilkes (Simon MacCorkindale and Jane Wymark) play a young couple who have just moved to a cottage in the country. Peter is a vet. He has come from the city, from "constipated poodles and sick old budgies", and is relishing being a "real vet" now, dealing with farm animals. Perhaps it is intentional on Kneale's part, perhaps not, but there seems to be more than a hint of James Herriot and Siegfried Farnon in Peter and his bluff, hard-drinking boss, Dick (the marvellous T.P. McKenna). The story opens, however, with two workmen, Mr Grace and Mr Biddick, finding a nest full of eggs on the cottage roof.

"None of 'em hatched," Mr Biddick observes.

"They'll be addled," opines Mr Grace.

And indeed they are. In fact, the only birds that seem to inhabit this patch of land are the ceaselessly cawing crows, traditional harbingers of doom.

Jo, six months pregnant, arrives at the cottage, having been to her father's house to fetch the family cat, which promptly runs away. This, of course, parallels the disappearing dog in "During Barty's Party", and may be included as a subtle joke by Kneale, to the effect that in a series about "animals", the domestic ones are always seen to be fleeing as if to make way for their malevolent counterparts.

Jo has already had one miscarriage, but she tells her father over the phone, "It's going to be all right this time." However she is clearly apprehensive, even more so when a large clay jar that Peter finds in a hollow whilst demolishing a wall in the kitchen proves to contain the hairy, wizened carcass of a long-dead creature.

The impact of this scene, and countless others within this episode, is made immeasurably greater by Jane Wymark's performance. In effect the story is told from Jo's point of view, and the camera is forever focused on her, showing us her reaction to the events around her, lingering on her face which is often etched with fear, and most particularly on her eyes, which flicker this way and that like those of a trapped animal.

Again, Jo is a character haunted by a dreadful sense of foreboding. As Peter begins to scrape at the tallow which seals the lid of the jar, she says quickly, "I don't know if we..." She feels an instinctive fear of the creature once it has been 'released', and tells Peter, "Get rid of it... it's *horrible!*"

The creature itself is a grotesque creation. Curled up like a foetus, it appears to be part pig, part monkey, part squirrel. It has no discernible features, long claws and the suggestion of tusks. It seems to exert a subtle hold on Peter. Certainly he fails to comply with Jo's request—though this may simply be as a result of his personality. Throughout the episode he is presented as selfish and insensitive, spoilt and immature. When Peter dreamily says of the creature, "I'm not sure it was ever actually born," we focus once again on Jo's face, where she wears an expression of dawning horror, as though she senses something of what is to come, but can do nothing to change it.

The more elderly of the two workmen, Mr Grace, is like an old sooth-sayer. He seems to know more than he is letting on—though on several occasions both he and Biddick exchange knowing, fearful glances, as if they are sharing some terrible secret which they cannot reveal. "I should get shut on it . . . get it gone," the old man tells her, and indeed Jo *does* try to burn it, but the creature is rescued by Peter, who tears around the corner in his Land Rover and leaps to snatch it from the fire as if somehow forewarned.

Jo's fears are further intensified when Peter's boss, Dick, tells the Gilkeses about the last couple, the Jacksons, who lived in the cottage. Mr Jackson tried to start a dog farm, but his prize bitch "made a fool of him every time . . . blew it!"

"Lost her puppies?" says Peter. The two men laugh about the matter, especially when Dick tells Peter that Jackson blamed the land. Jo, however, is uneasy, and is hardly reassured when Dick tells her that the land is prone to brucellosis, "contagious abortion", which affects cattle, but which she has no chance of catching.

Jo's anxiety causes her to reacts angrily. "A germ?" she shouts. "A germ? You don't know!" She asks whether the Jacksons, who had lived in the cottage for years, had ever had any children and receives the reply she is both expecting and dreading. They didn't.

Peter and Dick decide to do an autopsy on the creature to try to find out what it is. Dick is all set to take it to the surgery, but at the last moment Peter stops him, telling him he'll keep it at the house, bring it along tomorrow. In a moment of great irony, he conceals it in a cupboard in the

WE ARE THE MARTIANS

room that he and Jo are converting into a nursery. The next day, Jo and Mr Grace have a conversation about the creature.

This is a pivotal scene in the episode. The exchange between the two characters is odd, almost oblique. We are given the impression that Grace is trying to warn Jo, but that they are both edging around the subject, as though fearful of the consequences. Grace tells Jo that the thing would have had "purpose."

"Bad purpose?" says Jo.

"Most like . . . if nature wouldn't bring it about, then such as that might serve."

"Bring what about?" asks Jo cagily. "You mean make something bad happen?"

"In them days," Grace tells her, "they believed they could put harm on a person or a place."

"Who do you mean?" asks Jo.

"Somebody . . . wise in them powers. To cast 'em. And to fix 'em. That little brute you found . . . that's the way . . . to hold the power. To bind it . . . A thing like that . . . it'd have been suckled. Human suckling. To set it to work . . ."

Jo goes to look for the lost cat in the nearby woods. All is quiet except for the relentless, ominously threatening cawing of the crows. She finds a stagnant pool from which part of what appears to be a dead animal is protruding. Crouching beside it, she pokes it reluctantly with a stick—and is relieved when the object turns out to be nothing but a piece of wood covered with moss and weeds. However, at that moment, the sound of the crows seems to change pitch. It slows down, becomes distorted, begins to sound not unlike a guttural voice trying to form words. A shadow creeps across the pond. Jo looks up and sees what appears to be a column of darkness rising from behind the trees. She flees in panic, pursued by the distorted cawing sound. From here on in, the sound stays with her; she becomes haunted by it.

Just as the Truscotts seemed to be offered a brief hope of escape when their neighbours arrived home in "During Barty's Party", so Jo is offered a similar hope when Peter arrives home, covered in dung and raging that he has had enough, that he is getting out. He is like a child throwing a tantrum, but Jo is eager to fuel his desire to leave for her own reasons. She tries to articulate her fears to him, but is unable to. "There's something wrong here," she says. "Today I heard...I thought..."

Then Dick and his wife turn up with a bottle of whisky, full of good cheer and her hopes are dashed. Within moments Peter's tantrum is forgotten and Jo knows that her last chance has gone. There follows a raucous, drunken evening, which only emphasises Jo's isolation and unease. She retreats to the kitchen, the laughter fading into the background. Again she hears the low, guttural cooing sound and spins round. There is nothing there. Dick's wife, Dorothy, enters the kitchen, but she is oblivious to Jo's fears, fobs her off with empty platitudes. Jo turns to the sink for a moment, and when she turns back Dorothy is gone. However we catch a glimpse of a dark, hunched, shambling shape disappearing around the corner that leads upstairs. It is a terrifying moment—not least because when Jo re-enters the lounge, Peter, Dick and Dorothy are all there. The fear is stark on her face, but they are all too drunk to notice.

The climax is a sustained masterclass of terror. Jo is woken by the sound of splintering wood in the dead of night. Unable to rouse Peter from his drunken stupor, she goes to investigate the sound. She finds that the cupboard in the nursery has been smashed open as though something has erupted from it. She creeps downstairs, where she hears a greedy sucking sound coming from the direction of the lounge. Slowly she turns her head, and is confronted by the sight of a hideous, cowled shape, which brays and caws at her, sitting in the ancient rocker. The creature from the jar, now restored to life, is suckling on it.

"No!" Jo screams. "No! No!" She collapses to the floor, clutching her belly. The camera pans up to the rocking chair, now empty, which then fades to black as the titles once again run across a silent screen.

In many ways "Baby" is a simple story. It takes as its theme the fundamental, specifically female fear of being unable to bear a child, and encapsulates it within a traditional, intensely creepy horror story that brings to mind the tales of H.P. Lovecraft and Algernon Blackwood. The characters are boldly wrought, but work superbly within the confines of the plot. As with the Truscotts in "During Barty's Party", there is a real sense that whatever she tries to do, Jo will not escape her fate.

We Are The Martians

In the fifth story, "What Big Eyes", Kneale toys with two of the staple ingredients of horror movies, werewolves and mad scientists. Typically, however, he subverts these ingredients, mixing them into a dark, modern fairy tale, which takes as its twin themes the often corrosive effects of obsession and the moral questions associated with the subject of vivisection.

Inspector Bob Curry (Michael Kitchen) of the RSPCA is investigating the dubious business dealings of animal trader Duggie Jebb (Bill Dean) when he discovers that a number of Hungarian timber wolves have recently been purchased by an innocuous back street pet shop. In yet another link back to an earlier episode, these early scenes display an immediate parallel with "Buddyboy". Once again we are presented with the callous attitude of human beings towards his fellow creatures. Animals are seen merely as commodities; Jebb refers to the cheetahs he keeps in cramped conditions as "fur coats" and says that he possesses "a hundred and odd monkeys for research." Bob Curry is a rare, compassionate idealist in a cynical world. He arrives at the pet shop and is introduced to reclusive geneticist Leo Raymount (the incomparable Patrick Magee at his splenetic, creepy, eccentric best). Raymount is described as a "genius" by his downtrodden daughter, Florence (Madge Ryan). She has subjugated her life to him, even though he reviles and bullies her.

Raymount tells Curry that his particular subject of interest is "lycanthropy". He gives a convincing and committed argument for its existence, talking of race memory and evolutionary links. Curry is unconvinced, however, and when he discovers that Raymount bought the wolves in order to extract their brain tissue and spinal fluid, he speaks in horrified tones of "vivisection".

"An emotive word," observes Raymount drily.

Curry accuses Raymount of cutting up the wolves for his own amusement.

Raymount refutes the accusation zealously. He argues that his work has a serious scientific purpose. This, of course, raises the moral question of where to draw the line where vivisection is concerned. What may seem to entail relevant and important research to one person, could appear trivial and not worth the suffering of the animal to another.

Beasts

Raymount talks of "a case history", which he claims is "straight out of folklore." He then proceeds to tell the story of Little Red Riding Hood. Only in his version Grandma is not eaten by the wolf, she *was* the wolf. Curry scoffs at him, tells him that it is only a fairy story, but Raymount is adamant. What he has related is not a fairy tale, but a "folk memory".

He tells Curry that he has developed "the Grandma vaccine" to kick-start the race memory. He has been injecting himself with it daily. When Curry suggests that his deteriorating health is because he has been poisoning himself and is more likely than not suffering from septicaemia, Raymount refuses to accept his diagnosis. He dismisses his recent health problems as inevitable side effects of the drug.

Curry urges Florence to get her father to a hospital. She agrees, but the old man refuses to go. When Curry later returns to the pet shop, having discovered that Raymount has taken possession of yet another timber wolf, he finds the place wrecked, debris all over the floor. We wonder whether Raymount's experiment has borne fruit, after all, whether he has in fact transformed into a werewolf and run amok. Curry hears the sound of equipment being smashed and rushes to the laboratory, where he finds not a werewolf, but Florence, destroying her father's work.

Raymount is dead and Florence is raging bitterly, having realised that she has wasted her life serving a man she thought was a genius but who has turned out to have been nothing but a crank. In a way it is Curry who has wrecked her dream, who has dismantled the belief system that she has dedicated her life to.

"His work... all rubbish... you showed me," she wails. "Was that it?" she asks. "Both of us mad together, all the time?"

Curry tries to placate her, but she is inconsolable. "He *made* me believe in it... by despising me," she tells him. But now she realises that, "the reason I couldn't understand was because there was nothing *to* understand... He took all of my life and he used it up as if he had a right to it... wasted it."

Curry follows her into the squalid room where Raymount is lying dead on the settee. Leaning over the shrouded corpse she begins to bitterly recount the story of Little Red Riding Hood. As if the tale itself is a magical

invocation, she sees the sheet over the corpse begin to stir, sees the face beneath it appear to change shape. Immediately her expression changes from bitterness to rapture. "It's true!" she cries. "I knew it!"

Curry steps forward and whips the sheet back. Beneath it her dead father's form is unchanged. But Florence's faith has been restored. Mad glee in her eyes, she hisses, "Just for a moment...it was true."

In the end it is up to the viewer to decide whether Raymount's mad theories have turned out to be not so mad, after all, or whether Florence is simply deluded. One is left wondering sadly what Florence will do now that the sole purpose and meaning of her life has been taken away from her.

The final episode, "The Dummy", is both a full-blooded Hammer pastiche and a comment on the British film industry. Nigel Kneale commented that this was one of his favourite episodes. Perhaps he enjoyed it so much because it allowed him to get a number of long-standing grievances off his chest. It is widely known that he was never a fan of the movies that Hammer made of his Quatermass TV serials. At least in the fifties, though, the British movie industry was thriving, whereas by the mid-seventies it had all but ground to a halt. 'The Dummy' is about the making of the latest in a long series of films featuring the episode's eponymous monster. Early on, a visiting journalist, Joan Eastgate (Lillias Walker), is introduced to Sid, the director (Glyn Houston), who is told that she is writing an article on the British film industry. "What are you calling it?" he asks. "Down the plughole?"

Certainly everything about this sixth Dummy film, 'Return of the Dummy', is low-key and make-do, lacking in both budget and ambition. It is a world of cardigans and Styrofoam coffee cups and ancient equipment. The sets are flimsy and the Dummy itself is a shoddy, unconvincing thing which plods clumsily about the set. When Joan asks what the Dummy is supposed to be, PR man Mike Hickey (Ian Thompson) tells her it's "*the* monster—a mixture of animal, vegetable, mineral, immortal, bullet-proof, indestructible...I mean, the customers don't really care."

This attitude is indicative of almost everyone on the set, bar perhaps the beleaguered director. There is no artistic integrity, no love of the material. One of the film's guest stars, Sir Ramsey (Thorley Walters), is doing his day's filming purely for financial gain before jetting off to the Bahamas for a holiday. He comments jovially, "If they don't shoot my scene today, they can take my name off their nasty posters." Even the Dummy itself is regarded as a clapped-out concept that has been dragged into action once again simply in order to make a quick buck.

Perhaps fittingly, the man who plays the Dummy, Clyde Boyd (Bernard Horsfall), is a mental and physical wreck. Here again one of Kneale's recurring themes raises its head. The episode examines the predilection human beings have to prey upon one another. Boyd is a self-confessed failure. He has been chewed up and spat out by an uncaring industry and an equally uncaring world. His wife and most of his friends have deserted him, he has been clobbered for income tax, his career is down the tubes and he is drinking heavily. He is contemptuous of the role he has become famous for. "I was just the man who played the Dummy," he says of his efforts to secure other acting work. "No one wanted to know." Even when his "close friend", Bunny, the film's producer, who knows nothing of his recent problems ("You lose touch—you know how it is," he remarks glibly), tries to reassure him, Boyd remains unconvinced. When Bunny (Clive Swift) reminds him that he has a big international fan base, Boyd sneers, "They can all understand grunts."

Joan Eastgate talks to Bunny about "masks". In a scene redolent of Jo's conversation with Mr Grace in "Baby", she says, "That's what all this is about . . . the psychological thing . . . primitive tribes believe the mask itself is alive—the man is just helping."

Armed with this information, Bunny talks to Boyd, who has retreated to his dressing room after finding out that his wife's lover, Peter Wager (Simon Oates), has been given a part in the film. Bunny himself wears a mask, in that he is all things to all people, manipulative and two-faced. He uses his particular skills on Boyd, persuading him to resume his role in the movie. He does so by plying him with drink and convincing him that he is something more than a mere actor. He tells Boyd that his portrayal of the Dummy "happens deep down . . . where words don't function any more...the rules are different . . ." Boyd is so weak, so malleable, that Bunny almost hypnotises him. "Can't you feel it, Clyde?" he murmurs. "The power in you? I can feel it...taking over . . ."

Beasts

When Boyd emerges from the dressing room in his Dummy suit minutes later, he does indeed seem to be imbued with a new power. Everyone seems to feel it—the camera pans around a ring of awe-struck faces. The scene they have been trying to shoot all day—the Dummy strangling a grave robber in a studio-bound, fog-shrouded churchyard—is set up once again and the director calls 'Action!' This time the scene is perfect... except that Boyd doesn't stop when Sid tells him to. Before the horrified eyes of everyone in the studio, he (or rather the Dummy) strangles the man to death, then goes on a snarling, shambling rampage. Bunny has done his job rather too well. Boyd, who has been told all his life that he "lacks presence", has been subsumed by the mask that he wears.

Terrified of the beast that Boyd has become, the crew flee the studio, trapping him inside. Left alone, the Dummy destroys the polystyrene sets, showing them up for the bits of cheap tat that they are. A police sergeant (Michael Sheard), tries to retrieve the body of the strangled extra and receives a slashed face for his trouble. Boyd's wife, Sheila (Patricia Haines), enters the studio in the hope that she can placate him, but quickly realises there is nothing left of Boyd within the costume. In a moment of high black comedy, she slips in a pool of fake blood and becomes covered with the stuff (anyone switching on at that moment would doubtless have thought they had stumbled upon the goriest TV programme ever made). Finally it is left to Peter Wager, armed with a shotgun, to confront the Dummy face to face. He spots it sitting with its back to him, its energy apparently spent, and shoots it. It topples over and Wager rushes forward in triumph—only to discover that the suit is empty. Too late he hears the Dummy's familiar, phlegmy snarl and turns to see a bestial, drooling Clyde Boyd, his wiry form grotesque in white vest and Y-fronts. Boyd leaps on Wager and savagely strangles the life out of him. Interestingly the close-up of his savage expression as he kills his rival is almost identical to the scene which had caused Mary Whitehouse such concern a week earlier when the same actor, playing Chancellor Goth, strangled Tom Baker's DOCTOR WHO at the climax of part three of "The Deadly Assassin". The similarity of the two shots must have been a coincidence, of course, given the proximity of the transmission times of the programmes, but it is a startling oddity nonetheless.

WE ARE THE MARTIANS

This, then, was BEASTS, a major triumph of script-writing and production, but a failure in commercial terms. The fact that the series was ultimately sabotaged by poor scheduling is an indication of the network's uncertainty over how to promote what it must have regarded as a curate's egg. Rather than receiving blanket coverage and support, different regions ended up running the episodes in different timeslots and in different orders. Perhaps for this reason BEASTS remains largely forgotten, or at best dimly remembered—a state of affairs which endures despite the fact that the series is now available in its entirety on DVD. When I showed 'Baby' to a friend recently, he was astonished to find himself watching a programme which had terrified him as a child, but which he had vaguely and mistakenly assumed to be a particularly harrowing episode of TALES OF THE UNEXPECTED. However, even when set against a career characterised by astonishing work like the Quatermass serials, THE STONE TAPE and THE YEAR OF THE SEX OLYMPICS, BEASTS remains, in my opinion, Nigel Kneale's crowning achievement.

IT WOULD HAVE BEEN SUCKLED, YOU KNOW

Beasts and Baby—an appreciation

Jeremy Dyson

1

THIS IS HOW I REMEMBER IT: IT WAS A FRIDAY NIGHT AND I'D been looking forward to this for days—the start of a new series of 'supernatural chillers' by Nigel Kneale. I was only 10 years old but I knew Kneale's name well. He had written *Quatermass* and I had to see this show. I just had to. The film of **QUATERMASS AND THE PIT** had been on earlier in the year and I hadn't been allowed to watch that. How did I even know about Kneale? My father spoke in hushed tones about the fear *Quatermass* had generated on its broadcast and the character's name alone caught my imagination. It was so strange—it sounded frightening in itself. And references to Kneale cropped up often in many of the books I cherished—be it Alan Franks' Horror Movies', or in various anthologies of ghost stories (Kneale's story "Minuke" was in more than one). I had a fan boy's brain—even then. I delighted in making connections, tracking provenances, creating lists of the things I'd dearly love to see. Any young-

WE ARE THE MARTIANS

sters reading this—and by that I mean anyone under the age of 30—will find it hard to imagine a time when there was no on-demand access to media one has an interest in. Then the only way was to scour the TV pages in newspapers or the *Radio & TV Times* and see if you could spot an upcoming screening. Home video had yet to come in, so those rare 'Appointment with Fears' or 'Horror Double Bills' couldn't even be taped. We were a good five years away from being able to do that. I still can't quite remember how I would have known BEASTS was going to be on. A piece in *The Observer* perhaps? A lone trailer? Whatever—it had lodged in my consciousness as something I simply had to see. The only trouble was that no one else felt like that. This meant I was despatched upstairs at 9.00pm that Friday night to my parents' bedroom, home to a little black and white Sony portable.

Ah, that stretch between upstairs and down—to a boy of ten with an all too active imagination it was fraught with terror in itself. Downstairs, you see, was the safety, warmth and light of the family. Upstairs—and they were very narrow stairs with a right turn into a long, gloomy corridor lit by a lone 40 watt bulb—was my parents' room. It might as well have been in a hut in the middle of a forest– so far did I feel from human company.

As the episode of BEASTS unfolded I felt a spell was being cast—a growing pall of dread that had an almost tangible quality—as if some force of evil was leaking out of the screen and filling the room, coming to get me. I was too scared to move—that would only make things worse. The beasts were dangerous and they meant me harm.

The experience of viewing those episodes—and I think I watched five of the six—never left me. I carried individual moments and images into adulthood. The memory of the final scene of "What Big Eyes" is with me now, as is "The Dummy" which I had to turn off through fear (the only one I didn't make it all the way through).

I didn't get a chance to revisit them until well into adulthood. Before a commercial DVD release (which didn't come until 2006) Mark Gatiss had located a copy of the episode "Baby" on VHS—in the late 90s. Expecting its power to be diminished now we were in adulthood we were both a little shocked to find it at least as scary as we remembered it. Why shocked? Because not that many things are truly scary—not really—and certainly

344

It Would Have Been Suckled, You Know

not much television. "Baby" was. And still is. As a some-time practitioner of this difficult art—the question I keep coming back to is "why?" The answer I find increasingly fascinating—and I think it shows that Nigel Kneale was one of the greatest writers of TV we've ever had. Often it's only time that truly reveals these things—and each passing year serves to demonstrate how unique and glorious Kneale's talents were. Certainly we've yet to see his like.

2

To some extent Kneale was a beneficiary of the times he worked in, although he wouldn't agree with that. He always felt ill-served by the powers that be. What writer doesn't. Nevertheless if he were with us now he might see that the occasional wrong-headed obstruction he got from TV executives was but the buzzing of a mildly-irritating fly compared to the swarms of hornets most writers have to contend with these days. His earliest pieces went pretty much untrammelled on to the screen—and much of his output through the 60s and 70s was of the 'what do you want to do' variety. In other words he basically had carte-blanche to write whatever caught his imagination the most. If I sound envious, it's because I am. As Ben Miller has observed about Monty Python: they were playing in virgin snow, and creatively there's no more exciting place to be. BEASTS is as peculiar and singular a series as ITV ever broadcast. The fact it went out peak-time on a Friday night is even more remarkable.

BEASTS grew out of a play of Kneale's called "Murrain" which was one of a series entitled AGAINST THE CROWD shown by ITV in 1975. "Murrain" was well-received enough, and a happy enough experience for Kneale and producer Nicholas Palmer to want to work together again. They came up with the idea of an anthology series of unconnected plays—written around a theme, which might loosely be described as the conflict between the civilized man and the animal within. Of course, Kneale being Kneale, it wasn't his intention to explore this theme literally—rather he would use his fascination with the tropes of horror and the supernatural to cast light on the bestial inner darkness of his characters. Ghosts, psychokinesis, intelligent super-rats straight out of James Herbert, lycanthrophy and psychosis filled the stories, combined with Kneale's instinct for a telling location and rich characterisation. Kneale's sensitivity to the importance of a story's setting marks him out as one of our finest writers of uncanny fiction—who just happened to be working in television. Both QUATERMASS II and QUATERMASS AND THE PIT made substantial use of recognisable yet eerie locations: the sprawling, seemingly empty and bleak chemical plant at Winnerton Flats; the deep-excavations of the building site in Hobbs Lane. BEASTS is full of similarly singular and evocative locales: an abandoned dolphinarium; a seedy, colourless supermarket; a lonely old farmhouse in bleak countryside. And vivid characters to populate them. Kneale had a comic writer's ear for characterful dialogue and grotesquery. Pauline Quirke's Noreen in "Special Offer" and Patrick Magee's crazed Raymount in "What Big Eyes" would have been quite at home in Royston Vasey. (Me and Mark Gatiss were forever lifting bits of Kneale's dialogue—including many lines from his superlative 1989 TV adaptation of Susan Hill's THE WOMAN IN BLACK).

None of this esoterica seemed to put off ATV—who made the series for the ITV network—and Kneale and Palmer were left to get on with it. The

It Would Have Been Suckled, You Know

series was broadcast in October and November 1976 and pretty well-received, though not enough for a second series to be commissioned. Perhaps that was never on the cards. This was the golden age of the single TV drama and each of the episodes of BEASTS feels much more like a play than, say, an edition of a genre anthology series such as THE OUTER LIMITS — or the later HAMMER HOUSE OF HORROR. Kneale emerged from it with enough kudos for ITV to go and produce the final part of his Quatermass series on a very grand scale. In fact this single play feel is one of the keys to understanding what makes BEASTS so special. Each of the episodes were character studies — where the external phenomenon that troubled the protagonists somehow echoed whatever conflict was going on within their lives. The drama was powerful to begin with and the supernatural element served to heighten and focus it further — telling us more about these people and their problems, the working of their psyches — than a more vanilla rendering of their stories would have done. As with the best genre tales one could absolutely imagine non-genre versions of each of their stories. I always remember Simon Ashdown (my co-writer on the series FUNLAND) telling me how you could run **ROSEMARY'S BABY** as a straight drama and imagine it being almost as powerful (man prepared to have wife raped to further his own career). "Baby" is not so far from **ROSEMARY'S BABY** territory and Jo and Peter's abusive relationship could certainly be used as the basis for an hour of conventional drama in its own right. Likewise, without the rats the empty nest syndrome suffered by the Truscott's "During Barty's Party" could completely be imagined as a PLAY FOR TODAY over on BBC1 — certainly Anthony Bate's constant whiskey slugging reminds me of that. But throw in those rats running round the Truscott's walls — seeking to destroy them, to gnaw the floorboards from beneath their feet — and you feel the true terror of a failing relationship on a visceral level, in a way most drama would find hard to communicate.

To me this is a Hitchcockian model. I don't know if Kneale was an admirer of Hitchcock's — he never mentioned him in the few interviews I've read — but both their worldviews have much in common. **REAR WINDOW** is the quintessential version of the Hitchcockian story. Essentially it takes drama — or melodrama — and turns it into myth —

WE ARE THE MARTIANS

taking a genre story and projecting it through a psychological lens. There are not many writers (or writer-directors) who can pull this off. It seems to demand an expansive skill-set: a feel for the genre (whatever the genre might be), a command of dramatic storytelling, but above all a deep sensitivity and delicacy of touch—one might call it a feminine sensitivity. In **REAR WINDOW** L.B Jefferies (James Stewart) is a professional photographer, a masculine man of action. He is literally and figuratively immobilised—injured in an accident and wheel-chair bound—and emotionally frozen, unable to commit to marriage, even to the most beautiful woman in the world (Grace Kelly). Why is he unable to commit? Well—the contents of his psyche are played out in his own back yard—which he watches through a telephoto lens—numerous instances of marriage observed in acute detail—some comic, some tragic, until he hits on the one that resonates with his darkest fear: the murderous. His shadow side is played out before his very eyes and it threatens to destroy the woman he loves. Of course, one can watch and enjoy all of this and remain completely on the surface with it. No need to even think about the psychological reading. Nevertheless it's these Jungian underpinnings that regularly propel this seemingly bright and breezy comic thriller to the top of 'greatest film ever made' lists more than 60 years after its initial release. (My favourite comment about Hitchcock comes from the American academic Mark Crispin Miller: he said that Hitchcock's regular description as 'The Master of Suspense' was a bit like referring to the painter Turner as 'The Seascape Whizz').

These kinds of stories have their roots earlier in the twentieth century with Kafka—who himself grew out a Dostoevskian tradition. They are essentially religious stories for a secular world—and it seems to me they are increasingly popular. One could draw a straight line from contemporary TV series like HBO's TRUE DETECTIVE all the way back to Dostoevsky but in terms of popular culture—Hitchcock would be the first major flagpole on the way. And Kneale might just be the first TV writer you hit. I think Kneale got there first on television and BEASTS (with THE STONE TAPE as its direct antecedent) is perhaps the first the full fruiting of this new way of writing—consciously fusing the fantastic with a real psychological depth.

348

It Would Have Been Suckled, You Know

3

So how does this work in practise—or to put it another way—what on earth am I going on about? To put it simply Kneale establishes a problematic situation between his main characters—in "Baby" it's a fatal flaw in their relationship—and then reflects this emotional trouble in a supernatural event which intrudes in to the characters' external world. "Baby" begins with a young couple, the Gilkes, who have moved into an old farm cottage in the countryside. Peter Gilkes, played with glorious bombast by Simon McCorkindale (aka MANIMAL), is an ambitious and driven veterinary surgeon keen to make his way in the country practice he's bought into. His wife Jo, played with an effective air of brittle hysteria by Jane Wymark (daughter of Patrick)—seems uneasy with their move to the country from the get-go. Their cat runs away from the house as soon as it's released from its travel basket just as the workmen find a nest of addled eggs in the chimney. This is merely foreshadowing, for soon Peter's unearthed something far more troubling from the internal wall they're having knocked down (to make way for a new freezer). In an extraordinarily staged sequence director John Nelson devotes a dialogue free 2 minutes to McCorkindale hammering away at a decidedly real wall. He excavates it brick by brick—until he reaches an empty arch—containing an earthenware jar. The jar is sealed, ancient looking and when McCorkindale prises it open it contains the mummified body of some hunched indeterminate creature. It's very hard to tell what it is/was but it looks very real. In fact everything looks very real. The bricks and their plasterwork seem ancient, the jar dusty and authentic. The designer, Richard Lake has had a field day—all the more impressive when you look at his previous credits and see he was a veteran of 20 years of ITV variety shows. He evidently jumped at the chance to flex his muscles here. In fact it makes you think of one of those great pieces of 1970s theatre like David Storey's THE CONTRACTOR where a huge tent is erected for real on stage. The reality of the action serves to ground the fantasy that follows, making it all the more frightening when we get there. The two local workmen who see the item the next day know its provenance only too well. A witch's curse to blight the land—make it infertile—unable to bring forth new life. In a typical Knealian flourish the older of the workman (Mark Dignam) reveals all this in the colourful West Country dialogue of a character from a Hardy novel: "That little brute you found they always had such as those. It would have purpose... A thing like that—it would have been suckled you know—human suckling—to set it to work."

Oh and in the very first scene—as the cat struggles to get out of its basket and away from the benighted building—we've discovered that the heavily pregnant Jo has already miscarried once. An air of great unease is quickly established around her pregnancy—and the evil thing in its ancient pot resonates like a dissonant bell. Of course what we don't realise is that Arthur the workman's beautifully evocative dialogue is also setting up one almighty climactic call back that when we get there our eyes will scarcely believe.

This carefully set-up canvas allows Kneale to paint a realistic portrait of a unnervingly dysfunctional marriage. Peter wants to keep the mummified familiar to impress his new boss/partner in the practise Dick Pummery. It's clear that this relationship is more important to him than his marriage—because Jo begs Dick to take the thing away from the house only to

It Would Have Been Suckled, You Know

discover in the end that he's done no such thing. A small betrayal perhaps—and then again not. And Jo's discovery of this betrayal (in the nursery of their unborn child) leads directly to her final horrific epiphany. This is a man who does not listen to his wife—and who has no interest or respect for anything she might have to say—even as he pays lip service to loving and caring for her. The feeling is that she is trapped in the socio-economic structure of her times (perhaps witchcraft was one of the few options that women such as Jo had in earlier ages to empower themselves—even if it was a fantasy empowerment).

So Kneale has ratcheted up the tension with consummate skill—attacking us on several fronts at once. We have a vulnerable pregnant heroine with a history of miscarrying—fearful for her unborn child. We have a sinister occult object straight out of M.R. James unearthed from the heart of her home. We have a brutally unhappy marriage—at least in embryo—and we have an unfolding backstory of dark enchantment (via the local workman) of the cottage and its surrounding lands: the land and house are specifically cursed to disrupt pregnancy in animals and, it seems, humans. We learn from Dick Pummery that the fields all around caused cows to abort and dogs, and that the couple who lived their before Pete and Jo were childless. This slow accumulation of detail, menace, threat and emotional tension takes place over the first 35 minutes of a 51 minute drama and the remaining 15 minutes are reserved for the super-natural manifestations. These amount to no more than six individual beats—each one simple (until the last one that is) and understated: a shadow passes over a pond; a rocking chair moves of its own accord; the edge of a hunched figure is glimpsed exiting where there is no door, and yet their combined effect is quite devastating. The emotional drama interlocks perfectly with the supernatural. The fact that these events are so simple and yet so unnerving is a fantastic lesson in the generation of fear in a supernatural narrative. In a lesser piece they might be laugh-able. Here, because the tension has been sown so skilfully on several fronts—grounded in emotional truth via believable (if heightened) char-acterisation—the reaping of this fear pays off to tremendous effect. And I don't believe this is just a fan's hyberbole. I was speaking to friend and collaborator Andy Nyman only yesterday, telling him I was writing this piece and he recounted his memory of me lending him 'Baby' about five years ago. He'd never seen it as a child, only in adulthood and had no particular connection to Kneale (other than his first professional TV acting role having been in Kneale's THE WOMAN IN BLACK). He sat down to watch it thinking 'oh there's this thing Jez said I should watch'—not expecting it to be anything other than a curio from another time. And he told me he was devastated by it: disturbed, frightened, genuinely, authentically unsettled and troubled.

For me one of the things that marks out "Baby" as a very special genre piece (and is characteristic of what Kneale achieved elsewhere) is the depths of the emotional truth it articulates through the tropes of the supernatural. It's what I always hope to find—am always looking for—and what I respond to in the material I cherish. It's there in Robert Aickman, in Ramsey Campbell, in THE HAUNTING OF HILL HOUSE. Perhaps it's easier to find in literary material than it is in film and television. The best stuff, for me at least, doesn't just tell us about the human condition, it teaches us something, it has a moral component—it's authentic and particular—not a cliché—it's felt, it's earned, the writer's pulled it burning out of his own experience. Don't behave like Peter and Dick, Kneale's telling us, because that behaviour is insidiously awful. You can get away with it, for sure—men in particular. The structures of our culture and our society enable men to get away with it. But if revealed—properly looked at—it's ugly, it's terrifying and it will kill that which you profess to love. It will abort it.

As if in confirmation of this truth an elderly acquaintance of mine was recently telling me about her family—how her mother was married to a man who outwardly was a loving and supportive husband but who much of the time was a childish bully, not in a dramatically abusive way—he never hit anyone or even threatened violence—but he was selfish and controlling and given to sulking and snapping. In a quiet way he made her's and her mother's life utterly miserable—to the extent that they could never relax in the family home and that she herself wanted no family of her own—robbed of this possibility by the drip drip effect of her father's low level selfishness and cruelty. To me this is as ugly and frightening as the phenomenon Jo witnesses at the end of "Baby"—the monstrous witch suckling her bestial familiar mapping perfectly on to the hidden uglinesss and violence that can be concealed within the heart of a family home.

There's not much of this stuff in film and certainly not in TV. I think it's more difficult to pull off on screen than on the page (and it's not that easy, there) because Film and TV is so literal. The skill set required to translate it effectively into a visual and dramatic form—where you have no interior monologue (or reported interior monologue if it's third person) to get at a character's subjective experience where this stuff takes place—is a rare one. Kneale had the requisite ability with character, together with an authentic and deep feel for the uncanny (one might call this facility 'scary-bones'—akin to the funnybones a comedian or comic writer requires to successfully practise his craft) and a decades-honed ability with narrative structure that's almost musical. The way he manipulates tension in the viewer across the 50 plus minutes is exemplary. He has an epic sensibility too—bursting the imaginative banks of what appears to be a constrained chamber piece set in one location. It's a Knealian trait in evidence across much of his strongest work: QUATERMASS AND THE PIT, THE ROAD, THE STONE TAPE– where he peels back layers and layers of time lurking beneath the surface of his story's present. Not so much back-story as back-mythology. And it's always believable and compelling. This is a huge and penetrating imagination at work. Kneale also has a strong feminine sensibility. "Baby" is written from its female protagonist's point of view (as is "During Barty's Party", and "Special Offer") and it's evident where Kneale's sympathies lie. If you were told it was written by a woman you would nod and say of course.

All of the above goes some way to accounting for Kneale's ongoing legacy and influence. Thus far it's been felt in not just one generation of practitioners but two. Via them—and thanks to DVD reissues for some of his work—it may well continue. John Carpenter, Spielberg, Joe Dante all openly professed their love for Kneale. My own generation are still following his lights—Mark Gatiss and Russell T. Davies to name but two. Kneale achieved incredible genre peaks across four decades— Quatermass and his adaptation of NINETEEN EIGHTY FOUR in the fifties, THE ROAD and THE YEAR OF THE SEX OLYMPICS in the Sixties, THE STONE TAPE and BEASTS in the seventies and his adaptation of THE WOMAN IN BLACK in the eighties. As a writer he is a beacon for the principle of being true to your own voice whatever that voice might be. In its strangeness and distinctiveness, BEASTS may well be the pinnacle of that approach, and "Baby" the pinnacle of that series. I for one can only express my unending gratitude to this extraordinary writer for showing me who he was in such a pure and effective way.

QUATERMASS: Rebirth and Resurrection

Jez Winship

THE FOUR-PART 1979 SERIAL ENTITLED, WITH AN AIR OF REDUCTIVE finality, QUATERMASS has not generally been considered an essential part of the Nigel Kneale canon. Little loved at the time and subsequently regarded as a compromised project from the outset, it has none of the legendary cachet of the earlier Quatermass trilogy or hugely influential works such as THE YEAR OF THE SEX OLYMPICS and THE STONE TAPE. The return of the venerable professor, Kneale's signature character and an emblematic figure in the post-war TV landscape, after a 20 year absence from the small screen created a high level of anticipation.

The popular and critical response was muted at best, with a widespread disappointment that Quatermass' resurrection didn't recreate the epochal moment which his first appearance had come to represent in people's minds.

The bleak, ruinous future Britain of social and economic collapse, political corruption, ingrained cynicism and casually brutal violence through which the bewildered professor stumbled was considered a sour and relentlessly pessimistic extrapolation of contemporary trends. John Mills' portrayal of Quatermass as a frail elderly man adrift in a post-catastrophe world which his optimistic techno-futurism had singularly failed to transform was viewed as a betrayal of the spirit of the 1950s trilogy. Many found the Planet People tribes, with their hippie-gypsy attire and manner and vague new-age spirituality an anachronism in the angrily disaffected and politicised post-punk period. There were also hints of a reactionary conservatism in the division of the young into mindlessly warring tribes, and in the implicit and derisory rejection of the pop culture and experiments with alternative philosophies and ways of living which characterised the late 1960s and early 70s.

Even critics normally favourable to Kneale's work tended to regard Quatermass as a qualified failure. Kim Newman, reviewing a video release of the truncated feature-length compression of the series known as **THE QUATERMASS CONCLUSION** in the March 1989 issue of the Monthly Film Bulletin (the old review section of the BFI's Sight and Sound magazine) stated that 'it remains the least of the four Quatermass experiments'. Peter Nicholls, in an entry on Kneale in the Science Fiction Encyclopedia which is suffused with antagonistic iconoclasm, describes it as 'curiously old-fashioned'. Kneale didn't necessarily disagree with such criticism either. He added his own voice to the general consensus, reflecting in an interview with Paul Wells included in the 1999 I.Q.Hunter-edited essay collection BRITISH SCIENCE FICTION CINEMA that he "was quite unhappy about it really". He admitted that the Planet People "were a bit out of date; flower children instead of punks". He concluded that "by then Quatermass had had his day, I think", tacitly conceding that it might have been a mistake to bring him out of retirement.

I for one am glad that he did. I watched the serial when it was first broadcast, still bathing in the afterglow excitement of **STAR WARS**, which had set me on a quest to watch any science fiction which registered on my watchful childhood radar. My parents also encouraged me to watch it, recalling the thrilling, terrifying impact the original serial had had on their childhood selves. This was the science fiction which they had grown up with. There was a sense of generational exchange there and then. I had seen none of the Hammer Quatermass films at this time, and there was certainly no way I could have come across the original trilogy of BBC serials. I was really too young to appreciate this Quatermass fully, its underlying themes and contemporary concerns failing to imprint themselves on my brain, addled as it was by sizzling and pulsing light-sabre neon and blinking **CLOSE ENCOUNTERS** mothership light-shows. But there was something about it which stuck with me. Its title character, an iconic presence whom I was clearly supposed to know about, was decidedly unheroic, a weary figure out of his time in the violent chaos of an irrational world he had given up on some years ago. He won my sympathy through his very vulnerability, and his dogged refusal of humanity's descent into Darwinian survival of the fittest savagery. His effective rebirth, the revival of his sense of purpose and intellectual curiosity, felt genuine and moving. Even if I was aware of who he was only by hearsay, I could sense that the essence of the old character was being gradually restored as the story progressed; the revivification of a legendary figure whose exploits were passed down across the generations, related with a hushed awe. I also loved the contrast between the barricaded urban warzones and the ancient southern downlands and the cracked grey conduits of barren, rubbish-strewn motorways which connected them. The tone excited me, even if the substance passed me by.

Many years later, in 2005, the series was finally released on DVD, and I immediately bought it and sat down to watch it. In the manner of things heard or seen at an impressionable age and then reviewed after a significant period, it delivered a heady rush of nostalgic recollection. It affected me forcefully once more, in a way which was both similar to and wholly different from its impact on my childhood self. Historical and cultural shifts, personal and political, had inevitably altered my perspective on the material. I still loved its elegiac tone, the sense of a world passing, the mourning of lost ideals and opportunities which is perhaps an unavoidable corollary of aging. And the ending simply moved me to tears. It became affirmed as a favourite in my personal canon. I'll try to elucidate, to you and to myself, the reasons for my favouring a work which has found so little favour elsewhere.

QUATERMASS is set in a near future Britain in which the major institutions no longer function, resources have all but run out and the city streets have become battlegrounds between rival gangs, principally the Badders and the Blue Brigades. The elderly Quatermass has wholly given up on his researches, his dreams of the future, and has retreated to a cottage on the shores of a Scottish loch. He travels down to London to appear on a TV show, giving his opinions on the Hands-in-Space meeting between US and Russian space modules. On his way to the studio, he is mugged and rescued from a probably fatal beating by Joseph Kapp, a young scientist who is to be his fellow guest. Quatermass' real purpose for leaving his remote retreat and re-entering the world is to seek his granddaughter Hettie, who had come to live with him in Scotland but walked out one day and never came back.

The empty space spectacle ends in disaster, the vessels mysteriously crumpled and torn apart by an unidentified force. Joe drives Quatermass out to his home in the downland countryside, where he has built a small

Quatermass: Rebirth and Resurrection

array of radio telescopes to study the skies. The telescopes are adjacent to a small stone circle, known colloquially as 'The Stumpy Men', and there is a larger megalithic site nearby, Ringstone Round. This becomes the destination for a pilgrimage by the Planet People, a youth cult whose followers believe they are to be transported to another planet. At Ringstone Round, to which Joe, Quatermass and Joe's wife Clare have travelled, an intense beam of light shafts down from the skies, shining brilliantly for a few seconds before retracting back into the heavens. Those caught within its radius are vaporised, leaving behind only a few metallic artefacts and drifts of a bleached crystalline deposit. Quatermass and the Kapps rescue a girl on the periphery who has been blinded by the 'lovely lightning' but still lives. Her skin is covered with crystalline accretions similar to those littering the stone circle.

They take her from the arms of an aggressive Planet Person named Kickalong, who soon takes on the role of barbarian chief, picking up a machine-gun from a dead policeman and leading the Planet People along a more violent path. Back at the Kapps' home, they receive a visit from the District Commissioner, Annie Morgan, a strong but compassionate woman. Joe and his small team of scientists (his extended work 'family') are picking up reports of events similar to those they experienced at Ringstone Round via their satellite dishes (rolling news); gathering of thousands annihilated by concentrated, focussed columns of incandescent light. Ancient sites seem to be the major locus of these disasters. The Planet People maintain that those caught within the light have been transported to another planet, and that the holy light will return for them imminently. "Soon, soon", they chant. It is decided that Quatermass and Annie should travel to London with the young Planet People girl, whose condition is worsening.

On the journey eastwards along the cracked and debris-strewn motorways, Annie waxes nostalgic about the good old days before the fall. Quatermass, meanwhile, begins speculating in earnest, his imagination and intellect warming up once more. He posits an immense power approaching across the vast gulfs of space, homing in on the earth and somehow affecting those most vulnerable, most sensitive—the newly born. They carry this newly-intuited sense of impending contact with

WE ARE THE MARTIANS

something other into youth. The widening generation gap becomes more readily explicable to Quatermass and Annie with such a freshly-minted fable in place. The approaching entity widens the inherent generation gap, cracking it apart until it is a yawning gulf, stirring up "all the rage of the world", as Quatermass puts it.

When they reach the outskirts of London, Annie runs into the middle of a street battle. Quatermass is snatched from the car and Annie, unable to rescue him, is forced to retreat to safer territory. Back at the Kapps', the territory is being swamped by Planet People, who are gathering in and around the 'Stumpy Men' stone circle just by the makeshift shack which is Joe and Clare's home. Whilst Joe is stranded elsewhere due to an oil leak in his van's tank, the light comes down. He returns to find that his wife and children as well as his scientific colleagues are all gone, disintegrated, his house a shattered chaos of wreckage.

Quatermass somehow finds his way to a car breaker's yard where, amongst the precipitously piled-up carapaces of now useless cars, he discovers a gerontocratic ghetto. A supportive society of old folks eke out a communal existence in the catacombs they've created beneath the maze of automotive husks. Quatermass discovers a fellow scientist, albeit one who was involved in the commercial manufacture of soap and perfume. This man, now in the extremity of old age, tells him about the extraction of a tiny secretion of musk from a deer's glands, which produces the most exquisite scent. The rest of the body is discarded. Quatermass draws an analogy with the alien force, fumbling towards some model of its nature and purpose. The army sweep down on the underworld of the old and take Quatermass away, and he is reunited with Annie. The Planet People child had died after briefly levitating above her bed, exploding into a particulate shower of crystalline fragments. Quatermass is accompanied by the army to the TV studios, which they take over in order to communicate with the Americans. Quatermass speculates that megalithic sites might be markers, indications of cursed places which were visited in prehistoric times. He further suggests that there might be beacons buried deep beneath the stones which are attracting the young to come together in gathering hordes and which also guide the alien force. He concludes that what is happening is a harvesting, a great gathering, the

Quatermass: Rebirth and Resurrection

alien power effectively something akin to an interstellar combine harvester.

Quatermass and Annie take part in government meetings discussing the response to the alien threat, which is now a global issue following numerous 'visitations' across the planet. They come up against bureaucratic divagation, an ineffectual prime minister (Kneale's novelisation makes his delusional state apparent) and a young pretender who is affected by the planetary calling. He seizes his chance when the prime minister has a heart attack and takes control. Trying to do something to stop a mass gathering at Wembley Stadium, Quatermass and Annie suddenly find that he has directed the army to fire on them. They drive into the underground car park beneath the 'sacred turf' to evade their pursuit. Annie dies when she drives into a concrete pillar. Quatermass stumbles out just as the light engulfs the stadium above him. When he emerges aboveground, he finds the stadium dusted with the organic crystalline detritus of the crowds who had filled its terraces. When the sun rises, it illuminates a sky which has turned an emetic green. Quatermass reconnects with the government and sets to working on a way of fighting the alien harvester. He teams up with the Russian scientist Professor Gurov, who has flown in from the East, and recruits a team of elderly colleagues, including those who had helped him in the car breaker's underworld. They will be immune to the calling of the harvest, he reasons. He has now concluded that what they are dealing with is a machine rather than a sentient intelligence; something which has been programmed by distant, unimaginable beings. He wonders whether their visitation even has any utility, or whether it is just an amusement.

The team works to create an analogue of the scent of humanity which, combined with other sensory prompts, will draw the alien power down. Quatermass plans to set a trap and, whilst he harbours no illusions about their ability to destroy it, he intends to give the alien machine a sting powerful enough to send it on its way. He chooses Kapp's observatory as the ideal place to carry this plan out. He finds Kapp there, living in the wreckage of his radio telescope equipment room. Initially delusional, he regains his senses and insists on joining Quatermass for the final stand. They will set the simulated gathering going, beaming it out via Joe's dishes. When the light comes, they will detonate a controlled nuclear explosion. Their plan is disrupted by the arrival of the Planet People in person, who join their electronic analogues. Kickalong shoots Kapp with casual indifference as he tries to warn him away from the bomb. As the light begins to descend, Quatermass spots his granddaughter and freezes, his heart experiencing a terrible seizure, bursting with emotional overload. His granddaughter sees him, comes over to him and, with a smile of recognition and love, lifts his hand. Together they press the detonation button. A short epilogue lets us know that their sacrifice has been worthwhile. The alien force has been driven away, and there have been no more visitations.

QUATERMASS is something of a summary work, a gathering together of the abiding concerns of Kneale's writing career. The primary theme of the empirical scientific exploration of supernatural or folkloric events, the meeting of rational and magical worldviews, is central. There are also re-iterations of other strands which run through Kneale's oeuvre. The Planet People and rival urban gangs are descendants of similar irrational youth cults in the unmade 1965 script THE BIG, BIG GIGGLE, which centres on a craze for suicide amongst the kids, and the 1969 WEDNESDAY PLAY "Bam! Pow! Zapp!", in which three kids act out in the real world the fantasy violence they have absorbed from the screen. They could also be

Quatermass: Rebirth and Resurrection

seen as the antecedents of the youth-centred future of THE YEAR OF THE SEX OLYMPICS (1968), whose date is set at a prefatory 'sooner than you think...' The portrayal of women as subjects and victims of a blindly reflexive or more calculated chauvinism recurs from THE STONE TAPE and the dramas "Baby", "Buddy Boy" and "What Big Eyes" from the BEASTS anthology series. Kneale continues to place female characters in positions of authority, and has them play an active role in scientific and technological endeavours.

He renews his satirical attacks on the televisual medium he had been instrumental in developing, and whose potentially insidious effect and possible use for purposes of passifying population control he had savagely and presciently dissected in THE YEAR OF THE SEX OLYMPICS. And, as ever, Quatermass has to fight the forces of bureaucracy, military inflexibility and government corruption as much as the threat of alien invasion. This compendious thematic summation brings a further air of reflection, of belatedness to QUATERMASS. It's as if Kneale somehow intuited that this might be his last major original work, his final statement. It also marks the closure of a significant period in British post-war political and cultural history, a period which the Quatermass character neatly bookends. The professor had first appeared in 1953. It was a strange in-between time. Churchill had returned in 1951 to become prime minister once more, a revenant from the war who now inherited a newly constructed welfare state. In the same year, the Festival of Britain had been staged on the specially developed South Bank site. The airily suspended Skylon sculpture and the smooth metallic canopy of the Dome of Discovery reflected the dreams of a technological utopia the likes of which Quatermass was working towards. The Skylon was a manifestation of his rocket dreams. Churchill's Conservative government swiftly swept away these props of the future, the visions of the brave new world which Atlee's post-war Labour government had begun to construct. Skylon's streamlined hull was unceremoniously dumped into the Thames.

1953 saw the more backward-looking pageantry of the coronation, a restitution of a different and more deferent order. Kneale was explicit in drawing the connection between the broadcast of the coronation, which had been seen by one of the first mass TV audiences, and his own

WE ARE THE MARTIANS

staging of the climax of THE QUATERMASS EXPERIMENT in Westminster Abbey, where the regal investiture had taken place. He wanted to puncture the mood of optimism, he later wrote in the introduction to the 1979 re-issue of his script in paperback form. "1953 was an over-confident year", he wrote. "Rationing was coming to an end, Everest had just been climbed, the Queen crowned, and our first Comet jets were being deceptively successful. A sour note seemed indicated". And was duly struck.

The new Elizabethan age, draped in suitably patriotic liveries, was soon to be derailed. In 1956, prime minister Anthony Eden sent British troops to the Suez Canal Zone after the Egyptian prime minister Gamel Abdel Nasser had nationalised this vital oil supply route. The failure of this dubious military venture, jointly planned with the French and the Israelis but terminally truncated by American refusal to lend financial assistance, effectively heralded the end of Empire and the retreat of Britain from the world stage. It was US power and economic clout which was now resurgent.

Quatermass was effectively a man out of his time even in the fifties. Making his final TV appearance at the dawn of 1959, he missed out on the true technotopian age of the early to mid-60s. An era of rising affluence and expanding consumer appetites was allied with a sleek pop modernity which revelled in synthetic materials and electronic gadgetry. The spirit of the age was cannily summed up by Harold Wilson in his pre-election speech of 1963, when he talked of the "white heat" of the 'scientific revolution' in which a new Britain was to be forged. There was no place for Quatermass in this new world, however. Scientific invention was directed towards commercial and domestic applications, fuelled by consumerism rather than the thirst for discovery as an end in itself. Rocket science had migrated to America and Russia where the space race continued apace. It was another anti-establishment scientist character who was left to express the hopes and fears of the period through his spatial and temporal adventures in a show which spanned the decade and beyond (and which Kneale affected to despise); a series which started in the same year as Wilson's white heat speech — DOCTOR WHO.

When Quatermass did make his appearance in the 1960s, in the

364

Quatermass: Rebirth and Resurrection

Kneale-scripted 1967 Hammer adaptation of **QUATERMASS AND THE PIT**, it was significant that the action took place in a maze of dingy Victorian terraces, still punctuated by the absent spaces of bombsites. This was the London which modernity had passed by, a lingering shadow of the Victorian city. There were no clean-lined steel and glass edifices here, neither were there sharp-suited mods or colourfully clad hippies. The people around Hob's End might as well still have been living in the pre-MacMillan austerity years. When Harold MacMillan made his oft-misquoted comment that "most of our people have never had it so good" in 1957, he was drawing attention to a decisive shift in British society, a shift which would also dramatically affect its culture and even, to an extent, its character. 10 years later, Kneale suggested that this shift hadn't reached beyond certain concentrated centres. The film of **QUATERMASS AND THE PIT** is defiantly not of its age. The summer of love is taking place somewhere else entirely.

12 years later and Quatermass once more seemed out of time. Some of this can undoubtedly be put down to the tangled production history of this final serial. In 1968, Hammer had proposed a further Quatermass instalment should **QUATERMASS AND THE PIT** prove a success. QUATERMASS IV, as it was putatively titled, was slated for production in 1969, and was to be a joint venture with the BBC. It never happened. But the desire for a further Quatermass adventure was clearly in the air. Kneale was commissioned to write a four part serial by the BBC in 1972. He wrote the script and filming was scheduled for 1973. However, there were increasing concerns over costs, particularly those involving location shooting. When permission to film at Stonehenge, a key setting for the story, was denied by the English Tourist Board, the whole production was shelved. Kneale also believed that the BBC was unhappy with the down-beat tenor of his writing. He parted company with the corporation shortly thereafter.

The independent production company Euston Films, who were affiliated with ITV, stepped forward in 1978 to revive the project once more. Their reputation for shooting on location was particularly attractive to Kneale. The Euston deal involved making a four part serial, but also a condensation of the material into a feature length film which could be

365

WE ARE THE MARTIANS

shown in cinemas outside the UK, thus helping to recoup costs. The producers may very well have had the success of the Hammer adaptations of the 50s Quatermass serials in mind. Rather than wait for another company to create a lucrative cinematic version, they decided to make it themselves, effectively fashioning a dual format release. As much as anything, this indicated the cinematic ambitions of the TV series, which was shot on 35mm and featured extensive location shooting.

Kneale himself edited together the script for the alternative feature-length version, which was entitled, with a definite air of finality, THE QUATERMASS CONCLUSION. It wasn't widely distributed, however. As Kim Newman points out in his Monthly Film Bulletin review of the VHS release, "a few token appearances at film festivals apart, (the cinematic release of the film) never came to pass". It's certainly not mentioned in any of the standard SF film histories or encyclopedias, which routinely cover the three Hammer movies. QUATERMASS was, in fact, a tripartite release. Kneale also wrote an accompanying novel. Given that it included much detail and background absent from the TV series, along with reflections, dreams and memories which considerably deepened our understanding of Quatermass and his previous adventures, Kneale considered it a standalone work in itself rather than a tie-in book content merely to reproduce the action and dialogue of the series in prose form. As Tim Lucas, in his chapter on "The Literary Kneale", points out that this was, in fact, the one novel of his writing career.

QUATERMASS was shot in the summer of 1978 and broadcast in October and November of 1979, heading into the first winter of the new Conservative government led by Margaret Thatcher, who had been voted in the previous May. It was perhaps unsurprising that many considered it outmoded. People were hoping to move beyond the feeling of incipient collapse which the winter of discontent had engendered at the beginning of the year. And with a script first mooted in 1968 and written in 1972, there was an undeniable sense that it was looking backward, creating a retro-post-catastrophe scenario. Quatermass is still a man out of time. But rather than looking forward, fixing his gaze on a space age future, he is now looking backward. In a sense, this is a series imbued with far more punk nihilism than stoned hippie benevolence. The costumes might be

Quatermass: Rebirth and Resurrection

the rainbow headband and poncho tatterdemalion of the free festivalgoer, but the underlying ethos was much more in line with Johnnie Rotten's declaration "there is no future in England's dreaming". There's certainly a distinctly punk shade to the offensively snot-green colour of the sky in the post-visitation Wembley dawn. "It's like vomit", Quatermass observes. It's an incandescent, eye-scorching lime green, a deliberately tasteless standard for punk graphics (including the US release of The Sex Pistols' Never Mind the Bollocks). It takes a minor linguistic shifting and adding of letters to turn punk into puke. The emetic was a prime element in punk's brief, spattering moment. Puking out the past, demonstrating disgust with the present by sticking your fingers down your throat. With the sky turning an emetic green towards the end of QUATERMASS, the whole world has gone punk.

Its very downbeat tone also set QUATERMASS apart from prevailing trends. In the wake of **STAR WARS** and its many imitators, science fiction had once more become seen as escapist entertainment, formulaic space operatics which could safely be despised or patronised by highbrow critics. It was a development lamented by many SF writers, who saw the significant advances of the previous two decades instantly vaporised with the buzzing swish of a light sabre. JG Ballard, writing in Time Out in 1977, called it a "technological pantomime" from which "what is missing...is any hard imaginative core". He worried that, from SF as a fiction of ideas, "with **STAR WARS** the pendulum seems to be swinging the other way, towards huge but empty spectacles where the SFX...preside over derivative ideas and unoriginal plots, as in some massively financed stage musical where the sets and costumes are lavish but there are no tunes". Harlan Ellison, writing in the Los Angeles magazine in 1977, called it "a classic simpleminded shootout movie" which, lacking real people, "is merely a diversion, a cheap entertainment, a quick fix with sugar-water, intended to distract, divert and keep an audience from coming to grips with itself". The phenomenal success of **STAR WARS** effectively instigated a new era. SF was now expected to be an escapist spectacle, with challenging ideas and speculations a very low priority. QUATERMASS was stranded on the wrong side of the genre fault-line, and was judged accordingly.

It had much more in common with the SF of the earlier 70s, again harking back to the period in which it was written. Michael Moorcock edited an anthology in 1971, alongside his fellow NEW WORLDS author Langdon Jones, called THE NATURE OF THE CATASTROPHE. In fact, the catastrophe was multiform, and much on the minds of 70s writers. The future seemed a lot less certain, progress less assured. Only a few years on from the Apollo 11 moon landing and visions of moonbases and lunar shuttles already seemed like hopeless daydreams. The rocket ship futurism to which Quatermass had dedicated his life was on the wane even at the moment of its greatest triumph. The focus was now much more earthbound, more concerned with the fallout from the technological revolution rooted in the war. This was a collection of stories in which various writers took on Moorcock's mutable creation Jerry Cornelius, a modern myth-figure who skipped across the flux of the multiverse, appearing in varying guises in evershifting alternative versions of the present and near future. 1970s SF offered a multiplicity of catastrophes, their nature comprehensive and wideranging. In the cinema there was

NO BLADE OF GRASS (1971), based on John Christopher's n
famine and social collapse in England; SOYLENT GREEN (1973), based
on Harry Harrison's novel MAKE ROOM! MAKE ROOM!, which dealt
with unsustainable population growth; George Romero's THE CRAZIES
(1973), about the outbreak of a viral plague manufactured by the military
to induce psychosis, and the imposition of martial law to contain it; and
Stanley Kubrick's A CLOCKWORK ORANGE (1973), whose tale of
violent youth gangs, behavioural control and government corruption is
very much in Kneale territory, although taking a more disengaged, cynical
approach to the subject matter. Two films released in the year of
QUATERMASS' broadcast also provide an interesting point of comparison
and contrast. Robert Altman's QUINTET is set in a newly glaciated world
in which the remains of humanity imbue their frozen lives with a sense of
urgency by participating in the life and death game which gives the film
its title. Its dour, downbeat tone is very much in line with QUATERMASS,
although it is considerably more brooding and taciturn, moving at an
appropriately glacial pace. MEMOIRS OF A SURVIVOR, based on the
novel by Doris Lessing, has Julie Christie's character passively observing
the world beyond the bay window of her Victorian semi as it falls into
social decay and violent anarchy. She increasingly retreats into a dream
past of Victorian domesticity, turning inward and wholly disengaging from
the reality beyond her walls, from endemic problems to which she can
offer no solution.

TV drama also contemplated the nature of the catastrophe in the 1970s,
bringing a sense of impending doom into living rooms across the land.
Terry Nation's SURVIVORS afflicted the world with a deadly viral plague
brewed up in a laboratory which wipes out 95% of humanity; THE
CHANGES saw the British population turning violently Luddite under
the influence of some inexplicable power, smashing all technology, new
and old, and reverting to old fears and superstitions; DOOMWATCH
offered a variety of potential disasters and featured another anti-establishment scientist whose surname began with a Q—Dr Spencer Quist, who
heads the Department for the Observation and Measurement of Science;
and Jon Pertwee's Doctor fought against industrial pollution and corporate
mind control in "The Green Death".

E ARE THE MARTIANS

QUATERMASS is particularly congruent with the British science fiction literature of the 1970s, which also explored themes of social collapse and environmental catastrophe. The Jerry Cornelius mythos is germane, its anti-hero of the ruins having his origins amongst the more wild and anarchistic flowerpunks and urban guerrillas inhabiting the squats and communes of Ladbroke Grove and Notting Hill in the 1960s; the antecedents of the Badders. Christopher Priest's novel FUGUE FOR A DARKENING ISLAND charts Britain's descent into chaos and racial violence in the wake of a nuclear war in Africa. M.John Harrison's THE COMMITTED MEN is a post-apocalyptic novel whose action is centred on the semi-ruined motorway network. His short story SETTLING THE WORLD has a particularly Knealeian cast. God has returned to the world and manifests itself to a group of would be deicidal assassins in the form of a giant beetle towering over the strip of a motorway. A number of 70s British post-apocalpytic novels travelled out of the cities to the southern downlands and beyond into the West Country, just as Quatermass does. Richard Cowper's ROAD TO CORLAY series is set in a West Country which, in the wake of rising sea levels, has become a series of islands. Christopher Priest's A DREAM OF WESSEX finds a group of experimental subjects mentally projecting themselves into an imaginary Dorset of the future from their bunker beneath Maiden Castle. The savage caravan of Angela Carter's HEROES AND VILLAINS makes its way through poisoned wastelands down to Brighton and the Sussex coast.

One of the more unlikely points of conjunction can be found in Pete Townshend's post-60s concept for a Who album which would reflect the fading dreams of an alternative culture with the communal experience of music at its heart. His grand 'Lifehouse' project was never realised at the time (another parallel with Quatermass), partly due to his failure to lend the inchoate ideas brewing in his head coherent form. When he finally put it all together for a radio play broadcast on 5th December 1999, the similarities with QUATERMASS became strikingly clear. The story features a family who have retreated to a remote corner of Scotland to escape from an England which has become a blighted wasteland. The father, Ray, a bitterly disillusioned man (one of Townshend's self-lacerating alter-egos) travels south to try to find his daughter, Mary, who has run

Quatermass: Rebirth and Resurrection

away from home to go to an illicit and mysterious festival. It aims to subvert the government's control of the population, who live in environment suits supposedly protecting them from the poisoned world. These suits are also connected to a communications web known as the grid, through which they are fed a constant stream of multi-channelled entertainment, perceived as directly experienced reality (the live life show). People live within stories which mould their emotional responses, media immersion effectively used by an autocratic government as a means of social engineering. It's a vision of the future very much in line with Kneale's view of television's potential for pacification and population control. Townshend sees music, a more abstract and less malleable art form, as a potentially liberating force. The Lifehouse is a gathering which will bring people together, free them from the mediated dreamworld of the VR suits and create a communal experience to which everyone brings their own 'note', adding to a transcendent symphony which eradicates the boundaries between composer and audience. This festival, which the army tries to prevent, culminates in the disappearance of the participants, who apparently reach a state of ecstatic communion which leads to their disembodiment. Ray, a non-believer, is left behind, alone in the rubble of the fallen world. Townshend's gathered crowds really do seem to have been transported to another plane. There is a certain irony in the similarities between LIFEHOUSE, which still holds out the hope for some kind of counterculture, and QUATERMASS, which never entertains the possibility of its validity. Quatermass himself, talking of the younger generation in terms of possession, refers to the "huge assemblies", "mindless" gatherings. It's fairly evident that he's referring to the rock festivals of the late 60s and early 70s—to Woodstock, Altamont, The Isle of Wight, even to the Windsor Park Free Festival of 1974, which descended into violent clashes between the festivalgoers and the truncheon-happy Thames Valley Police.

The megalithic sites and chalk hill figures of the ancient southern landscape also crop up in much 70s British SF. Keith Roberts' cyclical story collection THE CHALK GIANTS is set in a post-apocalyptic Dorset in which humanity becomes reshaped by the power of landscape and the old gods latent within it. The ancient human landscape was a regular destination for TV fantasy in the 70s as well: Avebury for CHILDREN OF

THE STONES, Glastonbury for SKY, Wayland's Smithy and the White Horse of Uffington for THE MOON STALLION. QUATERMASS would have rounded this off with the best-known megalithic site of them all, Stonehenge, but in the end the art department had to fashion their own sarsens and menhirs as best they could. The cover artwork of subsequent DVD releases still cheekily uses the silhouetted outline of Stonehenge, however.

This fascination with the ancient landscape seemed like a pointed turning away from the space age futurism of the early to mid-60s. The fashion for modernity and the synthetic shaded into a fascination with the ancient past and the natural, the pre-modern crafts. This was accompanied by a shift from an urban-focussed culture to one which increasingly dreamed of an urban exodus, a rediscovery of the British rural landscape. "We've got to get ourselves back to the garden", as Matthews Southern Comfort sang, echoing Joni and translating her into a very English idiom. The silver space-suit 60s turned into the bark-brown, earthbound 70s.

Quatermass: Rebirth and Resurrection

The southern downland landscape through which Quatermass and Joe Kapp drive is the landscape of mid-20th century British artists like Paul Nash, Eric Ravilious and John Piper. There is a painting on the wall of the Kapps' home which combines golden corn, standing stones and clumps of beech trees in a very Nash-like manner. These artists brought a modernist sensibility to the British landscape tradition, and thereby gave full expression to the strange, magical quality with which these hills and plains are possessed. Paul Nash asked in a 1932 Weekend Review article "whether it is possible to 'go modern' and still be British". He and other artists were drawn to the ancient landscape of the southern downlands, with its megalithic sites, long barrows and giant chalk hill figures (whose spirit Ravilious evoked with brilliant idiosyncrasy) partly because there was something peculiarly modern about them. The blend of ancient and modern was particularly potent. The stones circle or outlined white horse could be as startlingly strange and alien as the parading pylons or glinting railway lines. The shock of the old meeting the shock of the new. Big science and modernity in the landscape has its own mysterious presence. The white disc of Jodrell Bank rising like a giant mushroom above a treeline at the edge of a field in which cattle graze makes for a stirring vista, and an oddly harmonious one. QUATERMASS places the ancient and the modern in direct proximity. When we first see the radio telescopes, the camera cranes up above them, placing them in the context of the rolling landscape in which they sit. A stone Georgian folly sits in between them, which turns out to have been an old 18th century observatory. The dishes are congruent with the stone circles nearby, both forms facing upward to embrace the skies. In between them is a concrete bunker, a defensive remnant of the Second World War whose blocky, grey monumentality also echoes the standing stones (and which anticipates the wartime spirit which Quatermass will raise when he assembles his elderly team and prepares to take his last stand). There are layered strata of human history, and of human endeavour concentrated within this localised landscape. Alan Garner found a similar congruity between the radio telescope in the landscape (Jodrell Bank) and more ancient markers of human presence in RED SHIFT and later BONELAND, his own summary work. Such proximities collapse time,

WE ARE THE MARTIANS

creating subconscious pathways fusing past, present and future into a single instant.

Director Piers Haggard captures the mystique of the English landscape in much the same way that he did in **BLOOD ON SATAN'S CLAW**. QUATERMASS at times has the same feel of human beings bound to the cyclical patterns of nature, prey to its occasionally pitiless and unforgiving harshness. There is a scene in which we see a procession of Planet People making their slow progress through a field of burnished, late summer corn. Their heads rising above the stalks, they are symbolically ripe for the reaping themselves. It's as if they were part of a new folk legend, or a modern variant of John Barleycorn. A folklore in which people are harvested like grain, ready to be sown and reborn again in the spring.

The catastrophe in QUATERMASS is, like those in the examples cited above, a very British affair. It is connected to the fears and anxieties of its period, but retains a timeless universality. It could equally well be envisaging a post-peak oil period. When Joe Kapp remembers a time when 'we' (i.e. Britain) thought that North Sea oil would solve all our problems, he is referring to an immediately post-OPEC world. But it was a dream which took a long time to fade. The highly politicised post-punk band Gang of Four were still singing about it with ironic mockery in their 1979 song Ether, which ends with the desperately chanted refrain "there may be oil under Rockall". The North Sea oilpipe dream stands for all the desperate attempts to eke out dwindling resources to maintain the established economic order. Kneale skilfully builds up a picture of social collapse through an accumulation of small details, often picked up in the background. Government posters recall the world of Orwell's 1984 which he had adapted in 1954. Their stark message reads "looting is a capital offence — offenders will be shot", which lets us know that martial law has been imposed. Graffiti writ large upon the jagged walls of a ruined factory reads "Kill the King". This is a new and barbaric civil war fought on the city streets. In the book, Kneale even has the prime minister imagine making himself Lord Protector, a new dictatorial Cromwell to re-impose order on the land.

The opposing street gangs who face each other over the barricades are divided along class lines, instinctive loyalties whose ideological bases have

Quatermass: Rebirth and Resurrection

blurred into blind tribalism. The Badders are descendants of the Angry Brigade, England's thankfully half-hearted attempt to emulate European far-left terror groups, and other revolutionary groups of the 70s such as the Worker's Revolutionary Party and the International Socialists (later the Socialist Worker's Party). The name is an etymological devolution from the Baader-Meinhoff gang, the reductive familiarisation making them sound like a chummy gang from an adventure serial; real violence turned into escapist fantasy. Their enemies, the Blue Brigades, descend from far right nationalist groups who were also prevalent in the 1970s. Not so much the National Front as the rabidly patriotic 'secret' organisations and would-be vigilante standing armies such as Unison, Civil Assistance and GB75 mustered by colonial ex-military types like General Sir Walter Walker and Colonel David Stirling to protect the country against the incipient socialist takeover they were convinced was imminent. We see Blue Brigade members wearing army surplus helmets painted with blue union jacks. In the book, Kneale incorporates cummerbunds into their uniform, turning them into Bullingdon Club boot boys.

Another dimension is added to the picture of collapse, of the passing of the post-war social and political order, by the presence of pay cops, a privatised police force who have absolutely no sense of civic duty beyond what is contractually required of them. The Metropolitan Contract Police bring the wholesale corruption of the Met in the 70s out into the open. A checkpoint is really a tollbooth where payments are made for permission to pass. The matter of fact swiftness with which Joe hands over his bribe, no questions asked, indicates the extent to which this has become accepted practice. The pay cops who police the crowds gathered at Ringstone Round, and who deliberately stoke up a riot so that they can indulge in a bit of "crowd control", are militarised ex-South African policemen. Kneale thereby hints that apartheid and white power has come to an end in the country. Their origins are made more explicit in the book, in which their speech is littered with Afrikaans words and phrases. Kneale doesn't disguise his utter contempt for them, and by extension for their racist ideology. He delights (again, in the book only) in having them blow themselves up through sheer stupidity; they drunkenly activate the self-destruct button in the plane Gurov and his pilot have landed in Hyde Park.

The pay cops are the official face of fascistic martial law, the rule of the gun. The army, too, prove politically malleable. The potential for fascism planting its poisonous seed and swiftly spreading is more dangerously present elsewhere, however. Kickalong is the violent male principle incarnate, a black clad rock god styled after Jim Morrison, although Kneale cites Charles Manson as another model. The machine gun he picks up completes him, giving easy vent to his unthinkingly destructive nature. He used it with increasing frequency and decreasing thought or restraint. He is utterly without compassion or empathy, even for those who are supposedly his own people.

Those whose remains are found on the edge of Ringstone Round are dismissed with a wave of the hand. "They didn't make it". The organic residue turning the sky green comprises "spillings", the rejected who weren't good enough to reach the promised land, the paradise planet; who weren't among the chosen. Signs of compassion are seen as weakness, a weakness that can be exploited. Kickalong pleads with an armed householder barricaded into his home to spare a tin of food "for the kids". When

Quatermass: Rebirth and Resurrection

the man proffers the promised food, putting down his rifle to do so, Kickalong immediately fires a round of bullets into his hideout. He also kills Sal, one of the Planet People who takes pity on Joe Kapp and says that she is going to stay to look after him. She is summarily shot in the back. Female compassion is weakness. The gun is strength, an extension and augmentation of the fist. Ready and cocked.

Kickalong is a false prophet, a cobra-like guru who mesmerises his followers, rallying them with violent, fevered rhetoric. The Planet People, like burned out hippies in the afterglow of the 60s, are ripe for exploitation, for being moulded by a strong leader who can implant them with his own ideology, or simply use them as a private army or slave labour force. In a way, these new age drifters are more dangerous than any punk, whose gestures at shock and rebellion were artfully fashioned or self-consciously appropriated from the detritus of cultural and political history. The Planet People have purged their minds of the tainted values of the world they repudiate and intend to leave behind. But they have yet to fill the empty spaces with a coherent philosophy which can offer a serious alternative. All they have is a deeply-rooted desire to escape, the urgency of which has been translated into a vague new belief system. This emptiness, the mental rootlessness which is made manifest in their dazed wanderings, leaves them open to exploitation. The Planet People can be turned and

We Are The Martians

used, manipulated like puppets. They can become Manson acolytes on a mass scale. When Quatermass staggers along the post-visitation terraces of Wembley Stadium, he sees two sets of graffiti directly adjacent to each othe. One is a Planet People slogan, "to the planet". The other is a Nazi swastika. It's like a prophecy.

Kneale has Quatermass and Kapp drive through a street market in the shadow of a ruined factory which serves as a neat encapsulation of the catastrophe. He emphasises in particular the resurgence of superstition and magical thinking and the concomitant decline of knowledge and the capacity for rationalism. Books are piled up on a table, but a notice reading "guaranteed to burn well" indicates their real value (shades of FAHRENHEIT 451). Charms and spells are on sale, including some deriving from a Hell's Angel called Gutsucker, whose uniform and remains are displayed hanging from a gibbet as if they were holy relics. The idea of hardened outsiders like the Hell's Angels coming into their own in a post-catastrophe world is one familiar from a number of sources, including the zombie apocalypses of George Romero's **DAWN OF THE DEAD** and the comic and TV series THE WALKING DEAD. This is a world which has rapidly regressed to Hogarthian street bedlam, suggesting that such tendencies were always latent beneath the gleaming technological surface of modernity.

Quatermass: Rebirth and Resurrection

The twin polarities of rationalism and superstition, science and the supernatural, and the interplay between them have always been central to Kneale's work, and they remain so in QUATERMASS. There is no simplistic dualism served up here, however. Joe Kapp's contempt for the Planet People shades into a fundamentalist's closed-mindedness, a refusal to even attempt to engage with them. "I give you up", he tells them, assuming a presupposed position of professorial seniority. He doesn't hold back when talking about them to Quatermass on their journey out of London. "I want a generation gap between me and them", he says with undisguised venom. Their mysticism is "violent to human thought". His rhetoric reaches a virulent peak when he says that "they infest the land". It's a dehumanising image, which reduces them to little more than locusts or, more appositely, rats (he refers to them as termites later). Joe, who cites the self-education of his Jewish forebears as their way of "holding back the dark", should know the Nazi's propagandistic equation of his people with swarming rats. His open contempt is very much in the vein of Richard Dawkins and his school of hardline scientific rationalism. Quatermass is more diplomatic and receptive, partly because he realises that it was his singleminded pre-occupation with his work which led him to neglect his granddaughter and drive her away. He is also interested in what the Planet People believe, particularly as he strongly suspects that Hettie has joined their ranks. When the light comes down on Ringstone Round, even Joe has to admit that the Planet People seem possessed by an intuitive knowledge, an inherent instinct. "They knew it would happen, and it did".

One of the central themes of QUATERMASS is that rationalism, the application of empirical knowledge and constant expansion of its borders, is not by itself enough to hold back the dark. The Enlightenment dream of a steady rational progress towards a rationalised utopian state has failed, largely due to the inherently irrational contradictions of human nature. Humanity needs something beyond its cold equations to infuse life with meaning, to illuminate what is universally important. Joe's wife Clare reacts to the shock of the Ringstone Round visitation and the return of the sick child to their home by bringing out the Jewish Menorah candleabra and turning the evening meal into a solemn ritual. Three candles are lit, one for each child in the shack. Clare is effectively welcoming the

WE ARE THE MARTIANS

Ringstone waif into the family and demonstrating that, for her, the Planet People are human beings worthy of her love and care. A connection with ancestral beliefs and practices is established, the light holding back the darkness sustained. Is this superstition worthy of Joe's contempt? Or a ritual observance serving to mark the sacredness of life and its continuation from the past through the present and into the future.

Clare's serious intentness, which brooks no refusal or mockery, gets through to Joe. Later, when he is entering the shack, he touches the Mezuzah, the small box containing verses from the book of Deuteronomy, which is attached to the door frame, after first touching his fingers to his lips in the accepted fashion. Such an observance recognises the home and family as sacrosanct, consecrated by God. Quatermass, who has made a particular connection with Clare, has previously had to remind Joe that his family need him when his consciousness has become entirely preoccupied with his work (and discussions with his work 'family'). It is through his Jewish roots rather than his scientific rationalism that he is able to express the centrality of his family to his life, to acknowledge that such feelings lie beyond reductive materialism. He opens his soul to the sacred.

The family is seen as the vital heart of humanity and of civilisation in QUATERMASS. Quatermass himself, on entering the Kapp's humble shack, declares "I like your home". When the light comes to the stumpy men stone circle, it not only takes away all those within its compass, including Joe's wife and children (and dog), but also destroys his home utterly. It effectively smashes the foundations of his life, leaving him bereft of reason in all senses; a hollow man. Quatermass' search for his granddaughter Hettie is a quest to reconnect with what remains of his family. We have encountered his daughter before in QUATERMASS II. She worked as an assistant in his rocket labs, as if this was the only way she could gain his attention. We learn in QUATERMASS that she and her husband were killed in a car crash, which is how their daughter came to live with Quatermass, her grandfather. Quatermass explicitly rejects the work which led him to neglect her when he makes his initial appearance in the TV studios. He condemns the huge waste involved in engineering the hands in space project, distancing himself from it in the strongest terms. He then presents one of his pictures of Hettie for the camera to

Quatermass: Rebirth and Resurrection

focus on, saying "that's all that matters to me now. A human face. The child of my child. I want to see her again — and to hell with all of this". His hopes for the future no longer reside in rocket technology and space science, but in a young woman lost somewhere in the wasteland. It is a hugely significant shift in perspective.

Women are also of vital importance to Kneale's worldview in QUATER-MASS, and to the professor's own revised priorities. They represent the possibility of renewal and the rekindling of a compassion which has been worn away by the harshness of the fallen world. The destructiveness inherent in the imbalance of a chauvinistic world of patriarchal power is one of the less commented-upon themes running through Kneale's work. It would be going too far to describe him as a feminist writer. His criticism of male chauvinism tends to focus on the damage done to female characters trying to exist and make something of themselves in a man's world. The psychological damage they sustain is made evident in "Baby", "Buddy Boy", "What Big Eyes" and "Special Offer" (all from BEASTS) and THE STONE TAPE, all of which feature scenes or scenarios of mental breakdown, in the case of "Buddy Boy" leading to suicide. Clare in QUATERMASS is another in this lineage. Kneale's women are generally a great deal more sensitive than his male characters, who are frequently self-absorbed, highly competitive and emotionally short-sighted. Sensitive in an empathic sense, but also in terms of being finely attuned to their surroundings, and to the supernatural currents with which they are charged. "Sensitive" is a word used repeatedly in THE STONE TAPE, used to describe the response of Jane Asher's character to the spectral presence in the old storeroom of the historic building she is working in; the only woman in a laddish team of industrial scientists. Clare is also "sensitive". She seemingly perceives the name of the sick Planet People child without any direct verbal communication. She, like Joe, is a scientist. But her discipline is an inverted reflection of his. She is an archaeologist, investigating the deep past, as opposed to Joe's astronomical exploration of deep space, his attempts to facilitate mankind's future expansion beyond the Earth. Clare is of the earth, and the megalithic stones planted in it. Joe is of the stars, his gaze craning upwards in synch with his radio telescopes, which glide above the earth on steel rails. In the aftermath of the

WE ARE THE MARTIANS

Ringstone Round visitation, and seemingly in a dazed state of shock, Clare wanders down to the stumpy men stone circle with her archaeological tools. Joe quietly tells her that it is not time. And yet Quatermass later surmises (after Clare has been discorporated) that the answer does indeed lie beneath the stones, possibly in the form of beacons planted there in the ancient past.

Clare talks to Quatermass about the connection she feels with the ancient peoples whose artefacts she has unearthed. She drinks fruit wine out of one of their beakers, conjuring an image of those who might have done likewise 5,000 years before. She marvels that they wore buttons. It's a detail that makes them feel ordinary, less distant, more like us. Clare's is a very human discipline, one which makes the human tribes seem less different from one another; a unifying science. It is also a science which delights in imaginative engagement, with coming to know the people whom it is studying. It is significant that it is after his conversation with Clare that Quatermass begins to speculate once more, making the imaginative leaps essential for forming new scientific models. He also begins to attempt an understanding of the young people who are drawn to the ancient sites, who know instinctively what his tired old brain must begin groping towards.

Clare's science is of a different order to the science of Quatermass and Kapp, which is a matter of grand technologies and cold equations. The struggle over the Planet People child is emblematic of the qualitative difference. Clare wants to keep her in the home, to care for her and, if necessary, ease her towards her death in the knowledge that someone is there for her, someone to love her. She knows her name, Isabel, and regards her as a precious life. For Quatermass and Kapp, however, she is a vital key to solving the mystery of what happened at Ringstone Round and elsewhere across the world. Quatermass' language dehumanises her, turning her into an experimental case as he refers to her as a "specimen" and as "evidence". Just as Joe used language which reduced the Planet People to the level of the animal, excusing him from the necessity of dealing with them on a human level, so Quatermass reflexively robs the Planet People child of her humanity in order to incorporate her into the distanced, objective framework of the scientific paradigm. He reduces her

Quatermass: Rebirth and Resurrection

to the status of an animal in a different way from Joe — to the lab subject. "As if you were putting down an animal", Clare wails as they take her away. It's interesting that Kneale equated cruelty to animals with the exploitation of women on several occasions, notably in "Buddy Boy" and "What Big Eyes". Quatermass' attitude is different from Joe's, but the end purpose is ultimately the same.

Annie is another central presence in Quatermass, its backbone in many ways (like the motorway she drives up and down in her armoured van). A strong woman, she also offers a link to the past, and retains a compassionate outlook despite the pervasive violence and divisive hatred which surrounds her. She responds to the news of the Ringstone Round visitation with tears, a display of genuine emotion which reinforces rather than diminishes her strength. She laments the loss of a past when "you could walk in the open and not be afraid", and expresses bewilderment at the world's descent into violent chaos. "Was it the kids?...What got into them all? The blind rage, in every land. As if we had to have it?" Her response is very different from Joe's "I give you up" though. "Poor all of them", she continues, after referring to the Planet People child as a "poor little wretch". "All those lost children wandering the roads, dragging their children...sometimes I've seen them and I've just wanted to gather them all up in my arms and hold them tight and...love them. Even the gangs, would you believe?" "I could feel for them all, I could", she adds. Annie is like a sustaining earth mother of the southern downlands, the district over which she is so appropriately a commissioner. Quatermass' first vague speculations as to the nature of their antagonist are spun in counterpoint to Annie's emotive outpourings, as if he were feeding off her open-hearted energy. He is later nursed back to health after he is left for dead in the city by Edna, the practical, presiding healer of the old folks' underworld. Along with Quatermass' central search for his granddaughter, the young woman who finds him in the end, it could almost be said that the three women who play such an important part in his progress represent the three traditional aspects of the Goddess: the maiden, the mother and the crone.

There is a danger in elevating the feminine principle to the sacred plane, of course, placing it up on an unreachable votive plinth. The human aspect is lost in worshipful generalities. In the book, Quatermass

WE ARE THE MARTIANS

lies with Annie after emerging from the automotive underworld and beginning talks with what remains of the government. He is exhausted, hollowed out. He's like a child in her arms, and she warms and comforts him. Her very human presence, the love she emanates, gives him sustenance, and leads him to the intuitive leap that what they are faced with is not alive but is a programmed machine. They embrace each other in the shadow of this death machine as if to prove what life is, what it means to be alive. A vital force defining itself in opposition to that which they face. Eros against Thanatos. In the novel, Kneale writes 'he looked down at her and it was like seeing half the human race. She seemed to guess the awe. "I'm me", Annie said. "I'm only me".' She is only human. But the apprehension of the fullness of that humanity, the completion which their coming together represents, contains the essence of the divine.

That divine essence is reduced to cheap spectacle elsewhere, a tawdry burlesquing of what should be sacred which Kneale had explored in previous work, THE YEAR OF THE SEX OLYMPICS in particular. The empty sexual stimulations offered by the TV landscape of the illiterate future envisaged by Kneale, used to pacify the population ("watch not do" being the byword), are encapsulated in QUATERMASS by the Tittupy Bumpity Show, which we see being staged and filmed in the TV studio the army is about to take over. Women in animal costumes (the equation of animal and human exploitation once more) dance before a giant figure of a hugely endowed woman like pornographic Pan's People. It could be one of the Artsex routines created for the all-pervasive TV channel of the future in THE YEAR OF THE SEX OLYMPICS. The routine reflects the highly sexualised, 70s-rooted future of **A CLOCKWORK ORANGE**. Kneale made his feelings about the sexual revolution of the 60s and 70s plain in an interview conducted by Julian Petley in *The Monthly Film Bulletin* of March 1989. "One of the more horrific and offensive things I found about the 60s was the "let it all hang out" business", he said. "Inhibitions are like the bones in a creature, and if you pull the bones out all you're left with is a floppy jelly". The giant woman is a gaudily mocking version of the exaggerated characteristics of a Venus of Willendorf-style Goddess figure. When the army invades the studio, the figure comes apart, thorax and lower torso bisected and drifting apart. It's a reversed replay of the technological coupling of the space modules which Quatermass had characterised with utter contempt as "the symbolic wedding of a corrupt democracy to a monstrous tyranny". Quatermass and Annie's union is an authentic human contrast to these grotesque, mechanised pantomimes.

Annie is human, warmly and wonderfully so. There is a distinctly religious feel to this Quatermass story, however. An alternate title might have been The Passion of Quatermass. He begins wandering in from the wilderness, lost in a dark land which he is no longer a part of. But he is awakened by the women he meets. He searches for Hettie but finds Clare, Annie and Edna. He passes through two underworlds, the old folks' catacombs and the underground car park at Wembley Stadium. And he rediscovers his faith, the faith of scientific enquiry and empirical rationalism, of human reason. But this time it is tempered with a more humane understanding, an empathy which he learns from his encounters with others. He once more finds the will to fight for the survival of humanity — rediscovers, indeed, that they are worthy of salvation. In the end, he is prepared to sacrifice himself to redeem them.

Joe Kapp is Quatermass' younger self, the action scientist, full of firm, unshakeable conviction. But he too is tested, his faith in reason and enlightenment values subjected to a trial by the fire of searing light. He is both John the Baptist and Job. He prepares the way for Quatermass with a ferocity the old man no longer possesses, and he is put through untold sorrows as if being punished for his hubristic attempts to penetrate the secrets of creation. Or for some more indeterminate crime or sin. In this sense, he is like his literary Jewish forebear and approximate namesake Josef K, whose attempts to find out just what he has been accused of in THE TRIAL are futile from the outset. Many have interpreted the mysterious and unaccountable power located in the void at the heart of THE TRIAL as being God, the novel a parable of the human condition. The temptation of Joe Kapp occurs when he is in the wilderness of his mourning, his reason torn and his once noble endeavours reduced to a scrabbling about amongst the wreckage in a pointless attempt to patch together smashed equipment and attempt communication with the alien presence. He is visited by the Planet People, led by Kickalong, who offers him the possibility of salvation through the great unlearning. In this mystical variation of newspeak, he must empty his mind of all his accumulated knowledge and adopt a new, reductive worldview. Its narrow limits are defined through a monosyllabic mantra, the leh-leh-leh which the Planet People incessantly chant. By reducing language to its simplest components, it flattens the world out into an undifferentiated whole. Nothing to understand since all is one, all is leh-leh-leh. If he subjects himself to this intellectual reconditioning, he can join them. He can become part of a new, extended family, a part of that which he once despised above all else. Joe can't do it, though. Something in him resists. A flickering ember of rationalism and the great learning of his forebears still glowing in the ashes of his despair.

It is a bitterly ironic inversion that Kapp becomes a cowering object of contempt (but not pity—Kickalong knows no pity) to the Planet People he once exhibited such scorn for. Quatermass is full of such ironic inversions. "The mad are sane" reads one of the Planet People's anti-logical dictums, scrawled on the walls of civilisation's ruins. One of the most prominent is the coming of darkness and death in the form of dazzling illumination. This is enlightenment which brings the opposite of spiritual awakening, or astral transport as the Planet People believe. Joe talks of his Jewish ancestors enlightening themselves to hold back "the dark". Here the dark comes in the form of light. The nature of the alien power remains purposefully vague, allowing it to become an overarching metaphor, a multivalent expression of the ills of the world. It is like a demiurge, the false creator of Gnostic belief systems which holds sway over malformed subworlds. Quatermass talks in terms of a pervasive presence, a skin enclosing the world. "Call it a film, a membrane, a bubble". An act of gnosis, or enlightenment, is required to break through, to achieve a new and truthful level of awareness. There's a wood engraving included in Camille Flammarion's 1888 book THE ATMOSPHERE: POPULAR METEOROLOGY which perfectly illustrates the idea of this conceptual breakthrough (the term used by Peter Nicholls in THE ENCYCLOPEDIA OF SCIENCE FICTION). A scholar looks up at the heavens from his rooted position on the earth's orb and his head breaks through the supposedly fixed sphere of the stars to perceive the mechanisms of the cosmos beyond. God here is a delimiting force, an antagonist whose illusionistic influence must be dispelled if the truth is to be perceived, humankind set free. Destruction of the sub-deity is preferable if possible. Kill God to discover the divine.

The Gnostic aspect of Quatermass invites comparison with another work from the 70s which also charts the fallout from the countercultural 60s, in this instance from a perspective more closely allied with the radical ethos of the period. Philip K Dick's VALIS posited an alien satellite orbiting the Earth, the Vast Active Living Intelligence System of the acronymic title. A benevolent version of QUATERMASS' vastly indifferent non-living machine intelligence, it fires concentrated beams of pink light which penetrate the barriers of the false reality imprisoning the Earth and maintaining a tyrannical imperium, and conveys information which triggers anamnesis (unforgetting) or gnosis. A form of divine invasion, in effect. M.John Harrison's ANIMA novels THE COURSE OF THE HEART and SIGNS OF LIFE also stumble towards intimations of a transcendent power which illuminates the harsh texture of the world for momentary instants. Whilst the quest to discover the source of this illu-

WE ARE THE MARTIANS

mination can be immensely harmful to Harrison's characters, it is also somehow essential to their becoming authentically human. Harrison quotes a passage from THE DICTIONARY OF SYMBOLS AND IMAGERY by Ad de Vries in the coda of THE COURSE OF THE HEART: "*It is easy to misinterpret the Great Goddess. If she represents the long, slow panic in us which never quite surfaces, if she signifies our perception of the animal, the uncontrollable, she must also stand for that direct sensual perception of the world we have lost by ageing — perhaps by becoming human in the first place*".

A similar process is at play in QUATERMASS. It is significant that it is an electronic analogue of the scent of human pheremones which is synthesised to lure the alien power to a particular spot in order to give it a shock unpleasant enough to drive it away. The most powerful of the human senses is recreated through the expertise of the oldest of Quatermass' assistants, Mr Chisholm, who in his day, working for the soap manufacturer Greeley and Prosser, could distinguish 1,032 separate odours. He can still recall the scent of the first girl he lay with. Scent as memory, the direct sensual perception of the world recalled even in extreme old age.

There's a cyclical, mythic quality to QUATERMASS, a sense of old tales being retold, history taking another turn upon the wheel. This circularity, the epochal patters of recurrence, are once more given overarching metaphorical form by the alien power. It was there at the dawn of human culture, history and sacred observance. As such, it is reminiscent of the semi-godlike power in 2001: **A SPACE ODYSSEY**, which plants its own megalithic trigger points on Earth and in the solar system beyond. 2001 has its own inversion, the obsidian mirror-image of that presented in QUATERMASS. The negative space of its jet black monoliths, bring about conceptual breakthrough where Quatermass' illumination brings darkness and breeds regressive ignorance and savagery. In the landscape around the Kapps' home, the circular dishes of the radio telescopes echo the circles of the megalithic sites, the stumpy men and Ringstone Round. Big science in the landscape is, in its own way, as congruent with its natural surroundings as the great stones. They face each other across the millennia, at opposite ends of the spectrum of human civilisation.

Quatermass: Rebirth and Resurrection

QUATERMASS' mythic quality is partly embedded in its title character, of course, his return like a late, redemptive iteration of a heroic saga. The story begins and ends with a storyteller's voice, initially telling us of how the world had fallen into a state of 'primal disorder'; civilisation turning full circle with a shocking rapidity. Quatermass' speculations themselves have the feel of stories being created, the imagination creating new models, useful tales which can never be fully tested, and will therefore always remain at least partly in the realm of the mythic. This storytelling aspect is made more explicit in the novel. Quatermass, lying in bed with Annie, says "I'm going to tell you a story". He proceeds to relate a tale about tiny mite-like creatures on Mars who are suddenly confronted with a huge monster which appears amongst them and begins scooping up the earth they live in with great long claws. It is, of course, a programmed probe sent from Earth. The story is a fable Quatermass has imagined to give them a new perspective on their own situation. The incomprehensible, the new and strange can only be dimly apprehended through the indirection of fiction and fable.

Quatermass' theorising performs part of the metaphorical function of myth, objectively analysing universal aspects of human behaviour through the magnifying lens of the gods, their activities and appetites. Quatermass surmises that the alien harvesting machine is simply gathering "a trace. A flavour. To enrich the lifestyle of inconceivable beings. Perhaps not even that. Just amuse them". Or as Shakespeare put it in KING LEAR, "as flies to wanton boys are we to the gods. They kill us for their sport". This quote was the central fulcrum of Robert Silverberg's story FLIES, written for Harlan Ellison's DANGEROUS VISIONS anthology. It's another fable about the human capacity for cruelty and destruction, with the godlike aliens known as the golden ones manipulating a single human being and feeding off the emotions he has been rendered hypersensitive to.

As with previous Kneale stories, THE STONE TAPE and QUATERMASS AND THE PIT in particular, myth, folklore and rhyme are important as carriers of forgotten knowledge, arcane secrets seeded within them, waiting to be germinated by the enquiring mind. In QUATERMASS, it is the Huffity Puffity Ringstone Round nursery rhyme which seems to bear the weight of ancient memory, a remembrance of previous visitations in the distant past. We first hear the rhyme recited by the Kapp children, who also read it from a book of nursery rhymes (where it is accompanied by a Kate Greenaway illustration). Quatermass recalls it from his own childhood. The rhyme is taken up by Kickalong, who uses it to seduce a soldier, part of a deputation sent to guard Ringstone Round, into the ranks of the Planet People (a scene which recalls images of hippies placing flowers in the rifle barrels of the National Guard who face them). In London, the rhyme becomes an aggressive route-marching chant, uniting the tribes which flood towards a common destination, and finally bellowed out in chorused waves from the terraces of Wembley Stadium. It makes the transition from a Blakeian song of innocence to a tarnished song of experience.

Quatermass initially appears insubstantial, a frail presence in this dark world. He is almost like a ghost returning to find everything utterly changed, leaving him an anomalous spectral echo of the past in its unforgiving landscape. Twice he emerges from the underworld, a double rebirth. After the Wembley visitation, he wakes covered in white dust and crystalline chunks of ectoplasmic matter. He really does look like an ashen revenant as he staggers up the slope and into the barren space of the

Quatermass: Rebirth and Resurrection

blasted stadium. There's a sense (a mythic sense) in which he dies at this point, returning for a brief time in order to make his final sacrifice. This story could be interpreted as the second coming of Quatermass. He returns as a spectre from the past, a mythic redemptive saviour come to protect a new generation (or preserve the world for a future one), even if they wholly reject his notion of salvation. If this is a second coming, then Quatermass has to rediscover a new sense of purpose, to struggle with his humanity in order to usher in a new world. His former beliefs, the old 20th century testament of scientific faith in a technotopian future, have been cast aside. They have proved misguided, co-opted by the divided cold war hegemonies ("the corrupt democracy" and the "monstrous tyranny"). Quatermass life's work has essentially ended in failure. He has to blindly reach towards a new belief system, blending science with humanism. Kapp, the younger incarnation of Quatermass, is still full of his absolute, unshakeable faith in the ability of the scientific method to reveal the truth, expand the boundaries of knowledge and thereby better the condition of humanity. Quatermass, older and wiser, knows that this is not enough on its own. His obsession with his work led him to alienate his granddaughter and, we suspect, his daughter too. This schism is somehow central to his failure. It has left him incomplete, his discoveries used for destructive ends, his revealed truth ultimately hollow.

By synthesising the smell, sound and presence of a gathered crowd, he unites science with the condensed, semi-mystical essence of the human. With his pipe clenched between his teeth, waiting for the end beneath the radio telescopes, Quatermass is returned to the idealistic model which Kneale drew on to create his character. The model who also provided him with his Christian name: Bernard Lovell, who developed the great radio telescope at Jodrell Bank. Joe and Quatermass are reunited to offer themselves as a sacrifice for humanity, for the younger generation. They are essentially divided halves of the same self, here brought together. The "sting" to be delivered to the alien force is a concentrated nuclear explosion, a redemptive adaptation of the destructive ends to which Quatermass' inventions were directed. Joe by this time is referring to the force as 'evil', the scientific fundamentalist reverting to a Manichean worldview of similarly stark, black and white absolutism. He even names it as "Satan. The enemy". Quatermass maintains a relativistic distance, however, a more Taoist sense of cosmic balance (akin to the worldview of Ursula le Guin's science fiction and fantasy). "Perhaps evil was always someone else's good", he muses.

Quatermass and Kapp wait for the moment when they can strike back at god. They are far too insignificant to contemplate killing him (and this mindlessly destructive machine is implicitly male, just as the destruction wrought in the world is the active result of people like Kickalong). But they can at least give him a bloody nose. It is still not enough, though. Quatermass and Kapp are two parts of a whole, their surnames headed by unusual and graphically striking letters which betoken their awkwardly individualistic stance in an increasingly tribal world. But they are still incomplete, and stand alone. This final stance is disrupted by the Planet People, led by Kickalong, his machine gun casually bandied about, the male principle at its basest. There is some underlying connection between Kickalong and Kapp, however, hinted at by the shared K of their names. Their worldviews might be poles apart but they orbit around each other like twin planets. Kickalong shoots Kapp with a contemptuous dismissiveness, barely even registering his presence. The gun has become an instinctive part of his persona, an extension of his arm with a reflex arc directly connecting to the violent centre of his mind. Quatermass sees his granddaughter Hettie, lost in enchanted Planet People dreaming. He freezes, grasping his heart. He cannot reach the detonating button. He is going to fail again. But she looks at him, and there is an immediate moment of recognition. She walks over to him, and smiles with seraphic serenity. They are bathed in actinic light. The visitation has begun. She reaches out to him. Together they complete each other. The family is reunited, the generation gulf spanned, scientific rationalism fused with intuitively felt mysticism. The elderly man is given power and life by the young woman. Perhaps Quatermass can't bring himself to press the button with Hettie present, even if he knows she will be destroyed in a matter of seconds anyway. This destructive act would seem like one final betrayal. But she gives him her radiant blessing. A new testament is forged. The component which has been missing from Quatermass' lifetime of scientific questing is fitted into place at last. It is love.

L I G H T

In a brief coda, in which the storytelling narrator returns to complete his tale, we see children playing around the stumpy men stone circle on a hazily dreamy summer's day. They dance around the stones, which are on a modest human scale, and chant the Huffity Puffity rhyme. The songs of innocence have been restored. The redemptive sacrifice of Quatermass and his granddaughter has not been in vain. They have brought about a new world. Together, they have led humanity back to the Garden.

BIBLIOGRAPHY

'Nigel Kneale, Not Quite So Intimate.' *Sight and Sound* (vol.28, issue 2, Spring 1959)

Nigel Kneale interviewed by John Fleming, *Starburst* no.16, 1979 (available online on John Fleming's blog: https://thejohnfleming.word-press.com/2014/10/03/writer-nigel-kneale-one-visionarys-view-in-a-pre-margaret-thatcher-world/)

Nigel Kneale interviewed by Paul Wells, 'Apocalypse Then!: The Ultimate Monstrosity and Strange Things on the Coast...an Interview with Nigel Kneale' in *I.Q.Hunter* (ed.), British Science Fiction Cinema

Tobias Hochserf, 'From Refugee to the BBC: Rudolph Cartier, Weimar Cinema and Early British Television', *Journal of British Cinema and Television*, 7.3 (2010)

Julian Petley, 'The Manxman', *Monthly Film Bulletin* (Issue 662, March, 1989)

Kim Newman, 'The Quatermass Conclusion', VHS review in *Monthly Film Bulletin* (Issue 662, March, 1989)

Nigel Kneale, *Quatermass* (Hutchinson, 1979)

Nigel Kneale, *The Quatermass Experiment* (Penguin, 1959)

Nigel Kneale, *Quatermass II* (Penguin, 1960)

Nigel Kneale, *Quatermass and the Pit* (Penguin, 1960)

Kim Newman, 'Quatermass and the Pit, BFI Film Classics' (British Film Institute 2014)

Roger Fulton, *The Encyclopedia of TV Science Fiction* (Boxtree, 1990)

John Clute and Peter Nicholls, *The Encyclopedia of Science Fiction* (2nd edition, Orbit, 1993 and online version: http://www.sf-encyclopedia.com/)

Daniel O'Brien and Kim Newman, *SF:UK How British Science Fiction Changed the World* (Reynolds and Hearn, 2000)

James Bell (editor), *Sci-Fi Days of Fear and Wonder* (British Film Institute, 2014)

Harlan Ellison, 'Luke Skywalker is a Nerd and Darth Vader Sucks Runny Eggs' (Los Angeles, August 1977 reprinted in Harlan Ellison's *Watching*, M Press, 2008)

J.G.Ballard, 'Hobbits in Space' (*Time Out*, 1977, reprinted in A *User's Guide to the Millenium*, Harper Collins, 1996)

Alexandra Harris, *Romantic Moderns* (Thames and Hudson, 2010)

Dominic Sandbrook, *Never Had It So Good: A History of Britain from Suez to the Beatles* (Little, Brown, 2005)

Dominic Sandbrook, *White Heat, A History of Britain in the Swinging Sixties* (Little, Brown, 2006)

Dominic Sandbrook, *State of Emergency, The Way We Were: Britain 1970-1974* (Allen Lane, 2010)

Dominic Sandbrook, *Seasons in the Sun, The Battle for Britain, 1974-1979* (Allen Lane, 2012)

David Kynaston, *Family Britain, 1951-57* (Bloomsbury, 2009)

Richard Cowper, *The Road to Corlay* (Gollancz, 1978)

Keith Roberts, *The Chalk Giants* (Hutchinson, 1974)

M.John Harrison, *The Committed Men* (Hutchinson, 1971)

Christopher Priest, *A Dream of Wessex* (Faber and Faber, 1977)

Pete Townshend, *Lifehouse* (Pocket Books, 1999)

Philip K Dick, Valis (Bantam, 1981)

The Kneale Tapes documentary on *The Quatermass Experiment/Quatermass II/Quatermass and the Pit* DVD (BBC, 2005)

Andrew Screen, 'Production Notes for *Quatermass* DVD' (Clear Vision, 2003)

THE QUATERMASS CONCLUSION
An Interview with Nigel Kneale

David A. Sutton

Nigel Kneale has been for many years one of the foremost scriptwriters in British television. Audiences have been treated quite a number of times to exciting and original stories that have often been more than a little frightening. Kneale was born in 1922, the son of the owner-editor of an Isle of Man newspaper. After leaving school he studied law, but became disillusioned and turned instead to writing fiction and to acting. His first collection of short stories, TOMATO CAIN & OTHER STORIES, won him the 1950 Somerset Maugham Award and stories from the book have been reprinted in various anthologies over the intervening years. Kneale joined the staff of the BBC shortly afterwards and scripted a wide variety of programmes before he became well known with his famous serials, THE QUATERMASS EXPERIMENT (1953), QUATERMASS II (1955) and QUATERMASS AND THE PIT (1958). All three were bought by Hammer Films and made into feature films in 1955, 1957 and 1967 respectively. (U.S. titles were **THE CREEPING UNKNOWN, ENEMY FROM SPACE** and **FIVE MILLION YEARS TO EARTH**). In 1954 the BBC screened Kneale's adaptation of George Orwell's NINETEEN EIGHTY-FOUR, which had an unexpectedly sensational effect. Apart from the three Quatermass serials, his original TV scripts include THE CREATURE (1955), MRS WICKENS IN THE FALL (1956), THE ROAD (1963), THE CRUNCH (1964), THE YEAR OF THE SEX OLYMPICS (1967), "Bam, Pow, Zap!" (1969), WINE OF INDIA (1970), THE CHOPPER (1971), THE STONE TAPE, (1972), JACK AND THE BEANSTALK (1974) and "Murrain" (1975). In 1976 ATV produced his six-part anthology with the umbrella title BEASTS. Individual titles were, "Buddyboy", "During Barty's Party", "Special Offer", "The Dummy", "Baby" and "What Big Eyes". 1979 saw his new QUATER-MASS serial on British television, screened in four weekly episodes commencing 24th October. A theatrical version entitled **THE QUATER-MASS CONCLUSION** has been made for export, while the novel has been based fairly loosely on the same story and was published in September by Hutchinson (paperback from Arrow Books, along with reprints of the three original Quatermass TV scripts). I met Nigel Kneale recently in Birmingham, where he was promoting the new books, and asked him about his career as a scriptwriter.

DS: *I think the first thing I should like to ask you is how the notion of the original Quatermass serials came about?*

KNEALE: Well, it was a long time ago and it's hard to remember how the idea came. The necessity was to fill an empty summer slot quickly. I knew they hadn't had anything like a science fiction piece on BBC television, so I dreamed up a story for them. I can't imagine somebody hadn't thought of something similar in outline, but the style of writing and presenting it was certainly new to television. Up to that time TV plays had been rather stately. They tended to be adaptions of stage plays with subtitles like "That Evening" and "Next Morning". My serial was written purely for television and it was very fast moving—I think that was partly what caught the audience, the sheer speed. The space element, if you could call it that, was very small. It wasn't possible to do any elaborate special effects and it had to be done wholly in terms of people on Earth which meant doing it in terms of characters for actors to act. That became the most interesting part

The Quatermass Conclusion

for me, writing it as a character piece. There was actually quite a lot of humour in it

DS: *That was presumably THE QUATERMASS EXPERIMENT. How did the others follow on from that?*

KNEALE: Well, I didn't intend any sequels. As far as I was concerned that was it. But a couple of years later the BBC said they'd like another and after some hesitation I wrote one. The obvious problem was to avoid dropping into a repetitive formula, and I think I managed it. The EXPERIMENT had had an alien-infected crew returning to Earth to spread chaos. In QUATERMASS II an alien colony had been established here for a year before Quatermass realised the horrid fact. Then with QUATERMASS AND THE PIT we had a Martian colonisation of the Earth that had happened not one, but five million years before. In tackling that, Quatermass was having to fight against his own heredity.

DS: *Although you spoke at the recent World Science Fiction Convention, SEACON '79, in Brighton, you've not really been involved with the fans like many other SF writers. How do you feel about this incestuous world of the fans and the authors?*

KNEALE: First of all, don't count me in as a science fiction writer. The bulk of my TV scripts don't fit into that category at all. I like to think of them as strange or mystifying stories but they can be anything from social satire like THE SEX OLYMPICS and WINE OF INDIA to what I like to think of as funny or just plainly human. As to the Brighton convention— I was rather taken aback by it. I just went down there to give a talk and found thousands of people running about with tickets on them. I simply can t make any sense of this fan thing. I find all the worshipping and gossiping pretty silly. Harmless but juvenile. Perhaps it's only to be expected. A lot of science fiction itself is juvenile. A kind of imagination-substitute for people who aren't blessed with much. Like painting-by-numbers. What was interesting about the Quatermass TV shows was that they were aimed at a big general audience who didn't even recognise them

We Are The Martians

as science fiction and would certainly not have thought of themselves as science fiction buffs or whatever the grisly term is. I was asking them to use their imagination and use it hard, because the whole story was put over in terms of implication and hint. And those millions of viewers did what was needed. They made an imaginative investment in the story, and when people do that they're committed. You've really got them on your side. You've won them.

DS: *The Quatermass serials were enormously popular on television and I think it was a bit of a surprise to see the best of them, QUATERMASS AND THE PIT, at the World convention. Do you know why the BBC have never re-screened those serials?*

KNEALE: On television? They can't. Their rights expired long ago. They have archive copies that get shown once in a while by special arrangement, at the National Film Theatre or something like the Brighton convention.

DS: *The rights for all three serials were bought by Hammer Films, I know. You scripted two of the feature film versions, but not THE QUATERMASS EXPERIMENT. Have you a personal favourite?*

KNEALE: Well, the last one, **QUATERMASS AND THE PIT**, is the only one I can bear. The **EXPERIMENT** I detested. It had almost none of my dialogue in it and the whole idea was coarsened and lost. I think it's a terrible film. **QUATERMASS II** is if anything worse—the leading actor was dire. I've been able to do something about that one at least. The story rights have reverted to me and it will never be seen again, thank God: **QUATERMASS AND THE PIT** I quite like. I think it was by far the best directed and acted. Of course the advantage of the TV versions was that they were much fuller. They were twice as long and you could be far more subtle in approach.

DS: *How do you feel the TV versions of the famous Professor Quatermass compared with the film actors?*

The Quatermass Conclusion

KNEALE: Brian Donlevy played in the first two films and I didn't like his performances at all. He turned my troubled professor into a hectoring bully. Andrew Keir played in the PIT and I liked him a lot. An intelligent rendering. Of course the TV professors were the originals. The first was Reginald Tate, a good actor with a lot of intelligence and vigour. Unfortunately he died before we made the second serial or he would certainly have played again. John Robinson took over. Well, then we have a long gap and Sir John Mills plays the new one in a way that's exactly right for the story. I find his performance very moving.

DS: *You've worked in television, off and on, for about twenty-eight years. Obviously there have been a lot of technical changes in that time, so how do you rate the later productions of your work against the early ones in the 60s?*

KNEALE: Tricky to answer this. The purely technical assets, the use of videotape and improved special effects, have made a big difference of course. And for the new QUATERMASS there's been the added quality of putting the whole thing on 35mm film. There's been time and money to give a fine polish to it. On the other hand the early plays of mine had something that's gone now—the fact that they were all done live. That used to give an extraordinary nervous excitement to the performances, the knowledge that you were acting in front of millions of people, right at that moment. The technical roughnesses that you always got were counter-balanced by that tension in the acting that simply over-rode the snags to a point where people didn't notice them. Today everything is cut and dried, perfected and timed. The danger is that it may be a little bit flat, over-processed. It's rather interesting that when we were in the studio with one of the BEASTS plays, it turned out to be almost a throwback to the fifties. It was about a couple whose house was invaded by a rat swarm, and it was basically fifty minutes of real time. When the director had done the usual collection of short takes he found he had just enough recording time left to try it in one non-stop run. So he said, let's try it: And they did, exactly as they would have done in an old live performance in the 1950s. And it was beautiful. Everything worked. The actors were excited and gave their best, a marvellous, thrilling performance. The cameramen were on their toes

WE ARE THE MARTIANS

and didn't make a single wrong shot—they hadn't realised they could keep it up like that. It worked so well the whole crew were high on success afterwards, thrilled with the quality they'd got.

DS: *The rat swarm in "During Barty's Party" was ostensibly a straight horror piece. How did you heighten tension without resorting to crude horror?*

KNEALE: The couple were eaten in the play, at least, that was the implication. But may I hasten to add that it all happened in the mind of the audience, not on camera. That play was a technical exercise for me—I wanted to try something like Hitchcock's **THE BIRDS** but without the birds. This was rats without rats—they existed only through the audience's imagination and the actor's conviction. Not a single rat was seen and even the sound of them was deliberately synthetic. Yet it held. And the effect was heightened by introducing a completely contrasting element. The only lifeline the victims had was to a commercial radio station, a sort of comic phone-in show called Barty's Party. Their terror was crossed with jokey commercials about bedding sales and deodorant.

DS: *A lot of your work is a blend of the everyday and the strange. You seem able to juxtapose and jigsaw your material to powerful dramatic effect. Do you have a personal philosophy about this or is it something that intrigues you?*

KNEALE: I just like writing stories. I have no particular philosophy about it but my starting point always has to be some kind of contradiction or paradox, two elements that don't obviously fit together. Otherwise there's a kind of flatness and I can't get started. For instance take THE STONE TAPE. This could have been a simple ghost story, but I set it in a big old house that was being used as an electronics research establishment. The whole concept of ghostliness and haunting was investigated in terms of a new recording medium.

DS: *Which writers appeal to you?*

The Quatermass Conclusion

KNEALE: Well, let's see. H. G. Wells of course. Orwell. Currently Joseph Heller, Anthony Burgess, Kingsley Amis, Len Deighton. I'm fond of the earlier work of Ray Bradbury, particularly his MARTIAN CHRONICLES. I see that's been turned into a film, by the way. I'll be interested to see what they've made of it.

DS: *You adapted Orwell's* NINETEEN EIGHTY-FOUR *for television. Have you scripted any other writers' books that come into the science fiction category?*

KNEALE: I did an adaptation of Huxley's **BRAVE NEW WORLD** a few years ago, which was due to be made in Spain by Jack Cardiff. The company went bust just before they were ready to start, otherwise it would have been a big one. I also did a co-script of one of Wells' novels, **THE FIRST MEN IN THE MOON**. I've scripted quite a number of films, some of which were made and some not—the usual history of anybody who works at screenwriting. Most were not science fiction but subjects like **LOOK BACK IN ANGER**.

DS: *Do you want to do more film writing?*

KNEALE: You mean original subjects? Those are the hardest to get launched. In this country the industry is moribund, apart from spin-offs—even those Quatermass films were spin-offs, don't forget. In a sense we've never had a real, native industry except for short periods when Hungarians or millers put some strength into it. Not like the French or Italians. At best ours was a kind of appendage to the American—and it's still like that. The English special effects teams seem to be blossoming as never before, servicing American projects in British studios. Perhaps the smoke and slime come cheaper here. If they go on making things like STAR WARS here it'll be good for the special effects boys anyway, if nobody else. They're having a bonanza.

DS: *Do you think the sheer quality of special effects is a good thing? Or are the movie moguls too reliant on technology?*

WE ARE THE MARTIANS

KNEALE: Well, we seem to have a prime example in front of us. I haven't seen **ALIEN** yet but it does seem to be a classic example of a designer's film, with the actors secondary. It isn't the sort of film I would ever want to make myself. It wouldn't interest me.

DS: *Meaning I presume that, as a writer, you'd be surrendering your function?*

KNEALE: That's it. It's handing your pen over to somebody else. A screenwriter puts ideas and construction into a film script of course, but his special area is the dialogue. Through that he can contribute not just characters but suspense, tension, ambivalence, suspicion, misunderstanding, comic relief and all the rest of it. Dialogue contributes all the sharpness to a film. Try watching something like **CITIZEN KANE** with the sound off for proof of that. You can't tell a story in pictures alone, in spite of what some directors would like to believe. Throw dialogue away and you've dispensed with half the colours on the palette.

DS: *The subtler tones, perhaps?*

KNEALE: I think so. Certainly the ones I prefer to use.

DS: *I think you'd agree that there can be very different approaches to a horror subject?*

KNEALE: Completely. I'm happiest when I've brought off an effect that happens in the eye of the beholder, that is, imagined. The opposite of the bucket-of-guts or squeam-and-scream school. For that you need a good working arrangement with the local abattoir, or a butcher with a nasty mind.

DS: *But weren't there some gruesome visuals in the* QUATERMASS *serials?*

KNEALE: No. It was all done by suggestion. Show a tuft of brushwood or scratches on a wall, and let the dialogue make them infinitely sinister—

The Quatermass Conclusion

because they're all wrong, ordinary things out of context and therefore alarming. I think we're responding to something very primitive in us then, picking up danger signals. Watch a cat do it.

DS: *Now with the new QUATERMASS all these years later, do you use the same techniques?*

KNEALE: Even more so. The threat-from-space bit is so remote as to be almost unrecognisable. I think that's being realistic. If some alien life-form does ever appear, it's extremely unlikely to be on our wavelength. It might not bother to attempt any contact. It might treat us with total contempt, or make use of us in some way.

DS: *Which is a long way from the friendly aliens in CLOSE ENCOUN-TERS...*

KNEALE: The word is unknowable. So the story concentrates on the human beings in it, humanity at the sticky end of this contact, their world suddenly falling apart on them without their knowing why.

DS: *To go back to my first question—what gave you the idea for the new QUATERMASS and when?*

KNEALE: About six years ago. That's when I originally drafted it. There were ominous signs of what we've been suffering from all through the seventies—terrorism, financial panics, the chance of oil drying up suddenly. So if you extrapolate from there you get an option on a very grisly future, all fuel gone, anarchy in the streets, all social structures collapsing. It's possible. And it's certainly enough to give credibility to the story. At times I just hoped I could keep ahead of the facts—while I was drafting it we had the first IRA bombs going off in London, and then a first oil crisis.

DS: *Let's hope it remains fiction: Now the new QUATERMASS seems to have two titles?*

WE ARE THE MARTIANS

KNEALE: The four-part TV version is simply called QUATERMASS. But there's a shortened, export version called **THE QUATERMASS CONCLUSION**. About ninety minutes had to be cut out of it so to make up they put an extra word in the title!

DS: *And the book version—did you write that from the screenplay, or did it come first?*

KNEALE: As always, the television version was the original one. But when the idea came up of doing a book, neither I nor the publishers wanted the usual sort of crude novelisation of the script. So I tried to imagine I hadn't written the script and that I was starting on it from the outset as a book. It wasn't easy because I was simultaneously doing routine amendments to the screenplay while shooting was in progress, and also working out the shortened **CONCLUSION** script, which was far more than just a matter of cutting. So there were three versions in play at once. It was very confusing for a while. But I think the book's come out as a separate entity, as intended. It's got a number of characters and a lot of action that don't even appear in the TV of film version. I like it the best of the three now.

DS: *Would you like to write more original novels, having done this one?*

KNEALE: Having done QUATERMASS I'd certainly be tempted.

DS: *Finally, do you have any future writing projects you can tell us about?*

KNEALE: The most immediate is another TV series. Something different. Comedy.

DS: *That'll be a complete breakaway for you, then?*

KNEALE: Not so much as it sounds. The strange story, the grotesque, is simply comedy stood on its head. So in a sense I've been writing comedy all the time. Upside down.

The Quatermass Conclusion

DS: *Can I ask what the future series will be about exactly?*

KNEALE: *Well, I hope it won't upset your readers. It's going to be about SF addicts, UFO buffs. Fans...*

(First published in *Fantasy Media*, vol. 1, no. 5, Dec 1980)

CREEPING UNKNOWN PT 2
KINVIG

Kim Newman

IN 1979, NIGEL KNEALE WAS PERSUADED TO VISIT THE WORLD Science Fiction Convention, held that year in Brighton. The author was undergoing a resurgence, with the long-delayed QUATERMASS serial ready for broadcast, the earlier Quatermass scripts back in print (along with a novel version of the current show which remains his only book-length fiction) and small-press publication of three of his BBC plays. However, he was not impressed by the fans he met at the convention. "They were the craziest lot of people I'd ever encountered," he said later. "They were dreadful. The whole thing consisted of just dancing about in masks, giggling and having too much to drink. I was just disgusted. I said 'never again'." Though costumed attendees and heavy drinking were in evidence, and remain high-visibility aspects of s-f conventions to this day, it strikes me that Kneale was being a trifle ungracious. I was in the audience when he was respectfully and intelligently interviewed by Bill Warren and my impression of the reception accorded the writer was of general sober and unmasked appreciation for Kneale and his outstanding contribution to a genre he may never have cared much for.

WE ARE THE MARTIANS

Two years later, after QUATERMASS had come and gone, Kneale turned to his Brighton outing for inspiration and came up with a television series which might be labelled the anti-Quatermass. KINVIG is a situation comedy, complete with the then-mandatory laugh track, about another oddly-named Earthbound individual who looks to outer space and finds himself struggling against all manner of alien invasions. However, while Professor Quatermass was a visionary boffin, Des Kinvig (Tony Haygarth, Renfield from John Badham's **DRACULA**) is a dreaming loser who runs a failing repair shop and fantasises involvements with a shrewish customer, Miss Griffin (Prunella Gee), whom he sees as a Barbarella-outfitted alien from Mercury out to aid the human race against the evil Xux (who combine the insectiness of the QUATERMASS AND THE PIT Martians with the doppleganging infiltration techniques of the QUATERMASS II aliens). Kinvig has the requisite sit-com indulgent harridan wife Netta (Patsy Rowlands), allegedly amusing pet (dog Cuddly) and layabout best friend Jim Piper (Colin Jeavons, Inspector Lestrade in the Granada Sherlock Holmes series). Among the semi-regulars are **THE BLOOD ON SATAN'S CLAW**'s Simon Williams, unrecognisable under a Ferengi-look alien mask as a Mercurian sage, and Patrick Newell, slightly slimmed since his AVENGERS days, as the local councillor Des suspects is a Xux humanoid out to conquer the Earth.

In the inane chatter of Des and Jim, who pore over UFO magazines and debate whether s-f writers make stories up or reveal deeper truths, Kneale unaffectionately lays into science fiction fans. As a strategy for humour, it fails several times over. The writer clearly despises his characters too much to make them engagingly ridiculous or even tragically daffy, and skilled performers Haygarth and Jeavons are stuck with face-pulling in an attempt to chase laughs which aren't there. Even more oddly, the playright who could once write convincingly about groups as disparate as motorcycle enthusiasts (OUT OF THE UNKNOWN: "The Chopper"), a high-tech r&d team (THE STONE TAPE), porn peddlers (BEASTS: "Buddyboy") and supermarket employees (BEASTS: "Special Offer") clearly didn't bother with even cursory research into fandom. Kneale doesn't know or care that science fiction fans and followers of what now tend to be called Fortean phenomena aren't one and the same sub-

Creeping Unknown PT 2

culture, and he tends (like other s-f outsiders in the media from Jack Webb through Steven Spielberg to Chris Carter) to think that UFO interests are central to s-f, rather than (as was the case in 1981) an embarrassing fringe that admirers of, say, Philip K. Dick, Michael Moorcock, Brian Aldiss or (indeed) Nigel Kneale tended to look down on. Other UK television productions have been far more insightful: Howard Schuman's 1976 play AMAZING STORIES, set at a sci-fi convention, covers similar ground with much more success, riffing on the Pod People and the notion that pulp writers channel arcane truth; while the 2002 TV movie CRUISE OF THE GODS manages Joe Dante-like affection for misfit fans, poking fun at their devotion to a terrible old television show (which, weirdly, looks exactly like the s-f fantasy sequences of KINVIG) then revealing that the writer and actors who sneer at them are shallower and more screwed-up than these well-adjusted loons.

KINVIG managed seven episodes, didn't achieve any ratings success and was never recommissioned. As Andy Murray notes in his useful insert booklet for the Network DVD release, 1981 was the year that the BBC mounted THE HITCHHIKER'S GUIDE TO THE GALAXY on television. Later, RED DWARF became a long-running science fiction sit-com, so the combination of laughs and aliens was always doable on British TV. The problem with KINVIG is that, unlike HITCHHIKER'S or DWARF, it was written as an attack on science fiction, not an attempt to be funny within the genre—the results are bad-tempered, shrilly-acted and rather a tough watch even for Nigel Kneale completists. The episodes are "Contact", "Creature of the Xux", "Double, Double", "The Big Benders" (about Uri Geller-style cutlery-bending), "Where Are You, Miss Griffin?", "The Humanoid Factory" and "The Mystery of Netta". Every great artist is allowed one stretch of truly terrible work–Bob Dylan's Christian period and Jean-Luc Godard's video agit-prop come to mind–and, frankly, KINVIG is Nigel Kneale's depth-plumbing exercise. With its gaudy costumes, laser lighting and basic video effects, the show also looks horrible–but that's presumably part of the point.

IN PURSUIT OF UNHAPPY ENDINGS
Chris Burt & Herbert Wise on THE WOMAN IN BLACK

Tony Earnshaw

"Young solicitor Arthur Kidd is sent to Crythin Gifford, a coastal town, to tie up the estate of a Mrs Drablow. Despite warnings from the local inhabitants, he goes to the Drablow house across the bleak causeway and encounters the ghostly figure of The Woman in Black."

TV Times—December 24, 1989

THE WOMAN IN BLACK
Central Films / 1989

CAST: *Arthur Kidd*, ADRIAN RAWLINS; *Sam Toovey*, BERNARD HEPTON; *Josiah Freston*, DAVID DAKER; *Woman in Black*, PAULINE MORAN; *Sweetman*, DAVID RYALL; *Stella Kidd*, CLAIRE HOLMAN; *Arnold Pepperell*, JOHN CATER; *Reverend Greet*, JOHN FRANKLYN-ROBBINS; *Mrs Toovey*, FIONA WALKER; *John Keckwick*, WILLIAM SIMONS; *Bessie*, ROBIN WEAVER; *Stella's Mother*, CAROLINE JOHN; *Eddie Kidd*, JOSEPH UPTON; *Rolfe*, STEVEN MACKINTOSH; Jackie,

ANDREW NYMAN; *Mr Girdler,* ROBERT HAMILTON; *Farmer,* TREVOR COOPER; *Gypsy Woman,* ALISON KING; *Stall Holder,* PETER GUINNESS; *Lorry Man,* TIMOTHY BLOCK; *Fireman,* ALBIE WOODINGTON; *Gypsy Child,* MARY LAWLOR; *Gypsy Child,* CLARE THOMSON.

CREDITS: *Director,* Herbert Wise; *producer,* Chris Burt; *executive producer,* Ted Childs; *teleplay,* Nigel Kneale, based on the book by Susan Hill; *music,* Rachel Portman; *cinematographer,* Michael Davis; *editor,* Laurence Mery-Clark; *casting,* Marilyn Johnson; *production design,* Jon Bunker; *set decoration,* Ann Mollo; *costume design,* Barbara Kronig; *make-up,* Christine Allsopp, Caroline Clements, Vera Mitchell, Connie Reeve. Running time: 100 minutes.

IN THE 1989 CHRISTMAS EDITION OF *TV TIMES* THE FOLLOWING synopsis appeared in the film listings: "Nigel Kneale, who wrote the original *Quatermass* serials for television, returns to the field of the chiller in this ghost story for Christmas. Tuck the children up in bed to wait for Santa and enjoy a polished late-night quiver and quake."

On the pages for Christmas Eve an image of Adrian Rawlins, playing Arthur Kidd, and Pauline Moran, as the spectral woman in black, dominated the schedule, which also included a presentation of another TV film, PIED PIPER, starring Peter O'Toole. Those were the days when regional broadcasters could make viable one-off dramas. THE WOMAN IN BLACK was certainly one of them—a subtle shocker that exemplified all that was good about intelligent British television in the late 1980s.

A quarter of a century later and times have changed. Many of those companies—THE WOMAN IN BLACK was made by Central Television in association with Carglobe Limited—are defunct. So how did THE WOMAN IN BLACK make her way to the small screen? Producer Chris Burt and director Herbert Wise discuss the bestselling book that became a smash stage play that became a chilling teleplay from the pen of legendary screenwriter Nigel Kneale.

In Pursuit of Unhappy Endings

How did the TV version of THE WOMAN IN BLACK *come to pass?*

Chris Burt: I wanted to make it so I rang Susan Hill's agent, who said the rights had gone. I was pretty depressed about that. I checked and found that [it was owned by] three film technicians—a make-up artist, a costume designer and an assistant director. It was really bizarre. So I got hold of them and said, "What are you doing with THE WOMAN IN BLACK?" And they said, "Well, we can't get it going." So I said, "Look, can I join in and try and get it going?" The make-up artist didn't want to make it with us. The other guy didn't, either. But Barbara Kronig, the costume designer, wanted to stay with us so she was the costume designer on the film. And after about two weeks they said yes.

Then it took me about four months to get it going, and it happened in a funny way. Central had just made something called ESCAPE FROM SOBIBOR. They were going to do ESCAPE FROM SOBIBOR PART II and suddenly the whole thing collapsed. So the Director of Programmes, Andy Allan, came down to see Ted Childs, the Head of Drama, and said, "Have you got anything *now*?" He looked at me and said, "You got anything?" and I said, "Well, I've got this book in my desk." Andy looked at it and said, 'I'll read it overnight.' He rang me up the next morning and said, 'If you can make it for this money, it's yours.' So there we started.

That was a very fast turnaround.

Burt: It was, wasn't it? It's never happened to me again. That was amazing.

How much was the budget?

Burt: Just over a million. It was a two-hour film. That makes it five hundred thousand an hour, which was about the same as every other drama that was being made at that time. And when I say drama I mean top drama. Five hundred thousand was about it. So I couldn't choose stars but then the parts didn't really need it.

Having got the right to make it did you then go back to Susan Hill?

WE ARE THE MARTIANS

Burt: No. I went then to her agent and said, "We can get it going" and she said, "Fine". I'd given Nigel Kneale a copy of the book some time earlier. He loved the book and he loved writing. Being him he'd actually knocked it off very quickly indeed. I remember him telling me it only took him six weeks. He got really into it.

Susan had reservations about the script because she preferred Stephen Mallatratt, who had written a play [from her book] and was still doing very well with that. So she was keen on Stephen writing it. I didn't think that he was nearly as good a writer as Kneale so I was adamant it went to Nigel. That was where Susan and myself didn't get on so well.

So you did it regardless of whether you had her blessing?

Burt: Absolutely. Central had bought the rights to it so it was up to them.

And with respect to Susan Hill she wasn't a scriptwriter.

Burt: She wasn't, no. And also I tried to get THE MIST IN THE MIRROR, the next book of hers, this time written by Stephen Mallatratt and the script was terrible. So that got elbowed. It cost me a lot of money.

What was so special about Nigel Kneale and why did you want him to adapt THE WOMAN IN BLACK *for TV?*

Burt: A) Because he's a brilliant writer. B) A really charming man with a great, great brain. C) He's so clever at getting into a script and getting out of it what you need to really make it work.

He also had an affinity with the genre.

Burt: Yes. It was a great book because it was horrifying but clever. He was very good at getting all these great things out of the book and really making it work. And also it was a very visual book. There wasn't a mass of chat. And that's why Herbert Wise thinks it's the best film that he made because

In Pursuit of Unhappy Endings

it's mainly up to him. The visuals on the film were very, very good. I thought that it was a much better film than the one they made later on [Hammer Films' **THE WOMAN IN BLACK**, 2012].

When you passed the project to Kneale to adapt did you provide him with any instructions or did you just let him go?

Burt: Oh, I let him go. You would never say that to Nigel. I gave him the book and said, "See if you want to make it. If you do, please do it." It was as simple as that. He was a brilliant, brilliant writer. Really great.

And what he delivered was precisely what you wanted?

Burt: Absolutely. That's why Susan got so cross—because of the changes at the end, which I thought were terrific and better than what she'd written. But she got very upset about it.

The process of adapting a book, and the journey from page to screen, can be difficult. What's your take on what happened in this case?

Burt: It's pretty close to the actual book in many ways, actually. The feel of it had the same feel as the book. I read the book again about five years back and, to be honest with you, it's only the end that he changed that really made it different. The actual film, and the feeling of the film, was pretty close to what Susan wanted, I'm sure. But you can't make them all do the things that you want to do.

Were you happy with the changes and that's why you went along with them?

Burt: Absolutely right. I wouldn't have changed them otherwise. I didn't have any discussions about it with Nigel. I turned round to him after six weeks and said, "How's it going?" and he said, "I've done it." I was totally amazed. But he got into it so quickly and with such energy. Great writer.

It's an issue of trust, too, isn't it? You don't want to be interfering.

WE ARE THE MARTIANS

Burt: There are some writers I would interfere with but not with Nigel.

Why did you invite Herbert Wise to direct THE WOMAN IN BLACK? *What made him the right man for the job?*

Burt: I first worked with Herbie on [an episode of] LYTTON'S DIARY. He was a very interesting director; terrific brain and I thought he had the right eye to be able to make this. And he bloody had, too. A lot of people look to him and say, "He made I, CLAUDIUS" and that was wonderful. But he said to me that THE WOMAN IN BLACK was the best film he ever made.

Wise: The initial getting together was completely fortuitous as far as I know. Chris may have done work on watching me [because] my work goes back to the '50s. I've done so many bloody films! I don't ever remember saying [about THE WOMAN IN BLACK], "This was my best film" because I don't know what is my best film. It is certainly one of my better films, let's put it like that.

[At the time] I was working as a freelance and I was engaged to do a series called LYTTON'S DIARY. I liked the script and Chris happened to be the producer on it. He more or less picked me or rather agreed for me to do that. In many ways we had to get used to each other. He's quite what I call an interfering producer. He likes to be in there and it often worries me. I try to elbow them out of the way.

What was the attraction of the project?

Wise: I like doing features like THE WOMAN IN BLACK because I never show the horror. I hint at things. It's much more powerful to let the audience *imagine* what it's going to be like rather than showing some Heath Robinson clobbered-together bit. The moment you show it I always feel that they think it's made up of papier-mâché or whatever. You have a device.

I love horror stories that are not what are normally called horror stories where there is a subtlety, where you have to think, and you have to anticipate and you are already worrying about what's going to happen next

418

In Pursuit of Unhappy Endings

because you know it's all insecure. This is the sort of thing I like. I don't like horror as much. There are a lot of inexplicable things in life and I like mirroring that in drama.

Do you believe in the notion of parallel worlds, in ghosts...?

Wise: I certainly don't believe in ghosts, foretelling, or life after death. None of that. Absolutely not. It doesn't mean to say that there aren't things that are inexplicable to us in life.

Was it rare to do something like this at the time: a quintessential English ghost story? Was it a big opportunity?

Wise: It was quite rare, mostly American in those days so it was very gratifying to be able to do this. But I wanted it to be a feature. When I was making it I was trying very, very hard to persuade Ted Childs, who was in charge, to give us the money but he wouldn't. He said he hadn't got it but producers *always* say they haven't got the money. It was a great shame because I think it's actually a theatrical piece.

Do you see any great difference — apart from the budget — in creating films for television and films for cinema?

Wise: There is no difference in the making of it. The difference is that if you were making a film for television you were really making it for one person. [There is] a direct contact between you — the actor, the director, the television screen — and the viewer whereas in the cinema it is a collective experience and the collective experience contributes to enjoyment or not or whatever. So in that sense it is different. As a director I've always kept that in mind. I prefer television; I would say that, because I have complete freedom in television. I was considered to be one of the top directors at the time and I had a very long career.

If you like horror stories what sort of material were you reading when you were a child?

WE ARE THE MARTIANS

Wise: I was born in Vienna and brought up in Austria. Funnily enough my childhood reading was DOCTOR DOLITTLE and things like that. As a more grown-up child, some Swedish literature. I remember THE WONDERFUL ADVENTURES OF NILS by a woman called Selma Lagerlöf. It was about a swan and a little boy who shrank and could tuck himself into the wings of the swan. And the swan would take him on all these travels. That sort of reading. Classical reading would be Schiller and Goethe and stuff like that. Once I came to England I was then reading more contemporary novels rather than classical material.

What was your opinion of Hill's book when you read it?

Wise: I thought it was extremely good. It touched the very basis of things that we don't understand and that we are afraid of, the guilt about things that we have done or may not have done, the retribution which may or may not await us [and] the whole question of what's the point of our existence? What are we here for? All of that. It seemed to touch all these things and I loved that.

Did you see the play? If so, what's your opinion of that?

Wise: The play is very good. And it works as such. But to dramatise the book as a film seems to me to be much better because you can open it out in a way that a theatre can't. But on the other hand it is very much an internal sort of experience.

So you had read the book and seen the play prior to beginning production. When it came to filming did you only work from Nigel Kneale's script?

Wise: Yes. I read the book and then his treatment of it and I liked what he did. He dramatised it. As Chris points out Mallatrat, who wrote the play, was a playwright. I don't know what else he'd written. He's not in my view a great playwright but he did do very well on this. But Nigel Kneale was a dramatist in the sense that he was a film writer.

In Pursuit of Unhappy Endings

Did you know Kneale before THE WOMAN IN BLACK?

Wise: I knew him before but I'd never done any of his work. I thought he did an extremely good job [on THE WOMAN IN BLACK]. He entered into the story absolutely positively and, to me, he didn't alter it. He went along the rails that Susan Hill laid out for him, in my view. So if you ask me how right was he, I think he was quite a good choice. Nigel was Chris's choice. He found the book. It was up to him to find an adapter. When I read it I approved of it.

Was this the only occasion that you collaborated with Kneale?

Wise: Yes. It's just the way it worked out. Also, very often, when one was wanted, one was not free. If I wanted him he was busy doing something. It's so difficult. You work with a DoP that you love. You do the film for four, eight or ten weeks or whatever. You finish. You now go through months of editing or colouring. He's onto two other films. To hang on to people like this becomes very difficult. Some directors manage to do it.

Did you have any involvement with Susan Hill?

Wise: None whatever. She disliked the whole project because she didn't like the script. I very much tried to get in touch with her to talk to her, but she wouldn't. I would have welcomed her co-operation. A lot of writers don't come. Can't be bothered. She obviously disliked the script in the sense of what he had done with that. That's her privilege.

I always respect writers. I'm not one of these directors who say, "Leave me alone". I'm very happy to talk to writers. I often have writers on the set. But I am very clear *that you keep your mouth shut*. And you talk to nobody except me. And you talk to me *after* I've shot a scene. You don't come to me telling me your ideas and what you want. I'm not interested in those.

In other words I don't invite them to take part in the direction, if you understand what I mean. I'm very much in favour of inviting them to hear

WE ARE THE MARTIANS

their comments. I know what I want. But if you have any objections or you want to know why I did a certain thing or you want to add something, I'm very happy to listen. I don't always claim to be original but I only pick the best. [Laughs]

She wanted Stephen Mallatrat.

Wise: I know she did. But she knows nothing about filmmaking. [Veteran British producer] Verity Lambert said to me one day, "I took a copy of the film out of the library. I wanted to see the first ten minutes because I was interested in that boy called Adrian Rawlins. I wanted to use him and wanted to see him. I put it on and I couldn't switch it off. I was on my own at home and I was terrified!"

I've known Verity since we were contemporaries. She's not easily frightened by anything but she said she found it absolutely terrifying. A lot of people seem to think that it's in fact very much more frightening than that film that they did [for Hammer]. It was what I aimed for.

You set out to terrify people.

Wise: I don't *set out* to scare people but this was material that will scare people so I went along with it. I like touching those areas in an audience which frighten me and which we are all of us frightened of and which we really have no explanation for. It doesn't mean to say that you believe in ghosts but there is something in our psyche where we are aware of the possibility of things like that: all the uncertainties are levelled because *that* is what will frighten an audience. I knew it would.

Did you invite Nigel Kneale onto the set?

Wise: He didn't ask for it and [so] I didn't, no. He was not interested in being a participant in the thing. He liked writing his stories. That's it. And handing it over. Authors come in all colours and he was one of those who, once he's written his thing he hands it over and that's it. Goodbye.

In Pursuit of Unhappy Endings

Burt: Nigel came on the set twice. Such joy. He saw the inside of the house and thought it was absolutely brilliant. And he came [on location] when we were outside the house itself with the noises and everything else. He enjoyed all those sorts of things.

Was there any sense of fascination for Nigel of seeing the translation of his work from the page to the screen?

Burt: Obviously he saw the end of the film. I sent him a cut and he had a couple of moments where he wanted to do this and that. We took his points and did what he wanted. What he really enjoyed was the whole path of the film. The sound on this film is absolutely brilliant, I think. He loved it when he heard all the neighing and shrieks, which were very cleverly and subtly done. It was very complicated when we were mixing that film but great, great fun to make.

When Kneale was on set was he fairly free with suggestions and commentary? Or did he step away?

Burt: He stepped away. On the other hand I'd never worked with him before when he hadn't. That's maybe why he and I worked together so well. We didn't have a feeling that there was any trouble between the two of us, you know?

How much did the ending of the film—your suggestion—change from what was in Kneale's script?

Wise: I can't remember that, to be quite honest. It's too far away and I haven't got the script anymore. It certainly wasn't my ending. It wasn't the tree falling [in Nigel's script]. But I love the idea that at the very end they're on the lake and she's still there, standing on the water.

But to me it's how life is. Life doesn't let you off. It catches you in the end. My experience of life is not that all the endings are rosy. That's me doing *my* film. Whether an audience gets it or not is immaterial. I've said my piece. It's there for them to pick it up if they want it.

WE ARE THE MARTIANS

If you are faced with two people, one who has never read the book and who loves your film, and another who hates your film because it's messed with his book, how do you balance those two points of view?

Wise: Well I don't have to, actually, do I? I feel that a writer has every privilege to write whatever he wants to write and I feel as a director that I have the freedom to do with it, if he has handed it over to me, what I want to do with it. Because I don't want to do what *he* wants to do with it. I can't.

He's in his mind. I'm in my mind. He's in his experience of life. I'm in my experience of life. And I can only put that into it. But, as I say, if he then comes to me and has a discussion about his view of the thing and mine I'm perfectly happy with that. And if I find his idea better than mine — because I know my own mind; I've been with it for umpteen years — that will fire me and I'll think, 'I'll use this.' As I said, I only pinch the best and I don't claim to be original.

What light can you throw on the changes to character names? In Kneale's version Arthur Kipps becomes Arthur Kidd and Sam Daly becomes Sam Toovey. Any thoughts on that?

Wise: We had to submit all these names to the legal people. They're always terribly careful about names. Maybe there was a Sam Daly who could possibly sue. They don't use somebody who can then say, 'You're making a caricature of me,' or whatever. I'm not saying that's the case. I have no idea about why that was changed.

What can you say about the casting?

Burt: The money wasn't very good to make this film and a lot of money had to go onto the production side to make sure we got all the spookiness correct. So we didn't have an enormous amount of money.

Had you had a much bigger budget would you have been pressured to cast stars who might have been inappropriate for the parts?

In Pursuit of Unhappy Endings

Burt: No, because I would have said no.

So you ended up with the right actors for the parts.

Burt: We did. Adrian Rawlins as an actor was going up and up and up. He was becoming a very important actor. Unfortunately this was about as far as it went. He never got much beyond *The Woman in Black*.

What made him right to play Arthur Kidd?

Burt: I'd seen him in a couple of things and really enjoyed his acting. I thought he was perfect for the part and naturally I think I was right. I had a deep discussion with Herbie about it, too.

Wise: Our casting director [Marilyn Johnson] suggested Adrian. He was an up and coming actor and I thought he was very good. I liked him and I approved of him.

Bernard Hepton, who plays Sam Toovey, arguably provides the film's best performance.

Wise: I'd done a lot of work with Bernard before that. He was one of what I called my rep along with John Cater, a little character actor who was with me in Dundee Rep, who I used over and over again. I had a certain number of actors that I really admired whom I would use again if I had the opportunity. Bernard was certainly one of those.

As Sam Toovey he had a sort of sardonic quality where you couldn't quite believe what he said. Did he really mean what he said or did he mean something else? It's not that he acted that but he had a sort of quality in him where I always felt you had to be a bit cautious: "Is that what he *really* thinks?" I liked that ambiguity. And he was extremely competent as a technician.

Hepton as Toovey in THE WOMAN IN BLACK *is almost the keeper of the secrets. Rawlins is doing some detective work and whenever he gets close you*

WE ARE THE MARTIANS

cut to Hepton looking shifty. He knows Arthur's going to get there, so does he help him or not?

Wise: Precisely why I liked his work. This is why I cast him in that part because he had that quality. He didn't have to act it. There was something in his personality that made one feel, 'Wait a minute. Be careful' and I liked that.

Pauline Moran as the woman in black is seen from a distance and then we have that wonderful close-up. The character is rationed throughout the film because she has to make an impact. Given that she is a figurehead and her appearances have to be rationed what was it about Pauline that made her right for that key part?

Wise: I don't think she had a specific quality that I looked for. What was important [was] that she was this icon: dressed in black, mysterious, distant. The point is that I deliberately didn't show her close up except on one occasion because, again, the audience can then imagine what she's like. If you don't see her clearly you as the audience will construct a face, which is horrible to *you*. If I show it I'm showing *my* thing. I'm saying to the audience—and this is how I like to do horror stories—it's up to *you*. You tell me what she's like because the horror that you feel will be your personal horror, not mine.

My son then was aged about 12 and of course I brought the rushes home. I was playing them here every night to look at them. He'd seen the film backwards and frontwards over the six weeks that we shot it and when it was shown at BAFTA he asked if he could come and see it. So I got him a seat and he went on his own. At the end of the film he came to me and said, "Dad, can I talk to you? Do you know why I wanted to see it again? Because this time when she came in through the window I kept my eyes open!"

Burt: She was horrifying, wasn't she? You only see her about three of four times in the whole film.

Were you a hands-on producer? Were you on the set to keep an eye on things?

In Pursuit of Unhappy Endings

Burt: Yes, I was at the beginning. We had to find a house that was in the middle of nowhere, probably in Essex or Suffolk or Norfolk with a place for a horse and trap to be able to go up and down. That was quite tough. Then we had to find somewhere that was much closer and matched the same house. Then we had to find the house's inside, as well. Then we had to find the little places outside—the little outhouses and all those sorts of places. So it was quite complicated.

The house is as big a character as any of the actors in the piece. It has to be right.

Burt: Yes, it is. That and the dog. Don't forget the dog! We had to sew a sausage into Adrian Rawlins' trousers to make sure the dog would follow him.

If the house hadn't been right the whole project might have imploded.

Burt: Yes. And we only found it about two weeks before we were about to shoot it. It was quite tricky. It was designed by two great people—Ann Mollo and Jon Bunker—who had just come in from feature films. They really did a great, great job on it.

What was so vital about that property that made it right for the film?

Burt: It had to look rather creepy. It was as simple as that. We found it just outside Henley, believe it or not.

What are your memories of the production, the use of sound effects and any particularly challenges you may have faced—with the weather, for instance?

Wise: The locations were difficult to find. Of course that causeway [to Osea Island in Maldon, Essex] is unique. You don't find that every five minutes. The overall challenge was that at every tide the bloody causeway was under water so we had to do our shooting and our scheduling according to the tides.

WE ARE THE MARTIANS

We had a terrible problem with fog and mist, where you could only just see the thing. All these [elements were an issue] because it was all out in the open. You accept those sorts of things when you're a filmmaker because this is what you have to do. I don't remember particular [problematic] things other than the causeway. I remember one occasion when we filmed too late and we had to spend the night on the island. We couldn't get out because we were too slow, so we got locked in. It was particular to this location.

We managed to match the exterior of the house with the exterior of what we're looking out on. It all seemed to fit together and they were miles apart. I had a very, very good director of photography [Michael Davis]. He understood what I was after, which is that the lighting mustn't be too mysterious. Let the audience do [some work]. You know, lamps swinging are much more important than showing anything else. They think, "Jesus, something's been here!" and you then construct the horror as the audience [sees it].

Did you face any constraints in terms of making a horror film for TV? And was there anything unique about the content of THE WOMAN IN BLACK *that gave you pause?*

Wise: I had some constraints. I can tell you one story. It is against Chris although I love him dearly. One of the things you have to do with a producer is agree the money. I said I wanted a crane—a really big, big crane—on two, three or four occasions because they cost a great deal of money. He agreed and said I could have it. And then I got the idea for the very end of the film, which was mine: when the tree falls and she gets them. That's what I was after. I got this idea of them in the lake with the tree over, and of course I was going to need a crane because the camera was pretending to be the tree.

I said, "I want another day's crane."

He said, "You can't have it."

I said, "Come on," and I told him the idea.

He said, "I don't care. You can't have it. I haven't got the money." Anyway I tried and tried and tried. I've been in the business since the

In Pursuit of Unhappy Endings

mid '50s and I know about producers telling me they haven't got the money. Anyway he wouldn't give way. I was talking one day, we were having a drink in the pub and the crew were there. I was saying, "I've got this idea for the end of the film" and the lighting cameraman said to me, "What a wonderful idea. Wait a minute." And he did some phone calling. He said, "I'll pay for half of the crane if you're prepared to [pay the rest]." I said, "Wait a minute." And do you know the whole crew chipped in. They all wanted to pay for the crane, and I said, "Absolutely no. I'll pay for it."

I can't remember now but I think it was about eight hundred quid. In those days, 25 years ago, it was worth a good deal more money than eight hundred quid is now. But I was prepared to pay that. And we got the crane. And on the day—we shot it on a Sunday in a park with a lake somewhere in northeast London—we were there at eight o'clock in the morning. Eventually Chris turned up at around ten, looked around and said, "What's this crane doing here?"

I said, "Don't worry, it's mine."

"What do you mean, it's yours. What's it doing here? I told you, you can't have it!"

I said, "It won't be on the charge of the budget."

And I told him that everybody had chipped in. He shut up then. When we did the editing the next day I turned up—I had an office in Wembley—and there was a note from the audit department saying the charge for the crane would be due to me. I accepted that. But the bill never came.

When we were editing, three months later, I said to Chris, "What happened to this bill for the crane?" He said, "Oh, forget about that." And that was that. Of course he had the money. It's a story against him but he acknowledged that he was wrong not to let me have that money. To me it really added something. And that was one of the things that Susan Hill didn't really like.

Ridley Scott once said that the sets on **ALIEN** *were so creepy that when the crew were off the studio floor and the lights were down they wouldn't go back onto the set because they were frightened. Was there an essence of that with* THE WOMAN IN BLACK?

WE ARE THE MARTIANS

Burt: Yes, but not as big as Ridley's film. That was *so* creepy. He's quite right. On THE WOMAN IN BLACK, no. It was all designed by lighting, good acting and some very good direction.

Did the cast buy into the mood and the vibe and the atmosphere or was it just a job?

Burt: A bit of both, to be honest with you. It was very different for a lot of people because you didn't often get a horror film — or this style of film — on television at that time. Therefore there was a big buzz about how you lit it. There was a big buzz to be on the floor every day.

Wise: That's down to me as the director. That applies to anything that I do. They have to come in to my world, if you see what I mean, without forcing them and without being in any way unpleasant about it. This is what I'm offering and you're part of that, part of the story. You have to be part of it and I don't remember any difficulties.

Was there also an attraction for people to be involved in a Nigel Kneale script?

Burt: Yes, but this was different to *Quatermass*. This had more subtlety than a lot of his stuff. That's why I loved working with him because you'd get so many different ideas out of him. In that way there was a terrific buzz on the floor every day. But it was a very tough schedule. We had to make it within four weeks. We were shooting five minutes a day.

Was that four-week schedule the norm in TV at that time?

Wise: It was the norm in the sense that we were encouraged to do it as quickly as possible, and it was a challenge. I did it. It was tough shooting this sort of stuff in four weeks with all those separate locations.

How much of it was shot in the studio?

Wise: We did little bits at Shepperton. I would say 90 per cent was on location.

In Pursuit of Unhappy Endings

Burt: We used Shepperton Studios for when the solicitor's place gets burned.

What's your preference as a filmmaker: location work or studio?

Wise: Whatever gives me the best opportunity to do what I want to do. Obviously [I like to film] an exterior scene on a big exterior and not pretend to be exterior in a studio, which sometimes I've had to do. Other than that I have no preference.

How did you create the scene of the woman in black standing on the surface of the lake?

Wise: The lake was in a park and wasn't very deep. We built a platform, which was anchored in some way just below the level of the water. Looking from a distance you couldn't see it. And she just stood on that. It just looked as if she was standing on the water.

Is it particularly tricky to film on water?

Wise: If you're out at sea and it's deep then you can't do anything. If you're in a park with only eight or ten feet of water you can actually anchor it and once you anchor it, it's fine. But it can still float a bit and of course the waves on the thing will make it look very unsafe for you and the actors standing on it because you haven't got a fixed ground. And that has to be overcome. Most of that shot was at a distance so it wasn't an issue.

What was the reaction to the film on transmission and were you pleased?

Burt: I was a bit dismayed because I thought that we'd get a bigger audience. It was about nine million and I expected to get 11 or 12 million. Andy Allan, the Head of Programmes, said, "Don't be so stupid. It's a Sunday night. It's late. You got a terrific viewing figure. Don't worry about it."

Wise: People were suitably frightened. I liked that. Whether it got 8

WE ARE THE MARTIANS

million or 11 million or 12 million [in the viewing figures], I don't know. That's the producer's job. I just get on, do my bit and hope I'm satisfied with what I've done, which I rarely am. But I was more satisfied with this than with most other stuff that I've done.

Were audiences unprepared for the subtleties of the piece?

Burt: Good question. I've never thought about that. You're probably right in many ways because it wasn't a straight horror show. It was more subtle than that.

Did you have any communication with Susan Hill afterwards?

Burt: Only once. She said she didn't like it.

It was her right to dislike it but did you feel she missed the point?

Burt: Yes, totally and utterly. We had done her a great favour. I thought it was a wonderful film, beautifully acted, beautifully made and wonderfully directed. I was very upset about what she had to say. She was into Stephen Mallatratt. I thought the play [of THE WOMAN IN BLACK] was very good. I'd been to see it twice before I did the film. I thought it was a good play but he was a playwright, not a filmmaker.

Were you in any way stung by Susan Hill's negative opinion of the film?

Wise: Things that I can do nothing about I learn [to say], "Don't bother" because you just make yourself miserable and you can't do anything about it. If this is how she wants to react there's nothing I can do. If I could do something about it like saying, "Can I come and talk to you?" then I would have been there.

She didn't want to and that's okay. I just did my film. And there it is. I had a most wonderful experience. People want to watch it. If people do retrospectives of my work when I'm gone THE WOMAN IN BLACK will be there, I know that. People can then pass judgment on it.

432

In Pursuit of Unhappy Endings

Did it ever trouble you that you made **THE WOMAN IN BLACK** *for television and not as a film for the cinema?*

Burt: No. It was still a film, just for TV.

The film has a substantial legacy. It has acquired a mighty reputation. People still talk of it and people are still frightened by it. Did it achieve everything you wanted it to?

Burt: I remember going to see it again with Herbie at the British Film Institute. We turned up thinking it would be about half full. It was *absolutely* full. We managed to grab the last two seats just in time. I was amazed and so thrilled to see that people still enjoyed watching a great film.

THE WOMAN IN BLACK has never received an official DVD release. Would you like to see it out there?

Wise: I certainly would. Not because it's mine but I think it's a good film. I have shown it to students; I've done a lot of lecturing and tutoring. I stopped working ten years ago when I was 80 because I can't get health insurance. I've shown it to a lot of students and they've all been terrified of it. I showed it for my own reasons, to show what I was aiming for. I would be very pleased if it was out there.

I have to admit I have not gone to see the recent film or the one that is supposed to be a prequel. Why [Susan Hill] should take such a violent dislike to what we did, I don't know. Maybe just because it's not her. I don't know her at all. I did the first PD James, for example, and I got to know her terribly well. We were great mates and we understood each other. It was all great cooperation. But Susan Hill...[he shrugs]

Burt: I've never found out what went wrong, but something did. There was allegedly trouble between the people that owned it—those three film technicians and Central. I never really understood why and I'm still trying to get to the bottom of it.

WE ARE THE MARTIANS

This joint interview was compiled from separate conversations with Chris Burt (January 20, 2015) and Herbert Wise (March 26, 2015). I am grateful to both gentlemen for their generous support. I also wish to acknowledge the assistance of Sheldon Hall.

WHERE'S KNEALE WHEN YOU NEED HIM?

Thana Niveau

"THERE ARE NO GOOD ROLES FOR WOMEN." SO GOES THE familiar lament, especially for those actresses past their ingénue days. However, even those ingénue parts can be tiresomely one-dimensional. There's The Girlfriend. The Sex Object. The Victim. And today we can add The Manic Pixie Dreamgirl to the list.

One female stereotype that occasionally managed to transcend her lot was the film noir femme fatale. She was sexy, certainly, and she used her sex appeal to get what she wanted. But she had her own reasons for doing so. She had a mind and an agenda of her own, and that's what made her believable—and watchable. Even if she ultimately got her comeuppance at the hands of the nominal hero, she still seemed like an actual person. She seemed real.

In recent years we've seen BUFFY/FIREFLY creator Joss Whedon lauded for creating 'strong women characters'. Asked repeatedly why he wrote so many, he had multiple answers. This was the best one: "Why aren't you asking a hundred other guys why they don't write strong women characters?" He went on to say that what he was doing shouldn't be remarked on, shouldn't have to be remarked on.

He's right, of course. And you could almost believe that the writers of mainstream films had taken that to heart. Now every other movie has

WE ARE THE MARTIANS

some badass girl with a sword. Or a gun. Or a bow. She probably also knows martial arts. And she's always young and sexy. But is she "strong"? More importantly, does any of the above make her a strong character? Of course not. Which is why the question keeps being asked.

Writers have catastrophically misunderstood what's meant by the phrase "strong female character". They've given her a sword, then gone and hamstrung her with it. Her "strength" (ie, fighting ability, brains, sweariness) is more about enhancing her sex appeal than making her a believable character. But she doesn't always have to be tough and wise-cracking. She can be vulnerable too. In fact, she should be. She should be every bit as weak and flawed as a real human being. She can be a bitch and she can even be a victim. She just has to be real. If writers would stop focusing on gender when writing characters, they might come closer to the mark with the female ones. If they would write a character who serves the plot—rather than being moved around by it—they would achieve the balance that's sorely needed.

One writer was doing this long before Joss Whedon, to great effect. Nigel Kneale was far ahead of his time in many ways and he was no by-the-numbers writer. He didn't write ordinary stories about ordinary people. And that went for his female characters as well.

Rather than relegate talented actresses to the stock roles of Wife, Mother or Damsel In Distress, he gave them interesting roles in the story and made them active participants. They were every bit as important as the male characters, and often more capable.

Perhaps it helped that he came from a theatrical background, having initially trained to be an actor at RADA. The classical stage has always offered women a variety of juicy roles and it's possible that Kneale took that away when he moved into writing for film and television.

In 1967's **QUATERMASS AND THE PIT**, Barbara Judd (Barbara Shelley) is a good example of what's meant by a 'strong female character'. In a lesser film she might have been Professor Roney's leggy secretary, who freaks out at the sight of a skull and has to be slapped when she gets hysterical. Or she could have been a feisty journalist, one who acts more like a bratty teenager than a strong-willed woman, and gets herself into trouble from which only the hero can save her. Kneale gives her much more to do.

436

Where's Kneale When You Need Him?

She's Roney's assistant, a fellow scientist, and she doesn't spend her time making coffee or being a nurse for injured men. She's cool-headed and highly efficient and she's the one who makes the connection between the Hobbs End discovery and ancient sightings of Hob's Lane ghosts and dwarfs. True, she isn't the hero of the piece, but she's instrumental in helping Quatermass solve the mystery. She also gets the best line in the film: 'So far as anybody is, we're the Martians now.'

It's interesting to note that the first person to see 'ghosts' in the unearthed rocket ship is a male soldier, who reacts hysterically and has to be dragged out. The second is also a man, who panics and winds up babbling madly about what he's seen.

When Quatermass decides to don the optic-encephalogram to record his own visions, he is soon overwhelmed and has to remove the device. Barbara is the one who takes over, claiming she is already seeing things. And when she herself experiences the violent vision of the Martian purge of the hive, she is stricken and disturbed, but she acquits herself better than her male counterparts. The blustering Colonel Breen and the pigheaded minister try to write her off as an overwrought female with too much imagination. In fact, Quatermass is far more overwrought than Barbara ever is.

It's unfortunate that Quatermass has to knock her out at the end, when she's succumbed to the Martian programming and is roaming the streets looking for a fight. But I can forgive that bit of clumsy sexism in an otherwise excellent film.

"Murrain" is a contemporary (1975) tale written for the series AGAINST THE CROWD, about a witch hunt in a small Yorkshire village. The story revolves around Mrs Clemson, an old woman who lives by herself in a bleak cottage, alongside the local pig farm and a stream which has run dry. When the pigs fall ill, veterinarian Alan Crich is called in to assess the problem. Soon he's also being asked to look at a little boy whom the villagers believe has been cursed. They never come right out and say the word 'witchcraft', preferring instead to list their grievances and whatever flimsy connection they might have to Mrs Clemson's arrival and solitary nature. She also had a cat. They killed it.

The character build-up is excellent, with Kneale painting a picture both of the ignorant villagers and the scary, warty old witch who has allegedly cursed them. He's made her a fascinating character before we've even met her. I don't know how this story would have been received by the kind of rural community Kneale was writing about. Certainly, it's difficult for a modern audience to feel anything but disgust for the superstitious villagers, who are no better than a torch-wielding mob. But Kneale's work has a timeless quality, and despite the primitive nature of the villagers, once Crich tells them off and goes on his own to visit Mrs Clemson, we find ourselves in unsettling territory.

The old woman (compellingly portrayed by Una Brandon-Jones) is indeed peculiar, but is she really anything more than a bit eccentric? To modern eyes, the villagers seem far more eccentric, with their insistence that she is the cause of the dry stream and swine flu. And the reaction of the boy's mother, who freaks out when she realises that the money she has just taken came "from HER", is just laughable. No one will listen when Crich tries to explain that the mother's subsequent illness is nothing more than hysterical conversion. But after scoffing at his advice that they call a doctor, Crich should know they're not about to listen to reason. "The power of suggestion," he tries to tell them. "She believes this influence to exist and that it can do this to her and so it has."

Where's Kneale When You Need Him?

The angry mob only hear what they want to hear and they're happy to mock his logic until they can mould it to fit their own prejudices. "Suppose she believes too, that she's—that!"

Crich defends the old woman for as long as he can, but even he finally finds his rational nature tested. After bringing her food and supplies, he finds a tattered doll and asks her about it. She says it belonged to a little girl who used to come and visit her. But the villagers made her stop coming. Mrs Clemson strokes the doll, lost in bitter reminiscence as she laments the children she never had. "I'd have put all my strength into them, every bit." Crich is disturbed as much by her vehemence as by her unsettling words, especially when she says she'd have "worked them just so, and they'd have been mine—to give me pride. It was meant to happen!" She clutches the doll, crying out, "But I was me!" For the first time, we (and Crich) sense that there might be something sinister in her after all.

The 'is she or isn't she?' question is never answered. Brandon-Jones does a fine job with the character, keeping her ambiguous throughout. While we immediately feel sympathy for her when we first meet her (and before that, when she's being accused by the villagers), Kneale cleverly subverts our expectations and, by the end, even a modern viewer cannot help but question whether the old gods are still about.

In 1976, on the strength of "Murrain", Kneale wrote six episodes of the show BEASTS, a series of character-driven pieces that showcased his favourite themes: science vs the supernatural and reason vs superstition. Some episodes are better than others, but the ones with stand-out female characters are "Baby", "Special Offer", "During Barty's Party" and "Buddyboy".

"Baby" is a highly disturbing story about a couple (veterinarian Peter and his pregnant wife Josephine) who move into a cottage in the country. The weather is bleak, the landscape is gloomy and, in contrast to Josephine, the fields are barren. So, apparently, is everyone who ever lived there, animals included.

During renovations, the couple uncover an ancient clay pot buried inside a wall. It contains the mummified remains of some sort of creature, and Josephine unconsciously touches her belly as Peter extracts it from the

WE ARE THE MARTIANS

jar, as though already sensing something about it, possibly even bonding with it against her will. Josephine wants the thing out of the house, but Peter isn't interested in her objections.

In fact, he doesn't seem terribly interested in anything his wife has to say. He's very full of himself and his wild mood swings keep her constantly off balance. He's sarcastic and snappy with her one minute, then jubilant about their future the next. She only lashes out herself when Peter and his boss make light of her concerns that the history of "contagious abortion" among the animals in the area might also affect her. Both men reassure her and then roll their eyes at her behind her back.

When Josephine shows the creature to the workmen, they are just as disturbed by it as she is, and there's an eerie moment where they explain that such things would have had a purpose—a bad one. "If a thing wouldn't happen by nature, if nature wouldn't bring it about, then such as that might serve." They go on to tell her how certain people were "wise in them powers" and could "put harm on a person or a place." Josephine is clearly afraid for her baby and her fears seem more than justified, especially by the suggestion that "a thing like that" would have needed "human suckling—to set it to work." Kneale does an excellent job of highlighting a special kind of horror unique to women, one that would be further developed so successfully by Canadian director David Cronenberg.

Josephine decides to destroy the 'baby'. Even so, she is psychically linked to it and she hesitates before trying to burn it. Peter rescues it from the fire and berates her. Then he hides it in the worst possible place—the nursery. One has to suspect he is under its influence too, as he is clearly more interested in this 'baby' than his own. True to form, however, Kneale never spells it out for us. We just have to trust Josephine, the only reasonable character in the story.

The next day Peter's in a rage over a childish prank played on him at work. Now he hates his boss and wants to quit. While this is stressful for Josephine, it's also music to her ears. Now they can get away from this place and forget all about the monstrous 'baby'. But as soon as his boss turns up with a bottle of whisky and a few blokey jokes, Peter's back to being friends with him, his tantrum forgotten.

Where's Kneale When You Need Him?

Josephine's fears are written off as the product of an overwrought imagination. And at the end, she witnesses the ultimate horror—a hag suckling the hideous 'baby'. This emphasises, both for Josephine and for female viewers, the fear of what one's offspring might turn out to be. And for those not keen on children, there's also the inherent horror of being the one on whose body new life feeds.

"Baby" is an interesting companion piece to "Murrain", exploring similar themes of witchcraft and ancient evil blighting the land. Perhaps the hag at the end of "Baby" is all in Josephine's mind and there is a rational explanation for everything, just as it's more likely that Mrs Clemson is simply a misunderstood old woman. But perhaps the hag is real and Mrs Clemson is a witch. Perhaps they are one and the same. It's to Kneale's credit that he rarely spells things out for us. As dated as these teleplays are, the stories still reward repeat viewings, even decades later.

Possibly the least imaginative episode of BEASTS, "Special Offer" is a British variation on Stephen King's CARRIE. But it deserves mention for its complex central female character, the pitiable Noreen (Pauline Quirke). Like Carrie, Noreen is awkward and unattractive, and she nurses an equally awkward crush on her boss, the callous Mr Grimley. She also harbours powerful telekinetic abilities and these powers come to the fore when her bullying coworkers push her too far.

Briteway Billy is the 'beast' of this episode, an indeterminate cartoon rodent who is the mascot of the Briteway store. When cans fly off shelves and bags of frozen peas explode before their eyes, Noreen points and exclaims that she sees some kind of animal. Naturally, no one else can see it and Mr Grimley sneeringly dubs it "Briteway Billy. A woman scorned, however, is nothing to sneer at. And as Noreen's secret crush becomes apparent, the attacks on the store intensify in concert with her feelings— both passion and rejection.

Noreen is made a figure of loathing throughout, and the viewer is invited to hate her too. Pretty coworker Linda calls her a "stupendous, giant-sized unrefutable drag" and "dead gruesome" while one nasty old woman senses "a badness in that girl". They may be right. Certainly her one attempt to use makeup transforms her into something resembling the Joker. And her insistence that "Billy" is responsible for the disturbances

WE ARE THE MARTIANS

does nothing to endear her to anyone, least of all Mr Grimley, who tries to sack her. Even her supervisor June is only nice up to a point. Like all borderline bullies, any kindness she shows for Noreen is swiftly followed by laughter or anger as she hurries back to the safe company of her coworkers, who despise the girl. June clearly doesn't want to be dragged down with her.

At first Noreen doesn't seem like much of a character—or a role—but, as her hidden feelings become clear, we begin to wonder about her. Just as we're never sure whether Mrs Clemson is really a witch, Kneale never makes it clear whether or not Noreen has actually conjured the creature she calls Billy. Is Billy a natural manifestation of her unrequited love? Or is she consciously and deliberately wreaking havoc and then playing dumb, playing on the others' (and our) expectations of her? Certainly there is nothing ambiguous about her actual powers, which by the end she wields remorselessly.

When Mr Grimley invites a flirtatious girl into his office, supposedly to interview her for Noreen's job, it's the final straw. Bags of sugar and flour burst open in the stockroom and form a blizzard while cans and other hard objects pursue the fleeing pair.

"It was Billy again!" cries Noreen. She reminds me of a child who seeks attention at any cost, preferring abuse to being ignored.

But Mr Grimley is furious. "I don't care! Get out of here and don't come back—ever! Ever!"

And with that, the whirlwind of debris dies out, leaving the broken-hearted Noreen standing there, devastated.

Mr Liversedge, from the Briteway head office, stands in for the usual Kneale scientist. He talks to Noreen alone, suggesting that sometimes things get blocked inside a person. And "once in a while, much more gets blocked. And then something erupts, tears loose". Noreen looks as though she understands what he's getting at, but by this time she's too far gone to be saved.

She sits in the coffee shop across the road, pining for Mr Grimley as she makes more objects fly around. But he's had it with her psychic antics. He drags her into the store, shouting at her and calling her a "mad, foul horror". He tries to force her to admit she's the one doing it, that there is

Where's Kneale When You Need Him?

no Billy. But this time she lashes out at him, burying him beneath an avalanche of cans. Afterwards she sits there, lovingly stroking his corpse. Her final words are pathetic and delusional: "He loved me really. He took me by the hand."

Unlike Carrie, Noreen never fully elicits the viewer's sympathy, and by the end she is more a figure of horror than of tragedy. Quirke does an excellent job of keeping Noreen ambiguous, and leaving us to question just how much she was ever in control of her powers.

In "During Barty's Party", elderly couple Roger and Angie Truscott (wonderfully performed by Anthony Bate and Elizabeth Sellars) face a more familiar and mundane horror—an invasion of rats. This episode is a masterclass in creating suspense and terror with sound alone, never giving the audience even a glimpse of the monster.

The story begins with Angie hearing screams. She thinks it's just a nightmare and we learn that she hasn't been sleeping well. Roger patronises her by saying it was brought on by alcohol and sleeping pills. She wants to believe that's all it is, but she trusts her own perceptions. She is distraught by the scratching she can hear beneath the floorboards. A lesser writer would have made her a stereotypical female who is terrified of rats. And in a lesser programme she would have run around screaming and smashing things up. But, despite her initial distress, by the end she proves to be the more resourceful one.

Roger is stubborn and practical to a fault, insisting, "we've got to keep our problems strictly practical, things we can find a way to cope with." Once he realises that Angie is not imagining the rats, his solution is to shout and stamp on the floor, and then gloat when the creatures are silenced for a while. He thinks that simply asserting his authority will make the problem go away. When the noises return, he blames the dog for being a "lazy brute" and not earning its keep. Then he shifts his blame to Angie for choosing the dog in the first place.

Rejecting Angie's suggestion that they simply leave, he plants himself in his chair and angrily declares that he won't be driven out. He's the kind of man who has an answer for everything and he doesn't want to be confused with the facts. He's so invested in blaming others and trying to rationalise the situation that he's completely unprepared when the moment of truth

WE ARE THE MARTIANS

comes. "Hoax! Hoax! Hoax!" he snarls at the radio, refusing to believe the reports of rat swarms, "super rats" or even the purely reasonable idea that they have evolved an immunity to poison.

"So they don't have to be afraid of us," Angie whispers over the phone to Barty at the radio station. "And if that happens, if they've stopped being afraid . . ."

At first Barty belittles her too, assuming she's just a frightened old woman jumping at shadows. But her chilling account soon has him convinced that they are in genuine danger.

"Now it's time for us to be afraid of them," she says, fully accepting the horror of the situation. While Roger simply rants and raves, Angie acts. Their individual world views have been shattered, but Angie is better able—and more willing—to face the awful truth. She is terrified, but she manages her fear better than Roger does. It's a common trait of Kneale women, this willingness to accept the fantastic. Perhaps they are simply more attuned to the unseen forces at work beneath the mundane, more able to see the extraordinary in the otherwise ordinary.

Which also begs the question: Was her nightmare actually a vision?

When Barty mishears their surname and it becomes clear that no one will be coming to rescue them, Roger loses it completely, succumbing to eye-rolling hysteria. Angie still manages to marshall her wits enough to get them kitted out in coats and fencing masks ("They go for the eyes"), unfortunately to no avail. Nonetheless, she remains the stronger one until the very end, when we hear the crumbling timber and the stampede of little rodent feet as the poor couple await their dreadful fate.

"Buddyboy" is generally considered by most to be the weakest episode. It's certainly no one's favourite. But I actually find it one of the most intriguing, even if I don't think it quite works the way Kneale intended it to. Its fascinating and provocative central concept is hampered both by its low production values and the histrionic acting of its period. Perhaps it's too ambitious a story for its humble medium, but Kneale gives it his best regardless. And, of course, it has a compelling female character at its core.

Ostensibly a story about the vengeful spirit of a mistreated dolphin, "Buddyboy" is actually a strange tale of supernatural affinity. Perhaps my own love of dolphins predisposes me to be more forgiving of this story than others are, but I genuinely do believe there's a great idea here, with a powerful subtext about the plight of the downtrodden.

Porn mogul Dave inspects a derelict dolphinarium (sporting the cheesy name *Finnyland*) with an eye towards turning it into a 'classy' adult cinema. The owner, Mr Hubbard, is a frothing, overacting and cowardly man who claims his star attraction, dolphin Buddyboy, drove the place into the ground; first by being so presumptuous as to have "a very definite personality" and then by using that personality to "refuse his tricks". In other words, the highly intelligent animal didn't want to spend his life swimming around a squalid little tank, performing for the unwashed masses. "He wouldn't be taught," Hubbard insists. "He thought he knew better than we did." As a final (and to Hubbard's mind, personal) insult, Buddyboy apparently did himself in. Dave isn't really interested in any of this. All he wants is somewhere to show his films and make money and he is suspicious of Hubbard's low price for the dolphinarium.

When they discover a squatter, a young waif named Lucy who used to work with the dolphins, Hubbard is even more disturbed. He clearly thinks the place is haunted by the ghost of Buddyboy and Lucy only seems to reinforce his fears.

Dave is rather taken with Lucy, and becomes a little more interested in her stories of Buddyboy, and especially her theory of what actually happened to him. Hubbard's claim of a spiteful suicide doesn't mesh with Lucy's understanding of the dolphin. Hubbard has already alluded to needing to show him who was boss. Lucy believes that Buddyboy was lured out of the water by the cruel man and kept there overnight, where simple gravity and the weight of the dolphin's body would have done Hubbard's dirty work for him, crushing Buddyboy's lungs.

It's a horrific thought, even more horrific than the idea of dolphins trapped in such an awful place as *Finnyland*. Lucy is distraught at the idea. She misses her dolphin friend terribly and she launches into the introduction to an imaginary show while Dave watches, bemused. When she climbs the ladder out over the empty pool and calls to Buddyboy, however, Dave's confusion turns to fear as he hears the unmistakable clicks and squeals of a dolphin.

It's at this point that Lucy becomes something else, in more ways than

We Are The Martians

one. While Dave's initial reaction is one of terror, he soon decides that Lucy simply made the dolphin noises herself. He feels inexplicably protective and affectionate towards her and takes her under his wing, moving into Hubbard's glitzy sleaze palace of a flat with her. There he is safely back on his own turf. Soon he's promising to make her a star. In porn, naturally. It's clearly all he knows. And however much he might actually like the poor girl, it's ultimately only the passing fascination of someone who likes shiny new things. Once they become tarnished, they can be discarded. Lucy is sweet and innocent and Dave quickly sets about corrupting his latest conquest.

"It's funny," he tells her, "how you can make use of a thing and not know how it works. That's what I did with you."

It's also exactly what Hubbard did with Buddyboy. Both men are incapable of seeing the similarities between their methods—and their victims. Dave claims his prize and rips Lucy's clothes off, taking her to bed. While he enjoys himself, Lucy lies there thinking of Buddyboy, her expression mournful. In her mind she sees herself turning from the empty pool and walking away. She clings to Dave and says she wants him to love her. But all he can offer her is a future in porn, because she's "much too good to keep private". Lucy's happy expression fades and she wanders off while Dave brainstorms names for his new club. After she fails to respond to him, he goes into the bathroom, where he finds her drowned in the immense tub. He stares at her body in horror, hearing the squeals of a dolphin.

Now, I don't want to go too far with metaphors and symbolic readings of what is ultimately just a little is-it-a-ghost-or-isn't-it? story, but this is Nigel Kneale we're talking about here. So it's hard for me not to read a bit more into all of this. Certainly Hubbard's comments about Buddyboy echo similar sentiments expressed towards women in less enlightened times and places. The parallels between animal rights and women's rights are hard to ignore.

Lucy clearly has an affinity with the dolphin, who was exploited just as Dave exploits the women in his porn palace. I think that when Lucy calls to him during her fevered performance for Dave in the dolphinarium, Buddyboy answers and his spirit enters her so they can be together again.

446

Lucy naively thinks she can find happiness with Dave, but, like the poor dolphin who probably trusted all humans in the beginning, she ultimately finds herself betrayed and facing a similar prison of exploitation and abuse. Buddyboy calls to her one last time, luring her into the water as he himself was lured out of the water. It's a bittersweet ending. Now they can be together forever and Lucy will never face the inevitable cruelty and pain of the life Dave envisions for her, the 'thing' he knows how to use.

Like Mrs Clemson, Lucy is left a mystery for the viewer to solve. Was she really possessed by the spirit of Buddyboy? Or did she just miss him so much that she couldn't go on without him? Either way, she is a fascinating character, the fey waif who is more than she seems. And even if she is a victim, she, like Buddyboy, has "a very definite personality" and hidden depths of her own. She quite literally refuses her tricks.

But before BEASTS there was 1972's THE STONE TAPE, my personal favourite Kneale story. And Jill Greeley (Jane Asher) is arguably his best female character. She not only has the central role; she is, in effect, the scientist of the piece. I like the description of her in the script:

We Are The Martians

"There is a very feminine, strong directness about her, so that what she is seems far more important than what she does."

What she does is work as a computer programmer, and she is at least the equal of her male colleagues. And like Barbara Judd, she is more sensitive to the occult than they are. In the opening scene, we see her strongly affected by the atmosphere of Taskerlands as she narrowly avoids a crash, presumably an attempt by the malevolent forces to keep her out. Once inside, she is the first to experience the haunting of the end room.

The others can't write her off as an overwrought female, however, because soon everyone hears and sees the ghost of the unfortunate maid at the top of the stairs. Even so, Peter Brock, the head of the research team, tries to belittle Jill when she becomes upset by the disturbing event. It's clear they have some personal history and he feels he has the right to talk down to her, as though his authority extends to their private life. "Oh, my Jilly," he tells her, "you're a very female one."

And she is—but she's a very Kneale female. She handles the other-worldly experiences better than the men do. She prophetically realises the true horror of the poor maid's fate: "It's just the thought of it. That there being nothing left of you but just enough to repeat the worst moment of your life, over and over again." She can't believe the stone is only a "dead mechanism" and she is certain there is more going on than Peter wants to accept. He's quite happy to pat her on the head and give her some credit, however, once he believes she has discovered the new recording medium they were after.

It's obvious that Peter feels threatened by Jill. She's the key player, the one who sees things clearly, the one who is really running the show. She's empathic and compassionate without ever being weak. She has a telling exchange with Collinson, who has to leave the haunted room because he "just can't take a woman's screams". Jill affectionately teases him, calling him soft-hearted. "A living person in that pain," he says, "you can try to help them. Here—you can't." He behaves in a protective and fatherly manner towards her, but never patronises her the way Peter does.

Peter is a typical Kneale man, by turns shouty and sulky. In fact, he's a lot like Roger in "During Barty's Party", pigheaded and insistent that he can bully nature into doing what he wants. He pushes the team so hard that several of the men crack under the pressure. And when he realises he has effectively 'wiped' the stone tape, rather than acknowledge his failure or try to fix the situation, he throws his toys out of the pram. He refuses to listen to Jill when she tries to tell him what she's discovered. When ordering her to stop doesn't work, he resorts to insults. He accuses her of trying to destroy him, as if her motive for trying to solve the mystery is all about him.

Now properly obsessed, Jill continues on her own, bashing away at her computer all night until she comes to the terrifying realisation of what is actually going on. The tragedy and horror of her subsequent fate is all the more effective for her strength of personality. But even then, Peter won't give her the respect she deserves. He denounces her mental state and orders all her work to be destroyed, as though trying to 'wipe' her too. He gets his comeuppance, though, when he returns to the haunted room and hears Jill's endless screams, proving she was right all along.

All of these women are 'victims' in some sense, but they are still strong, believable characters. They drive the stories they're a part of. You won't

WE ARE THE MARTIANS

find any scantily clad hotties wielding swords in a Nigel Kneale story, and that isn't just because of the period in which he was writing. "All stories," he said, "should have some honesty and truth in them, otherwise you're just playing about."

Kneale's women have their own strength and their own powers, coupled with a natural affinity with the unexplained and unexplainable. He puts a unique spin on the concept of 'women's intuition'. His female characters seem predisposed both to sense and accept the uncanny while the males are often practical, rational or scientific to a fault.

It's also interesting to note that, while he is generally sympathetic to his female characters, he can be very unflattering with his male ones. They're often either close-minded and bullying or weak and ineffectual. Perhaps he simply enjoyed writing about women more than men. Or perhaps he understood that female characters could be just as interesting as male ones, if not more so, and just as important to the plot.

We can't ask Kneale that troublesome question Joss Whedon keeps having to answer, but we can guess what his response would be.

CREEPING UNKNOWN PT 3:

"Sharpe's Gold" & "Ancient History"

Kim Newman

"SHARPE'S GOLD" (1995)

"THE MIND'S A VERY FUNNY THING. I HAD AN UNCLE ONCE, who thought the fairies were after him?" "What happened to him?" "They got him."

IMDb comments from Bernard Cornwell/Sharpe fans rate this as the worst of the TV movies adapted from Cornwell's novels—though Andy Murray, in his Kneale biography, says it's "more interesting" than the conventional derring-do in the others. Kneale said he threw away most of the book—perhaps because the novel SHARPE'S GOLD had already been partially used up in earlier films so he was forced to come up with his own story. Tom Clegg does a decent job of directing and Sean Bean is a craggy, compelling hero—but a kind of ITV blandness makes this far less gripping and pointed than **H.M.S. DEFIANT**, a Kneale-scripted historical drama with a similar background (albeit in the navy rather than the army) but a much more challenging subject.

It's a bitty episode in the hero's career, set in the last days of Wellington's peninsula campaign, and Kneale hops from one plot thread to the next as

WE ARE THE MARTIANS

if he were running together several episode ideas. Early on, it seems to be about the clash between gruff Yorkshire soldier Major Sharpe (Sean Bean) and a posh ponce lieutenant (Ian Shaw) of the Provosts (military police) and focuses on military discipline with looters and deserters...then Wellington's cousin Bess (Rosaleen Linehan) and her daughter Ellie (Jayne Ashbourne), a potential love interest, show up in search of a missing husband/father (Peter Eyre), who's mapmaking in the hills, and—after a shooting contest with Ellie which he gallantly tries to lose—Sharpe winds up stuck with the ladies as he takes a consignment of guns to be exchanged for British deserters captured by Spanish guerillas.

It takes a turn into the weird when it's revealed that El Casco (Abel Folk), the cuirassed guerila leader, is one of a band descended from shipwrecked Aztecs and practicing heart-ripping human sacrifice. The climax, in which Sharpe saves Ellie from the ritual knife, is very like the finish of Kneale's script for **THE WITCHES**. Sharpe is a Quatermass-like character, clashing with established order and commanding the loyalty of subordinates...as in most of the Quatermass stories, it's the hero's sidekick (Daragh O'Malley) who actually saves the day. Hugh Ross is good as Wellington and there are lots of mucky-faced, strangle-accented, bad-teeth lower rankers.

"ANCIENT HISTORY" (1997)

Nigel Kneale's final produced work was this effective episode of KAVANAGH QC, a vehicle for a post-Morse John Thaw created by Ted Childs and Susan Rogers which ran for six seasons of issue-based courtroom drama with ongoing family/workplace soap elements. Kneale skimps a little on the continuing characters and the comic sub-plots (not much room for that in a holocaust story) that were a feature of the series, though it is interesting to note that Kavanagh shares a few things with Kneale himself (including a son called Matthew) and even has one of those K-Q character names which recur in Kneale's work and subliminally make many of his protagonists semi-stand-ins for the writer.

This is the only Kneale script which mentions the internet...as Kavanagh has his son look up Holocaust history (and Holocaust denial)

Creeping Unknown PT 3

sites. The formula of the show works against ambiguity—whether prosecuting or defending, Kavanagh is always in the right, which means that the outcome of the story is seldom in doubt (he does sometimes lose, but he tends to be on the side of the righteous). When Kavanagh conducts a war crimes prosecution against a retired GP, Alexander Beck (Frederick Treves), who claims he was a prisoner at Dachau but is accused by an array of now-elderly victims of running inhumane freezing experiments, it's plain from the outset that Beck will turn out to be guilty...and Treves has a nice moment at the end, when exposed, as he shows a still-fierce pride in the ground-breaking research into the nature of death.

Other characters have to be sketched, but there's good work from Anna Cropper as Beck's devoted if obviously dim wife, Peter Firth as his businessman son, and Charles Simon (still on his deathbed eleven years after THE SINGING DETECTIVE—he lasted til 2002), Warren Mitchell (laying on the *kaddish* a bit thick) and Jonathan Adams (who admits that the villain could make people like him) as the witnesses, with Sara Kestelman in old age make-up as a last minute witness who is supposed to exonerate Beck (she says he saved her life) but actually confirms his guilt (he killed her and revived her). The best moment in the piece comes as Kavanagh realises this won't turn out the way smug defence counsel (pre-stardom Bill Nighy) expects as he interprets the old woman's grin with "she isn't smiling".

The case is presumably based on the real-life story that inspired Leon Uris's QB VIII, which was about a libel trial but also featured a concentration camp doctor who had lived a long useful post-war life as a medical practitioner; in that book (also an early US TV miniseries), a doctor sued an author for libel when he mentioned his concentration camp work in a novel, so there was a more audience-friendly situation of the good guy being in the dock and the villain persecuting him with the law seemingly on his side until the verdict (the real case involved Uris and a Polish GP called Wladyslaw Dering, who was awarded a contemptuous halfpenny damages).

ON WISHING FOR A
NIGEL KNEALE CHILDHOOD

Lynda E. Rucker

THE QUINTESSENTIALLY BRITISH NIGEL KNEALE WASN'T A PART of my American childhood, but I sure wish he had been. The odd thing is, it feels like he was. The psychic geography of much of his storytelling maps my own obsessions.

Like many American children, my childhood was at least as steeped in British fantasy as in its American counterpart. For many of us, thanks to writers like Susan Cooper and John Gordon and Lucy M. Boston and Joan Aiken—and the American writer Lloyd Alexander, who rooted his Prydain stories in Welsh myth—the landscapes of England and Wales became fantasy lands every bit as potent as Narnia or Wonderland, just as inaccessible and heaving with magic as those places. It is surely one reason so many Americans romanticise Britain, just as an Irish friend tells me that American television from the 1970s and 1980s was endlessly fascinating for a boy growing up in the Dublin of the time: the cars and freeways and sunshine and seeming availability of *everything* in shows like CHiPS and the DUKES OF HAZZARD promised their own fantasies of infinite freedom and ease and modernity that seemed just as impossible and wondrous to him as the idea of contemporary people living alongside the remnants of ancient Britain like the green man and standing stones and ancient manuscripts and the last resting place of the Holy Grail did to me.

In America, it felt like our television and movies were all about the new and the now: there were no ghosts or fantasies or ancient curses to be found in our sunny suburban American homes—Steven Spielberg's **POLTERGIEST** notwithstanding—but in dank English houses, and on gloomy roads like those traversed by the young veterinarian Alan Crich (David Simeon) in the opening of "Murrain". As Crich makes his way into the isolated and inhospitable northern English village, the sky looks like it's bearing down on him and the hedges and stone walls closing in, just as the paranoia and delusions—or are they?—of the villagers will soon close in on him as well, trapping him and Mrs. Clemson (Una Brandon-Jones) in their collective madness. The colours are muted. The fields are green but the trees are broken and bare. There is a chill about the place both literal and metaphorical: suspicion of outsiders, and worse, educated outsiders, runs deep.

Even as an adult, watching this opening scene, I feel a sense of frisson — *yes, certainly there* must *be witches here* —that is rooted in those childhood impressions. I think such imaginative attachments to places formed at a young age, entirely separate from how those places measure up in reality, create for us a strange sense of familiarity, of home, however alien those places may actually be. Something similar must occur sometimes in immigrant families where children grow up steeped in stories from a culture and a time and place that is no more (and perhaps never was) for the simple reasons that time marches on and memory tells lies. It means that signifiers will be off-kilter as well: I can see the opening of "Murrain" now through a dual set of perceptions. The adult me notes the grimness of the setting, the ignorance, the poverty, while at the same time I can imagine how I'd have viewed it as a child. The setting would have had a strange uncanny beauty. The sense of isolation would have been enchanting as would the suggestion that the old ways are still very much a reality here. The rural England of my childhood imagination, nursed by English writers, exists simultaneously with the real place that I know, and however odd it may seem, creates almost no sense of dissonance for me.

It is stories like "Murrain" and "Baby" and even, to some extent, **THE**

On Wishing for a Nigel Kneale Childhood

WITCHES (which some might argue should not even be properly discussed as a Kneale work, but for several reasons I feel it should be touched upon here), stories that draw on a sense of English village traditions and the rural landscape, folk horror, and paganism that embody one aspect of what attracts me to Kneale. The other aspect is his marriage of science with the paranormal found in works like THE STONE TAPE and QUATERMASS AND THE PIT. Such stories hearken back to a type of "nonfiction" book I loved as a child, compilations of alleged supernatural and paranormal events that often came accompanied by some crackpot pseudo-scientific explanation that I found absolutely thrilling. It was the scientific overlay of such stories that tipped me over into a state of awe: *surely* that meant that these stories could be true! Long before THE X-FILES made it a catch phrase, I desperately wanted to believe.

I don't know what effect Nigel Kneale had on British television in the decades that followed his work, although I know it was significant. I didn't become a writer because of Kneale; his work was not an integral part of my early imagination because I didn't know that he existed. Yet he joins other work that I only encountered as an adult—along with things like the fiction of Alan Garner and the film **THE WICKERMAN**—that I almost feel I remember having read or watched as a child. In the same way that you occasionally meet a new person that you connect with so powerfully and quickly that you feel that you've known them for years in a matter of hours or days, newfound art sometimes strikes an old chord, feels more like a recognition than an introduction.

Like many Americans, I eventually found my way to Kneale by way of the Quatermass films. I was already in my twenties by then though and although I imagined I'd have enjoyed them as a child, it was THE STONE TAPE some years later that first gave me that sense of watching my favourite childhood film that never was .

It was Sunday afternoon of the H.P. Lovecraft Film Festival in Portland, Oregon. I don't remember the year; it would have been sometime around 2002. I was tired and a little grouchy as I always am on the final days of these types of events, overstimulated and weary but not really wanting the weekend to end either. I don't remember exactly, but I'm pretty sure it was listed as a 'secret screening' that I slumped into that afternoon; at any rate,

I had no idea what was on the bill, and as it began, I was none the wiser. I knew who Nigel Kneale was but I didn't know until the credits rolled that this would be a feature by him, and I'd never heard of THE STONE TAPE.

It's so rare, these days, to come upon something utterly without knowledge of or preparation for what we are going to see. Most of the time, we experience so much about a movie or a television show before we actually sit down to watch it. We've seen trailers; we've read interviews with the stars and the director and the creator. We've seen stills and talked about it with our friends. We go in primed for the experience we are about to have.

There is a wonderful purity about simply stumbling across something with no foreknowledge of it at all, and this is how I came to THE STONE TAPE. For the next ninety minutes, I was transfixed.

This is the story of a team of researchers who are in search of a new recording medium. After moving to a new recording facility in a Victorian mansion, the researchers learn that work was stopped on one room due to builders' reports that it was haunted. They find that the foundations of the

On Wishing for a Nigel Kneale Childhood

building date to Saxon times, and then the team's computer programmer, Jill (Jane Asher), sees the figure of a Victorian maid screaming.

Eventually, the team realises that the stone acts as a kind of recorder with humans as the device for transmission. This is the discovery they need to compete with their Japanese rivals, but in attempting to study the phenomenon, they accidentally "erase" the recording—only to realise that it was only the most recent, and the structure is built upon stones that hold the echoes of an ancient force of evil.

THE STONE TAPE is Kneale's most effective marriage of science with the idea of places that are haunted by atavistic, malevolent forces. It is that dedication to playing it straight that makes a final scene that might have been laughable in less committed hands into one that is both harrowing and evokes the ineffable: as Jill is desperately climbing the Victorian-era stairs in an effort to escape this ancient evil, represented by a green glowing light, she is suddenly clambering across a much older landscape of stone thrust up through a young and very different earth. The production values here are not amazing. This ought not to work. It does. Oh, how it works.

There's also an interesting battle-of-the-sexes thread running throughout THE STONE TAPE that emerges as well in some other works including "Baby" and "Special Offer" (discussed elsewhere in this book) in which women are in touch with the seemingly irrational while men remain oblivious to it. Inasmuch as the logical man and intuitive woman may simply reinforce traditional stereotypes, there is an interesting dichotomy in that each of the three initially portray the women as unstable to varying degrees—and they are certainly considered to be so by the male main character in each story—when in fact they are the only ones who understand the situation for what it is. In fact, the entire research team, with the exception of Jill, is notably incurious and lacking in any sense of the potential profundity of their discovery beyond how much money they can make off it.

The pursuit of science devoid of humanity is taken to task as well; Jill has been engaged in an unsatisfying affair with the unpleasant Brock, who alternates between praising and attacking her, accusing her of trying to lure him away from his family although we see absolutely no evidence of

WE ARE THE MARTIANS

such behaviour, and in a particularly cruel moment tells her, "Oh, my Jilly. You're a female one," managing to make "female" sound like an insult. In the end, THE STONE TAPE also becomes a morality tale as well, with Brock forced to live the rest of his life with the resonance of his mistreated lover's final, despairing screams ringing in his ears.

I was so taken with THE STONE TAPE on that initial viewing that I—ever a skeptic and a rationalist—walked out of the cinema asking myself *but do you think stone could record things? And what if it did? And what if...? And if...?* This is one of Kneale's great strengths, that he makes the irrational seem plausible, even likely.

I watched **QUATERMASS AND THE PIT** years before I saw THE STONE TAPE, but after seeing that film, **QUATERMASS AND THE PIT** (pulpily retitled FIVE MILLION YEARS TO EARTH in the U.S., a title I confess I have always loved) took on a different resonance for me as I began to understand its preoccupations as quintessentially Kneale. "I suppose it's possible for ghosts, let's use the word, to be phenomena that were badly observed and wrongly explained," Quatermass muses, and this is at the heart of so much of Kneale's work. In this film, Kneale sets out to use science to explain no less a being than Satan himself.

I find the central conceit of this film irresistible: that humanity was enhanced by a race of Martians that resembled our conception of the devil (shades of Arthur C. Clarke's CHILDHOOD'S END), and that along with that image, the madness and violence that resulted in the Martians eventually exterminating themselves in a vicious planet-wide war is embedded in us as well. Quatermass also ruminates on the origins of all supernatural phenomena: "Poltergeist outbreaks, second sight, they've been reported the world over throughout the ages—myths, magic, even witchcraft. Perhaps they all came from there?" Once again, supernatural phenomena is explained through science—a wonky, Fortean science, to be sure, but within the world of the story at least, via a rational method-ology. How I longed for that kind of proof of the supernatural when I was a child!

Yet there are a few reasons that my initial viewing of **QUATERMASS AND THE PIT** along with the two earlier Quatermass films did not have the same effect on me as THE STONE TAPE. At its heart, QUATER-

On Wishing for a Nigel Kneale Childhood

MASS AND THE PIT is very much about a world of men: the older, grandfatherly scientist who is accustomed to being called in to save the day at its core, the marching in of the military and government officials, the world-shattering scope of the discovery are all in contrast to THE STONE TAPE, a much more intimate tale which has ordinary people — including a woman! — as its main protagonists and a ghost story at its centre. For me, in the end, the unknowable evil, the small scale storytelling and the triumph of the supernatural at the heart of THE STONE TAPE will always prevail over the science fiction horrors of Quatermass for no better reason than because it is what I like best.

It should be noted, however, that although she is not the central character that Jill is in THE STONE TAPE, once again, a woman proves to be a conduit to the paranormal — and in this case, Barbara proves herself to possess a mental resiliency lacking in the two men who preceded her. Eventually all of humanity, including Quatermass himself, are nearly consumed by the madness that is the remnant of our Martian origins.

In "Murrain", Kneale would again put rationality to the test, and would come up with perhaps his most subtle and ambiguous exploration of the tension between science and the supernatural. This episode from the anthology series AGAINST THE CROWD is the story of a man's loss of faith, and in this story, I am that man. As much as I love the supernatural in my fiction, I have little patience in real-life for belief in it. It isn't that I don't still want to believe — I do — but more than that, I think such beliefs are anything but harmless but do active injury to us, individually and collectively — as we see in "Murrain". Or do we?

So, I am Alan Crich, the skeptical veterinarian, believer in science, warts and all — we Criches see ourselves as modern and thoughtful and rational, but maybe, just maybe, we are a little bit contemptuous, a little bit judgmental, a little bit self-righteous. Not to put too fine a point on it: nobody likes a Crich. And yet wisely, neither Kneale's writing of Crich nor David Simeon's portrayal of the character are that of an unlikeable man. That would make it too easy, and "Murrain" isn't interested in making it easy for us. Crich *is* an outsider, a do-gooder, an I-know-better-than-you-er. He's a bumbling well-meaner who sticks his nose into affairs he knows nothing about and tries to make them better. And yet who among us

would not act precisely as he does here, shocked that no doctor has been back to see the sick boy, bringing the groceries to Mrs. Clemson? Who can blame him for being openly furious at the mistreatment of a sick little boy and a helpless old woman? And Mrs. Clemson's appreciation is so touching. "Lovely things," she says in wonderment, she who has been denied even access to running water by the rest of the village. This village may be stuck in time, but Crich is not.

"Murrain" is an archaic word for a pestilence or plague, and seems straightforward enough a title for a story that opens with farm animals dying of a plague. As the story progresses, however, the source of the true pestilence destroying the village becomes less clear. The fabric of this village is under threat less from a disease killing pigs than from ignorance. We are still in a rational world at this stage, and this impression is only reinforced as we meet the pathetic Mrs. Clemson for the first time, shortly after the villagers attempt to persuade Crich to play a cruel prank on her. Not a prank to them, of course—a deadly serious attempt to cut out the evil at the heart of their village. By the end of the piece, the choice of an

On Wishing for a Nigel Kneale Childhood

archaic word for the title has taken on a different resonance; this village is as outside of time as the word itself.

Mrs. Clemson *seems* like such an innocent victim of small-minded, small-town ignorance. From Crich's point of view, which we share as viewers, it's hard to sympathise with people who ostracise a helpless old woman, cut her cat in two and even attempt to deny her access to food and water. This is the madness of crowds. This is a contemporary version of THE CRUCIBLE. Crich invokes the modern world and we sigh with relief: he will be in touch with social services. He will make things right. Like us, Crich has entered in the middle of the story. We don't know why Mrs. Clemson is the way she is, whether she or the villagers set the cycle of antagonism in motion. We think we don't need to. We think we know best.

In the last few minutes of the story, Crich's rationality begins to falter. "Hysteria! Suggestion!" he insists at the sight of the sick mother who handled Mrs. Clemson's money. He seems unwilling to consider any other explanation, and yet why should he? What other explanation can there possibly be? And there *are* such things as somatic disorders; people do experience physical symptoms as a result of mental illness. Yet his explanations seem increasingly knee-jerk, as though he has abandoned science as a rational way of explaining the world and is now merely clinging to it in the same way the villagers cling to their superstition.

And then, in the final moments, everything changes. Science is not the force here that it has been in the previous two pieces; here it has inhibited rather than revealing the truth, or has it? The story balances on a perfect knife-edge of ambiguity. The question we ask ourselves at the end of this piece is not 'Was it real?' but what it is that we believe. "Murrain" is very much a fable about how we interpret the world, and it is told with such skill and precision that there are easily two stories in one here, one about how a village and eventually an outsider as well are gripped by an ancient hysteria, the other about witchcraft as an actual malevolent force in the modern world.

"Murrain" gives us signals in the first act that all may be not as Crich believes: the cattle are suffering from a disease they cannot diagnose and Mr. Beeley's water supply has inexplicably dried up. However, if there is a single moment in the piece that might tip the balance for us, the viewers, it is the look upon Crich's face in the final frames. He has just finished explaining away the final, shocking incident in the film, almost reflexively, and then the moment stretches, and a mixture of doubt and disbelief steal across his face. He exchanges a look with Mrs. Clemson—and it is clear that whatever has unfolded from an objective standpoint, she certainly believes herself to be a witch just as certainly as the villagers do. Crich has been deceived by everyone, but the villagers, at least, have been as honest with him as they can be. His entire body language changes; he slumps, and staggers back up the path and out of the frame.

This village—these old stone buildings, this grey sky, these farmers farming, this is a place where witchcraft might flourish. These modern clothes are just trappings. This might be the same village two hundred, five hundred, eight hundred years ago. Here, it is science that is ephemeral. This land is old; this conflict is ancient; and it will keep playing out whether we Criches of the world survive or not.

Kneale explored more rural horrors with "Baby" from the six-episode

On Wishing for a Nigel Kneale Childhood

series BEASTS. "Baby" opens with two foreboding incidents that we do not recognise as such until later: an abandoned bird's nest, its eggs rotten rather than hatched is discovered, and a terrified cat runs away. The natural world reacts instinctively to the wrongness at the heart of the cottage that a young city veterinarian and his pregnant wife have just moved into. Jo (Jane Wymark) is the first human to notice something is wrong, first in her observation that the cottage is what frightened the cat, and then in her own growing unease.

"Baby" would have been one of those horror anthology episodes I would have fallen in love with as a child. It has all the right elements: a young female protagonist at its centre, a rural English setting, folk magic, old evils, its grounding in realism, and its subtle, understated sense of growing horror and bleak denouement.

The central conceit of "Baby" is that in the walls of the old cottage, the couple finds an urn containing a strange creature, one none of them can identify, and they attempt to do so alternately as perhaps a cat, a lamb, a pig, and a monkey. Successfully building that sense of growing menace is all about choosing the right details, what Ramsey Campbell once called, in reference to M.R. James, a "gradual accretion of details." When Peter, the husband, first pulls the decaying thing from the urn, it's the phrase he uses that chills: "I'm not sure it was ever actually born."

It's this careful choice of words in Kneale's script—not that it is a fetus, for example, or even that it is unborn but *not… actually born* that makes it seem weird and unearthly and wrong. Later, and worse, another character tells us that a human would have suckled it. When I was a child, I watched **THE OMEN** with my mother, and at the moment that Father Brennan says, "His mother was a jackal," I missed the final word and asked my mother what he said. When she told me, I was so horrified I couldn't reply. Peter's words here and the imagery of the beast suckled by a human, reminds me of that moment, of an unnatural communion between animal and human that speaks of something dark.

Then, later still, we are introduced to the concept of contagious abortion: as with "Murrain", another disease of farm animals ostensibly making the leap to humans, and once again, the scientists—the veterinarians—dismiss Jo's concerns. Like Crich, they fall back on science as a dogma, and she calls them out on it: "A germ—a germ! But you don't know! Put a bit of Latin on it!" In Kneale's world, there are two types of science and rationality: one which is as dogmatic as religion and one which is open to possibility, and the first type of rationalists are always doomed.

All the same, Kneale's own affinity for exploring rural folk magic was overcome by his rationality when he approached the script for **THE WITCHES**. It's a shame, really, because this is another favourite of mine, marred by a campy, ludicrous finish. Kneale reportedly couldn't take the idea of a coven of modern-day witches seriously and wanted the screenplay to be more comic. That ending, along with the unfortunate stereotypical portrayal of African 'tribal magic' and 'witch doctors' (Joan Fontaine, as Gwen Mayfield, portrays a teacher in rural Africa who had a breakdown following a 'tribal rebellion'), detract from what is otherwise an underrated and understated film of a quiet English village where all is not as typical as it seems.

I read the Norah Lofts novel from which it was adapted as a teenager though I didn't know it had been made into a film and at any rate if I had at the time it would not have been available to me; it wasn't until years later that I saw the movie (prior to THE STONE TAPE, and I didn't know for several more years that Kneale had written it). There are so many elements of this that I love: we have another female protagonist at its centre, a rural setting, and witchcraft—one of my favourite horror tropes—plus a slow burner of a story that builds its menace gradually. Unfortunately, even though it seems on the surface tailor-made for a Kneale adaptation, ultimately he and the material were not the best match. Worse, Fontaine had acquired the rights to the book and brought it to Hammer, so her final major film role and one in which she was clearly invested (not just literally) ended up a somewhat uneven affair. A part of me wishes that someone other than Kneale had penned this screenplay, and yet the parts that are good are so very good—might we have lost that with someone else on writing duties?

THE WITCHES divides audiences, with some people arguing it's ludicrously bad from start to finish. Obviously, I disagree, but it is inarguably compromised. Still it has all the elements I love best from Kneale's other work—save for his utter sincerity, and that makes all the difference. I can't

On Wishing for a Nigel Kneale Childhood

help wondering why he was able to approach equally far-fetched concepts at the heart of his other works seriously and not this, and I suspect it might be ultimately a question of tone. Despite one character who claims to see belief in witchcraft as a psychological problem rather than a supernatural one, **THE WITCHES** lacks the underpinning of rationality that can be found in Kneale's other scripts as well as the contemporary realism that anchors so much of his 1970s work such as "Murrain", BEASTS and THE STONE TAPE. Although it was made in only the previous decade, the setting feels like another era entirely.

As a writer of horror fiction, I have often pondered, why we are drawn to the things we are. For myself, for example, I cannot remember a time when I was not attracted to gothic and supernatural imagery and, as soon as I was old enough to read them on my own, by the age of seven, stories in this vein. Certain types of stories attract us as children, and—for those of us inclined to seek out stories at all—we seek out more in that vein. It becomes a bit of an ouroboros, this work of teasing out the influence from some innate affinity, for that affinity then grows and we continue to feed it and so on.

I am less enamoured than many of my generation of the reification of my own childhood and juvenilia, yet my own affinities in the present are undeniably grounded in that childhood. For a long time I didn't have the vocabulary to talk about what some of those affinities were: it was more a *feeling* I got, one I wouldn't have been able to describe any better than with general words like *longing* and *awe* and *melancholy* and *wonder*.

It is those same feelings I get from Kneale, that I so often get from story-telling that I love best. He wrote about many different things, but these are the ones that speak to me: old evils, and how they clash with science, about the tension between science and magic, about old beliefs, about the origins of things, about how little we differ from our forebears although we believe the opposite, about the ancient and primordial forces that move us—the supernatural ones and the nonsupernatural ones. About the power of *places—and* if there is any supernatural idea that tempts me the most, it is perhaps this one: that, as we learned from THE STONE TAPE,

WE ARE THE MARTIANS

places encode strong emotions, places remember us, places are haunted, not perhaps by ghosts but by some essence that living beings can leave behind.

Wishing for a Nigel Kneale childhood? I think I had one—without knowing it.

One of the most satisfying aspects of creating stories is when others tell us that the story connected with them in some way—that it expressed something or moved them in a way that was meaningful. And this is one of the reasons that some of us feel so passionate about the creators that we love—and so disappointed when they fail to live up to the ideals that we impose upon them. It's because they express things that we feel and do not have the words to say. It's not even necessarily in what they express outright; it is the feeling they evoke with their stories, the ones that make us want to go up to them and say *you, too?*, (but we don't, because we are not stalkers), that makes us feel we *know* them in some intimate way when of course we do not, or perhaps we do? Do we not know some part of them, really?

So Kneale evokes that recognition in me: and this is also why it feels like he is part of that bedrock of stories that made me into the person and the writer I am today even when he was not. Science increasingly finds that our memories are utterly unreliable anyway, perhaps no better than (or just as good as) a book of stories at getting at the truth. As L.P. Hartley told us, "the past is a foreign country". The past, moreover, does not even exist just as the future does not, only the present moment, and so Kneale might as well be a part of that childhood, that wild untamed region of the imagination from which terrors and fantasies and stories emerge. Perhaps childhood is even the wrong word; it is that expanse of amoral Blakean innocence from which a myriad of influences unconsciously steer us all, writers and creators or not. It was a country Kneale understood well, and what he knew also was that we could, as Jo cried, put a name on it—a bit of Latin even—but it remains essentially unknowable, even with the tools of science at our disposal, and leaves us in its thrall.

CONTRIBUTORS

STEPHEN R. BISSETTE is a writer, film critic, comics artist, publisher and teacher. Justly celebrated for his groundbreaking work with Alan Moore and Rick Veitch on DC's SWAMP THING, he broke boundaries in comics storytelling as a publisher with TABOO, and with his classic dino story TYRANT. His film writing has appeared in *Deep Red, Gorezone, Video Watchdog Magazine, Monster!* and others. He has also provided artwork and essays for the Arrow Film And Video BluRay releases of Wes Craven's **THE PEOPLE UNDER THE STAIRS** and Jack Hill's **SPIDER BABY**. His book length study of David Cronenberg's **THE BROOD** is available as part of the 'Midnight Movie Monographs' series from Electric Dreamhouse Press and PS Publishing. He is currently at work on a follow up book about **CARNIVAL OF SOULS**.

RAMSEY CAMPBELL. *"Campbell is literature in a field which has attracted too many comic-book intellects, cool in a field where too many writers—myself included--tend toward painting melodrama. Good horror writers are quite rare, and Campbell is better than just good."* So says Stephen King, and who am I to argue? Campbell is a beacon on the landscape of horror, drawing lost souls toward it, and pointing the way ahead. We all aspire to be Ramsey. Perhaps less known, however, is his expertise as a film critic. A service he provided for BBC Radio Merseyside, and which continues in his essential 'Ramsey's Rambles' column for *Video Watchdog Magazine*.

WE ARE THE MARTIANS

MARK CHADBOURN is former journalist, turned novelist and screen-writer, Mark Chadbourn is perhaps best known for his AGE OF MISRULE trilogy. An expert on British folklore, he has twice won the British Fantasy Award for short fiction, and been shortlisted for the August Derleth award for Best Novel no less than five times.

JOE DANTE is the director of **PIRANHA, THE HOWLING,** 'The Good Life' episode of **TWILIGHT ZONE: THE MOVIE, GREMLINS, EXPLORERS, INNERSPACE, THE BURBS, GREMLINS 2,** EERIE INDIANA, **MATINEE, THE SECOND CIVIL WAR, SMALL SOLDIERS, LOONEY TUNES BACK IN ACTION,** stand out episodes of MASTERS OF HORROR 'Homecoming' and 'The Screwfly Solution', and one of the best 3D movies to date **THE HOLE,** Joe Dante is one of the most subversive and satirical directors ever to work in Hollywood. Equal parts Preston Sturges, Gahan Wilson, Harvey Kurtzman, Frank Tashlin and James Whale, his films effervesce with ideas, imagination and witty visual gags. He is also the founder and curator of TRAILERS FROM HELL, where he and other movie makers share their love of cinema, via great trailers and personal commentaries.

JEREMY DYSON is an author, screenwriter, playwright, and the least visible member of THE LEAGUE OF GENTLEMEN (in that he is not an actor), Jeremy is also the author of BRIGHT DARKNESS: THE LOST ART OF THE SUPERNATURAL HORROR FILM. His short story collection THE CRANES THAT BUILT THE CRANES won the 2010 Edge Hill Award, while his play GHOST STORIES (written with Andy Nyman) broke box office records at the Everyman Liverpool and the Lyric Hammersmith. Currently writing a new take on Quatermass for Red Productions, he can also be seen playing keyboards for the band, Rudolph Rocker.

TONY EARNSHAW is a Partner in Reel Solutions, working on an array of UK film festivals. Film critic for the Yorkshire Post and BBC Radio Leeds, he is also the author of BEATING THE DEVIL: THE MAKING OF NIGHT OF THE DEMON, MADE IN YORKSHIRE, THE CHRISTMAS

470

Contributors

GHOST STORIES OF LAWRENCE GORDON CLARKE, STUDIES IN THE HORROR FILM: TOBE HOOPER'S SALEM'S LOT, and UNDER MILK WOOD REVISTED: THE WALES OF DYLAN THOMAS as well as monographs on Eric Portman, Peter Cushing and Stanley Baker.

MARK GATISS is an actor, comedian, screenwriter, novelist and director, who made his name as one of THE LEAGUE OF GENTLEMEN, before writing and appearing in the regenerated DOCTOR WHO upon its return in 2005, for which he has continued as a regular contributor. His prodigious output includes far too many credits for radio, stage and screen to possibly mention here, but the documentaries A HISTORY OF HORROR, HORROR EUROPA and M.R. JAMES: GHOST WRITER are of particular note as examples of Mark's passion and erudition on the subject of Horror on the screen and on the page. As a novelist he has written four original DOCTOR WHO adventures and three original novels featuring the character Lucifer Box. More recently Mark has appeared in GAME OF THRONES, WOLF HALL and the modern reinterpretation of SHER-LOCK (which he co-created, writes for, and co-produces with Steven Moffat) as Sherlock's older brother, Mycroft.

KIER-LA JANISSE is a film writer and programmer, founder of The Miskatonic Institute For Horror Studies and Owner/Editor-In-Chief of Spectacular Optical Publications. She has programmed for the Alamo Drafthouse and Fantastic Fest in Texas, co-founded Montreal Microcinema Blue Sunshine, and was founder of the CineMuerte Film Festival. Her writing has appeared in Fangoria, Rue Morgue, and Video Watchdog Magazine. Her book HOUSE OF PSYCHOTIC WOMEN: AN AUTHOBIOGRAPHICAL TOPOGRAPHY OF FEMALE NEUROSIS IN HORROR AND EXPLOITATION FILM was hailed by no less than Iain Banks, and is essential reading for genre fans, and fans of great film writing. Her most recent book SATANIC PANIC: POP CULTURAL PANIC IN THE 1980'S co-edited with Paul Corupe, is available now.

JUDITH KERR is the much loved author and illustrator of THE TIGER WHO CAME TO TEA, MOG, WHEN HITLER STOLE PINK RABBIT and many others, all of which are now regarded as Classics of Children's Literature. Fleeing Nazi Germany as a child in 1933, she and her family eventually settled in London. Her novels WHEN HITLER STOLE PINK RABBIT and THE OTHER WAY ROUND tell the story of the Nazi rise to power from a child's perspective. They were written to show her children that life in those times was not as it was shown in THE SOUND OF MUSIC. In 2012 she was awarded the OBE for services to Children's Literature and Holocaust Education. She was married to Nigel Kneale for 52 years and is a National Treasure.

STEPHEN LAWS is the author of 11 novels and numerous short stories (collected as THE MIDNIGHT MAN). He is also a columnist, reviewer, film-festival interviewer and pianist. His novel DARKFELL was optioned by the Weinstein Company. He wrote and starred in the short Horror film **THE SECRET**, while his expert knowledge of the genre lead to a long association with the Festival Of Fantastic Films in Manchester, where he interviewed many genre stars, writers and directors from across the world. The best of these interviews will be collected in forthcoming book, THE LAWS OF HORROR. He is the co-founder of Novocastria Macabre, with Editor Neil Snowdon, an umbrella organisation bringing genre events to Newcastle and the North East of England.

TIM LUCAS is the Editor and Publisher (along with his wife, Donna) of *Video Watchdog Magazine* which was instrumental in changing the way movies were reviewed for home cinema. His critical writings have appeared in the pages of *Gorezone, Cinefantastique, Sight & Sound* and many more. His ground breaking book about the life and work of Mario Bava, ALL THE COLORS OF THE DARK was a monumental achievement, praised by the likes of Martin Scorsese, Guillermo Del Toro and Quentin Tarantino as well as the Bava family themselves. Tim can regularly be heard on commentary tracks for BluRay and DVD, on films as diverse as **THE ABOMINABLE DR PHIBES** for Arrow Video, the films of Alain Robbe-Grillet for the BFI, and the films of Mario Bava for Anchor Bay, Arrow Films and others. Not only critic, but also a creator, Tim is the author of the erotic horror novel THROAT SPROCKETS, and THE

BOOK OF RENFIELD—an inspired and unsettling exploration of the character, that weaves new material into the fabric of Stoker's novel, to explore the life of the titular character in depth. His screenplay THE MAN WITH KALEIDESCOPE EYES, about Roger Corman and the making of **THE TRIP** (co written with Charles Largent) is currently in development with Joe Dante attached to direct.

MAURA MCHUGH is an award winning writer of prose, comics and scripts for stage and screen. Her books include TWISTED MYTHS and TWISTED FAIRTALES and the SONG OF THE SEA PICTUREBOOK which accompanied the film, while her comics work includes a trip into the Mignola-verse for SIR EDWARD GREY: WITCHFINDER co-authored with Kim Newman, and the Eagle Award Nominated JENNIFER WILDE. Her short story BONE MOTHER is currently being adapted as a stop-motion short produced by the National Film Board Of Canada. She is currently writing a book length study of David Lynch's TWIN PEAKS: FIRE WALK WITH ME for the 'Midnight Movie Monographs' series from Electric Dreamhouse Press and PS Publishing.

MARK MORRIS is "One of the finest horror writers at work today" (just ask Clive Barker, who supplied that quote). He's also written original novels for the BBC DOCTOR WHO range, and audio drama for Big Finish and Hammer. His short fiction is widely anthologised, while his work as editor of THE SPECTRAL BOOK OF HORROR STORIES was nominated for a British Fantasy Award. His most recent books are the hauntological horror novella ALBION FAY and the three volumes of his genre busting OBSIDIAN HEART TRILOGY available now from Titan Books, with NEW FEARS a brand new genre anthology series from Titan Books looming large on the horizon. Mark Morris is at the heart of British Horror.

KIM NEWMAN is a film critic, author and semi professional kazoo player. He is the author of 'Nightmare Movies', monographs on **CAT PEOPLE**, DOCTOR WHO and **QUATERMASS AND THE PIT** for the BFI, and more fiction than seems feasible. His novels include the

WE ARE THE MARTIANS

delirously satirical ANNO DRACULA series, JAGO, THE QUORUM, LIFE'S LOTTERY, AN ENGLISH GHOST STORY. His critical writing can regularly be found in the pages of *Sight & Sound, Empire Magazine* and *Video Watchdog*.

THANA NIVEAU has twice been nominated for the British Fantasy Award—first for her collection FROM HELL TO ETERNITY and then for her short story "Death Walks En Pointe", Thana Niveau is one of the leading lights of the New Wave of British Horror Writers. She inhabits a crumbling Gothic tower with fellow scribe John Llewllyn Probert, where she is currently at work on her second novel.

DAVID PIRIE is the author of A HERITAGE OF HORROR, the seminal text on British Horror Films. He is also a novelist and screenwriter of repute. His first TV play RAINY DAY WOMEN was directly inspired by aspects of Nigel Kneale's QUATERMASS II. Later work includes the acclaimed MURDER ROOMS series of novels and TV which explored the origins of Conan Doyle's Sherlock Holmes stories, an adaptation of Wilkie Collins' THE WOMAN IN WHITE for TV, uncredited work on Lars Von Trier's **BREAKING THE WAVES**, and MURDERLAND starring Robbie Coltrane.

JOHN LLEWELLYN PROBERT won the 2013 British Fantasy Award for his novella THE NINE DEATHS OF DR. VALENTINE. He is the author of over 100 published short stories, 7 novellas and 2 novels, the second of which, a new novel in the ZOMBIE APOCALYPSE series edited by Stephen Jones is due soon. He is also a tireless film reviewer, chasing every horror movie ever made. His monograph on classic Vincent Price movie **THEATRE OF BLOOD** is available from Electric Dreamhouse Press and PS Publishing as part of the 'Midnight Movie Monographs' series.

JONATHAN RIGBY is an actor, film historian, and author of ENGLISH GOTHIC: A CENTURY OF HORROR CINEMA, CHRISTOPHER LEE: THE AUTHORISED SCREEN HISTORY, ROXY MUSIC: BOTH ENDS

BURNING, AMERICAN GOTHIC: SIXTY YEARS OF HORROR CINEMA, and STUDIES IN TERROR: LANDMARKS OF HORROR CINEMA. His voice can be heard on commentaries for numerous horror films (particularly the classic Hammer films), he also acted as series consultant for Mark Gatiss' A HISTORY OF HORROR and it's follow up HORROR EUROPA. His most recent book completes the 'Gothic Trilogy'—EURO GOTHIC: CLASSICS OF CONTINENTAL HORROR.

LYNDA E. RUCKER is an American writer with one foot in the American South and the other in Dublin, Ireland. Her delicately weird, quietly creepy, heartfelt and utterly haunting writing has appeared in the likes of THE MAMMOTH BOOK OF BEST NEW HORROR, THE YEAR'S BEST DARK FANTASY AND HORROR, THE BEST HORROR OF THE YEAR, THE MAGAZINE OF FANTASY AND SCIENCE FICTION, BLACK STATIC, POSTSCRIPTS, NIGHTMARE MAGAZINE, and SUPERNATURAL TALES. Her collection THE MOON WILL LOOK STRANGE is essential reading. She is currently at work on a book length study of John Hancock's mesmerizing 1971 horror film, **LET'S SCARE JESSICA TO DEATH** for the 'Midnight Movie Monographs' series from Electric Dreamhouse Press and PS Publishing.

RICHARD HARLAND SMITH is a film critic whose work first appeared in *Video Watchdog Magazine* and can now be found at moviemorlocks.com , the official blog of Turner Classic Movies. He is the author of NORTH AMERICAN FILM DIRECTORS: A WALLFLOWER CRITICAL GUIDE, BRITISH AND IRISH DIRECTORS: A WALL-FLOWER CRITICAL GUIDE and VAMPIROS AND MONSTRUOS: THE MEXICAN HORROR FILM OF THE 20TH CENTURY amongst others.

NEIL SNOWDON is a writer, editor, film programmer, and publisher whose work has appeared in the pages of *Video Watchdog*, *Rue Morgue*, and *FEAR*. He is the Commissioning Editor of Electric Dreamhouse Press, a new cinema imprint formed in conjunction with PS Publishing, Series Editor of the 'Midnight Movie Monographs' line, and co-founder of

Novocastria Macabre with author Stephen Laws—an umbrella organisation bringing genre events to Newcastle and the North East of England.

DAVID SUTTON lives in Birmingham, England. He is the recipient of the World Fantasy Award, The International Horror Guild Award and twelve British Fantasy Awards for editing magazines and anthologies (FANTASY TALES, DARK VOICES: THE PAN BOOK OF HORROR and DARK TERRORS: THE GOLLANCZ BOOK OF HORROR). Other anthologies include NEW WRITINGS IN HORROR & THE SUPERNATURAL, THE SATYR'S HEAD & OTHER TALES OF TERROR, PHANTOMS OF VENICE, HAUNTS OF HORROR and DARKER TERRORS. He has also been a genre fiction writer since the 1960s with stories appearing widely in anthologies and magazines, including in BEST NEW HORROR, FINAL SHADOWS, THE MAMMOTH BOOK OF MERLIN, BENEATH THE GROUND, SHADOWS OVER INNSMOUTH, THE BLACK BOOK OF HORROR, SUBTLE EDENS, THE GHOSTS & SCHOLARS BOOK OF SHADOWS, PSYCHOMANIA, SECOND CITY SCARES and KITCHEN SINK GOTHIC. His short stories are collected in CLINICALLY DEAD & OTHER TALES OF THE SUPERNATURAL and DEAD WATER AND OTHER WEIRD TALES. He is also the proprietor of Shadow Publishing, a small press specialising in collections and anthologies.

STEPHEN VOLK is perhaps best known as screenwriter of the infamous and groundbreaking BBC drama GHOSTWATCH. He also created the ITV series AFTERLIFE (with Lesley Sharp and Andrew Lincoln); wrote the screenplays for **GOTHIC** (directed by Ken Russell), **THE GUARDIAN** (for William Friedkin) and acclaimed ghost story **THE AWAKENING** (starring Rebecca Hall and Dominic West). He recently adapted MIDWINTER OF THE SPIRIT for ITV to much acclaim. A greatly admired prose writer, his 2014 short story collection MONSTERS IN THE HEART won a British Fantasy Award for Best Collection, while his novella NEWSPAPER HEART, won the 2015 Award for Best Novella.

Contributors

JEZ WINSHIP is a man of many talents: writer, storyteller, radio presenter, photographer. His work with The Folklore Tapes for their 'Calendar Customs' series, and as a storyteller at their live events has seen Jez become an integral member of that mysterious team, while his articles for *The Dreamers Oracle* are as incisive, accessible and illuminating as his work herein. His first book, a monograph about George A. Romero's **MARTIN** — the first book length study of Romero's criminally underrated masterpiece — is available from Electric Dreamhouse Press & PS Publishing, as part of their 'Midnight Movie Monographs' series. He is currently at work on his second entry in the series, this time focussed on the Czech fairy-tale horror **VALERIE AND HER WEEK OF WONDERS**. You can hear him on alternative Wednesdays presenting an eclectic selection of musical finds on Exeter's Phonic FM from 12-2pm and find him online at sparksinelectricaljelly.blogspot.com

ACKNOWLEDGEMENTS

THE PROCESS OF PUTTING TOGETHER THIS BOOK WAS THE process of putting myself back together, after a run-in with depression which stopped all creative activity in its tracks for over two years. Many people helped me in this endeavour and, by extension, helped rebuild my confidence and my creative life from the ground up. I'd like to take this opportunity to thank them...

First and foremost I must thank the contributors who stepped up to the plate to work with a then untested, rookie editor. Their passion, enthusiasm, and diligence was astounding. Each and every one of them went above and beyond the call of duty, to deliver a book that has exceeded what I thought that it could be. Ladies, gentlemen: I thank you, and I salute you.

Special thanks to Mark Morris and Stephen Laws, 'Men Of The Match' behind the scenes. Mark's kindness and generosity got the ball rolling, while both he and Stephen were stalwart in offering their help, their advice, and the benefit of their experience through high times and low (and of course, Stephen, for that celebratory Burger).

The path to publication was long and winding, and not a little fraught. Despite the difficulties, and my ultimate decision to change publisher, it would be remiss of me not to thank Siobahn Marshall Jones, who took a punt on me in the first place. Without that initial show of faith—in me and in the project—this book might not exist.

Immense thanks to Pete and Nicky Crowther at PS Publishing who stretched out their hands when it looked like we were drowning. It is a honour to work with you both, and all at PS (thank you Mike for making us look good).

Acknowledgements

To Mark Gatiss for his foreword, and enthusiastic support; to the Miskatonic Institute Of Horror Studies for hosting an amazing event which *should* have been our launch, but wasn't. That night was something very special — a gathering to praise the great man. It remains one of the best nights of my life.

To my wife Lili, and my daughter Mina, for giving me time and space when I needed it: you inspire me every day; to Josh Cudine for his pep talks in difficult times ("Nut up or shut up"); to Waitrose York and Waterstones Newcastle (who helped me pay my bills during the period I was working on this) for being flexible enough to accommodate the days I had to dash off to important meetings and interviews; to Stephen Durbridge for putting me in touch with Judith Kerr; to Wendy Thirkettle and the Manx Museum; to Daniel Marner (he knows why); to David Chatton Barker for the iconic cover art. To the utterly delightful Judith Kerr for inviting me into her home and taking the time to talk, and for permission to print THE BIG BIG GIGGLE: I hope you feel we've done Tom proud.

To you the reader for buying or borrowing this book. However you have come to it, I hope you have enjoyed it.

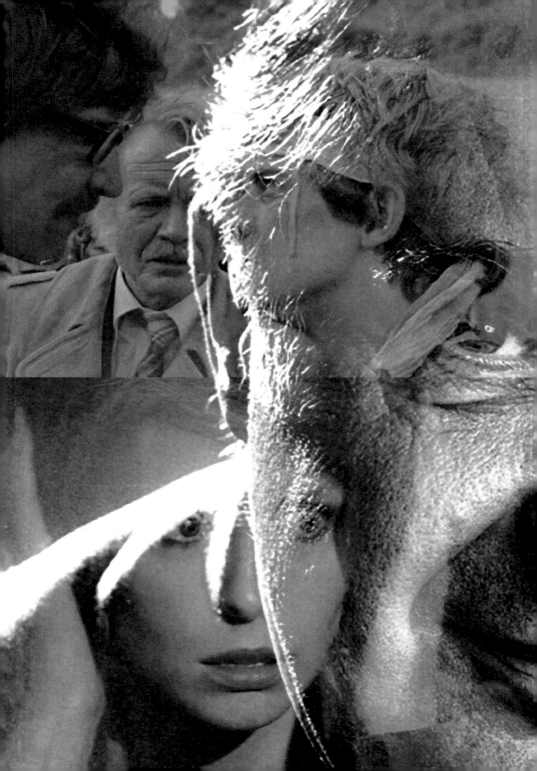